ERRANT KNIGHT

Also by Lou Paduano

The Greystone Saga

Signs of Portents

Tales from Portents

The Medusa Coin

Pathways in the Dark

A Circle of Shadows

Alpha and Omega

Greystone-in-Training

Hammer and Anvil

The Gifts of Kali

The Final Gauntlet

Greystone Lost Tales

Army in the Obelisk

The Last King

The DSA

Season One

The Clearing

Promethean

The Bridge

Spectral Advocate

Dark Impulses

Broken Loyalties

Season Two

The Wellspring

Foundations

The Missing

Cracked Chrysalis

Secret Histories

Terminal Point

ERRANT KNIGHT

Greystone Book Seven

Lou Paduano

Eleven Ten Publishing LLC

GRAND ISLAND, NEW YORK

Copyright © 2025 by Lou Paduano
All rights reserved. This book or any portion thereof may not be reproduced or used in any manner whatsoever without the express written permission of the publisher except for the use of brief quotations in a book review.

Eleven Ten Publishing LLC
282 Fareway Lane
Grand Island, NY 14072

Publisher's note: This is a work of fiction. Names, characters, places, and incidents either are the product of the author's imagination or are used fictitiously. Any resemblance to actual events, locales, or persons, living or dead, is entirely coincidental.

Printed in the United States of America
Edited by JP Services
Cover art design by GetCovers

First edition published 2025

Library of Congress Cataloguing in Publication Data
Paduano, Lou
Errant Knight / Lou Paduano

LCCN: 2025914439
ISBN-13: 978-1-944965-64-8 (hardcover)
ISBN-13: 978-1-944965-63-1 (paperback)
ISBN-13: 978-1-944965-62-4 (eBook)

For B,
and all the adventures we dreamed up as kids.

CHAPTER ONE

Portents burned. Flames rose along every city block. Smoke carried on the wind through the canyons of downtown, from Lowtown to Riverside, and out over the bay. The rain did little to mute the destruction. Instead, it pounded against those caught on the streets. Blood tinted the puddles pooling in the gutters a deep red.

No one was safe.

Malcolm Appleton wondered if he would ever feel safe again. The trek from his home in the coves, though ill-advised, was necessary. With the city at war with itself, with hell running rampant through the streets in the form of the Heads of Cerberus, time stood against Malcolm. There was only the need to act, to reach out to the people who would stand by his side in this desperate hour.

His travels took him into the deepening shadows of the city. Every step forward brought with it another faraway scream. Was it someone crying out for help? Was someone dying? Malcolm could do nothing but question everything, as no answers presented.

Arriving at his destination, Malcolm wound through the thick foliage. Hands bristled along the branches as he cut his way around sharp corners and overgrown brush. They pricked at his skin, which oddly comforted Malcolm. The sensation made him feel alive, something he wasn't sure he deserved with the constant background symphony of chaos emanating from the streets.

The city was lost. Cerberus, in all its mythological glory, controlled their fates. They were powerless to stand in the way of the multi-headed hound. War had come to Portents and threatened to spill out to the rest of the world.

Something needed to be done, though the options dwindled by the minute. Then again, that was the reason behind his trek, wasn't it?

He pushed the doubts aside. Fighting through the corridors of brush, Malcolm shuffled ahead. His heavy burden, chained around his neck, kept his mind occupied enough. So much so that he barely noticed the shadow before him until a heavy voice filled the air.

"You're late."

Malcolm slid to a halt. A hand shot out to the branches at his side, which offered little more than sharp stabs upon his flesh. He took a slow breath to calm himself. "Being cautious, I'm afraid."

Patrick Marsh nodded in agreement. He stared beyond his guest, down the corridor along the brush, wary of any uninvited visitors in their midst. The emptiness caused him to smile.

Malcolm approached his friend and extended his arms. Patrick accepted the hug, clasping tight to Malcolm's back. "It's good to see you, Patrick. Are the others—?"

"They've only just arrived," Patrick answered. He patted Malcolm's back, then led him down the wide corridor to a clearing.

Malcolm's steps were slow, an eye on his friend the entire way. Patrick's graying hair was thinner than he'd remembered. Dry patches of skin covered his hands and his neck. More wrinkles formed under his eyes. Age caught up with them both, but Patrick's reclusive nature cost him far more dearly, it seemed.

The others waited in the open space. At the sight of Jeremy Newton, the youngest of the group at forty-three, Malcolm's grin returned. Jeremy—with thick blond hair and a goatee on his chin—held tight to a small stone outcropping. His nerves ran high, his talents far from the physical.

Jeremy preferred books and history, which made him the perfect counterbalance to his neighbor, Geoffrey Michaels. In his youth, Geoffrey had served in the military. His years of training had given him a lean physique, but time had slowly chipped away at his more feral instincts. The hunting knife on his belt, always held close by a finger or two, gave him an extra edge against any threat.

The last of their group kicked at the grass beneath his feet. His hands plunged deep into his pockets with disgust. The weather matted down what little remained of his black-as-night hair. It certainly dampened any enthusiasm at being summoned, as well.

"Finally," Joseph Buchwald pronounced upon Malcolm's entry to the clearing. "The madman has arrived."

"Charming as ever, Joseph," Malcolm replied. He knew better

than to engage with the man. Their arguments never amounted to anything and only served as a waste of time. Something that was far too precious at the moment.

Geoffrey cleared his throat. "Buchwald might lack for manners, but he isn't wrong. It isn't safe on the streets. Not with the Heads of Cerberus prowling every district."

Malcolm nodded. "That is precisely why I asked you here, Geoffrey." He turned to the soldier's companion, always close to his side. "Jeremy, you brought it?"

"Of course."

"We all did," Patrick interjected. He ran a hand over the collar of his jacket. The chain underneath rattled at the touch. "But Malcolm—"

"It's about time," Buchwald announced. His teeth, stained and crooked, showed for the first time in a grin. Malcolm preferred the man's aggravation.

"Joseph?"

"Don't give me that look," Buchwald said at Malcolm's furrowed brow. "How many times have we met like this? Afraid of the future or even what tomorrow might bring? Portents is under siege. When it falls—"

"If," Patrick said, his voice booming despite his frail presence. "*If* it falls."

"Ever the optimist, Patrick," Buchwald said with a sneer. "Surprising for a hermit."

"I prefer the term guardian." Patrick held a hand to his chest and an eye toward the estate house on the far side of the thick brush. It loomed even at a distance, a deep shadow against the swirling storm.

"Yes, well, coward is more fitting," Buchwald grumbled. His throat seized, and he hurled forward in a fit of coughs. A hand shot up to cover the act. Jeremy rushed to his side, repelled instantly by the swing of Buchwald's other arm. When the coughing fit ended, Buchwald stood a little taller and refused to meet their troubled gaze.

"Joseph?" Malcolm asked, breaking the awkward silence.

The disgruntled member of their group scoffed at their stares. "It's a cold, you fools. Nothing more. Nothing like the death out there. The one that's been growing over the past year."

Geoffrey sighed, a hand on the hilt of his knife. "It has been getting worse. Buchwald may be right."

"Geoffrey!" Jeremy exclaimed. "I can't believe you."

The soldier's hand reached out to his companion and squeezed his shoulder. "Look at the evidence. Monsters on the streets. The Night of the Lights. Death and destruction. Isn't that why we took our oaths? Isn't that why you called us together tonight, Malcolm?"

The notion brought nothing but regret to Malcolm. He wanted nothing to do with the task. The chain around his neck felt more and more like a noose.

"There is still hope," Malcolm said, his voice little more than a whisper over the whipping wind. "There has to be."

"The hell there is," Buchwald shot back, spitting wildly in his frustration.

"Forces are gathering at Heaven's Gate Park for a last stand," Malcolm continued. The police—what was left of them at any rate—remained on the front lines against the enemy in their midst. Malcolm, however, knew there were other forces at work.

"They'll die," Buchwald said. "They will, Malcolm. The fail-safe—"

"Is a last resort," Patrick interrupted, standing between them. "I don't believe we're there yet, gentlemen."

Patrick shifted closer to Malcolm. His resolve brought comfort to Malcolm's shaking hands. It drove daggers through Buchwald.

"Well, I do," the angry man responded. He leaned into Patrick, his eyes widening. Malcolm pushed him away, looking at each through the pounding rain.

"That's why we are here," he bellowed over the storm. "I cannot make this decision alone. None of us can. We five have stood as the last line of defense for a long time."

Jeremy shook his head, gaze to the ground. "I hoped this day would never come."

"It's here, Jeremy," Geoffrey said in a solemn tone. He took the man's hand and clutched it tight.

"You don't know that," Patrick said.

"Open your eyes, Marsh!" Buchwald shouted. He kicked at the ground, his arms flailing before him. "This is the end! We have to do something!"

"We are," Malcolm said. He turned to each of them, begging for an answer he could not find on his own. "We vote, gentlemen. As we always must."

The sides drew quickly, Buchwald for action and Patrick for patience. Geoffrey surprised everyone by backing up Buchwald's assessment. Malcolm and Jeremy, however, remained hopeful that the Long Night would eventually end.

No action would come from them.

"You damn fools," Buchwald said. He squeezed the air before him, his eyes manic against the light of the storm. "If the Heads of Cerberus don't finish us, something else will. The fail-safe—"

"Remains, Joseph," Malcolm said.

"Until when?" Buchwald moved for Malcolm's side. His hand snatched at Malcolm's coat to pull him closer. "Until it is too late? You tempt fate. The world will fall from your inaction. Mark my words."

His grip fell away, and his steps carried him from the clearing.

"Joseph!" Malcolm called. The man refused to slow his pace and disappeared into the shadows of the brush.

"Let him go," Patrick said in a calm voice.

"He's wrong," Jeremy added. "There is still hope."

Only Geoffrey remained apart from them. He held the chain around his neck, the same worn by all five of them. Darkness filled his sullen eyes.

"What if he's *not* wrong?"

CHAPTER TWO
One Year Later

Time ran out. It started with the cough. Heavy with fluid, it dominated the day-to-day life of the aging Buchwald. His cold turned more complicated, with endless doctor visits and even more tests.

The analysis was clear from the start. His own demeanor changed from defiant in the face of their discovery to resigned to his fate. Cancer was never a willing partner. It ate away at people from the inside out. The disease broke spirits and hearts, shattering all positivity until all that remained was the end.

Joseph Buchwald suffered through an entire year with the disease. His cancer spread like wildfire through his body. A lifetime of smoking, heavy nights of drinking, and a dozen other risk factors had done nothing to stave off infection.

When the final illness started, the boy was at his side. He had been with Buchwald for a quiet evening in. They had shared tales from the past, grand sweeping epics and personal tragedies. It was how the boy had learned so much of the man's past, and why seeing him—bedridden and ghostly—brought tears to the boy's swollen eyes.

"Your fever is getting worse," the boy said. He dabbed at Buchwald's brow with a cold washcloth. It did nothing to abate the symptoms, but brought some color back to the dying man's face. "If you would let me call the doctor—"

"No," Buchwald replied in a soft whisper. The strain forced him to sit up, the words struggling to break through the surface. They had fought about the decision since the onset. The boy had begged for treatment, some hope of prolonging the man's struggle against the disease. Buchwald was clearly tired of the fight. "No more doctors. They've said their piece. So have I, Squire."

Squire. Buchwald had called him that for as long as the boy had known him. The name brought a smile to his face, in the fatherly way it connected them. Hearing it now, though, cracked the boy's false front until tears ran clear and heavy down his cheeks.

"But if you would—"

A coughing fit interrupted the plea. It was the clearest response to yet more treatment—to yet more delays of the inevitable. The battle had been fought, but time knew no measure and surely demanded its payment when the bill came due.

Blood spattered Buchwald's fist. The deep heaves calmed after a few seconds, but the toll they carried forced Buchwald to slide further beneath the covers until his head settled deep into his pillows.

The Squire moved to help, held back by the bloodied hand. "Come now. There's no more time for tears."

The boy swiped at his cheeks. He pushed away the pain, just as Buchwald did when he reached toward the torn collar of his stained shirt.

"I have a gift for you," Buchwald said. "A terribly necessary one, I'm afraid."

The chain slipped loose from the man's neck. Dangling from the end of it hung an ornate antique key. It was large and filled the man's palm. The surface was weathered from age with a looped handle.

The Squire's eyes sparkled in its presence. "Is that—"

A nod brought realization to the boy.

"I thought it was only a story."

"Not a story," Buchwald said as he passed the key over. "Prophecy."

He had believed them to be only bedtime tales to carry one to sleep at night or to share before a roaring fireplace and stir the imagination of the young. Buchwald had never intimated otherwise. Now, with the weight of the key against his skin, the Squire understood how every story, every great tale ever spun for him, was real.

"Then with this key…"

Buchwald swallowed hard, lifting once more from the pillows. "And four others, yes. You must take my place. You must become one of the five. One of the knights."

A knight. That was always how the Squire had imagined the

man—larger than life. Their time together sparked an unbreakable bond. The key solidified it. To take on the man's role like that, though? To replace him?

The Squire shook his head. "I can't. I'm not worthy. I—"

Buchwald squeezed the boy's hand shut with the key locked inside. He held tight, eyes locked on the Squire's. "You must be worthy. This is your time, Squire. Your mission.

"Portents nears its end. The monsters surround us daily now, and the people turn a blind eye toward it all. Myths and legends of long ago walk among us. They will be our ruin. And if Portents falls…"

A fit seized him. His gaze, once filled with power and dedication, was now consumed by fear. The coughs flowed through him like a wave, building with each one until he let go of the boy's hand and slammed back into the bed.

The Squire tried to help. He reached for the man—his knight— to provide comfort. With each attempt, the knight rebuked him. He could only watch as Buchwald suffered through the pain.

The fit subsided, and Buchwald lay winded upon the sheets. They were soaked from his effort.

"If Portents falls…" Buchwald repeated, his skin as pale as the moonlight.

The Squire peered to the window behind the bed. He looked beyond the crumbling edifice of the old city toward the horizon. "I understand."

"Do you?" Buchwald asked, his voice fading like the rest of him. "Will you act when no one else has? Will you save us all?"

The Squire stood from his chair. He kneeled at the bedside, the key before him like a crucifix. "I will. I swear."

Buchwald's lips curled at the edges. "I knew you would. I—"

He exhaled and settled against the pillows. His gaze drifted up to the ceiling.

The Squire leaped to his feet. "Sir? Sir, are you—"

Buchwald breathed, his chest slowing with every intake. He turned to the boy. "Save them, Squire. You have to—"

The breath left him. None took its place. Buchwald's head fell to the pillow. Dead eyes fixed on the Squire, their last entreaty clear.

The Squire, through tears of pain and grief, gripped the key tighter. He stood, placing the ancient item—and the task it bore—

against his heart.

"I will save them, my knight," the Squire proclaimed. "I swear it on my life."

CHAPTER THREE

The subway car thrummed along the track, cutting a swath beneath the downtown streets of Portents. The B Line started from the Grove and wound deeper north to the coves before circling across Allure and eventually reaching the central hub blocks away from Evans Tower.

Daytime routes transported thousands to their destinations—the proud shoppers carrying the economy on their backs and the employees who sought some privacy amid the chaos of their lives. Few spoke. Fewer still acknowledged their neighbors. One in particular kept his head low, yet his eyes watched every passenger carefully.

The vibrations of the subway ran up Gabriel Jordan's legs. His feet tapped against the floor, not to any song, but with impatience at the time spent in the seat, in the car, and in the very darkness at the heart of Portents.

An earbud hung from his right ear; his left was tucked close to the wall at the far end of the subway train. He gripped his phone tight in his hands, the illusion of music playing clear to any who bothered to glance in his direction. The ploy was necessary to keep up appearances.

That was all anyone did in the world. They went about their day in their own way, and only their way. They followed their rules, yet did what they could to fit within the framework society laid out for them, be it with their clothes, their shoes, their phones, even the type of glasses worn. All were judged subconsciously by those around them.

Or so the young man of seventeen imagined. The hours had been long, and he had cataloged all manner of characters during his time riding the rails. Glancing at his watch for the third time in less than ten minutes, the late hour surprised Gabe. The number of passengers in the car surprised him even more.

The old rules had fallen away over the last year. Danger stalked Portents in the shadows. It had always been the unwritten rule of the city to steer clear when the sun went down. Few adhered to the edict—not after the Long Night and the aftermath that had followed. Not after the coming of so many strangers to the city.

Myths and legends lived among them now. Even on the subway, creatures from centuries-old tales and beings plucked from the scariest of nightmares sat beside the so-called regular folk of Portents. Elves and imps laughed at profanity-laden jokes told in tongues while a family of elephant-tusked hybrids cuddled close in the corner, whispering hushed comfort from the dirty looks drawn their way by the crowd.

The arrival of so many strange beings failed to make the city any safer. If anything, it had the opposite effect, with nerves rising everywhere with everyone.

A jolt stirred Gabe from his thoughts. His feet quit tapping along the metal of the floor as the subway car slowed to a halt. Cambridge shone in bright letters over the doors. Another stop had passed in the blink of an eye.

Gabe had lost count of how many that made it for the night. When the passengers filtered out, and a few news ones entered, Gabe scanned them in turn. No one bothered to look in his direction. They merely stood or sat, waiting for their stop.

The car jumped ahead, and the dark walls of the tunnel streaked outside the windows. Gabe settled his head against the glass and sighed. "How much longer?"

A voice chirped through his headphone, a smirk behind the tone. "As long as it takes. Why? Got a hot date?"

Gabe groaned. He leaned along his knees, the phone before him and his voice a whisper. "You know how old you sound when you say that?"

"That's not a denial," the voice said with a laugh. "What's her sign?"

Gabe turned to the rear car of the subway train. He failed to see anyone through the dividing glass, yet knew his companion watched him. He raised a single finger casually. "I've got a sign for you."

"Nice," the voice said. "You're in a mood."

"It's been four hours," Gabe grumbled under his breath. The woman across from him eyed him nervously, then shifted away. Gabe rolled his eyes, leaning against the wall to his left and away from everyone else. "I can't look at another person sporting their pajamas for a night on the town. Doesn't anyone have any self-respect?"

His companion laughed harder. "Now who sounds old?" His joy made Gabe feel worse for his impatience. "Let's take the stop at King's Lane and call it a night."

Gabe's grip tightened on the phone. He snatched at the chair beneath him and squeezed the end to give his frustration some release. This wasn't how the night was supposed to go. For weeks, Gabe had been working on the case. People were terrified, ranting and raving about a ghost haunting the subway lines. There appeared to be no rhyme or reason behind the acts, not until the thefts started.

Gabe tracked each occurrence to figure out who was behind the hauntings on the subway system. All signs indicated the B Line as the next target. To him, it was clear as day, yet reality pushed against his so-called theory.

"I thought for sure they would strike here."

"Yeah, well, *for sure* isn't a thing in our line of work," the voice said. "How much homework is waiting for you at home?"

Gabe's eyes shot to the rear car, then back to the ground quickly. "Some."

"Got a handle on it?"

Gabe shook his head. Homework was the last thing he wanted to think about. Who cared about some stupid report on the US Constitution or differential equations when there was a freaking ghost terrorizing people?

"I'm fine," he answered.

"Gabe," the voice called, the worry clear through the earbud. "It's important. School is—"

"So is this." The weight of the stone in his pocket was ever-present. The burden it carried, the responsibility that came with the power at its command, kept him locked on his task—the only task that really mattered to him, no matter what his teachers demanded. "I..."

He trailed off. Shifting between passengers, a kid in a red-hooded sweatshirt and jeans scanned the crowd. His hungry eyes settled on every purse and wallet, noting their positions.

"Wait."

"What is it?"

The kid disappeared among the standing throng of people at the car's center. Gabe slowly stood. He tucked the phone away, a hand against the metal pole for support.

"I think…"

The overhead lights flickered and faded. The crowd shifted their gaze upward to track the growing darkness of the car. Then, everything fell to black.

"He's here."

A light billowed among the people. Each turned toward it, surprised and delighted. It appeared to be little more than the flashlight of a phone. In seconds, it brightened into an eerie luminescence that took shape in the middle of the throng.

Screams erupted before Gabe took his first step. From the middle of the crowd, the ghost hovered toward him. Hollow eyes marked its face. Hands made from spindly webs of ectoplasm reached for the closest occupants of the car.

All scattered in terror. They hugged the walls, pushing others closer to keep out of the ghost's reach. There was nowhere to run, nowhere to hide, as the train continued to streak through the tunnel for its next stop.

"Hey," Gabe said into the earbud. "Did you hear me?"

Static filled the line. "Ga… I…"

The voice cut out. "Great."

Gabe pushed through the occupants of the car. The ghost continued to moan, hovering ominously over the crowd. It passed like a shadow through people, groping nothing but air with its wiry fingers.

"Okay," he muttered. "I've got this. Now where are you?"

Ignoring the cries of those around him and pushing aside the creature at the center of the crisis, Gabe looked for the cause behind the ghost's arrival. He found it in the form of the hooded kid from earlier.

Crouched beside a pair of women in the car's corner, the kid held tight to an ornate box. Carvings of gold shimmered in the light provided by his ghostly companion. They ran along the open lid and in thick borders on every edge. In his other hand, he carried two wallets—both pilfered from the women at his side. He tucked them into the box, then shifted to a gentleman across the aisle.

No one noticed the thefts. Their attention was frozen on the ghost.

"Hey!" Gabe cried, pointing to the kid.

The gentleman before him turned suddenly to see his wallet out of his pocket. The kid smiled and tossed it back to him.

"Damn," the kid said, in mid-stride for the door. "Time to bolt."

His timing was perfect. The car reached its next stop within seconds of Gabe's discovery. The kid jumped over the neighboring seat, leaping behind a pair of frantically screaming co-eds, and landed right before the walkway as the doors opened.

"Stop!"

Gabe's cry did little to deter the rest of the subway car. They fled in a panic for the platform, half chased by the still-hovering ghost. At its arrival to the station, lights flickered and faded, but the length of the platform kept most of the crowd illuminated still.

Gabe pushed through them all for the kid. His red hood made him easy to follow, though the crowd waylaid Gabe's pursuit. The lid of the box closed. The second it did, the ghost vanished from view.

"I said, stop!" Gabe shouted again, struggling through the confused mob on the platform.

The kid offered a sarcastic salute. "Not a chance."

Gabe slammed into a passing pedestrian, and both tumbled to the cold floor. A nod of apology was all Gabe could muster before he was up and running again. "Why did I think that would work?"

"It never does," the voice replied through his earbud.

Gabe's eyes widened. "You're back?"

The subway car doors closed, and the train zipped off into the night once more. The hooded kid halted at the far end of the platform. Standing before him was a man with stubble on his cheeks, wearing a faded Superman shirt and black Dockers.

Greg Loren smiled at the thief. "What do you say, kid? Hand over the box."

CHAPTER FOUR

Loren looked the hooded kid over. Well-worn shoes covered his feet, with untied laces hanging loose on the sides. His jeans were even older, faded and torn in several places. Bags sat under his eyes, like he hadn't slept in weeks. He couldn't have been older than twenty.

"The box, kid," Loren said. He held out a hand for the ornate object in the kid's grasp. It was the cause of the trouble, its connection with the spirit plaguing the subway trains the past few weeks clear the moment the ghost vanished from view.

"It's a family heirloom."

Loren scoffed. "Whose family?"

The box, while pristine and shining under the platform lights, appeared older than anyone present. Designs were cast in gold along the edges. Dynamic lettering and an embossed emerald sat at the heart of the intricate work. The gem sparkled before Loren, almost begging for him to take hold of the object and release the spirit within.

Loren had heard of a recent theft at a downtown antiquity shop. The list of missing items stretched the gamut—from tacky earrings to the box in front of him now. The thief must have stumbled on something beyond what he had expected. Rather than fence it for a few bucks, the hooded figure took it a step further, with no idea of the danger it might bring.

"You can't control what's in there," Loren said, inching closer to the box. "Not forever."

"You want it so bad?" the kid asked, a hand on the lid. "Take it."

The box opened. In seconds, the ghost appeared. It rushed through Loren and headed in a broad sweep around the platform.

Its return certainly had the desired effect. Chaos ensued. Screams of terror rang out, and a frantic stampede erupted in a mad dash for the stairs and the streets above.

The kid took the momentary diversion and pushed through Loren. He rushed into the crowd, the box—and his nightly earnings—tucked tight to his chest.

Loren fell back a step at his assault. His feet stumbled near the outskirts of the platform. Swinging his arms out, he caught hold of a reaching hand.

Gabe pulled him back and steadied him. "Loren?"

Loren shook off the effects of his near fall. He stared after the fleeing kid, caught up in the mass of manic civilians. "They never make it easy, do they?"

"Why did you bother talking to him?" Gabe asked. "Why didn't you take him out?"

Loren shook his head. "I had to give him a chance, Gabe. Besides, I don't exactly like punching kids." Gabe cocked an eyebrow at him. "Keep it up, though, and I might make an exception."

They gave chase, pushing toward the stairs. The ghost continued to sweep through the platform, which caused people to scatter. Their frantic movements cut Loren and Gabe off from their target.

"These people aren't helping," Loren muttered.

Gabe pointed. "The ghost is the problem."

"A Yokai," Loren corrected. He had read about them at Atlas Books when the box turned up stolen. He recognized the artistry of the item as Japanese. Once the ghost sightings began, Loren had started his research with folklore from the area.

The Yokai were spirits. While typically malevolent or mischievous, they also sometimes worked with humanity. Some portrayed animal aspects, wings and the like, but this one stuck with standard ghost fare, it seemed. He wondered if the visage was tied to the thief's imagination or if it was a choice of the spirit.

Loren found such questions funny. There was a time when he only wanted to get through the day without hearing the word supernatural or monster. Soriya Greystone had opened his eyes to much more, so much so that even the moans of a Yokai failed to faze him any longer.

Gabe stared at him, shaking Loren from his thoughts. "What?"

"That's what I said," Gabe replied sharply. "You said something about the ghost?"

"Yeah," Loren said. "It's not a ghost. It's a Yokai."

Gabe stopped short. His shoes screeched loudly along the platform. "Looks pretty ghostly to me, Loren. You know, not everything has to be a homework assignment."

"That's not what I intended. You need to—"

"Lecture me later," Gabe said with a huff. He rushed past Loren for the kid.

The Yokai cut them off before they reached their target. Both halted, drawing back their hands at the Yokai's arrival. The spirit screamed at them. It raised its arms and spread them wide.

"I'll handle this," Gabe said. He retrieved an item from his pocket, one he never seemed to be without. Ever since being given the Greystone, Gabe treated it like a prized possession. The mysterious weapon never left his side.

He raised the stone to summon its arcane energies. Before Gabe could do more, Loren stopped him with a hand. He pointed ahead, through the Yokai towards the fleeing kid near the stairs.

"Handle him," Loren said.

"But the ghost?"

"Yokai," Loren clarified in a tired tone.

"Whatever!" Gabe exclaimed. "He's—"

"Controlled by the box."

Realization dawned on Gabe, and he slowly nodded. "Which the thief has. Right. And the Yokai?"

Loren stepped between Gabe and the spirit. He smirked and cocked his thumb at the moaning threat. "I'm not concerned. It doesn't seem to be harming anyone at the moment."

The Yokai fell silent at Loren's comment. Arms shot forward, and hands curled into claws. The cavernous, hollow eyes flamed to red, jagged in their rage compared to the desolate holes from before.

"Uh, Loren?" Gabe said.

"I'm sure it's fine," Loren answered. The Yokai closed in on him. Elongated and withered fingers snatched hold of Loren's Superman shirt and pulled him within inches from the ghostly visage. "Okay… I really stepped in this one, didn't I?"

The Yokai bellowed in anger. Lifting Loren up from the platform floor, it tossed the former detective aside as if he was an annoying toy.

"Loren!"

He crashed into the pillar between the opposing subway tracks. The spectators of the assault renewed their cries. They rushed away from the conflagration for the open exit on the far side.

The stunned figure slid to the floor. Loren rubbed at his head, shaking away the sudden jolt to his system. The Yokai headed his way for more.

"Loren?" Gabe called once more, still stuck in place. His loyalties won out over action.

"Don't worry about me," Loren shouted at him. "Get the box!"

Loren's command woke his companion to the fleeing thief. Gabe hopped to it, the stone still in his hand. "On it!"

The Yokai failed to care about Gabe's pursuit of its master. It remained committed to the task at hand, closing in on Loren with murderous rage in its crimson eyes.

Loren hugged tight to the pillar. "And, you know, hurry…"

CHAPTER FIVE

How am I not better at this yet?

A year of supposed training had done nothing for Gabe's confidence. Doubt trailed his every thought, fear of slipping up in front of a man who had done more than simply save his life at the hands of the Heads of Cerberus.

Loren had offered him a chance to take up the mantle of the Greystone. It was a role his parents and his brother had once carried. They bore the burden of the stone to protect those they'd loved. Gabe could do no less.

He needed to be better at it, though.

Quiet curses slipped from his lips as he raced after the hooded thief. He should have stopped him right away instead of letting the ghost—or whatever it was called—distract him. Loren had somehow known the correct course of action instantly.

Then again, homework wasn't Gabe's strong suit.

Gabe buried his feelings of inadequacy. His feet pounded the platform floor after the kid in the hood. He swiped the air at his backside, mere inches from his position.

"All this to pick a few pockets?"

The kid nearly tripped over his own feet as he scoffed. "You try paying for college?"

With the stairs within reach, Gabe leaped for the kid. His arms clasped tight around the thief's midsection, and the pair fell to the ground in a heap.

"I don't think you'll have to worry about college anymore."

The box remained locked in the kid's grasp. He kicked and thrashed against Gabe, who held tight. They wrestled for the box, the lid still open.

"Get off!"

"Not without the box," Gabe snapped through gritted teeth. He took an elbow to the cheek, but held firm. Out of the corner of his eye, Gabe glimpsed the ghost before a dazed Loren. Withered fingers reached for the man's worn shirt, the moan more of a scream now.

"It's mine," the thief replied. "You can't have it." A single hand let go of the box. Grabbing Gabe by the collar, the thief tossed him to the side, then scrambled for his feet.

Gabe recovered quickly to cut him off from the stairs. "That's far enough."

The thief stared at him. He weighed his options with his box filled to the brim with prizes from the night. Peering around Gabe for his freedom, the thief glimpsed his ghost and Loren. His desperate stare turned mischievous.

"G!" the thief yelled to his accomplice. "Kill the fool!"

The Yokai snatched Loren by the neck. The ethereal creature slammed the surprised man into the pillar once, then twice, before squeezing harder at his throat.

"Stop!" Gabe shouted. "You have to stop."

The thief shook his head. "Let me go, or the old man dies."

"Who… are you calling… old?"

Gabe sighed. A hand fell over his brow. "He's worried about a bruised ego instead of his life. Typical."

There was no time to consider the consequences of his actions. For Loren, there was no time at all, and that made the decision easy for Gabe. He stepped clear of the stairs.

"Fine. Go."

The kid took to the steps without hesitation. His only goal was his freedom. The box, however, remained open. With it, the Yokai continued to follow its last order, choking the life from a dangling Loren.

"Dammit," Gabe muttered. He held out the Greystone toward the ghost, then shifted for the stairs and the fleeing thief. "Good thing I didn't say how far I was willing to let you go."

Gabe closed his eyes. Every ounce of willpower channeled through his body and shunted into the stone. Along the surface of the ancient weapon, light formed.

It took him time to understand the power at his disposal. From Loren, Gabe learned about runes—from their meaning to the elements they manipulated in service to the Greystone.

Runes never worked for Gabe, though. Like his brother before him, he sought a deeper connection to the stone and his own power over it. While his brother preferred mathematical equations as the key to his connection, Gabe's teachings went back to his childhood in temple by his father's side.

The Hebrew symbol, Kaf, was only one such tool at his disposal. It represented the power to shape oneself, to give form to the spirit. With it, Gabe reached out and felt the swirling wind of the outside world. He drew it to him with closed eyes.

All forward momentum halted for the thief. With the summoning of the wind down the steep stairwell, he lost his balance. The gale slammed into his chest and he flew back. Crashing down the stairs, the kid fell to the ground before Gabe.

The force of the blow caused the box to slip from his grasp. Contents spilled out; the thief's earnings for the night skittered across the ground. The box skidded down the platform, over the edge, and into the darkness of the track below.

Light faded from the stone. Gabe took a sharp breath, winded from the effort. Still, he maintained his position over his target, a smile on his face.

"It's over."

"The box is mine!" The thief scrambled for the platform's edge. He failed to see the arriving subway train, caring only for the box and the power it held. Nothing else entered into it. He kicked off the platform's edge toward the track. "It's—"

Gabe snatched the hood of the thief's sweatshirt and yanked him back. "It's not worth your life."

The train rushed through the station. It shot forward without hesitation, and the box smashed beneath its weight. Shards spread along the track, the remains little more than splinters after the train passed by.

"No!"

Across the platform, the Yokai's scream turned to a bellow. The ghost dropped its victim to the ground before it shot through the air. One last desperate act carried it toward Gabe, murderous rage in its red eyes. As the ghost reached Gabe, withered fingers broke apart and vanished from the earthly plane. The Yokai dissipated—lost to the world because of the shattered box.

Gabe blinked hard, worried the Yokai would return if he so much as breathed wrong. Content with the ghost's passing, if such a thing was actually possible, Gabe's chest loosened. "Cripes, that was close."

Gabe shot to his feet and rushed across the platform. "Loren?"

The former detective stirred. His hand moved to his throat. "I'm good."

Another breath of relief escaped Gabe. He sidled next to Loren and helped him up from the cold floor. Looking back at the tracks, he realized the thief was on his feet as well, already rushing for the stairs.

"Crap," Gabe grumbled. "He's—"

"I've got him." Loren pushed off from Gabe. Hand on his holster, Loren removed the taser he carried lately. Twin electrodes cut through the air and slammed into the back of the hooded thief. Electricity funneled through his victim, and the kid fell to the ground in a spasming heap at the base of the stairs.

Loren grinned. The cartridge dislodged from the weapon. "See? I feel better already."

"Good," Gabe said with a laugh. The moment faded as rushing footsteps echoed throughout the platform. "Because we have company."

Police bolted down the steps with their weapons drawn. Loren pulled Gabe away from the fallen thief and toward the congregation near the opposite side of the platform. They filtered through the startled and confused group, ignoring their drawn glances.

A look back confirmed that the police had taken the thief into custody. Those at the front of the crowd were quick to confirm the situation for the befuddled officers late to the show.

"Come on," Loren said. Questions from the law were the last thing they needed. Those days were long over for Loren. "We need to get out of here."

CHAPTER SIX

The adrenaline rush didn't fade until they reached the coves. Traffic didn't help in that regard. Everyone seemed to honk at Loren. There was also the derogatory cursing and the ever-skyward middle finger directed toward him.

Did no one drive the speed limit anymore?

Sure, his driving skills were a little rusty. Loren had given up on the task years earlier, sworn it off out of fear of the death boxes and the lunatics on the road. Fear was what it truly came down to, though, and after Soriya's passing, he promised never again to let fear dictate his actions.

The car itself was an afterthought. Loren knew little of the current market, and even less of the cost involved. After running for the hills from multiple dealers at sticker shock, Loren found a cozy secondhand lot near the Allure Marketplace. His dream car lit up before him: a pre-owned Impala with a few rust spots and way too many miles. A sedan with character, as he called it.

Gabe still laughed about that decision.

Junction Cove sat alongside Rose Riley Forest to the northwest of the city. While more than half the district was designed for entertainment—shops, bars, and theaters—the rest contained residential neighborhoods and apartment complexes for those looking for a quieter space away from the rampant mayhem Portents provided.

At Landon near Derby, several doubles marked the lane. Most contained the multiple families the homes were designed for. One, however, had been remodeled to care for the extended nature of the family involved: Gabe's foster family.

The place was well kept. A vegetable garden on the side of the structure, and blooming mums around the covered porch, welcomed them to the home. How Curtis and Nicole Dunlop managed it on top of the five kids under their care astounded Loren on every level.

The loose belt under the hood of Loren's car dispelled the quiet of the neighborhood. Announcing his presence was something he should have inquired about at the dealership, as well as the insane maintenance schedule he had failed to adhere to since purchasing.

Jerking to a stop, Loren flipped the shifter to park. The Impala rocked from the sudden change until the engine settled.

Gabe rolled his eyes, a hand on the door handle. "How about I drive next time?"

"You just got your permit."

"Doesn't matter," Gabe said. "Anyone would be safer than you behind the wheel."

Loren huffed. "I'm getting better."

"Keep telling yourself that." Gabe gripped his stomach and lurched forward. "I'm glad we didn't stop for those chili-cheese fries."

Loren moved to slap the boy playfully on the arm. His hand hung limply in midair when the front light of the home lit up. Doors crashed open, and two figures rushed down from the porch to the front walkway.

"I think you're late enough as it is," Loren muttered.

"Crap."

Curtis held back at the base of the stairs. His hands hugged his hips, the shirt tight to his muscular frame. As a former cop, he stayed in shape to handle whatever his family might face on a physical level.

Not that he needed to with someone like Nicole as his wife. She barreled toward the car, fury in her brown eyes. Her hands flailed wildly. "What in the hell were you thinking?"

Loren nodded to Gabe, and both vacated the car in a hurry. Gabe jammed his hands deep into his pockets, his gaze on the ground. Loren kept the car between him and the yelling woman, surprised at her reaction to their arrival.

"Nicole, what's the—"

She ignored him and grabbed Gabe's arm. "Do you have any idea how worried we've been?"

"Yeah," Gabe grumbled. He pulled away from her to start up the walk. "You seem to be oozing concern."

"Hey," Curtis snapped. He stopped Gabe's approach, then leaned in close. "You don't talk to her like that, young man."

Gabe slapped his foster father's hands away. Quick steps carried him up the stoop to the front door. "I have better things to do than listen to this."

The door whipped shut behind him. Loren looked on in confusion, distraught at the argument on display. "Gabe!"

The storm door followed suit. Slamming the door ignited a series of lights in the upstairs windows. Shadows danced as the inhabitants of the Dunlop home sought a better view of the fight below.

Loren ran his hand over his brow. "I don't—"

Nicole spun toward him at the sound of his voice. "And you."

"Nicole, I—"

"No call," she shouted, hands before her. "No word at all that he was with you. Do you know what time it is? On a school night? We did you a favor by taking Gabe in, or did you forget that?"

"Of course not," Loren mumbled, at a loss for words. "I—"

"Gabe needs rules and boundaries," Nicole continued. "Not free meals and no discipline. What the hell, Greg?"

"I—but—"

Nicole threw up her hands and walked away in a huff. "I have to check on the others."

Loren could only watch her head back into the house. He settled on the hood of the car, hands running over his face at the dizzying whiplash that followed in Nicole's wake. He waited to open his eyes until the door closed again with a thundering crash.

Curtis leaned against the fence surrounding the yard. Loren pointed at him. "Thanks for the support."

"You made your bed, pal," Curtis replied. "Ain't no way I'm getting in Nicole's way when she's absolutely right."

"About what?" Loren asked, still in the dark. "You act like you didn't know where he was, but you dropped him off at my place this afternoon."

Curtis stared at Loren. "That what Gabe told you?"

The truth hit Loren. Gabe had shown up at his door and relayed the story behind his arrival. Loren hadn't bothered to confirm the details with his foster parents. "Aw, dammit."

"Yeah." Curtis rounded the gate to join Loren at the car. "He's been hopping the subway to the city."

How Gabe learned about the ghost sightings in the first place suddenly became clear to the former detective. The subway was no place for a kid, even during the day.

"How often?"

"Once is too many times for Nicki. She's not wrong there, either." He sighed; the long day had drained even a super-dad like Curtis. "Gabe's angry, Greg. At us. At school. Everything sets him off."

"I'm sorry. I didn't know."

Curtis chuckled. "That's because with you there's no responsibility and no rules. He sees us as prison wardens and treats us like it, too. But that's what he needs. He needs to feel like someone is watching out for him."

Loren thought he had been doing the same, only to realize he had been nothing but an enabler for the poor behavior he'd witnessed from Gabe with his foster family. He wanted to scream—not at the boy, though he certainly deserved it, but at himself for being so blind to the situation.

Their time together had been important to him. With him teaching Gabe about the Greystone, about the dangers lurking in the city, he felt closer than ever to fulfilling his promise to Soriya. In truth, he merely held Gabe back from getting the life he deserved after all the pain of his past.

"How bad?" Loren asked, afraid of the answer. "How bad has he been?"

"I've handled worse," Curtis answered. "Not by much, though. He's spiraling, Greg. Grades are down, he's skipping school, and you're not helping."

"I will," Loren said. Curtis, though, offered him a skeptical glare. "Curt, I will."

The officer sighed, standing from the car. "No more late nights. No more running off."

"I'll do what I can. I owe you."

Curtis patted Loren on the back. "Thanks."

"Thank *you*." Loren circled the car. He opened the driver-side door. "And tell Nicole… Well, tell her something so she won't rip me a new one next time."

His friend laughed and threw him a wave. "Better you than me."

Loren hopped into the car. The engine thrummed to life. Exhaust trailed up into the night sky in a gray plume. He waited for the front door of the house to shut and the lights within to fade to black. Loren started for the Knoll, wondering what else he'd been doing wrong with Gabe—and how the hell he could fix it.

CHAPTER SEVEN

Drawers turned over and spilled their contents onto the floor. Items scattered along the hardwood, clattering throughout the room and creating nothing but a walking hazard with each step taken.

The Squire cared little. There was only one goal on his mind—the object of his aggressive search through the sprawling estate of Patrick Marsh.

"Where is it?" he muttered as another shelf emptied under his sweeping hand. "It has to be here."

Marsh had only been known by name before a week ago. The man's reputation, or lack thereof, always garnered a headline or two, especially when a large check arrived at a local charity or ten during the holiday season. To the Squire, Marsh was nothing more than the idle rich until he learned differently.

It was among the knight's belongings: detailed dossiers on the others in the group. Every secret they carried had been hidden in boxes procured by the Squire from his fallen knight. From property holdings to habits, the knight had uncovered much over the years.

Those secrets had brought the Squire to the Marsh Estate in the dead of night. Outside, the wind whipped against the tempered glass of the windows. Tree limbs scratched along aging shingles and cast shadows over every room.

The Squire didn't mind the soundtrack to his frantic searching. It helped subdue his desperation to find the key to match the one he carried in his pocket.

This was meant to be a simple task. Marsh was unworthy of holding the key. For too long, the knights had stood idle against the growing nightmares of Portents. All culminated in the Long

Night and the rise of the Heads of Cerberus. The aftermath had left the city a twisted landscape. Monsters walked the streets like normal people. Freaks of ancient legend shopped and worked alongside regular folk.

There was nothing natural about the city. Portents accepted the devils as if that would halt the threat to come—and it would come. It had been the fear of Joseph Buchwald. The Squire had promised to make it right, and to do so, he required all five keys.

Reaching the den at the rear of the manor, a lingering fire greeted the Squire. He pushed aside chairs, upended the couch, and ripped books from the shelves. The key had to be here. He could not fail his knight, could not lose sight of the mission for even a second for fear of the consequences.

"Dammit." He tore through an old volume before grabbing another. "It has to be here!"

"What on earth?"

Patrick Marsh stood at the open pocket doors. A book dropped from the Squire's hand. He backed away from the dying flames of the fireplace for the shadows of the corner.

Marsh's slow, steady steps carried him into the room. He surveyed the destruction of his home with horror on his wrinkled and aged face. "What have you done?"

The question hung in the air. Marsh stood before him in flannel pants and a white t-shirt. Nothing spoke of his incredible wealth, yet that was all the Squire saw when he looked at him: a rich man in an oversized home, worried over his trinkets and possessions. There was no concern for the world outside, for the state of the city beyond his property line. Marsh cared nothing about the future.

The Squire clutched the key in his pocket. It served as a permanent reminder of the mission—the last wish of a dead man who had meant everything to him. Recalling the knight, coupled with disdain at Marsh's very presence, brought out the boy's rage.

"What have I done?" the Squire seethed. He slammed his hand against the adjacent shelf. Books toppled to the ground in a heap. "What have *you* done? While the city burns and people suffer daily? Nothing. Not a thing. You hide away and ignore those you've been charged to protect. You neglect your sacred task. How? With the threats bearing down on us? How can you do nothing?"

Marsh crept closer to the fireplace. At the corner of the insert, stood a metal bin. He reached inside and withdrew a cast-iron poker from the depths. He brandished the weapon before him like a sword.

"The only threat I see is you."

The Squire let go of the key in his pocket. His open hands fell to his sides. "I am no threat," he said, taking a step closer to Marsh. "I am the only one willing to sacrifice for the benefit of everyone else. It's my mission."

The hand returned to the pocket and removed the key. The Squire held it before him, evidence of his grand task.

"Joseph's key," Marsh whispered, terror in his pale eyes. "How?"

"He entrusted this to me," the Squire said. "I will not fail him."

Another step closer to Marsh brought the Squire within reach. Marsh backpedaled, a fallen chair stopping his retreat.

"Stay back," Marsh said, the poker clutched tight in both hands.

"Give me what I seek," the Squire said. "You know why I have to do this. You know what is at stake."

"That's not a decision for you to make!" Marsh shouted in defiance. He swung at the air between them, driving the Squire back. "It wasn't Buchwald's either."

"He was the only one who saw the truth."

Marsh shook his head. "He saw what he wanted to see."

The Squire held out his hand. "Give me the key."

"No," Marsh replied. A hand drew to his chest. From beneath the collar of his shirt, the Squire noticed the chain hanging around Marsh's neck.

The Squire chuckled at his idiocy. "Of course."

With the key in sight, the Squire charged forward, his mission his only concern.

Marsh swung out with the poker. "Stop!"

The poker swiped at the Squire's chest. He jumped back to avoid the blow, then shot forward. On the return arc, the Squire caught the poker in his grasp and ripped the weapon from Marsh.

"Enough," the Squire said. He tossed the poker aside. The iron rang loudly as it hit the floor. When silence returned to the room, the Squire loomed before Marsh like a massive shadow. "You refuse to recognize the truth. The danger is already here, and you do nothing. Out of fear."

"Please." The chair at Marsh's back pinned him in place. The

Squire snatched the man's collar. Hands wrapped around his neck and squeezed. "Don't—"

Eyes burning with fury, the Squire bellowed in the man's face. "I can save us all! I have to save us."

"Please…"

The Squire heard none of the pleas. Only the key around the man's neck mattered. The Squire held tight. He refused to relinquish control to the cowards who dared stand in his way. Couldn't they see the danger they were all in? Didn't they understand the risk of not fulfilling their sacred duty? They were supposed to be knights! They were supposed to keep everyone safe, not just themselves!

"Ple…"

Marsh's body fell limp.

"Marsh?" Fear sparked in the Squire's eyes. He let go of the man's neck, and Marsh fell to the floor. His lifeless body spread beneath him like a rug against hardwood.

The Squire reeled away quickly to the mantel. He stared at his hands, then at the dead man. "No. No, I didn't mean to… What have I done?"

Flickers of flame showered over Marsh's body. From beneath his collared shirt, the key shone in the dim light—blazing bright compared to the darkness that settled over everything else.

The Squire inched closer. "I… I did what I had to. For the key. For everyone."

He ripped the chain free from the man's neck. The key dangled between his fingers. The Squire took in every intricate detail of the item. It differed from his own in slight ways—the loop doubled around the head, with leaves etched along the shaft.

His steps carried him away from the dead man toward the floor-to-ceiling windows that dominated the back wall of the room. Staring down over the sprawling property behind the manor, the Squire grinned.

"You've hidden here for so long among your treasures. Among the great secrets no one else could ever possibly imagine." The Squire's gaze widened, his mission one step closer to success. "I have need of them. But not you. Not any longer. My mission is all that matters."

CHAPTER EIGHT

When people talked about Portents, they always mentioned the same sites. There was the Rath, the Vertrum Home, and the marketplace on Allure. There was shopping on the Knoll and the docks at Riverside with its eclectic bar scene. Everything was light and gentrified, clean and easy to handle.

Lowtown was none of those things, and the corner of DeFalco and Frenz especially painted a less than picturesque view of the city. The smell alone wafting from the fish market drove tourists away. The dead body, half-drowned in the gutter and covered by a dozen soggy newspapers, took care of the rest.

Samantha Myers lifted the police tape from the rope line. She held it high for her partner to join in the fun. Thel took the invitation, her purple hair shining even in the morning's gloom.

Angry residents dotted the sidewalks. Their glares made their intentions clear. They tired of the death that littered their neighborhoods. More than that, they wished for the area to regain the name it once held—Grant Park—instead of being considered the city's slum. The dead didn't help in that regard either.

Myers flashed her badge to the patrolman keeping watch over the deceased. He nodded, grateful for the backup. Concern filled his eyes over the scene, a youth Myers envied in him. The tag pinned to his uniform read H. MACKIE, a recent recruit like so many others over the past year.

The body continued to wait for them. So did the crowd in its own way. All wanted answers, yet none wanted to help facilitate them in the least.

Myers sighed at the predicament she found herself in on an almost daily basis. "Do you ever think the world doesn't like us?"

Thel, in her black leather coat and dark pants, swiped the wet hair from her face as she circled the scene slowly. "No."

"No?" Myers asked in surprise.

Thel didn't bother to look at her. "I'm well aware the world doesn't like me, Sam."

Myers smirked at her partner. Thel might have carried the appearance of a kid barely in her twenties—the hair certainly helped in that regard—but, in truth, Thel was an eight-hundred-year-old siren and the last of her kind. Despite the culture shock that had greeted her upon her arrival in Portents, Thel had acclimated well to life in the big city and to the job at hand.

Still, Myers couldn't help but jab at her colleague. "Is this another woe-is-me, I'm a freak thing?"

Thel stopped her pacing. Her hands fell to her hips. "Is yours the standard, why do murders only happen on my beat when I have to get home to my plants and my Netflix queue?"

Myers laughed. "I hate you."

"And you wonder why I feel persecuted," Thel shot back with a shrug.

Mackie cleared his throat. Water ran down his sleeves and dripped from his hands. Soaked from the storm, his patience for their banter appeared to be wearing thin.

Myers passed a glare to her partner to get serious, to which Thel rolled her eyes before joining Myers at the body.

"Who called it in?"

"Someone at the fish market," Mackie answered, checking his notes. "Guy named Hamilton. Must've been the smell."

"Like he could tell the difference?" Myers said with a hand over her nose. Fish guts dominated everything else. How anyone could stand around the area astounded her, let alone live or work within a mile radius of such a place.

Taking a deep breath, Myers slipped on a pair of gloves and crouched beside the body. She peeled off the newspapers, careful not to tear anything loose from the corpse hidden beneath. Each one revealed a little more of the victim.

He was clearly a man. His clothing was drab, but bore no marks or visible entry points. A jacket, pair of jeans, and t-shirt all seemed commonplace. With the body in the open, Myers noticed the pronounced state of decomposition already present. Time had passed since his death.

"Anderson on his way?"

Mackie nodded. "Should be here in a few."

"Hopefully, he can pull something useful." She turned the body over for a better view. The late-night storm bloated the cheeks and the eyes, but for the most part, the victim was fully intact. Something in the graying hair and the thin lips caused Myers to stare. "Huh. I…"

"What is it, Sam?"

She worked her way to her feet. "I know this guy."

"An admirer?" Thel chided.

"Funny," Myers shot back. She continued to look over the victim intently. "Where do I know this guy from?"

Thel left the body for the corner. She called back to Mackie, pointing at the traffic signal and the camera attached to the post. "Think we can get anything useful off these?"

Mackie chuckled. He directed their attention to another one down the block. "Those have never worked. No money in the budget. They sure look pretty, though, don't they?"

"Are you kidding?"

"Welcome to Lowtown," Mackie said. "Where the swamp meets the—"

"Marsh!"

Both turned at Myers' exclamation. Mackie's brow furrowed. "That's not how it goes."

Myers cocked an eyebrow. "Not how what goes?"

"The saying."

"What saying?"

Mackie approached, hands before him. "The one about the swamp meeting the—"

Myers waved him off. "What are you talking about? Thel, what's he talking about?"

"I—"

"You know what? It doesn't matter." Myers pointed at the body. "It's Patrick Marsh."

"Who?"

"Our victim."

Thel shook her head. "No. Who's Patrick Marsh?"

Mackie's hand rubbed his chin. "The millionaire?"

Myers spun on her heels toward Mackie. "He was worth that much?"

"That's what I read."

"From what?" Myers crouched beside the body once more. "Old money? Mob ties?"

"Textiles, I think."

"This fashion statement?"

Thel groaned at the comment. "Sam."

Myers took a breath. "I know, I know. Sorry, Thel."

She appreciated Thel's candor. Myers needed to be reined in numerous times over the course of the last year. Her commentary was a combination of nerves and exhaustion. There was always another murder, always another crime to solve. She wondered if this would be the one where they found her out for the fraud she truly was. Who was she to stop any crimes after the life she had lived?

Myers needed someone like Thel to keep her on task, while also allowing her the breathing room to work through her own self-doubts. It had been a great year with the siren of legend, and Myers grew to value her more with each passing day.

Thel, though, had more learning to do about the job. She kept her distance from the body—happy to work the scene rather than stare into the face of death. Myers wondered if it was a reaction to taking so many lives with her sisters, or if her youthful looks went much deeper into her very soul.

The victim didn't care either way, a point that became more and more obvious the longer Myers remained silent. She studied the dead man—a freaking millionaire, if she was right—for the cause of death. Deep bruising surrounded the man's throat.

"These markings could suggest strangulation," she said.

"Swab his fingernails," Thel called from the middle of the street. Myers shifted away from the neck for the victim's drooping hand. Sediment appeared to be caught beneath the nail. "There might be some particulates from the killer."

"Look at you," Myers beamed at her partner.

"Stop."

Myers pulled a specimen kit from her pocket. After collecting some samples from the man's nails, Myers locked up the small container for analysis.

"Any other insights, Detective?" she asked in a mocking tone.

Thel sighed. Her arms closed tight around her as she peered around the area. "Just a question. What was he doing in Lowtown?"

It struck Myers the second Thel said it. Myers stood from the body and groaned.

"Sam?"

She circled the dead, then looked up and down the street. Settling on the crowd on the other side of the rope line, her suspicions continued to grow.

"I have plenty of theories, Thel," Myers said. "With guys like Marsh, though? It always comes down to one thing."

One thing had always plagued Myers, no matter what she did or how far she ran from her former life. She had seen the worst in humanity, and even had the pleasure of taking some of it down while wearing a badge. But each one brought the same component to the party. Each one was plagued by the same thing, just as clearly as Patrick Marsh—textiles millionaire—must have been to find himself dead in a Lowtown alley.

"Secrets."

CHAPTER NINE

"You have that search and rescue form for the Runlow case?"

Thel paused at her desk. She was mid-stride, a dozen reports juggled in her grip. "You mean search and seizure?"

Myers sighed. She fell into her desk chair, letting the wheels carry her against the filing cabinets along the rear wall of the office. "Oh, right. I'm the one in need of rescuing."

A huff escaped Thel. She lowered the reports next to her computer, joining three more piles. "Sam."

Myers waved her off. She didn't need to hear it, not when she knew Thel was correct. Work had been too much of late—too many hours and too many dead. The city was on edge, just waiting for one more calamity to send it right over into the abyss. Myers couldn't help but wonder if Patrick Marsh would be the tipping point. The rest of the station certainly thought so.

Word had, of course, already spread throughout the precinct. Even in a building as disjointed as the Rath, with its multiple floors and divisions staggered throughout, somehow everyone had heard the news about the millionaire's demise. It practically buzzed through the corridor, creating a background noise neither Myers nor Thel could hope to contain. They had to ride the wave now, and hope for a quick resolution.

"Sam?" Thel looked at her with renewed concern. The only thing more unnerving than Myers' constant musings was when she fell silent, it seemed.

"Four new cases this week." Myers lifted the preliminaries on the murders dropped in her lap by her superiors. A pair appeared connected—a murder-suicide that simply required a post-mortem confirmation from Anderson's team. The Runlow case, however, hung over her head like a shroud.

Runlow had been a career-criminal lowlife. He'd broken into a residence and earned himself a bullet from the occupant. The problem? The occupant wasn't quite human, with more attributes of a fish than a man. Whenever one of the new residents of Portents—the myths and legends trapped by the loss of the Courtyard—were involved, be it as victim or perpetrator, there was always the added pressure of retaliation from both sides of the genetic divide.

Marsh, of course, took precedence.

Thel had her own take on the uptick of work. "Delegate," she said. "You are Head Detective."

The office was a constant reminder. Alejo Ruiz, her former captain, had once occupied the space. It was twice the size of any other on the second floor, with a view of Heaven's Gate Park across the square.

It was an office—and a position—Myers never deserved. Her time in Portents had been plagued with lies and betrayals, all of which continued to trail her every decision. Being Head Detective offered little time to dwell on anything, though. Reports from the rest of her team filled the office. They required a second glance and her approval before moving to the next level.

Then there were the schedules taped to the wall. Every detective under her (not the way she liked to phrase it by any means) was listed next to their current caseload, shift hours, and partner. All fell on her to manage, including the fresh cases cropping up.

"You're right," Myers said. "I am Head Detective. Which means doing the work without complaining."

"You're always complaining."

"To you," Myers said with a scoff. "Totally different thing."

Thel grumbled, "Lucky me."

"Damn right." Myers pulled close to her desk. Pushing aside everything else, she dug through the preliminaries on Patrick Marsh. Ever since Lowtown, Myers couldn't help but review everything they had on the man. Something in the location where he was found, something in the open questions left by Thel and Mackie, gnawed at Myers.

"Something's bothering you about this one," Thel said, reading her strained thoughts. "You want me to—"

Myers slammed the file closed once more. "Head down to Anderson's for the autopsy. See if the killer left anything on the body, or if Marsh had drugs in his system. Something to tell us…"

Her words trailed off. Thel was already at the door, her coat in her hand. She glared at the senior detective, too polite to interrupt her ramblings even when she should.

"You were about to say the same thing, weren't you?"

Thel nodded. She slipped the leather jacket on. For having only been in the department for a year, and the world itself not much longer, Thel's situational awareness was extraordinary. Nothing slowed her down, not even the manic thoughts of her partner. When Myers would learn to trust her instincts was a question she should have answered long ago. Trust remained a difficult thing for the troubled detective.

"What task will you be handling this fine morning?" Thel asked, snapping Myers out of her doldrums.

Myers tapped the side of her computer monitor. "Tracking Marsh's financials. Maybe this was about revenge or blackmail. Maybe a jilted lover looking for a payout. Or a former business partner. All of the above?"

"Doesn't feel right," Thel said.

Myers grimaced. "Nothing does. Wish I knew why."

"You'll figure it out."

Myers jumped to her feet and started for the door. Thel blocked her path, confused. "I thought I was the one leaving. Where are you headed?"

"Upstairs."

"Ah," Thel said with a smirk.

Myers rolled her eyes. "Don't start."

Thel retreated from the open doorway, hands in defense. "Don't let me stand in your way."

"Come on."

"I know how you like to check in with the boss."

Myers groaned. "What did I say?"

Thel rummaged through her pockets. She pulled out a thin tube and held it out. "Need some lip balm for after you're done?"

Myers slapped her hand. "Bite me, you old bat."

Thel's laughter followed her into the corridor. Looks flew from the detectives tucked inside their tiny cubicles or hanging around the breakroom. Conversations fell silent; all thought of sports or current gossip was lost behind the arrival of the Head Detective and the latest murder in their fair city.

Myers ignored them all. She moved for the elevator on the far side of the bullpen, the Marsh file tucked under her arm.

Thel waved from across the floor. "Tell the Commissioner I said hello!"

CHAPTER TEN

Thel continued to acclimate to the world around her. Noise especially, was a concept she'd understood on a contextual level, yet with each passing day, the decibel level continued to amaze and astound her ears.

Everything made noise. From the cars rumbling down the roads to the motorized scooters every kid seemed to have asked for during the last holiday. Pounding feet on the concrete, the shifting of bags in hands, the dinging of bells and every beat, bang, and bong overwhelmed her yet thrilled her in the same breath.

The world had changed so much in the last eight centuries. Crashing waves typically accompanied Thel's thoughts. Now there were no clear thoughts capable of passing through her mind without a song on the radio or the drumming of her idiot neighbor downstairs as accompaniment.

She missed the solitude of the past, yet hated the loneliness that came with it. Her sisters were gone, their second chance lost because of their inability to adapt. Thel refused to go the same way. Each day might have been a struggle—both of wonderment and frustration—but she was more than up for the task.

Sam helped. Her partner had a gift with words, grounding everything in the simplest of terms and somehow turning them into lessons at the same time. Even her sarcasm held a purpose. It pulled Thel along for the ride in every conversation. She always knew her place with Sam. More than that, she always *had* a place, thanks to her.

Thel's second chance would not be wasted like her sisters'. She held onto the life before her, half afraid that it would somehow slip away if she so much as looked at the wrong person in the wrong way, and half hopeful everything would turn out all right no matter the day.

With their tasks at hand, Thel watched Sam disappear into the elevator. She blew kisses to the senior partner. Myers returned the favor with a gesture of her own—one far less appropriate in public, though it caused Thel to laugh all the louder.

Her joy carried her from their shared office to the breakroom. Grabbing a spare cup—something Sam kept in hidden locations throughout the station somehow—Thel poured the remaining coffee from the pot. After starting a replacement, she peered around the tiny counter space for the creamer bottle. It nearly launched into the air with the force she used to lift the weightless bottle.

Empty.

A quick scan of the counter offered her no sign of a replacement. Thel lowered her mug and opened the cabinets above. Plastic forks fell loose, and she tried to catch them before they scattered to the floor. Once secured, Thel dug around each reachable shelf until finally surrendering.

"Where would I put a bottle of creamer?" she asked herself as no one noticed her conundrum or moved to assist her.

Spying a group within the confines of the breakroom, Thel grinned. She opened the door and peered inside.

"Hey," she called. "Any of you see where they keep the creamer?"

The four gentlemen in the room turned away from the baseball highlights on the television screen. They stared at her in silence for a long moment.

"Uh, anyone?"

Quick glances passed between them. Then, without a sound, they reached behind them and removed a set of headphones from their belongings. Each of them slipped on a pair to cover their ears to block her voice out.

"Cute," she muttered as the door closed. "Real cute."

It was not the standard reaction to a simple question, but occurred more often than Thel cared to admit. Those four had never taken to a *freak* in their midst.

Thel's talent came from vocal manipulation. Her singsong voice allowed her to control others. The talent came with trust issues, though she knew the quartet in the breakroom simply didn't care for her.

She snatched her coffee cup, the contents no longer steaming, and started back to her office. A quick call to Anderson before heading over was in order, though her mood soured thanks to her so-called colleagues. When was she going to be accepted into the group? When was she going to be accepted by the world?

A hand jutted out to bar her path, an unopened bottle of creamer in its grip. "Here you go."

Thel stopped. She covered her cup, afraid of spilling the contents. Her head spun to the mysterious hand's owner. He grinned at her with pearly white teeth.

"I'm pretty sure it's expired, but can a powder really go bad?"

The man was young. That was her first impression. He had wide brown eyes and a pair of freckles on his left cheek. Thin black locks were perfectly placed on his head and matched his pressed uniform.

His smile widened when she took the bottle from him. "Yardin. David Yardin."

Thel held back a laugh. "Is that like that spy guy? Ford. Henry Ford."

Confusion filled his face. "Uh, it's actually…"

The laugh erupted as his cheeks flushed deep red. Thel covered her mouth in embarrassment to match his own, and he shook his head.

"You were messing with me, weren't you?"

"Little bit." Thel moved for the counter. Cracking open the creamer bottle, she poured the contents into her cup. Yardin offered her a spoon to stir.

"Thanks." Thel noticed the silence from him. "Sorry about that. Part of my training with Sam was catching up on pop culture references. She was quite adamant about that."

"Sounds like a taskmaster."

"Oh, she's the worst," Thel joked, though when it came to the current lineup on every major network and the top ten of each streaming service, there was no fooling around with Sam. The concept of celebrities continued to confound Thel.

Yardin rubbed his neck. "Well, when you get a break, maybe we could…"

He fell silent at the opening of the breakroom door. The four morons waved at the young officer, slapping his back and laughing incessantly. At the sight of Thel, though, they merely offered her a blank stare and grabbed hold of the headphones still secured over their ears.

Yardin's cheeks flushed further, his cocksure attitude thrown off by the presence of his pals. After they passed, the stray glances back at an end, Yardin cleared his throat. "I was just going to say…"

"Yes?"

"Maybe we could grab a coffee or something?" he asked in a muted tone. Thel lifted her cup, and his eyes widened. "Outside of the Rath, that is. Obviously."

"Obviously," Thel chided.

He pointed to his colleagues, who watched from the far side of the corridor. "And forget about them," he whispered.

"Already have," she replied. She turned toward her office. Yardin though, held back for a moment. His gaze trailed the group for a long second before he rejoined Thel.

"I should get back to it," he said, a thumb to the stairs and the parking garage beyond.

"Me too," Thel agreed.

"See you around."

Thel waved. "See you."

Even after his departure, her hand remained in the air. Realizing how ridiculous she must have appeared, Thel bolted for her office. The door closed behind her, and she let out a long, calming breath.

Her heart raced in her chest. Her pulse refused to slow. She felt like those idiotic teens from the movies, crushing on anything and everything after the smallest of interactions.

Damn, it felt good.

Thel whistled a tune on her way to the phone, her coffee in her hand and a future date on her mind. Maybe she was part of the world, after all.

CHAPTER ELEVEN

Stepping clear of the elevator, Myers immediately moved for the open door on the right-hand side of the floor. On the left, behind a series of half-walls, were three executive desks. Staffers occupied them, including Janet Williams—personal assistant to the Commissioner.

Janet, easily in her sixties yet with the energy of a twenty-five-year-old, welcomed the latest arrival to the sixth floor of the Rath with a quizzical smile. It was as simple as that for the small, fiery woman to keep track of the comings and goings on the floor. Myers merely indicated the open door, and a nod gave her clearance.

Rather than knocking, Myers crept around the corner and halted in the doorway. The office was muted, both in color and lighting. Table lamps surrounded a large couch in the left-hand corner. They provided little in the way of actual illumination. A desk lamp flickered, the base molded from clay like a school project gifted to the owner of the office by one of his daughters. Awards framed the back wall, surrounding built-in bookcases in the center, which were covered floor to ceiling in reference guides, protocol sheets, budgetary tools, and who knew how many other ridiculous items necessary to run every precinct in the city.

The job took a toll on Alejo Ruiz. Just shy of a half-century in age, he appeared stretched thin from the role he'd accepted in the aftermath of the Heads of Cerberus' invasion. The pepper in his hair had completely surrendered to salt. His eyes, always carrying bags beneath, were set deeper and fell to shadow unless looked at directly. Even the way he sat behind his desk, hunched over another pile of forms and letters requiring his approval, made Ruiz appear far older than he truly was.

The work always had that effect on him. Myers recalled the

piles throughout his former office—now hers—and Ruiz's struggle to keep it all straight. That task paled compared to what lay around the expansive space.

Her staring eventually wore down his resolve. Ruiz dropped his pen onto the desk and sighed. "Are you going to stand there looming all day, or are you going to come in?"

Myers stepped into the shadowy office. "I didn't realize you were having a party, sir."

"A party?"

Myers showcased the piles of reports accumulated on every surface.

Ruiz grumbled, pushing from his desk to stand. "Yeah, me and fifty of my best friends. Good one, Myers."

"I thought so, sir."

"And cut the *sir* crap," Ruiz said with a huff. A pop ran up the length of his spine when he stretched his back. He rounded the desk to face his visitor.

"You prefer Chief?"

Ruiz shook his head. He caught sight of the time, hands on his hips. "I really wish I could stay and continue this lovely chat, Myers," he said, his tone less than genuine. "Your attitude is always a constant pleasure, but I have meetings I'm already late for."

Myers slowly backed away for the door. "I'll leave you to it, then."

As she reached the frame, Ruiz called out, "Wait." She turned to face him once more. His hand reached out for the file tucked under her arm. "Tell me about Marsh."

She held the report before her. "What about your meetings?"

"You think they won't ask me about one of the wealthiest men in Portents turning up face down in a Lowtown alley?"

Considering how many officers on the second floor were talking about the case already, there was little doubt about what was transpiring at City Hall and every major news network at the moment. The thought left a pit in Myers' stomach. Her fear of screwing up grew with each strained breath.

"Good point," she muttered.

She passed along the file. Ruiz opened it and started absorbing what little information they currently had. She wished she could offer more, wished she could figure out why the scene felt wrong to her. Instead, Myers remained silent to give her superior the time he needed.

"These the preliminaries?" he asked, knowing the answer. He wanted more as well.

"Thel is working with Anderson on the autopsy." Ruiz continued to read as she spoke, yet halted at the bottom of the opening dossier. A curious look spread across her face. "Should I be concerned, si—Ruiz?"

He lowered the file. "About what?"

"The smile on your face."

Ruiz sighed and headed for the couch. He settled on the center cushion. The contents of the file spread out on the small section of table left available. "After a morning of budgets and recruitment, I could use a few minutes of actual police work."

She certainly felt the same way after hours spent dealing with scheduling, caseloads, approvals, and officer complaints. When the work fell to the wayside, it was like an additional crime had been perpetrated—and the victim was her very soul in some respect.

Ruiz peered up from his reading. "He was strangled?"

"Looks that way."

"In Lowtown." It was a statement that hung between them like a question waiting to be answered.

"We found him behind the fish market on Frenz," Myers relayed. "What the hell was the name of it? Simmons or something."

"Never had the pleasure," Ruiz replied.

"You would be the lucky one." Every time she thought of the place, the smell returned. Two showers before coming into the office and everything still reeked of rotten fish.

"How did Marsh get there?" Ruiz held out the file for her.

Myers took it in hand, his query barely able to penetrate. "I'm sorry?"

"Where is his car, Myers?"

"I don't—" Myers cut herself off. She never thought about it. How did Marsh get to Lowtown? His place was in Riverside, wasn't it? Staggered by the question, Myers tried to recover. "Maybe he took a cab? I'll put in a call with the taxi services, as well as any ride-sharing platform he might have used."

"Don't bother."

Myers' brow furrowed. "Why not?"

"Waste of time," Ruiz said. He stood once more, wiping the creases from his pants as he met her face to face. "Patrick Marsh was a recluse. He never left his estate."

"Then why would he be in Lowtown?"

"He wouldn't," Ruiz said simply.

The words crashed down on Myers. That's what was wrong with the scene. Not just the missing car, but the missing motive for Marsh's presence in the first place. Suddenly, the veil lifted, and she saw the circumstances of the man's death much more clearly.

She slapped her forehead. "I'm a damn idiot. This was a body dump."

Ruiz nodded. "Someone needs to check out his estate."

CHAPTER TWELVE

The smile remained. For the first time all week—hell, if Ruiz was being honest, a lot longer than a week—he felt like he'd actually served a legitimate purpose in his role as commissioner. That sensation held a certain rarefied air in the office.

Most of his existence served others, never his fellow officers in blue, but those of higher stations in Portents. City Hall practically adopted him as one of their own. There were always arrangements to be made, reports to be reviewed or passed along to apprise everyone of the current status of crime throughout the city. Who in their right mind wanted to know the danger outside their penthouse window? Ruiz didn't understand the fascination, yet played the game as expected. That was his role, and he hated it.

Everything was pomp and pageantry. Nothing served the people he had sworn to protect. Budgetary debates ate up more time than any type of backstop for the officers under his purview. Scheduled visits, like he was a damn dignitary, took up most of his days, and even then the precincts spent more time hiding the dirt in the corners than passing along any useful information to be used to keep Portents safe for everyone.

Ruiz had become a bureaucrat. He had joined the Reginald Dunn's of the world, God rest the former mayor's soul. It aggravated him to no end. More than that, the new role made him feel old. Old and out of touch with the current status of the city, with the people in the very building he occupied.

Still, the smile remained. Being able to aid Myers in some small way cleared away every spiteful conference call and ignorant debate over police enforcement with those Ruiz had become forced to engage with daily. Myers certainly needed no assistance. Her instincts were on target; they simply took a moment longer than she had expected. It seemed to rattle her far more than he had meant when he'd suggested the reason behind Patrick Marsh's visit to Lowtown, but Ruiz was sure Myers could handle the case. He wouldn't have made her Head Detective if she couldn't.

Ruiz left the comfort of the sofa for his desk. Shuffling aside several daily activity reports—more unnecessary paperwork for review—he grabbed the binders along the edge and tucked them under his arm. When he started for the door, another shadow appeared across the frame.

"Why are you still here?" Janet asked. She was the true reason anything got accomplished on the sixth floor of the Rath. Janet was a tour de force, constantly supervising not only those under her, but those she served directly. How she came to work for the Commissioner's office remained a mystery considering her extensive training as an administrative assistant. Ruiz didn't much care. He was glad to have her by his side... most of the time.

"I was working," Ruiz replied, a hand toward the piles on the desk. "Janet—"

She cleared her throat to end his thought. A hand reached for his crooked tie and straightened the yellow silk monstrosity gifted to him by Teresa for Father's Day the previous year. Her hand settled against his chest, cold eyes boring through him. "The meeting started ten minutes ago."

"I'm aware." Ruiz checked the clock on the wall. "I was just—"

"You need to move it."

"I know." Ruiz turned for the mug at the corner of his desk. "If I can just—"

"Nope." She blocked his reach. Janet, hands on his back, edged him through the door hurriedly. "No more stalling. They need their commissioner."

"My coffee—"

"Will be nice and hot when you get back," Janet said.

"But—"

They were in the corridor before he could stop her. He gazed back longingly at the missed coffee, and Janet pointed toward the end of the hall for the closed door of the conference room.

"Go."

His grumbling carried him to the meeting. With firm control of the knob, Ruiz pushed the door open and slipped inside. Without a sound, he closed the slab with the same precision and filtered to the back of the room.

Voices boomed from the far side. All eyes were locked on the pair presenting their case. A projector offered a look at the deal currently under discussion, another capital improvement to the city in its recovery from the Long Night and the nightmare of Karen Winters.

Ruiz knew the speaker. Stuart Renfield ran a contracting company called LUMOS and served the city on a number of boards and committees. They had crossed paths a few times, but more and more over recent months. The balding figure had the crowd eating out of his hand, the image of Portents splayed on the wall behind him.

At his side stood Julia Tuttle, Lumos' Head of Public Relations. Why she was necessary with Renfield making the presentation might have been on Ruiz's mind, but noting the reactions from the other gentlemen in the room toward the petite blonde, the reason was clear.

"We call it Four Points," Renfield continued through his speech. The image of Portents changed. From the corners of the city rose four gleaming peaks, like obelisks shooting from the ground. "The spires, set up at the four corners that mark the city's borders, will serve as a welcome to visitors. Each will showcase the history of Portents while promoting a brighter future."

Astonished faces filled the room. Tourism was a slight problem when a fair portion of your population had been murdered by hairy beasts that had been posing as your neighbor, your colleague, or your spouse. Needless to say, the city needed a bulletproof idea to win people back.

Renfield grinned at their attentive gazes. "My associate, Julia, will go into more detail about each of the sites and what we are looking to build around them as time goes on."

Tuttle took to the main stage while Renfield edged to the corner. Council members whispered hushed congratulations as he passed.

Ruiz shook his head. The meeting was a preliminary discussion, and they were already acting like it was a done deal. It was yet another aspect of his job he disliked more and more. Corruption always remained. It only took on a different form with each iteration.

Rather than focus on the negative, or the busty blonde spinning her tale, Ruiz opened the top binder in his grasp. It detailed Renfield's proposal in much the same manner, but without the hard sell. The entire endeavor was called The Restoration of Portents. It was a revitalization of every area devastated by recent violence. From Rose Riley Forest to Olcott Curve, everything was within the scope of the project. An ambitious deal from the looks of things, that went into further detail with each page turned.

He didn't manage to read too far into it before a shadow passed over his binder. Ruiz looked up to see a middle-aged woman with auburn hair and sharp green eyes.

"Sounds intriguing, doesn't it?" she asked in a hushed tone.

Ruiz closed the binder. "Sounds expensive. Exactly what Folsom likes."

Gerry Folsom made Reginald Dunn look like a saint in some regards. Sure, there was a genuine quality of concern with Folsom. He cared about Portents. He merely cared about his legacy in the city more than the people living in it.

The woman sighed. "As long as it's not his money, right?"

"Exactly." Ruiz nodded, then shook the thought away. He knew nothing about the woman at his side. "I'm sorry. I shouldn't have—"

"It's nice to hear some honesty for a change."

She seemed familiar, as if they had passed each other a dozen times before, yet never connected in any meaningful way.

"Are you with the City Council?"

"I am," she confirmed.

Ruiz's cheeks flushed. "There's been so much turnover after what happened last year. I'm afraid I don't know your—"

"Leslie Gates."

The name sent Ruiz back on his heels. His eyes widened with surprise. "Gates."

"You knew my niece, Melanie."

He knew Melanie Gates all too well. A bright up-and-coming officer, her life had taken a tragic turn when a demon possessed her body. She'd fought back against the malevolent force and sacrificed her sanity to save Loren.

"She has your eyes," Ruiz said, seeing his former subordinate in the woman before him. "I didn't realize she had family left in the city. After her mother passed…"

"Another tragedy." A sullen gaze fell to the floor between them. It faded when she returned to him, as if she had tucked the memory aside. "It seems to follow my family like a shadow. I'm grateful I was able to be here for her at the end. I wanted to come back after what happened to Melanie, but work kept me away. It wasn't until the Long Night that I quit everything. So many were lost. I couldn't… I couldn't stand aside any longer."

"Yeah," Ruiz whispered. Even with the new carpet throughout the sixth floor, Ruiz could see the bloodstains from where Rufus Mathers had been slaughtered. He still felt John Pratchett's icy hand in his as the man left the world. Ruiz let out a long breath. "We lost too many."

Silence filled the room. The sudden loss of so much noise from Tuttle and Renfield shook the occupants of the meeting awake. Folsom caught sight of Ruiz and raised a hand.

"Ah, Ruiz," he called. "I didn't see you come in."

All eyes turned toward the startled commissioner, still lost on the past. Ruiz straightened his posture and threw on a false grin. "Didn't want to interrupt the presentation."

"I've just been informed about Patrick Marsh," Folsom said. "Do you have any suspects?"

"My people are pursuing their leads and gathering evidence," Ruiz answered over the growing murmurs of the crowd. "As soon as there is a break, I will update you."

"He was a good man." The details mattered little to Folsom. Ruiz could have fingered any of Folsom's cronies, and it would have barely fazed him. He was always too busy working on his next sound bite. "Quiet and kept to himself, but his fortune always helped the city. A significant loss."

Those around him agreed, their tone respectful and earnest. All tried to ignore the blatant comment about the dead man's money.

"Yes, sir," Ruiz said.

Folsom shifted back to the presentation. Attention returned to the pair of presenters with high hopes of securing a contract with the city.

"All right, Renfield. Tell us how much this Four Points project will cost."

Figures covered the wall; their numbers were meaningless compared to the prestige such a project would bring to Portents. Ruiz, his briefing concluded, happily started for the exit. Passing Leslie, Ruiz offered her a stern nod.

"Excuse me, I need to—"

He didn't bother finishing. His hand opened the door, and he was out in the hall before the next word could be uttered. He didn't expect to have company for the journey.

Leslie held him up, the door closing behind her. "I wanted to thank you."

"Ms. Gates, you—"

"Leslie."

Ruiz scratched his scalp. "You don't have to thank me."

"I really do," she said. "For what you've done for this city, and for watching over my niece."

"Melanie was a wonderful officer. I miss her smile. If I could have done more…" Ruiz settled against the wall and let out a deep breath.

"We all feel that way," Leslie said, joining him. "That's why the Four Points Project is important. With the fundraising we're hoping to procure, we can finally wipe away the dark stains of the past and start building a brighter future."

Leslie was a genuine believer, and the idea brought a smile back to Ruiz's face. It had been a long time since he had something to root for—or someone.

Fierce eyes caught his stare and locked on tight. "We're going to make a better Portents, Ruiz. Nothing is more important than that."

CHAPTER THIRTEEN

Secrets. What the hell had she been thinking?

Myers' foolish notions regarding secrets, because of her personal history, trailed her the entire way to the Marsh Estate. The look on Ruiz's face made it clear how off base Myers had been with her presumption. Her preoccupation with her own past of late clouded everything in her eyes, and she cursed her inadequacies in the silence of the drive.

She went alone—another mistake, but one Myers justified. Too many cases and too little time left Thel to pick up the slack while Myers cleaned up her own mess. Her partner could handle things better, at any rate. Anyone else could, the way Myers felt.

"Stupid," she mumbled under her breath, hands tight on the steering wheel. "A body dump. How could you have been so clueless? What is the matter with you?"

No one said anything, but it was clear from the looks that passed her way of late. Even Thel had picked up on Myers' behavior over the past few weeks. A year into the job and the pressure threatened to overwhelm her. Was it that simple, or was it more that she hadn't lived up to the expectations of her station?

Myers felt undeserving of the post, and what had she done in the interim to earn it, other than bury herself in the task and lose herself in the minutiae?

Something had to give. Perhaps the Marsh case was the tipping point. Myers needed to solve it and quickly, for fear of losing what little remained of the life she had carved out for herself in Portents.

Self-loathing and doubt vanished the moment Myers rounded the corner of Augusta and Twelfth. In its place, wonder and astonishment filled her eyes as she arrived at the estate.

The Riverside District had always been known as where the idle rich went to hide, but this went above and beyond. Where most roads contained the standard fare of housing with a modicum of property between them, Augusta Street held only one home. It stretched down the small hillside tucked behind a dozen immense white birch trees.

The manor stood three stories tall, yet filled Myers' field of vision with its depth. Black as night, the place stood as a massive shadow—almost certainly lost to the world when night arrived. Statuary decorated the cornices. Intricately carved creatures loomed over the driveway and along the rooftop of the estate toward the rear of the property.

Myers coasted up the driveway, then parked. She climbed out from behind the wheel, unable to take her eyes off the home—as if the statues above might leap out and grab her if she did.

"So this is how the one-percent live?" Myers said. "Only in Portents."

Leaves floated around her, carried by a chilly wind. The heat of the summer faded, and she pulled her jacket in tighter. Presumptions about her victim continued to present themselves, despite her track record thus far.

"This guy never worked a day in his life," she muttered to herself. Yet, looking at the home, Myers couldn't help but wonder why no one else had brought the man's death—or his disappearance from the estate—to the authorities' attention? Marsh must have had friends, right? A man with more money than God must have surrounded himself with *someone* to make the long days brighter.

The front door was locked. Myers glanced around for signs of life, anything that might deter her from entering the home, and saw nothing. Removing the lock-pick set from her inner pocket, Myers set to work on the door. Her father's gift never strayed too far from her, though with each use she cursed it more and more.

A creak welcomed her to the manor. The door lifted from the frame and arced into the darkness of the home. Nervous steps took her from the entry hall—a lavish foyer with vaulted ceilings and twin staircases to the second-floor landing—until she reached what appeared to be the den.

Smashed furnishings decorated the carpet. Broken glass lay next to shattered mementos, beside torn paper and shredded books, all spread across the room like an earthquake had struck the place.

"They were looking for something," Myers whispered in the

dark. She bent low and retrieved a discarded poker in front of the fireplace. It held no markings and no bloodstains, but it drew her attention all the same before she lowered the potential weapon back to the ground.

She replaced the poker with a flashlight from her pocket and let the thin beam of white guide her away from the den for the stairs. Thoughts raced over the trash piles strewn across the dozen rooms she passed on her travels.

The killer needed something from Marsh, more than just the man's demise. But why remove the body from the scene? They must have been aware of the man's reclusive nature, hadn't they? Why not leave Marsh to rot alongside his belongings? Had his death rattled the killer into a mistake?

Too many possibilities hounded Myers as she entered the bedroom of the deceased. She failed to trust her instincts with any of them and put them aside as she studied the spacious room that occupied the back half of the top floor. Windows dominated the rear, overlooking the property that trailed down the hillside. Myers shifted closer for a better view, and her eyes shot wide at the sight beneath her.

"You have got to be kidding me," she breathed in surprise. A large hedge maze occupied most of the estate. Gated at the front and back, tall walls of brush curved in sharp angles and spread toward a small clearing.

Squinting, Myers could almost make out an outcropping of rocks beneath a white tree at the heart of the maze. She whistled loudly, the echo filling the room. "A freaking hedge maze. Why not? He probably hosted the Tri-Wizard Tournament every year."

Myers shook her head. "Rich people. Even when it's not secrets, it's still…"

She trailed off. From the corner of her eye, she noticed the wall in the corner slightly askew from the rest of the room. Quick steps brought her to the crack. Hands delicately ran along the side and gently pulled the false wall free. A hidden room opened up for her.

A seven-foot-tall knight in gleaming silver armor brandished a sword over her.

Myers jumped back, a hand to her heart. Her flashlight slipped to the floor and rolled deeper into the revealed room.

"I take it back," Myers said, slow to recover from the shock. "Even when you think it isn't secrets… It's always secrets."

Every shelf was filled. Every nook and cranny in the hidden space held another memento or keepsake. From pennants to statues, from swords to shields, all appeared medieval. Dragons and other symbols decorated them. This went well beyond a hobby for Patrick Marsh, but meant something entirely different for Myers, who had seen too much during her tenure in Portents to write off her discovery.

"This case just got more complicated."

CHAPTER FOURTEEN

A sharp noise woke Gabe from his slumber. He lifted his head from his folded arms, his vision still blurry from the deep dream. Drool ran from his lip and he struggled to wipe it clear when the laughter in the room snapped him awake to the world.

"What the—"

The entire class stared in his direction. They pointed and snickered in disbelief, unashamed in their judgment of him. Mr. Phelps, his math teacher, looked down indignantly from behind his desk. A large textbook sat before him—the cause of Gabe's rude awakening.

"Welcome back to the land of the living, Mr. Jordan," Phelps said over the growing chuckles of Gabe's so-called peers. Before any could settle back down to the lesson of the day, one which appeared to be little more than Greek to the still-stirring Gabe—the bell rang.

Phelps immediately waved down those already on their feet, desperate for one last second of attention. "Don't forget to finish the problems on page fifty-three for tomorrow."

The class was out the door before the directive ended. Gabe did his best to join them, jamming his text under his arm and power walking for the hall. He kept his head down as he circled the back of the room. His subtle departure failed to dissuade Phelps from calling him over all the same.

"You can stay, Gabriel."

Gabe sighed. He approached the desk in defeat. "Listen, Mr. Phelps…"

"I don't think I will," the teacher interrupted. "You certainly seem incapable, so why should I bother?"

Phelps had been teaching for decades at the school and had

most likely heard every excuse under the sun. Gabe wondered if anyone had tried to explain what a Yokai was to him before. Gabe decided the truth was not the way to go. "I'm sorry, sir, I—"

"Fell asleep," Phelps continued in a disgruntled tone. "For the fourth time this month. I'd like to think it had to do with finishing your homework, but we both know you haven't bothered with an assignment from me, or any of your other teachers, in weeks."

"I'm trying—"

"To fail?" His constant interruptions grated on Gabe, but he couldn't fault the teacher for his frustration. Gabe had never been the best student. Now, the classroom was the last place he wanted to be.

"I know I—"

Phelps waved him down. The lecture wasn't over yet. "Don't bother with homework. Don't bother with classes half the time. It's an excellent strategy, I'll give you that." He leaned closer, concern in his tired blue eyes. "You have potential, young man. Live up to it."

That's what I'm trying to do, he wanted to say. A thousand other rebuttals rose to his lips, but Gabe sucked them all down. Instead, he nodded and said in a soft voice, "Yes, sir."

It did little to win Phelps over. "Get moving," he grumbled as he pointed to the door. "Or you'll be late for your next class."

Gabe shuffled into the hall, Phelps' words trailing behind him. He should have been more on top of things. His brother, Noah, had been a math genius, and here Gabe was, unable to even stay awake for the class.

It didn't matter to him. That was what it came down to in the end. Gabe found school, the life of an average, ordinary teenager, to be impossible to grasp and something he had no desire to attain. He felt the pull away from that life with each breath, and every time he reached inside his left pocket to make sure his Greystone was still there.

No one could understand the thrill of chasing monsters in the dark. No one could begrudge him the adventure he sought. Gabe was saving the city. How could homework compare to that?

Chaos ruled the hallway. Students rushed in all directions. Lockers slammed up and down the corridor, like a symphony of dissonant noise. Gabe ducked his head low and barreled through the crowds accumulating at the doors to their next classes. They passed around gossip like candy on Halloween, and it all seemed to center on the kid who slept his way through math class.

"Rested up?" A nudge on the shoulder caused Gabe to jump slightly. He cursed the instinct and turned to see Kameron "Kam" Rusch. Her nose ring sparkled under the torturous overhead fluorescents. Strands of stark black hair swayed over her forehead, the sides all but shaved off.

"Kam," Gabe said, already annoyed by the smirk on her face.

"The sleep thing isn't a stretch," she said. "I mean, Phelps is a major bore. But the snoring?"

She mimicked the sound. Laughter broke out from a passing crowd, and Gabe tucked his head even lower to push through them.

"Thanks, Kam. I appreciate the ribbing."

She batted him playfully on the arm. "What have you been doing, Jordan? I called last night and your parents—"

"Foster parents," he corrected.

"Touchy much?" she asked sarcastically. "Anyway, they said you were out. They didn't sound thrilled about it, either."

"I snuck out," Gabe admitted. "For a walk."

Her gaze drifted to the bunched-up sleeve of his shirt. Deep welts of blue and purple ran up his arm. He quickly pulled the sleeve down to cover them up.

"A walk," she repeated. "Where? A dark alley or ten?" Kam reached for his arm, and he pulled away at her touch. "Hey," she said, hands up in defense. "I like a little mystery. Keep your secrets."

"That's not—"

"I just hope you're awake enough for our US History test."

Gabe paused in mid-stride. His eyes snapped wide. "Is that today?"

The bell rang from every speaker in the building. Kam clutched her textbooks to her chest and passed by him for the door to Mr. Melvin's history class. "Today," she answered. "As in now."

She stopped at the door, head beckoning him to follow. He waved her ahead. "I'll, uh, be right there."

With a quick nod, she was gone. The hallway cleared in seconds, and Gabe found himself alone. History was actually his favorite subject, though he would never attest to that if questioned. Something about dates and facts always appealed to him. But to say he was prepared for a major part of his grade for the quarter?

"Yeah," Gabe muttered. "I'm not ready at all."

A quick glimpse of the exit at the end of the corridor made his decision for him. Gabe rushed toward his freedom and the life he truly desired.

CHAPTER FIFTEEN

The door slammed shut behind Gabe. He scanned the area for any eyewitnesses to his escape, then ducked around the corner of the building. Staying close to the ground to avoid the windows dominating the place, Gabe quickly moved for the parking lot and the street beyond.

Loren watched it all from his car on the far side of the campus. He leaned against the hood, arms crossed, and a clenched jaw that threatened to undo years of dental health in a matter of seconds.

Of course, Gabe cut class. He hadn't heard a single thing Nicole or Curtis had said to him the previous night. Why would he? Hell, when was the last time Loren took advice from someone close to him?

Loren slammed his foot down and caught the bottom of the front bumper. He pushed off, pacing hard toward the parking lot until he stopped himself. A loud huff escaped into the air, but little else. He wanted to rush over and grab Gabe—to scream bloody murder at having witnessed his inability to make it through a single day of school.

Yelling wasn't the answer. Loren wished he knew what the hell would help with his seventeen-year-old protégé. He worried about him. More than that, Loren worried he was to blame for the current swath of problems plaguing the kid. The late nights, the danger always surrounding them—none of it was right, yet Loren had clung to it so tight over the last year.

All because of a promise he'd made to a dead woman.

Soriya had been wrong to trust him with the task. Loren couldn't safeguard a kid, let alone the city. Why hadn't he said as much? Training Gabe seemed like a good first step, yet had he simply been deluding himself this whole time?

No one could protect the city. Even with the crazy myths and legends now present in their daily lives, few still understood the truth about Portents. They couldn't see what was right in front of them for fear of what it might mean to their existence. Loren had to keep fighting. Watching Gabe run away from his responsibilities, from school, and from his foster parents made Loren doubt the methods he'd employed since Soriya's death.

Something had to change. He wished he knew where to start.

His phone rang in answer. All thought of Gabe and his current whereabouts fell to the background thanks to the name listed on his screen.

MYERS

The ignore button screamed to be pressed. Every instinct demanded Loren run as far away from the call as humanly possible after everything Samantha Myers had put him through in the past.

Loren leaned along the side of his rusty Impala with a sigh. He accepted the call and held the phone to his ear. "Please tell me this is a social call."

"I wish." Her tone was jovial. Sarcasm had always been her main approach with him. He had once found it endearing. Now, though, there was a reticence with each word spoken. "Though I could waste your time talking about the weather for a few minutes if you'd like."

"What can I do for you, Myers?"

"I need you to take a look at something."

Loren shifted his weight against the car to reach for the handle. "Sounds ominous enough."

"Yeah, well, it looks worse," she said in a low tone. There was deep concern behind her words. "How soon can you get to the Marsh Estate?"

Plans fell into place. The details were thin, her concern hidden but palpable over the line. Loren noted the address as he slipped behind the wheel of the Impala. Hanging up, Loren turned the key, and the engine rumbled to life.

Gabe was long gone. Any chance of nipping the kid's latest mistake in the bud had passed. Loren had no idea what to do next with him.

All he had was Myers and her case. Loren ran his hands through his hair, then settled in for the drive.

Work never ends.

CHAPTER SIXTEEN

Loren secured the lock on the door. The Impala creaked and groaned, another worry for another day. Not even the shadows looming over the Marsh Estate affected Loren as he approached the spacious driveway to the left of the manor. The statues along the cornices—each one carrying the head of an eagle and the body of a lion—stared down upon him, almost waiting to strike, yet Loren felt unfazed by their stone-cold gaze.

His thoughts still lingered on Myers. A year had passed since her betrayal, when she'd framed him for the murder of Richard Crowne. The accusation had ended his career with the police department. While it was true Myers had been coerced to act in such a fashion thanks to the manipulations of Robert Standish, the betrayal continued to sting.

Myers, however, had done everything possible to mend the fence. She had stood against the Heads of Cerberus, even going so far as to bring Standish down for his role in the entire affair. Loren offered forgiveness. He saw the valor in her, a genuine goodness mired by a shady past and a need to keep it hidden.

Forgiveness was as far as the pair had taken things. Loren walked away from the cop life, content to try something new and rediscover who he should have been in the process. Now, circling back to Myers brought the old wounds to the surface again, and he struggled to head for the open front door of the home because of them.

The wrought-iron fence surrounding the back of the property pulled him closer. Loren looked to the gate and the opening through the hedges at the center, curious about what hid within. As he passed the front walkway, a shadow slipped from the inside of the home and started toward him.

Myers waved him down, an awkward smile on her face. "Thanks for coming."

Loren continued to stare in silence at the hedges, then left them for Myers. He tucked his hands deep in his pockets, the chill of the wind biting against his face. "I'd say thanks for the invite, but I have a feeling I'm not going to like what I hear, am I?"

Hitching her thumb for the front door, Myers took the lead. "Let's talk inside."

As if the shadows outside weren't creepy enough, the inside took the feeling to a whole new level. Dark and dreary failed to sum up the decor of the foyer that bled seamlessly down the hall, then opened up to the den on the right and the stairs to the left.

"Certainly an upgrade from your last apartment," Loren commented, trying to keep the mood light—well, lighter than his surroundings, at any rate.

"Which is still my apartment," Myers replied. Loren halted mid-flight up the stairs. A sniper had assaulted her apartment; her life had barely been saved, let alone the rest of the place. Myers shrugged at his reaction. "The bullet holes add character."

Loren let the subject drop and continued up the stairs to the third floor. "So this is the Marsh Estate."

"The very one."

A portrait of the owner hung in a place of prominence outside the master bedroom. Loren blinked hard, unsure why he hadn't put two and two together before. "As in Patrick Marsh?"

"Yes."

Loren spun around to scan the area with a fresh view of the home. "He's not big on company."

"Or breathing," Myers said, heading into the bedroom. "Not anymore."

Loren grabbed hold of the molding around the door. He leaned on the frame as if the wind had been sucked from his lungs.

A dead millionaire? This just gets better and better.

"Ruiz must be livid." He joined Myers near the back corner of the ridiculously oversized room. "The press has to be all over this case."

"The press, the politicians, and every charity in the state." Myers sighed, hands on her hips. The weight of the case was clear from the deep wells beneath her eyes. "Marsh had a lot of fans."

"Money has that effect," Loren said. "What happened?"

The details came fast. Myers started with the body dump in Lowtown and the signs of strangulation that Anderson's team had already confirmed.

The disarray of the property made much more sense to Loren. Someone was looking for something. Money more than anything else when considered with the choice of victim, but then why bother displaying the body at all?

"You think he made a mistake," Loren said in a quiet voice. "The body dump—"

"Put way more attention on the dead man than our killer could want," Myers continued. "I think Marsh's death wasn't intentional. I don't believe they meant for Marsh to die at all."

"That's a lot of anger to unleash and not expect the man to die," Loren said, imagining the victim's demise. "Strangulation is personal."

"An argument gone wrong, then."

Loren nodded. "The killer needed something from him."

"He gets frustrated at not finding it…"

"Marsh walks in…"

"And our guy loses control," Myers finished.

"Sounds straightforward enough."

"That's what I thought," Myers said with a low huff. "Until I found this."

Her hands caught the lip of an unseen edge thanks to the shadows in the room. With the slightest pull, the wall dislodged and opened. An armored knight at the precipice of the secret room loomed before Loren—sword at the ready.

"Holy!" Loren jumped back, a hand over his heart and the other at his belt, wishing he had packed his gun. "What the hell, Myers?"

"Loren?" She rushed to his side. "You all right?"

"You could have warned me," Loren said, brushing off her concern. He straightened and caught his breath. The statue failed to move. The light had played tricks on his senses. "I don't have a fondness for suits of armor."

He didn't bother to get into the details, though they replayed in his mind at the mention. During a case, Loren had paid a visit to the Library of the Luminaries and made the mistake of triggering a security protocol in the ancient repository. He had almost lost his head to a trio of self-activating suits of armor looking to protect their property.

Myers continued to watch him. Loren shook his head. "It's nothing. Let's just get this over with."

She headed inside. Loren took his time to give the suit of armor as much room as possible. He kept his hands tucked close to his sides, refusing to touch anything for fear of the repercussions.

The hidden vault of Patrick Marsh opened up for him. It ran the entire length of the home; the place was obviously originally designed to be a panic room that Marsh converted for his collection.

Swords and axes were displayed throughout. Maps and scrolls sat in bins or tucked in deep mail slots. Some covered the open wall space between exhibits. There were clear borders marked on each, but the country they depicted remained unclear at a glance.

Myers stood amid the collection, hands spread wide. "This goes well beyond a fascination with the Middle Ages, wouldn't you say?"

Loren peered around once more. His hand edged toward his neck, and he rubbed the skin deeply. "Everyone needs a hobby."

"Really? That's all you've got for me?"

Despite everything surrounding them, it made little difference to Loren. It made even less difference to the dead man they'd hoped to aid. "What do you want me to say, Myers? People are weird."

"I'm all for collecting, Loren." Myers brushed alongside a chain-mail tunic with a red cross emblazoned on the breast. "The hidden room tells me this is more. The swords, the shields, and everything else? These are the real deal."

She wasn't wrong. Loren simply failed to connect it with the case. "So Marsh was moonlighting at the local Renaissance Faire. I hear the maidens at those things are quite busty." Myers groaned at his flippant attitude. "I don't know what you want from me, Myers. It's been a year since I wore the badge."

"Officially, yes." A quizzical look spread across his face at her response, and she smiled. "Oh, come on, Loren. Don't play the whole retired cop bit."

"Myers—"

Her arms crossed her chest. "Why don't you tell me about the subway ghost?"

"What?" He felt his cheeks flush at her questioning, suddenly under the spotlight. "I don't—"

"Please," she snapped. "You want more? How about the Wendigo down on Forty-Seventh? Or the squid-looking thing a few weeks back? I have a whole list from the past year. Witnesses have been more than happy to describe a raggedy man with a Superman fetish as their would-be rescuer."

Loren scoffed. "It's not a fetish."

"It's a poor lifestyle choice, is what it is, but to each their own, right?"

"I'm doing what I can, Myers. I made her a promise."

"The Greystone," Myers said, the old anger still tucked behind her words. "That's how you've been handling things? Can I see it?"

Loren turned away. "It's not mine. I don't work that way." He paced the length of the room, eyes washing over the contents of the dead man's prized possessions. "I'm not Soriya. She would understand what all this means. She would see…"

He trailed off at an oddity among the rest of the collection. Medieval carvings, tomes from the period, and more dominated every square inch of the hidden room. Except for a single image hanging on the back wall, dead center between two crossing swords.

"Loren?" Myers called.

"That photo." Loren cautiously crept to the wall. He scanned along the frame for tripwires or any other traps. He had been burned too many times in the past with his impatience. Nothing jumped out at him as dangerous, though he could hardly call himself an expert on the subject. Unsatisfied, yet no longer caring, Loren carefully lifted the photo from the wall and held it before him.

"What about it?"

Five men wore armor in the image. The lack of helmets allowed their faces to be seen. Loren recognized the one in the middle from his portrait in the outer corridor.

"It's Marsh."

Myers was at his side, eyes wide over the photo. "Look how young he was."

"I'm more interested in what he's holding." The men held their right hands out before them. Lying along each of their palms was an ornate key. All appeared unique in design, yet the same in terms of importance.

"A key?"

"Have you found one?"

"No," Myers said. "Not yet, at any rate."

Loren passed along the photo. "Could be the reason for his death."

"It's a stretch."

"It's a lead, Detective," Loren shot back. "Because if someone took his, they'll probably want the rest."

CHAPTER SEVENTEEN

Patrick Marsh was dead.

Malcolm heard about it on the news. The report detailed the finding of the man's body in Lowtown, of all places, which brought Malcolm to his feet. Had it been a quiet death in the comfort of his home, the shock would have been just as great, but understandable. Death surprised all in the end. Those closest to Patrick—Malcolm liked to count himself in that regard, but knew the man had distant family as well—may have found the body.

To wind up in a gutter in Lowtown, though?

Alarms blared within Malcolm's mind. He immediately left his modest home in Venture Cove and hopped into the first cab to Riverside. He had to check the estate to know for sure. The presence of the police at Patrick's home cemented the situation for Malcolm.

Someone had murdered his friend.

Worse, the killer knew what they were doing. By publicly displaying the body, by allowing the media to showcase the event on every broadcast throughout the state, the killer was announcing his intentions.

The keys were in danger. Whoever had killed Patrick realized his role as a knight, which meant the rest of them were at risk as well. Not once in the decades spent safeguarding the keys had someone threatened their role in Portents. His predecessors were quiet souls who'd kept the secret from leaking out. They had prided themselves on their steadfast altruism. When the task passed down to Malcolm from his uncle, he believed himself to be the same.

The responsibility was too important to falter now. After everything that had happened in Portents over the past few years—from

Nathaniel Evans' return to Death's coming under the power of the Medusa Coin—the knights had never been more necessary.

"You all right, pal?" the cab driver asked.

The car had arrived at the corner of Augusta and Twelfth during Malcolm's musings. A tired hand reached for the handle of the door. "Yes. Yes, I'm all right."

"That'll be—"

"Could you wait a few minutes?" Malcolm interjected. A stiff wind passed through the open door and into the cab.

A grumble escaped from the driver, followed slowly by a nod. "Yeah, sure. It's your dime."

"Thank you."

Malcolm exited the cab. He closed the door softly, but held on to the roof of the vehicle. The estate loomed across the street, dark and empty. The thought of Patrick's death continued to eat away at his soul. His knees quaked and his legs wobbled to the point of almost giving way beneath his weight. Malcolm gripped the cab's roof, grief-stricken over his friend and panicked from his growing fear.

Maybe Buchwald had been right. That was what it boiled down to repeatedly in his mind. Their decision the previous year had been the right one. The police—with help from some very interesting parties—had fought back the darkness of Karen Winters and her Heads of Cerberus. Yet now, in the calm before the next storm, the threat was more direct.

If the keys fell into the wrong hands, no one would be safe.

Malcolm needed to check on the others. No one had answered during his first attempt. The news saw to that. The second Patrick's death hit the airwaves, he had no doubt Joseph, Jeremy, and Geoffrey fled from their homes to safer pastures.

With his fellow knights out of reach, what was the alternative? Malcolm pondered his options. The police were out of the question. Their reluctance to face the barest of nightmares in the shadows of their city proved their inadequacies. They did everything in their power to disprove the threats of myths and legends alike, turning a blind eye rather than staying well-informed.

Fear made them foolish. Malcolm, though, refused to follow their example. But where to turn for help?

As Malcolm took his first step toward the manor, the answer to his dilemma arrived. He stood in the chill wind near the front walk.

A vibrant woman with a badge attached to her belt accompanied him, but Malcolm locked on Greg Loren's presence like a lifeline.

He had read about Loren's dismissal from the force. It surprised Malcolm to see Loren in the company of the department that had spurned him. Malcolm, though, understood the man well enough to realize his unwavering dedication to the job—badge or no badge.

Malcolm stood in silence under the small cone of light near the corner. Loren offered a nod to his companion; their farewells were stunted and clearly awkward even from afar. The former detective made his way across the street to a beat-up sedan and hopped inside.

Rushed steps carried Malcolm back to the cab. He should have been in hiding. The killer was out in the world, and Malcolm was on the list of potential targets. Anyone else would have realized the meaning behind Patrick's demise and run like hell in the other direction. Instead, the weary knight slipped back inside the waiting vehicle.

"That it?" the driver said.

Malcolm ignored him. Twin headlights washed over them. The Impala, its driver all but oblivious to the outside world, passed by them without a glance.

Malcolm required allies. More than that, he needed intel on the case of his friend's murder. He held out a wad of cash for the driver.

"Follow that car."

CHAPTER EIGHTEEN

"Wait, what are you saying, Loren?"

"You don't need me, Myers. This isn't my world anymore."

The words stayed with him the entire way home. Loren replayed the conversation, his tone, his mannerisms, and every other detail in a constant loop that kept his foot on the accelerator and his squeezing hands along the steering wheel.

What had he been thinking? First, to answer the damn phone, knowing it had been Myers on the other end, and then to be pulled into an open homicide investigation for his perspective. That wasn't his life anymore. Sure, there were the monsters in the darkness, the ghosts on the subway, but police work? Those days were behind him. They had to be, for his sanity.

Yet the case persisted. His notion about the keys felt right to him. Maybe it was all the time spent with Soriya, where even the smallest detail turned into a walking, talking cataclysm. Loren couldn't get them out of his head. Myers, of course, didn't see it. How could anyone?

Was that why he walked away? Had it been a fear of being the odd man out again, always fighting for his theories to be heard and never knowing when the next struggle would end or how?

The question dogged him the rest of the way home. It clung to him during his brisk walk from the lot around the back of the building to his apartment, desperate not to be thrown off by the billowing wind.

He knew the truth. It was Myers herself. Her presence more than anything, kept Loren from diving into the case headfirst, without a care about the consequences. The very thought of Myers gave him chills and sent a rush of blood coursing through his extremities. She made him want to scream, but also stymied him into silence in the same breath.

Working with Myers was the last thing he needed. Their roller-coaster ride of a partnership never fit the mold. It was all risk and no reward, something Loren couldn't afford any longer.

There was Gabe to think about. He should have been the priority today. Loren still did not know where the kid had run off to rather than face the tortures of a normal high school day. Seventeen, and Gabe had written off the world at large. What was wrong with him?

"What's wrong with *me*?" Loren shut the door to his apartment. He slipped off his jacket and missed the coat rack behind the door. It dropped to the floor in a heap, and he let it rest there, too tired to care or too lazy to be bothered. Either way, the result was the same.

This isn't my world anymore.

Then what was?

Loren groaned. Gabe was in the wind. His friends, the couple who had bent over backwards to look after the kid, were pissed at him. Every move he made, every word he spoke, seemed to be wrong or simply ignorant.

He thought this last year would have been different. He had moved into a new place. While still in the Knoll, the apartment had offered a fresh start for Loren without the baggage that came from his wife's death.

Photos hung on the walls. Potted plants near the window offered life to the space. The kitchen remained clear of dishes and debris, mostly because they hid in boxes tucked beneath the small table by the window. Few groceries occupied the pantry. Mastering that task eluded Loren, even with the extra time on his hands.

Down the hall, on the left, was the bathroom. His towel drooped off the base of the tub in the corner. His untouched razor waited impatiently by the side of the sink.

The room to the right held his bed, unmade from the previous night's sleep. It took some getting used to after years on the couch, but Loren had tried to stick with his promise to move on with his life.

That all changed when he reached the spare room in the back of the place. Boxes were piled in towering aisles like a warehouse. Most of his belongings remained stored within. Mementos of the past—of Beth.

Not everything was stored away, though. Trailing back to the living room, forgetting the mess closed off in the spare space, Loren stopped before the image of Beth. She beamed at him, so young and full of life. They had been so happy together, their time cut far too short.

"Tell me what I'm supposed to do," he said to the photo. It was a silly request, but the words hung in the silence, wishing for an answer. "It's been a year. A year, and I still don't know how to talk to that woman. I still don't know how I'm supposed to feel about what she did."

Loren shifted closer and caught the sparkle of her eyes. "Why her, Beth? Why, of all the people in this stupid little world, did you help me save her? I wish you could tell me. Hell, maybe you did."

His head fell against the wall at his wife's side. "I don't dream anymore. I don't hear your voice in my head. It's been a year, and I still miss you. A year, and what's really changed for me?"

A knock at the door stirred him from his musings. Loren pushed from the plaster, eyeing the shadow beneath the frame suspiciously.

"Definitely not the number of visitors," he muttered under his breath. Instinct made him reach out for his holster hanging from the coat rack. He removed the taser. He'd forgotten to replace the spent cartridge from his subway adventure. The weapon itself would have to be threat enough. He tucked it to his side. Hand on the knob, Loren twisted and pulled the door loose.

"Hello?"

An older man stood in the corridor. Thin with graying hair, the gentleman straightened his posture at Loren's arrival. His hands were before him, clasped together.

"Greg Loren?" the man asked in a deep voice.

Loren kept his eyes on the clasped hands. "You have me at a disadvantage. You are?"

"Malcolm Appleton." His visitor extended one hand. Loren's grip loosened on his weapon. "Patrick Marsh was a dear friend."

"Oh." Loren tucked the taser away and took the hand. "I'm sorry, but I don't—"

"I need your help, Mr. Loren," Malcolm continued. "I think I know what Patrick's killer is after."

CHAPTER NINETEEN

Loren shuffled through his pantry. Besides a layer of dust and neglect, little else occupied the small cupboard. A choice existed between a stale pack of crackers and a couple cans of condensed chicken noodle soup. Loren grabbed the crackers and closed the door.

Malcolm sat at the table, a glass of water cupped between his hands. He remained dignified, even in his apparent grief. Tall and proud, he reminded Loren of his father—on the good days anyway, what few there had been. The man wore a tweed jacket over a dark button-down shirt and khakis. His foot tapped lightly under the table.

Loren dumped a sleeve of crackers onto a plate and joined Malcolm at the table. He slid the entrée over, wincing as Malcolm looked up and noticed the slim pickings of the apartment.

"Sorry there isn't more," Loren said as he took a seat across from his guest.

Malcolm hesitated, then reached for a cracker. "This is fine, thank you." He peered around while he nibbled along the corner of the bountiful feast provided. "I notice quite a few boxes about. Moving soon?"

Loren rubbed at his neck. "Still moving in, actually. I've been… busy." He hated the excuse. Whatever look he shared with Malcolm when he said it conveyed the same disgust, though the aged visitor made no comment. Loren cleared his throat and clasped his hands before him. "Tell me how I can help, Mr. Appleton."

"Malcolm, please."

"Then make it Greg." Malcolm nodded at the request. Loren leaned closer. "Who killed Patrick Marsh?"

Malcolm's eyes sparked. Shock filled his face. "I wish I knew."

"But you do know why he was killed?"

His guest's gaze fell to the table and the half-eaten remnants of the cracker. "That, I am afraid to say, is correct."

"Does it have anything to do with a key?" The question caused Malcolm to straighten. A hand shot to his collar. Loren noticed a chain around Malcolm's neck. "A key like the one you're wearing?"

Malcolm slowly lifted the chain over his head. The key dangled at the end. He set it down between them. Loren couldn't believe it. There was the key, just as he'd predicted. If only Myers had listened to him, not that he'd been certain of anything from his time with her.

Fascinated, Loren took the key in hand and ran his fingers along it. The handle was curved into a heart-shape and the jagged edges along the other end were like teeth. Content with its presence, Loren returned the prized possession to the table, where Malcolm's hand fell over it lovingly.

"To understand the key, you have to understand the story of the five knights."

"Knights?" Loren said, curious. "As in the Middle Ages? The Crusades?"

"As in Camelot."

"Really?" Loren exclaimed in disbelief. "King Arthur? Merlin? All that crap?"

Malcolm held his attention with a stony stare. "All that crap."

Loren ran his hand over his brow. "I'm sorry. I shouldn't have—"

His guest's lips curled, and he quietly chuckled. "It's quite all right. I have trouble believing it myself sometimes." Malcolm let out a long breath before settling along the back of the chair. "Camelot was the peak of human civilization. There were no wants, no needs. Everyone lived in prosperity under the king and his knights.

"But all kingdoms fall. Camelot proved to be no exception to the rule. Mordred's strike, Morgana's deceit, and Lancelot's betrayal shook the kingdom to its foundation. The great table of justice cracked, and everything fell into chaos.

"The loss of Arthur proved too much for most of the knights. Most struck out on their own.

"Those who stayed were unsure of their role or what good they might provide while everything went so awry throughout the kingdom. During this time, Merlin had become reclusive. They say he had taken refuge in the great maze at Gedref to collect his thoughts. Lost in the hedges, Merlin experienced terrible visions of the world to come. What he actually saw, I don't think anyone ever learned. But when he returned to Camelot, Merlin called forth the best of the remaining knights for a special task."

"Let me guess," Loren interjected. "He asked for five knights?"

"An astute assumption," Malcolm chided. "You must have been quite the detective."

"Please continue," Loren said with a slight nod.

"Thank you." Malcolm held the key as he collected his thoughts. "Where was I? Ah, yes. He spoke to these five brave knights of a well of darkness growing in the west. He had witnessed a terrible nightmare and knew the world would suffer if such a threat were allowed to go unchecked.

"It was a prophecy, you see," Malcolm continued. "Merlin saw the future of the world in all its dreadful glory. However, he also found a way to stop it. Five would stand against it. Five noble warriors would hold the line and beat back the final darkness, no matter the cost. There was no doubt in Merlin's mind about who should be sent for this task. None were braver than the knights of Camelot. He tasked the knights to seek the well of darkness and to do everything in their power to stop the evil. If that failed, they were to contain it so that it could not spread.

"The knights, their task at hand, departed Camelot for the last time at the turn of the twelfth century and were never seen again. Not as they were, anyway."

"They came here," Loren mused, hand to his chin.

"They did."

"And you?" Loren asked. "You're one of these knights?"

"Do I look that old to you?" Malcolm replied with a grin.

"I had to ask."

"Well, that opens up many questions of my own." Malcolm shuffled closer to the table.

"You'd be surprised what I've seen."

Malcolm eyed him curiously, then shook his head. "To answer your question, I'm merely a descendant of the knights. All of us are. Or were, in Patrick's case."

"That search of Merlin's? It brought them here, of all places?"

Malcolm nodded. "There is something more to Portents. Myths and legends may walk among us openly now, but they have been here since the founding of the city. The knights settled here in the early days of the twentieth century to protect against those threats."

"Who were they protecting?"

"The rest of the world," Malcolm answered in a calm voice. "How many times has Portents been on the brink of destruction? Where some menace has almost been released from the depths of the countless hells out there? The knights came here to fulfill their duty to Merlin."

"To stop the evil," Loren said.

"Only they couldn't," Malcolm replied. "They certainly tried. They battled all manner of wickedness, but more always came. Containment was their only option."

"What if that didn't work?"

Malcolm lifted the glass and took a long drink. When he lowered the beverage before him, his eyes locked on Loren, deadly serious. "They spoke about that for years. Endless debates of morality versus duty. Oh, the arguments they had. Some… some we carry to this day, Greg. But the course was decided long ago, and duty won out over all else. Should all else fail—if evil succeeded over every ounce of good in this place—the knights needed a way to keep the people of the world from falling with them. They built a fail-safe. A last resort."

"A fail-safe?" What was Loren hearing? Not only were maniacs and monsters around every corner, but there had been a way to stop them and it had never been used? "The key triggers this?"

"All five do," Malcolm confirmed.

"To stop the evil in this city? The keys can do that?"

Malcolm nodded. "Yes."

"Yet you've never used it," Loren said. "Even with everything we've faced lately. Why the hell not?"

"You don't understand, Greg," Malcolm said, his voice soft and restrained. "If we activated this fail-safe, if we fulfilled the prophecy handed down to us by Merlin himself, nothing would survive. Not in Portents."

Loren pushed from the table and stood. "What kind of fail-safe are you talking about?"

"The kind you never want to see activated."

A slow pace carried Loren through the narrow kitchen. What was Malcolm saying? A prophecy handed down from Merlin? One that foretold the dangers Portents would somehow unleash upon the world if left unchecked and the five needed to end the threat? Was such a thing possible? After everything he had been through in his life, how could he doubt it for even a second?

Malcolm's presence crystallized the case for Loren. As much as he wanted to leave it with Myers, to walk away from the life he'd lost, that decision came at too high a price. How had Malcolm come to realize that?

"Why me?" Loren finally asked. "Why didn't you go to the police with all this?"

Malcolm grinned. "I know about you, Greg. About Soriya and her Greystone. I know a fellow knight when I see one."

Loren nearly fell over with laughter. He gripped the counter behind him and leaned close. "Me? A knight?"

"You laugh, but who else has stood up to such menaces and lived to tell the tale?"

"I don't know if I'd call this living," he muttered. The boxes dominating his spare room and scattered throughout the apartment served as a constant reminder about the absence of life more than any attempt to live one.

Malcolm shook his head. He joined Loren at the counter. "I need your help, Greg, to protect the others."

"Why not go to them directly?"

"The second the news hit about Patrick, they went to ground," Malcolm said. "I think that was what the killer wanted."

"The body dump," Loren commented. "They used it to scare you out of your homes."

"And out into the open."

"You came here. Where would the others go?"

"I have some thoughts, but…" He looked away, ashamed at the lack of answers. "Will you help me?"

The decision was obvious the second he'd let the man into his home. No matter what his feelings for Myers and the Portents Police Department, Loren was and always would be a protector of the city. It was time to accept that.

"Of course," he said.

"Good." Malcolm wiped his tired eyes. "Where do we start?"

"We?" Loren pulled away, suddenly reticent about the decision. "Malcolm, I—"

Malcolm pointed to the table and the object at the center. "That key is my only purpose in this life. These knights are my family.

They're all I have left."

"Right." Loren sighed. He turned toward the open window across the living room. Night had fallen during their discussion. With the late hour already in place, Loren motioned for the hallway and led his visitor through the apartment. "Take the bedroom, Malcolm. We'll start in the morning."

CHAPTER TWENTY

Nightmares plagued Loren. His mind whirled from the dizzying tale spun by his unexpected guest. Visions of destruction—the Portents skyline in flames and crumbling—swam through the sea of his subconscious.

By the time morning arrived, Loren felt as if he had just lain down. His eyes were bleary, his head heavy with thoughts of the threat to come and the dead man at the center of it all. He leaned off the side of the couch, another reason for the lack of a restful sleep, and bent over his knees. Hands ran the length of his face as he tracked his swirling thoughts.

The danger was real in Portents. He'd said as much dozens of times. Murder and mayhem were the city's specialty. He constantly worried about it escalating, that the threat would spread faster than a plague to consume more and more innocents. Recalling Chaac's rise during his brief stint in Chicago cemented Portents' destructive influence on the world.

But to destroy the city as the only path forward?

Loren shook his head. He reached for his phone on the coffee table and flipped through the notifications piled high over the course of the last few hours. Before he had slept, he'd reached out to Myers to let her know about Malcolm Appleton and the other names listed by the man during his tale. Uniforms had been sent out to bring the surviving three into protective custody. Two had vacated their homes and were in the wind. Myers found the last, though the news wasn't any better on that front.

Joseph Buchwald was dead. His obituary had posted in the Gazette two weeks earlier.

Loren took the news in stride, gathering up Malcolm for a quick trip. Hearing about the death of another knight brought an additional layer of grief to Malcolm's weathered face. He quietly directed Loren north from the Knoll. They skirted the side of Allure and the old city until they reached the Corridor. The Courtyard building remained a ruined wreck. Few of the homes had been rebuilt in the aftermath of Cerberus' invasion.

Loren kept his eyes on the road, refusing to let the memory of those nights bog him down further. There was enough pain on the day and plenty still to come. Row housing turned into little nooks of life. Apartments sat atop shops, delis, eateries, hardware stores and barber shops, like something out of the past.

Malcolm pointed ahead to a six-story complex in the middle of the block on Janus. Loren parked across the street and stepped out of the car. Wind whipped his hair and bit into his skin. He tucked his hands deeper into his jacket pockets and cut through the middling traffic.

The edifice had been marred by time. Chunks of brick had shattered over the years. Some left gaping holes in the structure. The windows were stained from age, several with deep cracks on the surface. Shades blew behind those opened, but most hid the occupants from view. Along the corners of the rooftop, statuary loomed over the street. A pair of gargoyle-looking beasts stared down from their gray perches. Their similarity to Patrick Marsh's home struck Loren, but he said nothing when Malcolm joined him at the front door.

Instead, he held up the grieving man with a soft hand. "You can stay in the car if you want."

Malcolm thought the offer over for a long moment, then shook his head. "No. I... I have to see it for myself. The two of us grew up under the burden of the keys. Almost three decades together. Joseph wasn't much older than me. Neither was Patrick, for that matter. For two of us to pass so close together..."

Loren understood. Loss came quickly; the weight of the dead always overshadowed what life might remain for those left behind. "This is where he lived?"

"Since his divorce, yes." Malcolm led the pair into the building. The door stuck in the frame, forcing both to push for entry.

"There were children too?"

"A son, I believe." Sadness filled his face. "Joseph and I were never very close, Greg. We never saw eye-to-eye over our task as knights."

The pair passed along the mailboxes that dominated the right wall in the entryway. A small window sat open on the left, connected to what appeared to be an office. The superintendent of the building was listed on the glass, though the letters had peeled over time and the glass had become obscured with grease stains and spiderwebs.

A lone figure sat behind the glass. His jowls filled the window, his portly frame barely able to fit upon the lone stool in the space. Behind him, a door opened to what must have been his own apartment in the building. An acrid odor rose from within. It grew more powerful with every step Loren took toward the window.

"What do ya want?" He wore an undershirt no longer able to call itself white. His pants were torn in several places, his entire left knee exposed.

"Are you the super here?"

"I prefer landlord," the man said in a sharp tone.

"I'm working with the police on a case that may be connected with a resident here." Loren said. He wished he carried a badge to share or any kind of authority to make the work easier. Depending on the kindness of strangers had never worked well for him, but it was all he had at the moment.

"Who?"

"Joseph Buchwald."

Irritation crept onto the man's face. His massive hand slammed against his brow and pushed back the surviving strands of hair. "Christ. Even dead, the guy's giving me a headache."

Loren leaned closer. "If we could take a look at his apartment?"

The landlord grumbled, unsure of the request. Malcolm shuffled to the window, a hand to the glass. Between two fingers, he held a fifty-dollar bill. "It would help us a great deal."

"Fine." The man snatched the cash. He stood, and the stool groaned with relief. The landlord slipped from the makeshift office to join the pair in the corridor. "Follow me."

His staggered steps carried him toward the stairs. Malcolm moved to follow, but Loren held him back a moment.

"Let's not follow too closely." Loren pinched his nose and wafted the air between them. The pair stifled a laugh before trailing the out-of-shape landlord up the two flights of stairs to the third floor of the building.

His breathing grew heavy, a hand over his chest. Loren wondered if another death was in the cards and what would happen if the heaving landlord fell backwards when he finally dropped.

Thankfully, the obese super survived their jaunt to lead them to an apartment along the northeast corner of the building. He jammed his key into the lock and opened the door for them.

"Here it is."

Loren and Malcolm stepped inside. Cracked and peeling paint littered the walls. The hiss of the radiator in the corner sounded like a teapot boiling. The kitchen bled into the living area, with a single bedroom in the back. All stood empty.

"I'm sorry," Loren said as the landlord joined them. "Where are Buchwald's belongings?"

"No clue," the man said with an indifferent shrug. "Neighbor kid helped box everything up, and I left a message with Buchwald's son. Lousy prick never got back to me, but maybe he took it all. Looked like a bunch of junk to me."

Loren read the code well. The landlord had clearly pawed through the man's belongings and found nothing worth stealing. Rolling his eyes, Loren pushed it aside. He wished he could do the same to the man himself, but questions remained.

"You never saw Buchwald's son?"

The landlord shook his head.

"Did you happen upon a key by any chance?" Malcolm tried to hide his concern. "It would have looked quite old."

"No keys," the man said. The irritation returned. "And no rent for his last month, either. Probably won't be able to rent the place without fumigating. Guy couldn't even have the decency to croak in a hospital."

Loren sighed. "I feel your pain. Where does he get off dying like that?"

"Exactly." The landlord paused, catching Loren's tone. "Hey, are you putting one over me?"

Malcolm's hand fell on the man's shoulder. "My dear sir, he's putting them all over you."

The landlord rubbed his head. A confused stare passed between them.

Loren cleared his throat. "Look. Can you tell us anything else about Buchwald? Any surprise visitors? Angry neighbors—other than yourself, of course?"

"Nay." The portly fool hitched his thumb toward the hall and the door opposite Buchwald's. "Maybe he can. I seen them together a couple times, going for walks, getting their mail, and stuff."

"Thanks," Loren said.

"Yes, thank you. You've been…" Malcolm raised his hand toward the landlord, who had already headed out of the apartment and started back down the hall without another glance at them. "…a help."

"He was something, all right," Loren grumbled. He scanned the emptiness of the apartment once more, then moved for the door across the hall. "Shall we?"

Loren knocked. Steps rose from a distance, and a shadow passed beneath the frame as the pair was inspected through the peephole. After a quick peek, the door opened and a tall, well-built figure filled the frame. The youth in his face practically screamed early-twenties, though there was a heaviness in his deep blue eyes.

"Yes?" the young man said. "Can I help you?"

"I'm Greg Loren, and this is my friend, Malcolm. We're working with the police, and we'd like to ask you a few questions about your relationship with Joseph Buchwald, if that's all right?"

"I was an old friend," Malcolm stated.

The youth considered the request before shifting to the side of the door. "Come on in. Please."

The apartment was spartan. A small table occupied the kitchen. A single couch in the living room and a standing lamp in the corner made up most of the furniture in the space. Army posters decorated the walls, with the folded flag of a fallen soldier atop a narrow table like a shrine. Everything appeared put in its proper place, not kept locked up in boxes.

"Thank you," Loren said. "Mr.—"

"Adam," the youth replied with a smile. "Adam North."

"Thank you, Mr. North." Loren let the door close behind him. From his position, he could see exercise equipment in the bedroom. The sweat still upon the young man's brow made it clear the weights had been in use before their unexpected arrival. "You live here alone?"

"Yes."

"You became friends with Mr. Buchwald?"

Adam nodded. "He got sick. Cancer. He had trouble getting around. I went through it with my mother. No one should have to do it alone. I started helping him with his groceries, then with cleaning around the apartment."

"What about his son?" Loren asked.

Adam raised an eyebrow. "He would visit—rarely. Always un-announced, Joseph would tell me. I don't think he cared whether his dad lived or died."

Loren pointed across the hall. "The boxes in Joseph's apartment. Did you see who took them?"

"N—no," Adam answered, concern in his voice. "I assumed they were still in there."

Malcolm pushed forward. "Was there a key among Joseph's belongings, Adam?"

"A key? I don't—" Adam trailed off. His hand shot to his chin, as if he were weighing the question. His eyes stayed on Malcolm. A curious look ran up and down the elder statesman. Adam slowly shook his head. "There may have been. I… I didn't go through the chests and drawers he kept locked away. He was my friend, but his life was his own."

Malcolm let the answer settle between them, then fell back a step. "Of course."

Loren extended his hand, a soft smile on his face. "Thank you for your time, Mr. North."

"Yes," Malcolm said with a wave as he moved for the door. "Thank you."

"You're welcome to stay," Adam said, offering the couch. "I'm finished with my set for the day, and there's a fresh pot of coffee."

"Another time," Loren said.

The young man read their shared looks and nodded. "Not a problem at all," Adam said with a sad smile. "If you need anything else, don't hesitate to reach out. I'm happy to help any way I can."

Loren nodded from the hall. "We will. Thank you again."

The door closed, dropping them into shadow.

"What now?" Malcolm asked in a hushed voice.

Silence filled the corridor as Loren took the first step toward the exit. The dead had taken their secrets with them, leaving the pair with nothing but unanswered questions.

"I wish I knew, Malcolm," Loren muttered. "I wish I knew."

CHAPTER TWENTY-ONE

Frustration followed them to the street. Malcolm continued to gaze at the ground, mired in the grief of another friend gone from the world. Loren's focus remained on Buchwald as well, but from a different perspective.

They had come to the apartment for insight into the dead. If the key had been taken, it would have pointed to signs of another murder like the Marsh case. Buchwald, though, had died of cancer. The illness behind his demise complicated matters more than it helped.

"That went well," Loren said when they reached the sidewalk. The wind continued to pick up. Clouds rolled in from the south, but at the moment, the sky was bright.

"Joseph always had a way with people," Malcolm said. The landlord certainly attested to that. The only one who seemed to genuinely care about him was the lonely kid across the hall. Even Malcolm held a degree of irritation at the mere mention of Buchwald, which surprised Loren.

"He worried you, didn't he?"

Malcolm sighed. "I don't like to speak ill of the dead."

"Make an exception," Loren pressed, curious and in need of some insight.

"Joseph believed we were wrong to stay our hand," Malcolm answered. "He saw the events of the last few years as signs of the end. Our duty was—"

"To what?" Loren interrupted. He still couldn't believe Malcolm's story about the fail-safe. "What was your duty as a knight, Malcolm? To destroy the city?"

"To save the world."

It was too much power to put in the hands of so few. Five people determined whether a city of five million lived or died, and one of them had an itchy trigger finger. How did no one else know about this?

Why didn't Soriya tell me about this?

A year after her death, and Loren still floundered at the job. He knew next to nothing about the so-called true city, and what he had learned barely kept his head above water.

"I hate prophecies," Loren grumbled. "They never end with cake and ice cream."

The pair skirted through traffic to the parked Impala. Horns blared, angry gestures shot out from open windows, but Loren pushed ahead to step out from the shadow of the apartment building and the growing threat that rose with Buchwald's demise.

"Another key is missing, Greg," Malcolm said, reading Loren's thoughts.

"We don't know that," Loren replied. "Hell, we don't even know if Buchwald's death is connected with Marsh's."

"How could they not be?" Malcolm moved closer, hands tucked deep in his pockets. "Two knights are dead. One of them wanted nothing more than to activate the fail-safe and destroy this city."

"Buchwald had cancer."

"And the second he was gone, Patrick Marsh was targeted," Malcolm snapped. "Don't tell me they are not connected. They have to be."

Loren stepped over to the sidewalk, leaving behind the Impala for the grieving knight. "You're right. Malcolm, I'm sorry. You're right."

"No… No, I shouldn't have—"

"We need to locate Buchwald's son," Loren continued. "I'll call my… my friend at Central for help with that. She can also look into Buchwald's passing to see if foul play was involved."

"Thank you."

Loren waved him down. "You don't have to thank me, Malcolm. I know how tough this must be for you. But you've been rock solid throughout. You should be the detective, not me."

"You're too hard on yourself."

"Maybe not hard enough," Loren muttered. "Come on, let's get out of here and—"

A shadow swooped across the sky. It blotted out the sun for a brief second. A dozen bystanders along the sidewalk stopped to glance up at the quickly shifting darkness. They pointed up, terror and confusion on their faces.

"Greg," Malcolm called, joining the others.

Loren peered at the sky, and his brow furrowed at the streaking shadow. "What the hell is that?"

Large and gray, the shadow soared from Buchwald's building toward them. The statuary Loren had noticed upon arriving no longer loomed over them. Now it flew right at him.

Loren rushed for Malcolm. He pulled him to the sidewalk and out of the line of fire. The stone creature swooped over them, shot skyward into the light, and then descended rapidly.

"Wait," Loren said. He gradually noted the statue's trajectory. "No. Not the—"

The stone beast crashed atop the roof of Loren's Impala. Sharp claws dug through the metal, tearing at the frame of the vehicle as Loren and Malcolm cringed on the sidewalk.

"—car," Loren finished. The beast strode from the car, shredding metal beneath its stony paws with each step. The roof caved in from the impact, and the windows shattered. Loren let out a deep breath. "I only had forty-two payments left on that hunk of junk."

A hand fell on Loren's shoulder. "Back away, Greg," Malcolm said. "Slowly."

"Any idea what I'm looking at?"

Despite being made of stone, the beast was intricately sculpted. A tail whipped behind its hind paws. The body was that of a lion with thick legs and sharp claws. The wings and head, though, were clearly inspired by an eagle with an immense beak that screeched at them in anger.

"Malcolm?"

"A griffin," Malcolm said in a quiet, petrified voice. "It's a protector of King Arthur—and of his knights. Though I don't think this one will listen to me."

"Run."

Malcolm staggered back as the crowd dispersed in a panic. He nearly tripped upon turning away from the approaching beast, but Loren lifted him up to his feet and pushed him ahead.

"Go, Malcolm, go!" Loren yelled, trailing after his companion. He looked back as the griffin swiped at the air toward the fleeing innocents. "I'll try to buy you some time. I—"

The griffin screeched at his words and lifted into the air. It soared after Malcolm, claws at the ready. Loren jumped into the path. His jacket ripped away as the beast locked on. Loren felt pressure in his chest, then a weightlessness as the monster took off into the heavens.

Malcolm screamed from the ground as Loren left it. "Greg!"

CHAPTER TWENTY-TWO

The world spun. From the blues of the spinning sky to the deep blacks of the pavement, nothing remained stationary. Up was down and back again in seconds as clouds and people blurred together for Loren.

He couldn't catch his breath. The dizzying array, constantly spinning from the griffin's jostling claws, cost Loren any chance of finding his bearings in his struggles against the stone beast.

Screams carried on the wind. They were joined by honking horns and crashing cars. People pointed to the sky. (*Maybe they were pointing? Maybe they were people?*) Loren thought he heard the snapping of images and the narrating of videos over the screeches of his captor.

Weightlessness returned. The griffin let go of him and he fell. Five feet, then ten, and Loren could do nothing to slow his descent. Nothing jutted out to save him; no power line, street lamp, or building was within reach. It was open sky.

At fifteen feet, the griffin swooped down once more and snatched Loren by his torso. Claws dug deeper, cutting through his shirt and into his sides. Loren cried out and did so again as the griffin released him.

This time didn't last as long. A second later, the beast had him once more. It followed the same pattern again as the beast repositioned Loren for a better grasp.

Loren wanted to throw up. He begged for release, then countered that with a purely delusional plea for a man in a red cape to save his ass instead. There was no reprieve and no hope as the griffin clamped tighter.

His shirt cut away, the Superman symbol all but destroyed from the constant jostling. "Come on," Loren grumbled, caught between breaths. "Not the shirt. Not the—"

A sharp rip ended the debate. Loren's shirt dropped away toward the ground. His gaze moved to track the descent, and Loren cursed his stupidity. They were at least fifty feet up and climbing.

Turning back to the griffin, Loren reached for the beast's legs. "Hey!" he shouted. "How about we talk about this? I'm not a big fan of heights!"

The griffin's beak snapped at him. Loren's hands fell away. Claws dug into his back. Loren cried out, matching the beast's fury, but unable to do a thing about it.

The monster was in control. When it dove through the growing cloud cover, the city returned. Buildings took shape, as did the people below, including the flashing lights of police and emergency vehicles. The beast soared toward them all, its shriek carried along the wind like a battle cry.

To Loren, though, it was his death cry. All it took was one sharp turn, one drop, and his life was over. There would be no more worrying about Gabe, about Myers, or about all the other stupid crap that plagued his weary brain.

A tightness rose in his chest. The griffin's claws squeezed, blood trickling down its talons. Then they snapped open, and Loren felt nothing but air again.

"This wasn't what I had in mind!"

Loren closed his eyes and waited for the end. He crashed hard a second later. His side slammed into the rooftop of Buchwald's building. Momentum carried him from the impact, bounding across the gravel like a skipping stone on water.

Breath returned to Loren's lungs. Pain shot through every inch of his body. Still, Loren looked at the rooftop with a smile on his face.

"Oh, sweet asphalt," Loren said. "How I've missed you."

Across the way, the griffin landed. Gravel spread beneath the beast's impact. Stone kicked up and sprayed the recovering Loren. He glared at the screeching hybrid.

"I sure as hell didn't miss you."

Loren grabbed hold of a nearby exhaust pipe. His legs screamed, but he struggled his way to his feet. "Now, look, I don't know what you want from me—"

The griffin launched at him, claws first. Loren dove, instinct fighting through the agony of every muscle in his body. The right claw of the beast raked his heel, but Loren cleared the path of attack before more serious damage could be done.

The second he was out of range, Loren bounded away. His ankle cried out with each staggered step, but he pushed through it.

"Okay," he said. "I get it. You want my head. Why?"

The griffin bellowed. It offered no insight, no crucial clue to explain its preoccupation with Loren. Not that the former detective needed much, anyway. It was clear the second the beast arrived who it was after and why.

The beast was after Malcolm. Loren couldn't let anything happen to the knight, but his options were getting increasingly limited by the second. The griffin blocked the exit, and Loren was in no condition to reach the fire escape.

All Loren needed to do was survive, but the odds were not in his favor. The second the griffin struck out, he thought the fight was over. Claws extended, its beak wide, the griffin moved in for the kill.

A shadow dropped from above and slammed into the stony beast. It tackled the griffin to the ground, causing the pair to roll away from a startled and shocked Loren.

"Huh?"

"I'll handle this," a voice called from atop the creature. The shadow kicked the beast, then somersaulted backward into the sky before landing between Loren and the griffin.

Loren blinked hard at the lithe figure and nearly collapsed at her sudden presence.

"Soriya?"

CHAPTER TWENTY-THREE

It couldn't be...

Loren stood in stunned silence. He ran his hand over his forehead, then down to his neck to check his pulse. Even through the thrumming in his veins, he doubted the validity of his life. He must have fallen to his death, smashed against the pavement in a puddle of broken bones and sinewy goop. There was no other explanation for the presence of the woman before him, a woman he watched sacrifice herself to save everyone.

"Soriya..." he whispered. "How is it possible? You... You... Look out!"

Soriya ducked beneath the swiping claw of the griffin. The beast shrieked with renewed ire, not caring about the change in victims. It merely wanted whatever death and destruction it could carve out, and Soriya appeared more than happy to oblige.

Rolling under the sweeping arm, Soriya kicked off the side of the creature. It tipped over but didn't fall, propped up by an outstretched wing. With a shrill cry, the griffin jumped back into the fray.

The fight carried them across the rooftop and back again. Soriya said nothing; she let her fists speak for her. She pummeled against the stone in quick jabs, then leaped, ducked, and dodged from the frustrated assault of her target. The griffin failed to keep up with her dizzying pace, like it was stuck in slow motion. Minor scrapes turned to pebbles, which became chunks as the creature took blow after blow from the steadfast Soriya.

Loren could do nothing but stand in awe at the display. When the griffin shot forward unexpectedly and caught Soriya along her right leg with its twisted claw, though, he knew the time for standing still was at an end. He shifted forward as Soriya ripped the shards of stone from her bleeding wound and prepared for another strike.

"Soriya," he breathed, another step in her direction. "Let me help. Tell me how I can—"

The griffin struck out, twin paws reaching for their target. Soriya caught the paws and lifted the beast away from her. Spinning to greet Loren, a stern look conveyed everything she needed without a single word spoken.

Loren raised his hands and backpedaled to a safe distance. "Right. Shutting up now."

She pushed the beast back. The griffin landed on its hind paws, then twisted around. The beast's tail swung out and caught Soriya around her midsection. It twisted like a rope, stone somehow pliable in the movement, yet too rigid to break. The griffin tossed Soriya clear across the rooftop.

She crashed into the access door leading to the apartment building below. Frustrated, Soriya slammed her fist against the ground. The griffin screeched through its cracked beak. Shattered eyes searched for its victim.

Soriya reached to her side and the hand-woven pouch always tied tight to her belt. She removed the item locked within and held it before her.

Loren grinned at the sight of the Greystone. As the griffin pounced toward Soriya, Loren waited for the light to take hold on the small stone's surface. He'd studied the runes in her absence. He had hoped to pass along the knowledge to Gabe, but the kid had taken the lessons in his own direction—a perfectly acceptable tactic, though Loren had missed the runes more than he'd ever thought possible.

Stray glances shot to the heavens for signs of lightning in the morning sky. He held the air conditioning unit behind him as he imagined the wind rushing toward them. Loren made every preparation as Soriya clutched the Greystone before her, willing the griffin to its very destruction.

Nothing came, however. There was no stiff wind, no rising fire, and no lightning from the clear sky. The stone did nothing but sit along her palms. Soriya squeezed harder, to no avail, and as the beast raised its claws to strike, she lowered the weapon and dove clear of the blow.

Tucking the stone away, Soriya returned to the fight with renewed anger. A scream erupted, and she launched from her crouched position toward the griffin. She clutched the raised paw of the creature, then twisted to its backside and landed between its wings.

Furious fists pummeled the griffin. Chunks of stone flew free. The griffin's screeches, so full of rage and anger, changed to panic and terror. It clawed at the woman on its back, unable to reach, unable to do anything but take the punishment unleashed.

The griffin collapsed onto the rooftop. Life bled from its broken eyes until finally, with a great heave, the stone collapsed and shattered.

Soriya sat among the debris, fists clenched before her. Her chest rose and fell quickly in waves as she sought to contain the rage viciously used to subdue the threat.

"Soriya! I… That was… Well, brutal is the word." He rushed to her side as she struggled to stand. "Are you okay? I mean, not being dead is a plus, but… Soriya?"

The young warrior wavered before him, a hand on her brow. "It's good to see you too, Loren."

Without another word, she collapsed into his arms. Her eyes simply closed and her body gave way.

CHAPTER TWENTY-FOUR

The impossible rested in Loren's bed. Soriya was alive. An entire year of mourning, and she simply returned as if she had gone out for milk and eggs. The feeling of failing her last request had plagued him after her passing. Every decision he'd made came from a place of loss and regret. Those feelings had been for nothing.

Loren weighed everything by the door to his bedroom. He watched the steady breathing of the unconscious woman in continued disbelief. How had she come back after what happened? How long had she been back? More importantly, how long had she let him continue to spiral like he always knew he would?

Turning away from the room, Loren closed the door and moved for the living room. Malcolm sat in quiet contemplation on the couch. For as much as Loren had been through that morning, Malcolm had taken more than his fair share of gut punches. Another death had clearly worn him out, yet instead of resting, he continued to mull over the case and the missing keys.

When Loren arrived in the room, Malcolm stirred. "How is she?"

Loren couldn't help but chuckle at the question. "If only there were a simple answer." He took the chair opposite the couch and fell back against the cushion. "What was that thing back there? Did you say it was a griffin?"

Malcolm ran his hands over his knees. "Yes."

"You said it was a protector?"

"Of the knights, yes."

"It seemed more interested in murder than protecting," Loren said.

Malcolm nodded. He pushed off the couch and paced the room

to the window. "The statuary is controlled, summoned by a knight in a time of need."

"So someone sent that monstrosity," Loren said. "Someone who knows about the knights and what the keys are for."

He wanted to go further with the question. Someone had known they were at Buchwald's apartment. Someone had trailed their movements and didn't care for the questions being asked, be it about the dead man or his prized possession. Whoever sent the griffin to silence them had wanted to cover their tracks as efficiently as possible. Why put a scare into someone when you could silence them? And from a distance, thanks to the use of some damn statues.

"Malcolm?"

The knight shifted his creaking frame, then leaned against the wall. "Yes. I'm afraid it seems someone knows."

"Newton or Michaels?"

"No," Malcolm answered quickly. "No, they wouldn't."

Loyalty only went so far, but Malcolm appeared confident about the pair's innocence. That left only one explanation. "Anyone else part of the club?"

"I'm afraid not. Unless…"

Loren leaned off the edge of his seat. "Buchwald's son."

It kept coming back to the missing player in the drama. Loren had already reached out to Myers about their potential suspect. Myers promised to handle things on her end. He didn't bother to mention his entertaining morning, trying not to think about his swollen ankle, the cuts adorning his midsection, or the shredded shirt that could easily have been his entire body.

Malcolm stared at Loren; his musings offered little more than an awkward silence. Loren stood and joined the knight by the window.

"Do you think he told his kid about everything?"

"It's certainly possible," Malcolm said. "Despite his beliefs about Portents, Joseph always seemed quite proud of his standing with the knights. To be able to share that with an impressionable youth?"

"Have you?" Loren asked, catching the distant stare in the man.

Malcolm's gaze fell to the floor. "No. No, I… I never did."

Loren pushed off the wall. Slow, steady steps carried him across the room. "Buchwald was dying. Cancer. That can give you a lot of time to reflect, to consider your options."

"To make plans," Malcolm said.

Loren snapped his fingers. "Exactly. So what else does this guy have at his disposal?"

Malcolm shifted uncomfortably along the wall. "I'd like to say the knights have always considered themselves to be enough for the task. Unfortunately, you've met one of the many weapons we've accumulated in our arsenal."

"I don't like the sound of that, Malcolm."

"You shouldn't," he said. "Over the years, the knights have created or communed with many such guardians. Griffins are among the fiercest in strength and number, but there is also—"

The door to the apartment burst open. Malcolm jumped back against the wall. Loren spun to greet the intruder, snatching the taser at his side.

"Loren!" Gabe blitzed into the room in a panic.

The weapon lowered, though his heart refused to do the same. "Gabe?"

The kid stopped when he noticed the taser, then continued through the room, rushing for Loren. He hugged the man tight. "You're here!"

"What are you—"

Gabe pushed off, then looked him over. "Are you all right? When I heard what happened, I had to see if you—"

"Hey. Relax. What—?" Loren's hand fell on Gabe's shoulder. Glancing at his wrist, Loren noticed the time. It was still early afternoon. "Did you cut school again?"

Gabe blinked hard at the accusation. "Loren, I—"

Loren waved off the coming excuse with disgust. "Dammit, Gabe. You can't keep doing that!"

"Are you kidding me?" Gabe snapped. "I was worried about you!"

Loren turned away from the kid, hands on his hips. He started looking for his phone. "I'm fine. I don't need you worrying—" He stopped. "Wait. How did you hear about what happened?"

"Seriously?" Gabe grabbed the remote from the end table and turned on the television. "It's been all over the news." The footage came up almost immediately. Amateur video displayed Loren's flight in the griffin's grip for all to see. More images filtered on the screen, including a lovely one of a shirtless Loren falling, a scream on his lips. "They keep replaying the footage. You're trending on every major social network."

Loren's hand fell to his brow. "I'm trending. That's something I never want to hear again."

He snatched the remote away from Gabe and turned off the television. Tossing the control aside, Loren shook his head and started for the kitchen.

"What's going on?" Gabe asked with renewed concern. "What can I do?"

"Nothing, Gabe," Loren replied in a sharp tone. He caught the surprise in Gabe's eyes, as well as the hurt. Loren sighed, softening his voice. "I need to figure this out."

Before Gabe could respond, a voice called from down the hall. "Maybe I can help."

Soriya stood outside the bedroom door, using the frame for support. Gabe's mouth stood agape, a dozen questions demanding to be asked. They were the same ones Loren had, and he took the opportunity to step between the shocked kid and the resurrected woman.

Soriya beckoned him into the room. "We should talk, Loren."

CHAPTER TWENTY-FIVE

Everything felt different in the world. From the air in her lungs to the thin carpet beneath her bare feet, Soriya struggled to come to grips with reality. She kept the lights dim in the bedroom; the muted sun behind the blinds was almost too intense for her to handle.

She led Loren into the bedroom. When she heard the soft click of the door behind him, she knew her time was limited. There were so many things to say, and she didn't know where to begin.

Rather than jump into the deep end with Loren, Soriya motioned to the decor on the walls. "I like the new place."

Loren said nothing. He simply stood against the door, hands in his pockets. The shirt, while ratty from age, appeared to have been cleaned recently. His face, however, needed some attention, especially with the scrapes inflicted by the statue earlier in the day. Still, through it all, Soriya recognized the changes in the man. There was a brightness to him she hadn't seen in quite some time.

"I'm glad you were able to move on," she continued in the awkward silence between them. "How have you been?"

Loren struggled to hold back a laugh. "You… You're asking me how I've been? Talking about my apartment?" He pushed from the door. "Soriya, you died. I watched you die."

The shots rang out through her memory, like claps of thunder crashing in her ears. There were two of them, and with them came the heat in her chest and the sound of blood trickling from her body.

"Harvey," Soriya said in the softest of whispers.

Tears dotted Loren's eyes. "He shot you. And then—"

"The Bypass," she finished. The swirling green energy had been out of control. It threatened to explode and take more than just the

Courtyard with it. Portents had been in danger, and she had to stop it the only way she could.

She had leaped inside, pulling Harvey along with her to end his threat. With the Greystone in her grasp, Soriya fell through eternity to close off the Bypass from the world and save everyone. All it cost her was her life.

"It vanished," Loren said. "You vanished. How are you standing here now?"

She turned away from him, hugging her arms to her chest. "I don't know."

"Soriya."

Loren reached out to comfort her. His sympathy was the last thing she needed. It drove hot spikes through her veins, and she fought back a scream. Pulling away, Soriya spun around to face him. "I don't know, Loren! I remember the light and falling. Falling forever. But I was content with the decision. And then?" She closed her eyes to force down the flood of emotions raging within her. "The Bypass… it tossed me away."

"What do you—"

"I woke up in the chamber, Loren," Soriya said over him, afraid to let the memory slip—afraid if she didn't get through it all, she never would. "There was a shadow. I saw it, but only for a second, and then it was gone and I was alone. I found the strength to stand and face what I had done." She pulled down her shirt slightly. The bullet wounds from Harvey were gone, erased from her skin as if they had never been there. "The Bypass tossed me back to the cold. It healed my body, but my mind? There are holes in my memory, Loren. Things I can't remember. All I know for certain is I haven't earned my chance at forever."

The implications hung over them in a veil of heavy silence. Soriya sat along the side of the bed, her knees tucked tight to her chest. Loren hovered close by, always present, without smothering her. His sadness was clear, eyes heavy with pain.

"I… I'm sorry, Soriya."

She wiped her runny nose on her sleeve. "I'm fine, Loren. I am."

Loren joined her on the bed. "That's not what I saw back there. The way you handled the griffin? The violence you unleashed without a snarky comment or so much as a smirk?"

She pushed off the bed in a flash. "I handled it. That's the job."

"Of the Greystone," Loren pressed. "You took it out. Why didn't you use it?"

"I saved your life, Loren," she snapped in disbelief. "Some gratitude wouldn't be out of order."

"You think… You think I'm not grateful?" Loren shook his head, hands before him. "That I'm not ecstatic to see you again, to have you here and now? Soriya, this last year—"

"A year?" Her eyes shot wide. She clutched the dresser for support. "It's been a year?"

Loren's voice softened. "You didn't know."

The changes came into focus. So many more than she had thought possible. Loren's new apartment and his appearance topped the list, but there was also the boy outside—Gabe. He looked so much older than she remembered. She had thought only weeks had passed. A year had been taken from her. What else had happened? What else had she lost during her absence?

Loren stood at her side when she turned to face him. His hands fell to her shoulders, a soft touch running down her arms. "You should rest."

Anger welled up. The room blurred with her rising fury. She knocked his hands aside. "I don't need to rest!" Her hand shot back, and she delivered a slap across his cheek.

Loren said nothing at the act. Reeling from her toward the bed, he rubbed at his cheek, surprise and hurt in his troubled gaze.

Soriya cradled her hand. It pulsed from the blow. The world refocused as her rage subsided. "Loren, I…"

He waved her down as he slowly retreated towards the door. "Try to sleep, Soriya. You've been through… Well, you've been through more than any of us could possibly understand."

"I…"

"We can talk more later."

The argument rested on her lips, as did her apology. Rather than risk the former with the latter, Soriya offered only a slight nod.

Loren smiled, grateful, then exited the room without another word. The door closed, leaving her in the dim light of the bedroom, alone once more.

She sat at the edge of the bed. She raised her hands before her eyes. They appeared alien, like nothing she'd ever seen before. How could she have done that to Loren? What the hell was wrong with her?

Nothing made sense anymore. All she felt was anger and rage—a desire to do nothing more than fight against the world.

The question of her return echoed through her mind. Fingers rubbed deeply into her scalp, and she fell upon the bed's comforter to stare at the ceiling. The questions frightened her the more she considered them. Yet it was the lack of answers that terrified her the most.

CHAPTER TWENTY-SIX

Gabe paced the room. He wrung his hands as he created a circuit around the couch to the door and back again. Soriya was alive. How the hell was Soriya alive? The question made him dizzy, yet it failed to quell the pain in his chest or keep his blood from boiling at what else her return meant.

Loren had said nothing to him. Here Gabe was, rushing out of school—and his history exam, again—to make sure Loren was okay after the vicious attack that morning, and what had been his partner's response?

Another lecture. It was all anyone ever did with Gabe. From Curtis and Nicole, his so-called family, to the siblings who wanted nothing to do with him, all the way to Loren. Loren, who had been there for him through so much, who had stood by him in his darkest hour and offered him a purpose.

Their year together, hunting the monsters in the dark, had helped Gabe through the grieving process. Losing his parents to a devastating fire, and the murder of his brother, would have shattered him if not for Loren's actions. Instead, Gabe found strength in their memory.

But now?

Loren had joined the chorus of disappointed adults in his life. Worse, with Soriya's return, what the hell did Loren need with Gabe any longer?

On his fifth circuit through the room, Gabe stopped near the door to the apartment. The bedroom was still closed off, the discussion within merely a series of grumbling voices. As he moved to the hall for a closer listen, a throat cleared.

The old man on the couch leaned along the edge, his hands before him and a soft smile on his face. "They need time."

"I should be in the room," Gabe replied. "I deserve to be in there."

"I'm sure you do," the man said. "You look like you have seen much for someone so young."

"I'm not some kid," Gabe snapped. He reached into his pocket and let the small object within rest against his palm. "I'm the Greystone. Or, at least, I was."

The old man said nothing. He stared at the stone.

Gabe snapped his fist closed to cover the item. He couldn't believe he'd shown the stone to a complete stranger. Rational thought escaped him. Taking a deep, cleansing breath, he shoved the stone away and moved for the window.

"Why am I explaining myself to you? I don't even know who you are."

"You never asked," the man said, standing. He held out his hand as he approached. "Malcolm Appleton."

Gabe bit his lip. He swallowed his anger at being shut out from the bedroom, then took the hand. "Gabe."

"Nice to meet you, Gabe," Malcolm said. He cocked his head toward the closed door. "You care for him very much, don't you?"

"He…" Gabe stared over the streets of Portents. His mind, however, was on a different day in the city. "Loren saved my life. He gave me something to fight when I was ready to give up on everything. Now that Soriya's back though…"

"Jumping to conclusions won't help," Malcolm said in a soft tone.

"Yeah, well, neither will standing on the sidelines," Gabe answered, disgruntled. The old man was right, however. He could do nothing about Loren and Soriya. There were other questions left to answer, though. "Who are you, Malcolm? What are you doing with Loren?"

"I…"

A door closed, cutting Malcolm off from answering. Loren quickly entered the room.

"He's part of a case I'm working, Gabe," Loren said in a sharp voice. "That's all you need to know."

Malcolm stepped forward. "Is the young woman—"

"She'll be fine," Loren said. He peered back at the door as the light turned off. He was clearly shaken from his talk, though he set it aside. "She just needs some rest."

Gabe threw his hands in the air. "Guess you've got it all figured out."

"Gabe?"

"Soriya needs rest," he continued. "I need to be shut out of the case—what should be *our* case."

"That's not—"

"Then what?" Gabe shouted. "Tell me, Loren. What have we been doing this past year? I thought we were partners."

"We were," Loren said. "We are!"

"Yeah," Gabe muttered. "Sure feels that way."

"Hey!" Loren grabbed Gabe by the shoulder. "You're still a kid, Gabe. You have a chance at a home. A family."

"They aren't my family!"

"They could be, if you gave them a chance," Loren said. "If you gave anything a chance. School. Friends. A normal life."

"Normal?" Gabe said with a scoff. "No thanks. Those days are gone and I say, good riddance."

"I… I'm sorry you feel that way."

"I don't need any of that, Loren," Gabe said. "Don't you see? I can be more useful here. If there's something out there, we can track it down and—"

Loren shook his head. He moved for the door and collected his coat from the floor. The cup atop the small bookshelf near the entrance held his keys, and he snatched them up.

"Come on." He opened the door. "I'm taking you home."

"Let me help."

"You're not ready!" Loren yelled. Gabe fell back on his heels, staggered by the words. The pain in his chest grew and his entire world shattered before him. Loren took a deep breath. "I won't see you throw everything away. Not for this. Not because of me or that stupid stone."

"Stupid…" Gabe could barely hear himself. His heart pounded in his ears. "You think it's stupid?"

"Gabe, that's not… I…" Loren sighed. "Come on, kid."

Gabe held his ground. A hand patted his back softly. Malcolm was at his side. "You should go with him."

Gabe glared at the kindhearted man, but felt nothing of the sort. All he saw was a roomful of so-called grown-ups standing against him. He rushed for the exit, angry tears stinging his eyes. "Yeah. I can see when I'm not wanted."

CHAPTER TWENTY-SEVEN

Portents held many secret places. Some hid far away from prying eyes, tucked in the furthest corners of the city or buried deep where one would never find them—or so most hoped. Others, though, were lost in plain sight. There was no need for subterfuge, no hidden walls or passcodes or other safety measures to secure the treasures they hid. They simply existed side-by-side with the rest of the world and were promptly ignored.

The Armory was one such place. It sat on a corner in a section of Portents called the Grove, a quiet, out-of-the-way area west of Lowtown before Rose Riley Forest. Blink and you would pass it, not the Armory itself, but the Grove in general. One missed turn on the RDJ sent you closer to Caldwell Correctional than anyone would like to be, but exit the expressway too quickly and Lowtown would claim you as one of its own.

Tucked along the corner of the Grove, at the intersection of Kingston and Loyola, stood an innocuous building. The picture window wrapped around the front was blacked out, the contents of the shop obscured from view. No signage denoted the business. No hours were posted on the door, which was never unlocked.

Most passed by without a care on their way to the pancake house across the street or the liquor store occupying much of the neighboring building. Then again, most were unaware of the secret entrance to the rear of the structure or held the key to the lock for the door.

Dozens of displays were positioned inside. Knights in armor stood at attention within every door frame and loomed—with swords at the ready—in the corners of each room. Walls held plaques and lavish banners of fighting troops. Painted images hung in golden frames. They showcased warriors in twilight, maps of long-forgotten kingdoms, and massive battlefronts lost to history.

Why such a place existed was as little known as the Armory itself. How the owner came to hold such an impressive collection was another question to be asked, should anyone learn of the place's existence. But what one such inquiring mind had learned from a dying man's treasured belongings was the identity of the man behind the store.

Jeremy Newton rarely left his house. There was grocery shopping and the occasional film at the local cinema. His pattern of movement was rigid, too rigid for some, and a shock to the system was required to stir him from the trappings of his life.

The death of Patrick Marsh provided such a shock.

Within hours of the news hitting the airwaves, Jeremy had locked his doors and headed away from his humble home in Grant Park for the only place he believed to be secret from the world. Or, at least, *most* of the world.

"Jeremy?" a voice called from the rear entrance to the Armory. The metal slab shut behind the figure, his steps slow and cautious in the deep shadows of the night. He carried a large hunting knife. A hilt of gleaming silver shone beneath his grip.

"Geoffrey?" Jeremy said, confused. "What are you doing here?"

At the sound of his companion's voice, Geoffrey tucked the knife away and made his way over to Jeremy. He took his hand, squeezing gently before hugging the man close. "I didn't know where else to turn or who I could trust."

"You could always trust—"

Geoffrey nodded. "I know. I figured if you were anywhere…"

"You're welcome to stay." Jeremy led him through the display room. "The stairs lead to a small apartment I had set up in case of emergencies."

"Always the planner," Geoffrey said.

"Which you always hated, if I remember correctly."

"Jer—"

Jeremy smirked. "I'm sorry. No need to dredge up the past. These days are dark enough as it is."

"Darker than you can imagine." The voice boomed from the shadows.

The knife was back in Geoffrey's hand. His body acted like a shield for Jeremy, who scanned the corners of the room for signs of life.

"Malcolm?" Jeremy asked the darkness. "Is that you?"

"Step into the light, Malcolm, where we can see you," Geoffrey continued, the knife gripped tight. "Do you know what's going on? What this is all about?"

"I know a great deal, I'm afraid." The Squire stepped out of the shadows. He had waited patiently, hidden away in the secret place he had discovered in a journal kept among his knight's belongings.

"You're not Malcolm," Jeremy said, terror behind the admission.

Geoffrey continued to protect his friend as they inched backward across the display room. "What do you want?"

"Your keys, gentlemen," the Squire replied with an open hand. "That's all I require."

The request stirred something inside Jeremy. He lowered Geoffrey's protective hand and shifted to his side. "If you know about the keys, you also know why we can't give them to you."

The Squire sighed. "He always said you were the stubborn one, Jeremy. You see what is happening to this place. Portents is a powder keg waiting to explode. After everything that has happened, how can you stand idle? You were charged with protecting the world. Not yourselves. Give me the keys. I will carry out your charge. I will be the knight this city requires."

Jeremy shook his head. "You would doom this place out of fear."

Geoffrey held his tongue. His eyes peered through the darkness at the Squire, scanning and assessing the threat like the soldier he had once been. He didn't strike out, didn't make a single move against the threatening figure. His hesitation brought a grin to the Squire's face.

"Your companion understands the truth. He believed Joseph Buchwald was right."

Geoffrey took a sharp breath. At his silence, Jeremy nudged him along the arm. The former soldier patted the hand, then inched closer to the Squire. "For a time, perhaps, I saw what Buchwald saw. Not any longer."

"Then you are *both* fools."

"We are not the one outnumbered." Geoffrey lunged at their foe. "You should not have come alone."

The strike swiped nothing but air as the Squire backpedaled. He held up the twin keys already gained in his quest. "I am never alone," he said. "The guardians serve me now."

From every side of them, armor came to life. Empty shells atop pedestals and tucked in the corners, unsheathed their swords. They surrounded the pair of awestruck knights, yet held back at the slightest wave from their controller.

"Impossible," Jeremy whispered.

Geoffrey failed to lose himself to the incredible sight. He launched at the Squire, blade held high. "You cannot have them!"

Anger took the man, and he slashed the air like a crazed killer instead of the practiced soldier he should have been. The Squire continued to back away from the strikes, astonished at the lack of strategy and the feeble strength behind each swing.

Time had stolen Geoffrey Michaels' youth—his vigor and stamina. The Squire's mission would not be stopped by the foolish and the weak. His mission was pure.

Geoffrey continued his assault. The Squire easily dodged out of the way with each strike. When the knight brought the blade up once more for a downward blow, the Squire stepped forward. He caught the man by the wrist and squeezed.

"You…" The Squire slowly seized control of the downward arc of the blade. Sweat dotted Geoffrey's brow. Terror sat in his wide eyes. The blade was no longer his to wield. He was merely a puppet, and the Squire took the last step to swing the blade directly into the gut of his victim. "… cannot stop me."

The Squire twisted the blade hard to the right, before ripping it from Geoffrey's midsection. The stricken knight stood for the merest of seconds before he fell.

Jeremy rushed to his side. "Geoffrey!"

"No," Geoffrey breathed, blood running from his lips. "Run. You have to…"

A low gurgle escaped his lungs and Geoffrey's eyes closed to the world. With his companion dead, Jeremy turned and fled. Statues blocked the way on all sides. They closed in, forcing Jeremy back to the center of the room.

"There is nowhere to run," the Squire said. "Nowhere to hide. I never wanted this. You have to see that. I made a promise to my knight to see this through."

"Joseph was wrong," Jeremy said. "This place—Portents— deserves the chance."

"Not at the expense of everyone else. There is no more room

for selfishness. I'm sorry."

He gripped the knife with his right hand and swiped the air. The blade caught Jeremy across the throat. Blood sprayed the length of the room.

Hands immediately shot for the gaping wound, too late to do anything to avoid the end. Jeremy fought for his next breath as the Squire approached. The blade sank deep into Jeremy's chest. He staggered a step, then collapsed beside the body of his fallen compatriot and died.

The Squire stood over them. His heart pounded with excitement. It wasn't what he'd wanted, but the satisfaction that came in their deaths was difficult to ignore.

Gathering his wits, the Squire moved to his victims. He removed the keys chained around their necks and held them up triumphantly.

"Only Malcolm Appleton remains," the Squire said in the dark, surrounded by the empty statues. He had looked for the lone holdout for days without success, before reassessing his priorities for the others. There had been no sign of the last of the knights, or so he'd thought. It came to him like a bolt of lightning from the heavens. The detective he'd sent the griffin after. An old man had been with him.

Realization set in and his eyes widened. "Of course."

The Squire departed the Armory, his prizes firmly in hand. There was still work to be done. Now he knew where to strike… and how.

CHAPTER TWENTY-EIGHT

It took time for Myers to track down Buchwald's son. Jonathan Buchwald had hidden his employment records to escape a few tax problems he'd encountered in the past. Rather than face up to the errors and work within the system to clear his record, Jonathan was forced to work under the table at less than reputable businesses.

His latest gig was with a construction company in downtown Portents. MacKenna Corp served the city through several government contracts. Despite the strict protocols required to fulfill those contracts, the number of changing hands and shifting regimes allowed for certain things to slip through the cracks.

Personnel tended to be one of the main ones. Bodies were necessary to meet the extreme deadlines of the job. Where they came from was certainly questioned—especially during an election cycle—but when push came to shove, if there was a skilled laborer needed for the task, they were welcomed with open arms and a fat envelope of cash to avoid questions.

Luckily, one of MacKenna's underwriters hadn't received the memo on the less-than-ethical hiring practices of the supervisor at the site of their latest project and written Buchwald's name on one report. Thel had stumbled upon the paperwork, quick to note the location of the site as a new parking ramp off Pepperidge.

Breakfast was on Myers for that discovery, and the pair took their meal across the street from the massive traffic nightmare in one of the city's busiest areas. They sat in the car, needling their egg sandwiches on fresh bagels, coffee hot and steaming in the cup holders of Myers' sedan.

Workers arrived in waves, passing by the parked sedan without questioning the women waiting inside. They were caught up in their own worlds, their own lives, and cared little for outside drama.

"Myers, though, thrived on it. "Say that again?"

Thel grinned. "He asked me out for coffee."

"Get out."

"It happened."

"Yardin?" Myers asked in curious shock. "He's Traffic Division?"

"That's right," Thel replied. "Going on four months."

The details mattered little to Myers. How Thel came by them, though, brought a smile to her face. "You stalked his personnel file?"

Thel lowered her sandwich. "Isn't that what you always told me to do?"

Myers reached for a hug, immediately slapped away by the hungry siren. "I'm so proud of you I could cry."

"Like you still know how to do that."

"I'd fake it."

"Like everything else," Thel muttered.

Myers slapped Thel's shoulder. "Someone is feeling cheeky today. Don't let a potential date go to your head." She reached for her coffee and took a long sip. Despite the playful nature of their conversation, Myers was proud of her partner. To reconnect with the world after a centuries-long absence took a lot of guts.

Myers lowered her drink to the holder. Thel glared at her. "What?"

"What about you?"

Myers raised an eyebrow. "What about me?"

"Come on, Sam," Thel said. "I saw the way Devlin was looking at you during the Stane inquiry."

Myers winced. "The man's a perv."

Thel rolled her eyes. "And Atley? He slipped you his cell number just last week."

"He has weird hair."

Thel lowered her breakfast. "Weird hair?"

"Yeah." Myers shifted in her seat, hands over her head. "How it sticks up on the sides. Who does he think he is, Wolverine?"

"I don't know who that is."

"Hugh Jackman."

"Oh," Thel said in surprise. It quickly turned to confusion. "Atley doesn't look anything like Hugh Jackman."

"If he did, we wouldn't be having this conversation."

Thel swallowed down her clear bewilderment with a last bite of her sandwich. She finished, then wiped her lips with a napkin. "Weird hair?"

"It's a thing," Myers said with an exasperated breath. "You know it's true."

"Mine's purple."

"Punk-rock purple, Thel. Cute purple."

"Fine," Thel said with a shake of her head and a wide grin. "So Atley's out. What about Loren?"

Myers nearly spit out every ounce of coffee in her mouth. Choking it down, Myers slammed her hand to her chest. "What? Loren?"

"Yes, Loren," Thel laughed. "Is that why you called him for the Marsh case?"

"No," Myers snapped indignantly. Her cheeks felt flushed, and she cursed the reaction. "I called him—"

"Instead of me, by the way."

Myers' jaw clenched tight. "You were busy."

"So you thought, why not spend some quality time with Greg Loren."

"I did not," Myers exclaimed.

"Then why are you blushing?"

"Clam up."

"Oh, come on, Sam. Why not—"

Myers shook her head. She was no longer looking at Thel or thinking about the conversation at hand. "No, Thel. Check it out."

Thel tracked her gaze to the construction site. The shift had started during their chatting, with dozens at work throughout the site. Shuffling up from the far side, bleary-eyed and obviously exhausted, was a young man with tattooed arms and a hard hat.

"Is that him?"

Myers snatched the photo from the dash and held it between them. The mug shot offered a better view of Jonathan Buchwald—smug and arrogant in his arrest, because, of course, he had a record. Myers flicked the corner of the photo. "Definitely. Let's go."

They made their way across the street to the site. Before reaching the sidewalk, catcalls and hooting rose from the workers. A handful of men sat along a support beam, staring lustfully in their direction.

"Can I hurt them?" Thel said with clear disgust.

Myers hesitated to answer. She wasn't sure what upset her more—that there were still men like that in the world, or that all of them were looking at Thel.

"Must be the hair," Myers said, not bothering to give them a second of her time.

"Or the limited intelligence," Thel said loud enough for them to hear.

"Probably that." She strode ahead, hands deep in her pockets. When the calls continued, growing ruder with each addition, Myers pulled out her badge and flashed it at them. Silence fell over the site. It brought a satisfied smirk to her lips.

Jonathan continued toward the site, his steps slow and deliberate. Myers rushed to catch up. She preferred to avoid heading into the maw with such free-flowing testosterone rampant.

"Jonathan Buchwald?"

A furrowed brow turned to her. His eyes were completely bloodshot, as if he hadn't slept all night. "Yeah? Who are you?"

"Portents PD."

He rolled his eyes. "What do you want?"

"Late night, Jon? You look a little—"

"Inebriated," Thel finished. She edged away, fingers over her nose.

"I was celebrating," Jonathan answered. "That a crime?"

"Might be," Myers commented.

"What is this about?" the young man asked. "I have work to do."

"In this state? You must love taking risks." Myers inched closer. "It's about your father."

"He's dead."

Myers nodded. "And some of his possessions have gone missing."

"So?" Jonathan shrugged. "He ain't going to miss them, is he?"

His indignant behavior grated on Myers. The man's father was dead, and he couldn't care less. "There's also the matter of another man's murder."

Bleary eyes snapped open. "Murder?"

"Patrick Marsh," Thel said in a cold voice.

He lost it at murder. Panicked at their line of questioning, Jonathan whipped around. He bolted for the street, his steps too slow and his coordination clearly lacking for the job.

Myers grabbed him by the wrist. She spun him into the fence of the construction site. Murmurs rose from the crowd of observers, yet none rose to the defense of their colleague.

"Not a good idea." Cuffs slapped against Jonathan's wrists. "Thel? Do the honors."

"You have the right to remain silent…"

CHAPTER TWENTY-NINE

Loren kept playing with the visitor's badge pinned to his jacket. It felt wrong in every way, but he was lucky to have made it through the front doors of the Central Precinct without bursting into flames or starting a riot, let alone down the first-floor corridor for the interrogation rooms in the back of the building.

The desk sergeant—his name escaped Loren—offered little more than a grumble. It had been a year since Loren was part of the force, working to serve and protect Portents, but the man behind the desk made it clear some grudges stuck around.

Looks from the other officers lingering around the station or typing up reports shot his way. Loren tossed a friendly wave and a grin where he could. None were reciprocated. He couldn't fault them. He had burned every bridge during his time in the precinct. They had all stood by him in his grief. He'd returned the favor by skirting procedure and putting them at risk with his belligerent behavior.

Learning their names might have helped matters, but the damage had been done long ago. No amount of apologies could mend fences. It was part of the reason Loren fought against returning to the Rath. Myers' call had made it clear, though, she needed his help. After he had brushed her off last time, a clear mistake thanks to Malcolm's arrival, Loren felt obligated to lend a hand.

Still, surprise greeted him when he arrived at the interrogation wing. Myers leaped to her feet and joined him before the door.

"You came."

"You called." He tossed a wave to Thel, who sat nearby. She nodded, thumbing through a magazine as she waited.

"I heard you made the news," Myers said. "Shirtless, even."

"The less said about that, the better."

Thel closed the magazine. A grin spread from ear to ear. "Oh, I don't know. I'm sure *someone* would like to hear more about it."

"Thel," Myers intoned, nudging her partner away.

Thel patted her back, eyes locked on Loren with keen interest. "Shirtless, you said?"

Myers pointed to the stairs. "Be somewhere else."

Thel winked at Loren. Prodding hands pushed her for the exit. "Going. I'm going!"

Myers breathed a sigh of relief at her partner's exit. Loren held back a laugh. "You two seem like a good fit."

"For twin straightjackets, sure."

Loren waited patiently. Myers collected herself and the reports left behind by the departed Thel. When she seemed ready, Loren nodded toward the door to the first room in the wing. "You talk to him yet?"

"Just some preliminaries," Myers replied. "Daddy issues with this one."

"The things parents do to their kids."

Myers raised her hands and took a step back. "I'm not touching that one."

"No?" Loren wasn't surprised. Myers' father had been a notorious thief who had brought Sam along on multiple jobs to teach her the trade. It certainly added to their trust issues.

"Not a chance," Myers said. "I save it for Tuesdays and alternate Thursdays. She's a good listener, but damn expensive."

"Better than a stranger and a cheap bottle of booze."

"Debatable."

Loren chuckled. He reached for the door. "Want me to talk to him?"

"Have at it."

Now he was surprised. His hand fell away. "Just like that?" he asked. "Ruiz would have had kittens at that request."

"Too bad he's busy with that fundraising shindig our esteemed mayor is throwing tonight," Myers said. "Anyway, it's my case and my call. I trust you, Loren."

"I…" The words failed him. He wondered if he had misread the situation completely and for how long. Heat rose along his cheeks. "Appreciated."

As he grabbed hold of the knob, Myers' hand fell on his arm. "Don't fuck it up, Loren."

"Yeah," he said. "That's more like it."

She passed along the reports. Opening the door, Loren stepped into the heavily shadowed box of a room. The lone occupant sat on the far side of the table. His feet tapped impatiently on the floor; nervous and anxious eyes flitted through the room. He was clearly uncomfortable with his situation, but was it a sign of guilt?

Loren took a seat and opened the report. "Jonathan Buchwald," he read. "Construction worker for MacKenna Corp. Paid off the books now for what looks to be three years. Dropped out of school for the chance to build shopping plazas, strip malls, and parking ramps. How's that going for you?"

Jonathan ran his hands over his face, then slapped the table. "What the hell does this have to do with my father?"

"Not a thing." Loren closed the report and dropped it beside the chair before leaning in close. "I was making small talk. But speaking of your old man…"

"Let's not and say we did."

"That bad, huh?"

Jonathan's gaze hardened, a finger to the table. "He was a mean drunk. Never had a nice thing to say about me. He drove my mother to the grave, then finally had the decency to join her. Nicest gift he ever gave me."

Loren blinked hard, then settled against the chair. "Don't hold back or anything."

"He never did."

"No?" Loren shot a quick glance at the camera in the corner. The red light beamed down on him. Shuffling closer to the table, Loren rested his elbow on the edge. "Bet he was a great storyteller, though, wasn't he?"

"What do you mean?"

"Ever hear the one about the five knights charged with saving the world?" Loren read the man's body language with each word spoken. Jonathan's eyes flared with recognition. "How about the five keys to a fail-safe capable of destroying a city?"

Jonathan looked everywhere he could for an escape. Anywhere but at Loren. "You're kidding, right?"

"Am I?"

A low growl slipped from Jonathan's lips. "He used to spout that garbage constantly. Utter nonsense. Why would anyone pick that miserable bastard for some grand destiny?"

"You mean, instead of someone like you?"

Jonathan slammed his hands on the table. "I mean, it was crap then, and it's crap now. There were never any knights or keys or quest to save the world from this hellhole of a city."

Spit flew from the man's lips. Intense anger caused tears to well in his eyes, a side effect of being held in the interrogation room for suspicion of murder, or possibly from the memory those stories held for an impressionable kid like Jonathan once was.

Loren scanned the man's arms, noting the tattoos on his flesh. The iconography reminded him of the hidden room in Marsh's home. Swords and banners mixed with shining armor and castle ramparts. Sigils, crests, and keys were interspersed throughout, all lining up with the Camelot myths carried down the ages from those first five knights and Merlin's grand prophecy.

A soft voice slowed Jonathan's temper, and Loren crept closer. "I don't know, Jon. If that was me as a kid? Hearing about knights and fantastical deeds like that? I would have bought into it in a heartbeat. Maybe even gotten a tattoo or three to memorialize the only decent memories shared with a sad old man."

Jonathan fell back against the metal chair. He crossed his arms over his chest and sniffed back his tears. "You're wrong."

"Did you find the key in his belongings, Jon?" Loren asked outright. "Is that what set you off? Maybe you remembered Patrick Marsh from story time as a kid and realized the fairy tale was real. Did he fight back, Jon? Is that why you killed him?"

Jonathan leaped to his feet. "I didn't do anything!"

Loren slammed his hand on the table. "Where's the key, Jon?"

He stared at Loren with cold, angry eyes. A sharp breath filled his lungs and when he released it, Jonathan sat back down on the chair. He eased back to the table. "Go to hell," he said. "I'm done talking to you."

"That hurts," Loren said. He gathered up the reports from the floor and stood. "Not as much as jail time will for you."

"What?"

"No alibi for the night of Marsh's death," Loren said, checking the statement given to Myers earlier. "Really doesn't leave you many options but to deal with me. Think about it."

Content with his progress, Loren moved for the door. Jonathan Buchwald could stew for a bit. He wasn't going anywhere, anytime soon.

CHAPTER THIRTY

"Well?"

Myers waited across the hall when Loren closed the door to the interrogation room. He passed the twin screens monitoring their suspect. Jonathan stared down at the table, hands pressed tight to his temples. What thoughts passed through his mind, be it guilt or innocence, be it rage or regret, Loren could only guess, but he knew the silence would eat away at the man for as long as it took to find out the truth.

"What were you expecting?" Loren asked with a shrug. "A full confession?"

Myers shook her head. "Definitely more fireworks. I've heard some stories about your interrogations."

They were not cherished memories for Loren. The fact that he knew exactly which events Myers referred to sent a chill through his body.

"Those were different times." Loren shifted away from the monitors.

"Right." Myers led him to the stairs for the second floor. Her steps echoed as they ascended. "You still think he's our guy?"

"He's hiding something," Loren replied. "That much I know. For all his bluster and anger, he loved his old man."

"Enough to kill Patrick Marsh?"

"I don't know." Loren considered his options. The shock on Jonathan's face, the fear at the very accusation, brought doubt to Loren. "I don't think so."

Myers offered a slight nod, then pushed ahead. They wound through the bullpen—heads catching whiplash at Loren's presence among them. He tried to wave politely, but Myers dragged him away for the corner office.

"Huh," Loren whispered. "New digs?"

"Head Detective, remember?"

Loren said nothing. He stepped inside to scan the space. Ruiz had always kept the office in deep shadows, using only a desk lamp for a thin cone of light. Myers, however, preferred the overhead bulbs—bright and beaming over every inch. It helped blot out the view of the city outside.

When he finished his appraisal of the office, Loren found Myers staring at him. "What? Do I have food in my teeth?"

"You wear that shirt and you're concerned about food in your teeth?"

Loren peered down. He pulled at his Krypton Lives rocket-ship t-shirt. "I like this shirt."

Myers laughed.

"Now really," Loren said. "What was the look for?"

She circled her desk. She lowered her reports onto a pile in the corner and let them settle before straightening the entire stack to keep it from falling to the floor. Clearing her throat, she offered an innocuous grin.

"Tell me about these keys."

The door to the office slammed shut behind Loren. The sudden sound caused him to jump. Thel edged around him to get to her desk on the far side of the space.

"Tell us."

Loren let out a long breath and started. He relayed Malcolm Appleton's arrival at his apartment and the story he'd brought with him—everything from Camelot to Merlin's prophecy with the five knights. From there, Loren worked through the missing keys at the heart of everything, including their ability to activate a devastating doomsday device. Disbelieving glances passed between the pair of detectives, but no interruptions slowed Loren's tale.

Finished, Loren settled in the chair across from Myers and waited to be thrown out of the office. There was no way to believe such a ridiculous account. Then again, Myers and Thel had seen far more than the average person.

Thel remained quiet throughout the affair, an edge to her posture, like the tale had struck her hard. Myers, though, paced the length of the office. She stopped at the window and turned back to face them.

"That is some bedtime story."

"No kidding," Loren said.

Thel leaned forward, hands before her. "So this is happening because of people like me."

"Thel?" Myers asked.

"No, Thel," Loren jumped in. "It's happening out of fear. Fear of the unknown. Fear of change. Whoever is behind this is afraid. Plain and simple."

"Thanks, Loren," Thel said in a quiet voice.

Myers ran her hands through her hair and shifted for her desk once more. "We can't hold Buchwald for long. His lawyer is on the way, and she'll push for his immediate release."

Thel reached into her jacket pocket and removed a slip of paper. Slapping it on Myers' desk, she smiled. "I secured a search warrant for his place and his car."

Myers lifted the document. "Any singing involved with the judge?"

"Would I stoop so low?"

"I would," Myers answered with a shrug.

Thel snatched the paper back and moved for the door. "I'll head over there now."

"I can join you."

Thel shook her head, an eye toward Loren. "Stay. I got this."

"Thel."

"You can thank me later, partner," Thel called with a wave.

"Hold up." Myers lifted the phone from her desk, then dialed rapidly. It rang twice before the line clicked over. "Hampton? Myers. Hey, I could use a favor."

Loren looked to Thel for clarification, but she was as much in the dark. She inched away from the door, the handle still within reach. The phone clanged atop the base and both shot a glare at Myers.

Her grin widened. "Take Yardin with you."

"What?" Thel said. Her cheeks immediately flushed at the mention of the name. "Sam—"

"Already cleared it," Myers continued. "Take him and enjoy yourself. After you find my evidence."

Thel bit her lower lip. She started once more for the door. "Thanks."

Loren leaned over the desk after Thel's departure. "I feel like I missed something."

Myers settled back against her leather chair, hands clasped behind her head. "Yardin is a rookie who has a thing for our purple-haired diva."

"It's mutual, I take it?"

"Oh, yeah."

Loren ran his hand over his chin. "So you just set up their first date? Samantha Myers, matchmaker?"

Myers pushed off her chair. "Someone should have a life around here. Sure as hell won't be me."

Loren huffed. "Tell me about it."

Three quick raps on the door startled them into silence. The door pulled away from the frame and a head poked in. He was young, with black hair slicked back and an unlit cigarette hanging from his lips. He held out a single slip of paper.

"This just came in."

Myers retrieved the note. "Thanks, Hooper."

The door closed once more, the cop's eyes lingering a little too long on Myers for Loren's comfort, but the visitor let the notion drop. Myers scanned the note once, sighing in aggravation.

"What is it?"

"Double homicide in the Grove." She held the note out for him. "Looks like we've got a date of our own."

CHAPTER THIRTY-ONE

"Thanks for coming with me."

Her words were nearly lost behind the noise of the coffee shop. Yardin stood at the counter, cash in hand to pay for the drinks. Thel had offered to cover the cost, but he wouldn't hear of it. It was the only time they hadn't agreed on anything, from the music on the radio (classic rock all the way) to who brewed the best coffee in the city (Pablo's on Fifty-Sixth). In fact, it was also the only time the grin fell from his face. Thel preferred the smile.

Hers had come and gone sporadically throughout their adventure to the Buchwald home. Thel knew the purpose of their visit: the search for the key. It was the critical clue to confirm Jonathan Buchwald's guilt in the death of Patrick Marsh. She kept that detail to herself, however, rather than let slip the story behind the dangerous item.

Yardin had been there for moral support, shining his light wherever they went. Buchwald's home in Lowtown offered them nothing. She found none of the elder Buchwald's possessions on the premises and no key of any sort. The same results came with their search of the man's car, and the last hope of finding the smoking gun in their investigation.

Frustrated, Thel let Yardin take the lead to Pablo's and acquiesced on who paid for the pleasure of a large mocha. She was just grateful to be with him and his smile for the afternoon.

"Thank *you*." Yardin leaned along the counter as they waited for their order. "You got me out of traffic duty with Cliffords."

Thel winced at the name. "Oof. I hear he sings."

"All day," Yardin said, dragging out the words. "To 90s boy bands. I might never get *Bye, Bye, Bye* out of my head."

"Sounds pretty bad."

"It's the worst."

The barista stepped to the counter, two steaming cups in his hands. "Order up!"

Yardin took them from the man. "Thanks."

"How about a table by the window?" Thel asked, indicating an open section away from the crowd.

"Works for me."

The window offered them a clear view of the street. Small businesses ran the length of the block with a convenience store at one end and a tax preparation firm at the other. Thel took her seat on the far side, which allowed her to see the entire room as well as the neighborhood. Yardin joined her on the opposite side. He passed along the cup and she brought it to her lips, slow to sip though she felt tempted to chug the whole thing.

Satisfied with the drink and the company, Thel took in the view. Yardin joined her, content in their shared silence.

The city moved like a breathing organism. People ran up and down the block, rushing to their next destination. They grabbed cabs and hopped in cars on their way. Some tipped their hats to their neighbors, while others laughed and shouted and kicked and screamed, depending on the relationships that grew and broke all around them.

Not everyone could be considered human, either. Some refugees from the Courtyard mixed with the crowds. Horned females snapped selfies near the corner, with their shopping bags in tow from a fun-filled day. Boys with more in common with the dung beetle sniffed around the gutter for something more appetizing than what was being served at the eateries in the district. Their parents watched them intently through cavernous eyes.

"It's something, isn't it?"

Yardin shifted away from the window. "It takes some getting used to."

"Oh?"

"No offense," Yardin said quickly, a hand in the air. "There are some insane things in this city. Nothing like home."

"Then why come to Portents?"

Yardin shrugged. "For the work? I don't know. Don't get me wrong, I like it. I have a life, friends—"

"Not a bonus in your case," Thel said. She didn't need a reminder of the quartet of buffoons from the precinct. She lifted her cup to her lips. "Just my opinion."

Yardin chuckled and nodded. "Sorry. I guess I'm as close-minded, aren't I?"

"You're here. That's a good start." Thel settled along the seat and sighed. "It's an adjustment for me, too. The world has changed quite a bit in the last millennium."

Yardin shifted uncomfortably, focusing on the drink cupped in his hands. "You seem normal to me."

"For an eight-hundred-year-old siren, you mean?" Thel said with a smirk. "Normal doesn't really exist in this city."

"It could," Yardin said. He noticed her furrowed brow. "You make it work."

"Because I have to," Thel said. "A lot of others won't get an opportunity like mine, and that's not their fault. You see that, right?"

"Yeah, I..." Yardin's gaze fell to the drink on the table. He took a long breath, then straightened against the seat. "I just meant you look like you've got a good handle on it all."

"Thanks," Thel replied. "Sam helps. She's always teaching, even when she's trying to be funny. Which she's not."

"Better than Cliffords?"

"Anyone would be better than Cliffords." Their laughter filled the room. It made Thel feel lighter than air, and almost completely human. "This is what I needed, David. I..."

Reflected light caught her attention, and she turned back to the window. The crowds were gone from the block, but two men rushed into the convenience store at the corner. It was not an unusual sight, except for the ski-masks they both wore, and the guns they held in their hands.

"Thel?"

She pushed for the end of the bench and stood. "Something's happening across the street."

"What?"

Thel pulled out her sidearm and held it before her. "Come on."

"But—" She lifted him from the seat. He tossed a sad look at the beverages on the table, then followed her for the door.

Quick steps brought them to the front of the convenience store, and both ducked near the entrance. Inside, five people cowered along the back wall. They kept their hands in the air and their eyes locked on the guns of their assailants. One gunman hovered over the hostages while the other screamed at the cashier behind the counter.

"A robbery." Thel shifted to the entrance.

"There are hostages," Yardin said. His body hugged the wall. "Thel, we need to call this in."

She shook her head. "Backup will be too late. The gunmen are on edge. Probably drug-related. We can do this."

"Procedure says—"

Thel tucked her sidearm away. She was in the store before he could try to stop her.

"Thel!"

The door chime announced her arrival. Both guns spun for her position, and Thel's hands reached for the sky.

"Hi."

The crook in charge of crowd control was overweight. His gut spilled out from beneath his sweatshirt, and his pants hugged tight to his thighs. Gold chains hung from his neck like badges of honor. Sweat clung to the eyeholes of his mask.

"Down on the ground!" he shouted. "Don't make me shoot you!"

Thel continued to creep into the store.

The sweating thief turned to his friend, the gun still trained on Thel. "Hurry up with that cash!"

"I'm hurrying already!" his lithe partner snapped.

When the overweight crook looked back at Thel, he tightened his grip on his weapon. "I said, down on the ground!"

Thel smiled. "You haven't heard what I have to say yet."

A song rose from her lips. The words offered a melody that filled the entire store. While the hostages stared in silent confusion, both thieves immediately lowered their weapons. Their eyes flared as their bodies betrayed them. Once lowered, the guns fell from their hands and they kicked them toward Thel.

The song picked up; Thel's vocal talents consumed the two overwhelmed crooks. They started to dance to the rhythm. The overweight fool grabbed his partner by the hand and spun him around.

"What are you doing?"

"I can't stop!" he yelled, tugging the slim crook close.

The hostages watched the tango unfold before them. Fear turned to laughter, and their hands fell from the sky. They reached for their phones to record the incredible display. So did others from the street, who must have heard the shouting.

Thel focused on the song and the effect on the two crooks. She tightened their performance. The tempo increased, so that they were waltzing down entire aisles with no sense of control over their bodies.

Both cried for their freedom and when she split them apart with her song, they thought they had won some semblance of normality again. Instead, Thel pulled their strings once more. The pair ran like bulls toward each other. One head crashed against the other, and both men collapsed from the impact.

Thel held the note for an extra second until she was sure the crooks were unconscious. Her voice drifted from song, and the performance ended.

"That should just about do it." She let out a relieved sigh. "You're safe, folks."

The cashier jumped up and down behind the counter. "That was incredible!"

Cheers erupted throughout the store. People rushed in from the street. Thel slipped on a pair of gloves and retrieved the fallen firearms. The filming continued from multiple patrons and bystanders.

"All in a day's work," she announced. She glanced toward the door. "Right, David?"

Yardin stood outside. The smile was gone, replaced with a sneer. Thin eyes like daggers stared at her.

"David?"

He shook his head and stalked off down the street without a word. Thel moved for the door, then stopped.

"So much for our date." She wanted to chase after him and find out what she'd done wrong. Sirens rang out in the distance, though. There was still work to be done, and the hostages were her first priority.

"Is anyone hurt?" Thel asked. She forgot all about the quiet normalcy she'd attained for a few scant moments. It would have to wait. "Let's take a look. Make sure you're all right."

CHAPTER THIRTY-TWO

The sun waned in the sky by the time they arrived at the Grove. Traffic was gridlocked down the RDJ; the so-called rush hour left everything at a crawl. Once in the Grove, Myers took them through the twisting streets, passing residential neighborhoods.

Loren noticed the Bennett home to his right, the broken edifice repaired and forgotten to time, yet firmly ingrained in his memory. There was no going back, yet somehow the more he pushed ahead the more life wanted to drag him right to the beginning. Here he was, working with the police once more, chasing after murderers and getting caught up in a mystery he barely understood.

Myers seemed to roll with most of the punches. Dead bodies were nothing new to her. She rolled up her sleeves and dove in. Yet, behind it all was a reticence that surprised him. Her usual confidence typically covered up any doubts, but he realized her nervousness in her iron grip of the steering wheel and the way her eyes flashed with every stoplight that halted their drive.

Arriving at their destination, both vacated the car and made their way to the sidewalk. The place didn't appear to be open to the public, if it ever had been. There were no signs on the building, no hours posted by the door, which remained locked.

"Someone called this in?" Loren asked as he scanned the area.

"Anonymous tip," Myers confirmed. She trailed his footsteps around the shop.

"Not as anonymous as they would like."

"You think it was—"

Loren stopped, and Myers nearly rammed into his backside. A narrow stairwell led down into a shallow alley at the rear of the building. Loren took the steps and found a metal door slightly ajar.

"No one else would have found the place, let alone left the

door open for us. Don't you think?"

Myers said nothing. She held tight to her gun. Loren turned on a flashlight and led the way inside. They swept both walls of the small entry space, then stopped at the main hall.

"More armor," Loren grumbled. Displays and pedestals filled the room. Banners hung from the walls, and weapons were kept in cases on all sides. "Were you able to trace the call?"

Myers shook her head. "It was a recording. Too short to trace."

"You listened to it?"

"Before we left," Myers said. "Voice was scrambled."

"Lucky us."

"We might be. Forensics is looking into it."

Loren shot her a look.

She rolled her eyes. "Okay. We're not that lucky."

At the threshold of the second room, both stopped. The beam of light fell on two bodies sprawled on the ground. Blood pooled beneath them.

"Dammit." Loren closed his eyes.

Myers tucked away her sidearm and joined him by the bodies. She slipped on a pair of gloves and started her examination of the body. Loren kept the light focused on the top figure, a middle-aged man with blond hair. Myers let the victim's arm fall back to the ground. "How did he draw them out?"

It was a good question. Loren had asked the same of Malcolm in the hopes of protecting the pair now dead before them. Malcolm, though, had been at a loss to track down his fellow knights. Marsh's publicized demise had sent everyone into hiding, exactly what the killer had wanted.

"He must have known what they would do," Loren said. "Where they would go."

"He thought this through," Myers commented. "When it came time, though? He was angry."

"Myers?"

She indicated the slit throat and the stab wounds in the other. "Marsh's strangulation almost appeared accidental—like a struggle gone too far. But this? This was no accident."

She was right. Their deaths were never the goal, yet the killer decided they were necessary. The cuts were deep and final.

"Any keys?"

Myers double-checked for chains around their necks. "None.

Any chance they weren't carrying them?"

"No."

"Great." Myers shot to her feet. The back of her leg connected with the display behind her and she started to fall. Reaching out, Myers grabbed for the armor at her side. Instead of bolstering her, the armor toppled with her.

"Myers, watch out!"

Loren grabbed her by the wrist and pulled. The armor collapsed, splitting into a dozen pieces and spreading across the floor. He watched the destroyed artifact cautiously. Part of him waited for the pieces to move on their own to rebuild what had been lost. The other, more rational part, simply didn't want to look down in his arms.

Myers was still there, hugged tight to his body. He could feel her throbbing heart and her warm breath.

"Thanks," she said.

"You're…" Loren helped her up, then backed away a step. "You're welcome."

She grinned. "You have a knack for saving me." When his gaze shot to the floor, Myers shook her head vigorously. "Not just me, of course. I'm… I'm sure Gabe feels the same way. It must be nice having him around. Someone to lean on. To help carry the load."

It was a decent recovery, but did little to set Loren at ease. He rubbed at his neck as he drifted into the shadows of the space. "I'm not very good at it."

"What?"

"Talking," Loren said. "With Gabe. With…" He caught her eyes boring through him for more. Loren cleared his throat and nodded to the dead men in the room. "We should focus on the case."

"Right," Myers answered. "The case."

"Could Buchwald's son—"

"That's what I was wondering." Myers leaned over the dead men. "Time has definitely passed. He could have easily—though I hate to use that word considering what we're looking at—but he could have done this, yes."

"And then he just heads over to work like nothing happened?" Loren asked.

"He was late for his shift. Bleary-eyed. Exhausted from what I assumed was a long night of drinking."

"Did he smell—"

"He did," she said with a nod. "Said he was celebrating."

"Did he happen to say where?"

"Not so much."

Loren ran a hand over his chin. "Where the hell was he all night?"

"We might be looking at that answer."

"I don't know," Loren said with a deep sigh. "What I do know is we're at four dead knights now."

"Leaving us with…"

Their eyes widened at the same moment. The implication of the dead men suddenly brought home the urgency of their case. Four keys had been obtained and only one remained. One victim left to save, and they were on the other side of the city.

"Malcolm."

CHAPTER THIRTY-THREE

Soriya sat on the bed. The sun disappeared from view along the skyline. She had lost a whole day to endless thought and never-ending debate.

Every time Soriya closed her eyes, she imagined the Bypass. She heard the whooshing air of the swirling orb of green light and felt the cold of the chamber all around her. There were shadows, so many shadows, but only one dominated her view: a figure stood in the distance, freed from the prison of eternity. They never bothered to look back at her. Instead, they rushed away into the darkness before she could act.

She never saw the Bypass as a prison. The ancient crossroads to forever was meant to be her reward for everything she had suffered. She had saved the city from Karen Winters, from the Heads of Cerberus, and in the end, from Julian Harvey. Her sacrifice had kept Loren and so many other loved ones safe, yet the Bypass had rejected her. It had shot her back out into the world without so much as an explanation, and now nothing made sense.

An entire year had been lost, yet she held no memories of her time in the Bypass for that stretch. There was a void in her mind. Something was missing, and it went beyond a feeling or a misplaced item. This was her very being, and every thought about it left her emptier and angrier.

Soriya kicked off the bed and moved for the window. Her fist slammed against the molding, then she settled her forehead on the cold glass.

"Why did I come back?" Soriya whispered to the growing dark of her city. "What happened to me?"

The silence offered her nothing.

A soft rap at the door brought a necessary distraction. The door creaked open and an older gentleman stepped inside. He carried a tray filled with small snacks and a glass of water.

"Hello," he said. "I don't wish to disturb you, but I thought you might be hungry."

He placed the tray on the dresser, then retreated for the door. "It's not much. Greg isn't quite adept at grocery shopping."

Soriya looked over the selection. A pack of gummy worms rested beside a handful of graham crackers and a Hershey bar. At least Loren's diet hadn't changed in her absence.

"Where is Loren?" Soriya asked. She grabbed a cracker from the tray.

"Working the case."

Soriya lowered the treat. She had done nothing but rest while Loren kept working. Her guilt caused the blood to rush faster through her body, and her fist clenched at her side. "I should join him."

The gentleman barred her exit. "He would want you to rest. You've been through an ordeal."

Soriya shook her head, wanting nothing more than to scream at being held back. There was truth in his words, however. She had died—been free of the pain and suffering of the living—yet now found herself back in the world as if nothing had changed.

Everything had, though.

She fell to the bed once more, then leaned hard against her knees. The man continued to look at her.

"It's Malcolm, isn't it?"

He nodded, inching closer. "Pardon my staring," he said in a soft voice. "I've heard stories about the Greystone over the years."

"Not what you imagined?"

"Far more, actually," Malcolm replied. He joined her at the edge of the bed. "What you've done for Portents—you and Greg—well, it puts us knights to shame. I'm afraid we never did anything but wait for a day we hoped would never come. But you? What you've faced?"

They were memories, and like the rest of her previous life, they seemed far away. Each blurred into the next, lost in time from her long absence. Some remained, the strongest and most powerful from her time with Loren, but most slipped away when she tried to remember them.

"Those days seem like a lifetime ago," she said. She threw on a slight smile for the man. "Mentor... my teacher... he told me about the knights when I was young. He thought they were only a story, but part of me always knew the truth. Maybe it was the imagination of a child. Either way, it made me feel safer, knowing someone else was out there keeping watch."

Malcolm's cheeks flushed with gratitude. He stood up from the bed and started toward the door. "I'll leave you to your meal."

Reaching for the tray, Soriya followed him. "I think I'll join you. I'd prefer the company."

They headed for the living room. Images lined the walls, photos of Beth and Loren from happier times. Old maps and treasures Beth had studied and written about extensively hung beside them.

They made Soriya smile. "It's so different. Loren's apartment. He's changed."

Malcolm shook his head. He moved for the chair on the far side of the room. "He doesn't see it that way."

"Maybe it's not just him who's changed," Soriya said. "I—"

The apartment door opened suddenly. Soriya dropped the tray of food, and her glass of water spilled along the carpet.

"Stay back," she snapped, fists ready for a fight. "I'll—"

Gabe entered. At the sight of Soriya, he jumped back with his hands held in front of him. "Whoa! It's me."

Soriya held a long breath in her lungs to calm down. "Gabe. What are you doing here?"

Malcolm grumbled. "A fine question. Your foster parents—"

"Don't care about me," Gabe said, eyes like daggers.

"I find that hard to believe." Malcolm slipped into the kitchen. He was back in an instant with a towel in hand. Soriya took it and cleaned up the squandered beverage as much as she could.

Gabe joined her, tossing snacks on the tray. "Please," he said. "I've had enough lectures from everyone. Loren could have been killed yesterday. He needs my help, whether he knows it or not."

Malcolm took the empty glass from Soriya. As he turned to confront Gabe further, Soriya retreated for the nearby window. Night had always been her time in the city, when she felt most alive. Now, even the sounds rushing down the street below were foreign to her.

Everything felt foreign to her. Alien, as if it had all left her behind somehow.

"Gabe," Malcolm said in hushed tones. "You have to understand—"

"I understand plenty. I've been doing this for a year. He can't cut me out now."

"That isn't what he's doing," Malcolm said. "I'm sure once you've talked, you'll see."

She clearly wasn't the only one worried about being left behind. Gabe struggled with her return almost as much as she did. Soriya wanted to say something comforting, something to relieve the young man of the pressure he must have been feeling over his time as the Greystone—and as partner to Loren.

No words came, and she continued to stare out the window. Scanning the street, Soriya's gaze fell on a shadow at the mouth of an alley. The dark figure stared up at her. Tension immediately filled her body. She leaned closer, her head against the glass. The shadow backed deeper into the darkness until only two pinpricks of light remained.

"Soriya?" Malcolm called with concern.

She pushed from the window and rushed to the door. "Lock up after me. Stay away from the windows."

"What?" Gabe shouted. "What did you—"

"Do it!"

Soriya raced out of the apartment.

CHAPTER THIRTY-FOUR

Malcolm clasped the lock to secure the door. Gabe's jaw remained agape with incredulity. He glared at the slab like someone had tossed him in a prison cell without the key. His hands balled into fists and he screamed.

"You see? You see how they treat me?"

He ran over and kicked the door in frustration. Days of being on the receiving end of every lecture, and the blame for every problem, had pushed him to the edge.

Malcolm reached for him. "Soriya is trying to protect us."

"From what?" Gabe seethed. He pulled away from the kindly old visitor. "She couldn't even bother telling us that much! To them, I'm just a kid."

"Your time with come."

"Yeah," Gabe grumbled. "When they say so, right?"

Pacing steps brought him closer to the window. Malcolm called him back.

"Gabe, you have to understand," he said in a calm tone. It did little to appease the pissed-off teen. "The knights were put in place to keep certain dangers from ever seeing the light of day. This new player—"

"Knights?" Gabe asked. He felt stupid and useless. No one had said a damn thing about the case, or what was involved. "Like King Arthur, knights?"

"Yes," Malcolm said. He removed the chain from around his neck and held a key out for him. "The five of us carried one of these. To safeguard the world."

"You," Gabe muttered. "You're a knight."

"Not exactly what you pictured, I'm sure."

"My dad used to read me stories about knights. Noah always

said it was just a bunch of garbage. He never had the imagination for that kind of thing. But I…" Gabe swiped at his tired eyes. The thought of his family always stung him, though he tried his best to bury the grief. "It's all real, though, isn't it? Like everything Loren has shown me."

"It is," Malcolm said. "And there is a very real danger being sent after my fellow knights. Soriya and Greg are merely—"

"I can help," Gabe interrupted. He rushed to the window and started scanning for something, anything. "Now, what did she see?"

"Gabe," Malcolm called. "Soriya said to stay away from the windows."

"I'm not going to sit here and do nothing," Gabe snapped. "I can—"

He stopped, eyes locked on a small ball of light streaking across the sky. "What is that?"

Malcolm stood behind him, a hand against the frame. Gabe caught his reflection thanks to the lamp next to the couch. Both stared at the light dancing through the night. It glistened as brightly as the sun. Like a ping-pong ball, it shot over entire sections of the skyline and back again. As it grew larger, Malcolm's eyes widened. Terror filled his face.

No longer streaking back and forth, the light headed directly for the window.

"Get down!" Malcolm cried. He pulled Gabe to the floor and covered him.

The window shattered as the ball of light crashed into the room. Malcolm shrieked in pain as the glowing orb brushed against his arm before its momentum carried it through the living room and into the kitchen.

Gabe struggled to his feet. Malcolm, though, lingered on the floor. "Hey, are you all right?"

Malcolm's sleeve had been sheared off. Burns bubbled along the skin, and the smell of cooked flesh filled the room.

"Fine," Malcolm said in barely a whisper. "I'll be fine."

The light grew brighter in the kitchen; the orb was on a return flight for their position. Gabe grabbed Malcolm by his good arm and pulled him to his feet.

"We need to move."

"Sound advice," Malcolm replied.

They reached the door, and Gabe's fingers fumbled against the lock. When he opened it, the light was at his back. The massive orb bristled with energy that burned the walls with the merest touch. Crackling pops burst from the surface as the object spun furiously in place, waiting to strike.

"Come on!" Gabe yelled. They bolted for the hall, slamming the door shut behind them. Instinct led him to the left and the ascending stairs, Malcolm at his back. Reaching the next landing, both stopped.

A hole melted through the door's surface. Melted metal dripped down the slab for the floor as the light burst into the hall, then hovered to assess the threat.

"It's still coming," Malcolm said.

Gabe didn't need to hear more. He pulled at the knight, forcing him to climb faster and faster. They circled the landing for the next flight of stairs. Two more floors vanished beneath them in their climb until all that remained was the roof.

"Here." Gabe opened the door.

"Gabe, I don't think—"

The crackling stopped Malcolm from continuing. Gabe dragged his companion through the open door and outside. He crashed against the door to close it, then stepped away with a soft prayer on his lips.

"This has to work," he said. His hand hovered over the door. Heat built from the other side. The light was working its way through, as easily as it had downstairs.

Gabe rushed for the building's ledge, panic in his eyes. No fire escape existed for the property and the adjacent roof was too far away to jump.

Malcolm was at his side, holding tight to his burned arm. "Now where?"

The light erupted through the door. It blocked their only escape.

"We're trapped."

CHAPTER THIRTY-FIVE

Soriya rushed into the night. Feet pounded pavement, arms pumping at her sides, as she raced deeper through the darkness for a single shadow. Two blocks out from Loren's apartment, she paused.

Nothing looked familiar. Where once she recognized every corner of her city—for it was hers and hers alone to protect for so long—now everything appeared changed or new. No landmarks marked her path or guided her way.

"Where are you?" she whispered.

The city was alive and chaotic. The unwritten rule had once quieted the mayhem Portents stirred up. People would return to their homes as the night took over, fearful of the unknown dangers or unseen threats always hiding in the corners of their minds. Those rules vanished as easily as Soriya's knowledge of Portents. Too many changes during her absence unsettled her nerves.

Still, she persisted. A shifting shadow dove deeper down a nearby alley. The sound of crashing garbage cans rattled and echoed in the air behind them.

"There."

She was in the alley before the next breath. Nothing would keep her from the shadow. The second she saw it from the window of Loren's apartment, she knew the figure was tied to the case.

Winding through the darkness, Soriya crossed another street. Car horns blared in her direction as she leaped over an idling sedan, landing perfectly on the opposite side. Cheers broke out, astonished gasps as people reached for their phones to record her movements. She was gone before they caught another glimpse of her.

Water dripped from above; window air conditioner units ran to fight off the humidity that lingered between the canyons of the city. She barely noted their presence, letting the drips fall away behind her in her pursuit. Every breath recharged her. The fresh air filled her with a frenzy to act and end the menace plaguing Portents.

Ahead, the alley split in three directions. A path angled to the northeast to connect with the neighboring block. Another cut crosswise, offering escape routes to the right and to the left.

"Where now?" Soriya said as she approached at a run. A quick glance showed the shadow fleeing down the left path. But when she looked to the right, the shadow was present there as well. "How?"

Without hesitation, Soriya turned left. Feet stamped soundly through the dirt-ridden filth of the alley. When she came out the other side to the street, she stopped once more.

There was no sign of the shadow. No eyes trailed her, no movements caught her attention. It was gone, as if it had never been there in the first place.

Soriya circled back to the split. The moon glinted off reflective surfaces positioned at different angles surrounding the intersection.

"Mirrors," Soriya murmured. The shadow must have placed them there to prepare for the chase. This had been planned. She ripped one from the wall. "Tricked by mirrors, of all things."

The truth set in, and her eyes widened. "No. Worse than that."

Soriya tucked the mirror under her arm. Hurried steps carried her back through the city, around the squeals of passing cars and back to where her hunt had started.

Loren's apartment building loomed before her. A glowing sphere rose into the night sky above the structure. Small flickers of light shot off the spinning orb, illuminating the pair of innocents trapped on the rooftop.

"Gabe and Malcolm," Soriya said. "I left them unprotected."

Gabe wanted to scream. For all his demands to help, for all his dreams of being the partner Loren deserved, he had failed. He never deserved to be the Greystone. He'd been nothing but a fool to think otherwise.

"I can't believe how badly I screwed up," Gabe said under the crackling of the light.

Malcolm's hand fell to Gabe's shoulder and squeezed. Despite the clear pain on his face, he sought to provide comfort. "You didn't know."

"No shit," Gabe snapped. "I don't even know what this thing is."

It was another failing of Gabe's. Loren had tried to drill a sense of responsibility into the teen. That included learning about the job and the threats involved. Gabe had brushed it aside, just as he had everything else in his life.

"Unfortunately, I do," Malcolm said. "A will-o'-the-wisp. Highly effective. Highly dangerous."

Gabe's brow furrowed. "Loren told me about one once. He never described anything like this." He couldn't believe he was going to die—killed by a ball of freaking light. Tucking Malcolm behind him, Gabe raised his fists. "I should have been better. I'm sorry."

"No apologies necessary," Malcolm replied. "We'll face this together. No matter what happens."

The Wisp wailed into the night. It billowed light, brightening with each rotation, until the sphere practically screamed. With their deaths all but certain, the Wisp launched at them.

Soriya's foot smashed against the rooftop door. The burned and broken slab crashed against the brick as she leaped onto the gravel.

"Down!" she screamed.

Gabe and Malcolm didn't need to hear another word. They dropped to the ground, hands over their heads and their eyes shut tight.

Light streaked toward them. The air snapped and crackled with anticipation. Soriya pulled the mirror back and flung it at the diving creature.

It spun wildly, the perfect Frisbee, cutting a path to protect the cowering pair. As it crossed over Gabe's head, the glowing sphere slammed into the mirror. The light reflected into the night in a dozen directions, its scream a cry on the wind.

Gabe and Malcolm opened their eyes. They peered up in time to see the last flickers of light disappear from view.

Night returned to the rooftop.

Soriya made her way over, wary of another strike. She reached the pair and helped them to their feet.

"How did you know?" Malcolm asked in surprise.

"I... I didn't."

"Is it gone?" Gabe said.

Soriya scanned the skyline around the apartment building. The shadow was gone, as was the instrument of his attack. The threat remained, however, and Soriya could not let go of her anger at how close she had come to letting Gabe and Malcolm die.

She leaned along the ledge of the roof, fists scraping along the brick. "For now."

CHAPTER THIRTY-SIX

Appleton was still alive.

The Squire spat curses at his luck. His distraction had not lasted long enough to keep Appleton's protector away from the apartment. The second she'd ended her pursuit, he knew his gambit had failed. The dismal result trailed him down dark alleys and across the Knoll. He wanted to scream, to lash out at those around him, but held his emotions in check. He let the shadows of Portents swallow him for a time as he weighed what options remained.

Dim flickers of light snapped above him. Shards of white against the black sky whirled in place, spinning against each other. The Will-o'-the-wisp reformed in the air by pulling itself back together, one crackling firefly after another, until it completely coalesced from the damage inflicted by Appleton's protector.

To say the Squire was disappointed would have been an understatement, but he had pursued his final target indirectly in the first place for a reason. Appleton was the smartest of the group. Rather than run off and hide in the shadows, he had found allies. He had turned to the police and others, who now surrounded him at all times.

The knight always said Appleton was a thorn in his side. Of all the knights, Appleton always stood in opposition to Buchwald's beliefs. Because of that, the others fell in line. The two had hated each other. Their arguments had been sharper than any sword they might have held in a different age. They'd stood at opposite ends of the spectrum—one naïve in his flagrant disregard of his duties and the other a prophet with a clear vision of the end to come.

The Squire would not let ignorance win out. As the Wisp shook off its injuries, the light now a booming spotlight in the sky, the Squire left the confines of the alley. He looked back once and pointed to the heavens.

"Go," he told the sparking orb. "I will handle things from here. The time is fast approaching. Before tomorrow is through, it will be done."

Appleton was too well guarded. That would only increase thanks to the Wisp's attack. Something had to change, and thanks to the knowledge passed down from the knight, the Squire realized his next move.

It went against everything the Squire believed in. There were lines never to be crossed, ethical boundaries never to be so much as brushed upon for the slippery slope they unveiled and the spiraling descent they inspired. Honor dictated a better world, and wasn't that what the Squire had been working toward? To live in a place without fear, without the ever-growing nightmares and the monsters in the dark?

Portents was doomed. There would be no saving it, not at the expense of the world. If that meant crossing lines and questioning the morality of the mission, so be it. The Squire had tried to play it differently. Marsh had been an accident. The others, though, lingered in his thoughts. Perhaps the line had been crossed long ago, and he never noticed.

No. This is right. It has always been right. They will see. Everyone will see.

The mission was all that mattered. He needed the keys to unlock the end. How the Squire achieved that end was a small price to pay.

Appleton could not be reached directly. The Squire required a new path. For someone so steeped in secrets for the majority of his life, they had been incredibly easy to find, thanks to the foresight of the Squire's fallen knight.

No secrets remained hidden any longer. Appleton's walked steadily down the street. Her shift had ended minutes earlier, and she hastened to the bus stop at the end of the block. She was in her early twenties, pretty, with large eyes and rose-tinted cheeks. Her eyes were locked on the task ahead of her, never searching the area for danger, and never seeing it in the form of the Squire across the way.

He didn't want this. Appleton, however, proved reluctant to accept his fate and would fight to his dying breath. He required persuasion, and the girl would be the tipping point. She would open the way for the retrieval of the last key and the end of the Squire's holy mission.

At the intersection, the Squire crossed the road for the bus stop. He stood apart from the station to give her space as she sat in wait. When the bus arrived less than a minute later, she stood and started for the door. He rushed over to follow.

His sudden arrival caused her to trip up the steps. The Squire was quick with a hand to help her.

"Are you all right?"

"Yes," the girl said. She shook off the fall and moved deeper through the bus. "Clumsy tonight."

"It happens to the best of us."

She smiled at him, beaming with youth and innocence. "Thank you."

"My pleasure."

They sat across from each other, and she continued to smile in his direction. "Where are you headed?"

"Not sure yet." She offered a queer look at the notion. "I'll know when I get there."

"That's an unusual way to travel."

"Not if you know where the journey ends," the Squire said with a smirk. "Then you know exactly where you need to go and what you need to do."

CHAPTER THIRTY-SEVEN

"He did what?" Loren exclaimed into his cell phone. He pointed ahead for Myers, who parked along the side of the road a block away from his apartment building. "No. No, I haven't seen him, but I haven't been home. I'm almost there now. Curt's where? Yeah. Send him over. If he's not there, we'll… Nicole, we'll find him."

With an exasperated breath still on the line, Nicole hung up. Loren held the phone for a long moment, then let it fall from his hand to his lap.

"Gabe?"

"The kid is trying to give me a heart attack," Loren said. "Are they all like this?"

"I am absolutely the wrong person to ask," Myers replied. "My plants stress me out enough with their constant needs."

Loren smiled at the admission. He stepped out of the car. "Thanks for the lift." Myers was already outside and rounding the car. "What are you doing?"

"You might need help," Myers said. "For Gabe."

Loren nodded and started toward the apartment. "Hopefully, he's here. I don't know what I'm going to do if—" Loren stopped. The window of his apartment was shattered, tiny shards of glass barely hanging onto the frame. What remained swung in the breeze and beat against the outer edifice. The sound, though silent because of their distance, boomed through Loren's ears.

Myers tracked his gaze. "Is that—"

Loren raced across the street. He dodged passing cars, but refused to halt for one second. Panic held him in its grip, a terror not only for Malcolm Appleton, who Loren had sworn to protect, but for anyone else caught in his wake. He had just found Soriya again and couldn't take that loss again. Now there was Gabe to consider as well.

Each name pushed him harder. His steps slammed against the pavement until he reached the apartment building. He swung the door open and jumped inside.

Myers caught the door before it closed, calling after him. "Loren, slow down! Wait for me in case—"

He was already on the third floor when the "in case" hit him. A large circle had been burned in his door. Long drips ran beneath the wide gap left in his entryway.

"Gabe!" he yelled, knocking the door open with a stiff kick. "Gabe!"

The walls rippled with burn marks. Chunks of plaster had been taken out of the frame leading to the kitchen. Shattered glass lay along the carpet. Soriya stood near the broken window, fists clenched and ready for a fight. On the couch sat Malcolm Appleton, a washcloth on his exposed arm. Gabe sat on the armrest at his side, worry in his tired eyes.

"Gabe?"

"I'm okay." It didn't stop Loren. He rushed into the room and pulled the kid into his arms. "Hey. We're okay."

Loren didn't know where to begin. His chest refused to unclench, and his heart jack-hammered against his ribs.

Myers was the voice of reason from the door. "What happened?"

Soriya and Gabe fell silent, unable to meet the question head-on. Malcolm, despite the clear pain he felt with each shift of his weight, offered some insight.

"A will-o'-the-wisp," he said plainly.

Myers shook her head. "Never a straight answer with you, is it, Loren?"

"A wisp?" Loren asked, confused. "That can't be. To do this much damage? I handled one years ago." He turned to Soriya. "Remember?"

No response came. Her gaze faltered to the floor.

Loren wanted to press, but let it go. "It was small. Mischievous more than malignant."

"A youngling," Malcolm replied. "They grow up stronger and more controllable."

"Another guardian?"

Malcolm nodded. He winced when he reapplied the cloth to his arm.

"Soriya handled it," Gabe said. "She… She saved us."

Loren let the kid go, and his hands fell to Gabe's shoulders. "She shouldn't have had to."

"What do you—"

"Dammit, Gabe. How many times do I have to tell you? You can't keep sneaking out like this."

Gabe's eyes flared, and he retreated a step as if punched in the gut. "This again? So much for your concern."

"That's all I have for you!" Loren shouted. "You could have been killed."

"I wasn't."

"This time!"

Gabe shook his head in disbelief. "You can't stop me from helping, Loren."

"I sure as hell can try."

"You should listen to the man, Gabe." The voice startled everyone in the room. They spun quickly to see Curtis in the doorway. There were bags under his eyes. Loren wondered how many worried hours he had already put in on the day over Gabe. "He's trying to do right by you."

"You called him?" Gabe asked Loren, the betrayal written all over his face.

Loren shifted for the door, then opened it fully. "Thanks for coming, Curt."

"Thanks for the heads-up." Curtis said. He looked around the room. With each glance, his concern grew. From the battered people littering the room to the visible damage in every direction, all set off alarms for the former officer. "Something happen here tonight?"

"We're handling it." Myers took out her badge.

"Need anything?" Curtis asked.

"You've done enough." Loren shook the man's hand. "Go home, Gabe. We can talk more tomorrow."

Gabe scoffed. He scrambled across the room like a petulant child and snatched up his belongings. "You can talk more, you mean. When was the last time you listened to a word I said?"

"Gabe." The boy pushed through Loren to make his way into the hall. "Gabe!"

Loren tried to follow, blocked by Curtis. "I've got him, Greg."

"Sorry, Curt," Loren said. "I didn't—"

"I know. You did the right thing." Curtis nodded to the silent trio in the room, then headed after his charge. "We'll handle it."

Loren closed the door after him. He slipped the lock into place. Stepping back, he remembered the massive hole in the door, negating any safety the lock might have provided.

He sighed. "At least someone can handle something."

"Greg…" Malcolm called from the couch.

"You all right, Malcolm?"

He removed the washcloth from his arm. The burns were clear. Layers of skin were no longer present, and the wound appeared raw. "Singed," Malcolm managed to say through clenched teeth. "But breathing."

"I have some ointment in the hall closet." Loren looked to Myers. "If you wouldn't mind?"

Myers nodded. She moved for the couch. "Let me give you a hand, Mr. Appleton."

"Malcolm, please," he said, grateful for the additional support. They started for the hall and left the room to Loren and Soriya.

"A wisp," Loren said.

"Apparently," Soriya answered in a soft, distant voice.

"I'm glad you were here, Soriya," he continued, joining her by the shattered window. "If not, I—"

"You shouldn't be," she snapped.

"What? Why?"

"I screwed up." Her body shook with the admission. "I ran off and left them vulnerable. All to chase a shadow when the threat was here."

"You didn't know."

"Exactly!" she bellowed. Fingernails dug into her palms. "I don't know anything anymore. Everything is wrong."

"What can I do to help?"

"Nothing." Soriya reeled at his approach. She pushed past him and rushed for the door. "I have to figure this out. Alone."

He grabbed her by the hand to hold her back. "You can't. Soriya…"

"I have to," she said. "I'm sorry."

With that, she was gone. Loren stood alone in the dim light of the living room, his entire world flipped upside down.

"You sure have a way with people, Loren." Myers carried the ointment and a bandage for Malcolm, who struggled by her side.

She was right. Everything he had done of late pushed people away when he should have brought them together. He should have been the one to protect them. Instead, he'd been absent when the danger arrived on his doorstep.

He pulled the door open. "Can you keep an eye on Malcolm for me, Myers?"

"Sure," she said. "What are you going to do?"

The question demanded an answer. Not only for his current course of action, but for everything that had happened of late. Soriya. Gabe. Even Myers. All needed something from Loren, but he was too blind to see it. And Malcolm... Malcolm needed more help than any of them now.

"I just need some air."

CHAPTER THIRTY-EIGHT

Processing the robbery scene took time. Booking went even longer for Thel, who waited impatiently while her overweight perp visited the bathroom for the fourth time since their arrival at the Central Precinct.

No one liked the pair, but every last one of them enjoyed a good laugh at the video that had gone viral over their capture. Social media was a wonderland of such crap. Thel, however, appreciated the help in winning over some holdouts at the department through her inventive arrest technique.

As the final mugshot was processed, Thel escorted the pair down to holding. She caught a figure rushing through the crowd on the far side of the floor. Yardin did his best to keep his head low. Stares from others dogged his every step, including several jeers from his fellow officers. Thel easily ignored them, but could tell they stung the young man who had so quickly caught her eye.

"David!" Thel called. "Hey!"

Yardin continued without a glance back. He hunched over further, heading up the east stairwell. Thel moved to follow, then stopped. Her job was still tied up with the pair of morons in cuffs.

A sympathetic look passed from the booking sergeant. "Go," he said. "We've got this."

"Thanks."

Grateful didn't capture her accurately. Elated was more apt, as more and more of her colleagues patted her back and tossed her a wave of acceptance that had been withheld previously. Her viral video changed opinions. Unfortunately, not all of them appeared to be in a positive direction.

Thel caught David at the top of the stairs on the second floor. The detectives in the bullpen were all working diligently on the opposite side of the Rath. Privacy was at a premium, but somehow Thel had lucked out when she reached her coffee date.

"David."

"What?" Yardin said with a huff. "What do you want?"

His hostility set her back a step. She did her best to recover. "You took off. I didn't understand why."

"You're kidding, right?"

Footsteps rang out from below. A crowd of officers joked and laughed. The sound of their voices echoed through the stairwell. Yardin retreated farther down the corridor. His slow steps, though, kept him much too close, and he was discovered by the new arrivals almost immediately.

Yardin's so-called friends from the breakroom joined them. They didn't bother with headphones this time, though. They had a new target in mind as they passed Thel without so much as a glance and surrounded Yardin.

"There he is," the first said with a wide grin.

"With his protector, no less," the next continued, a thumb toward Thel. She was nothing to them, even after everything, yet her very presence seemed enough to set them against Yardin.

"Good work out there, rookie," another said with a scoff.

The viral video came with a downside. For a few seconds, as the bystanders outside the convenience store rushed over to check out the situation, they caught Yardin by the door with his knees tucked in tight to his chest. His body trembled, his gun locked in his shaking hands. Noticing the phones, Yardin did his best to sell his inaction. It failed to impress his precinct pals.

"Best cowering act I've ever seen," the first said.

The others laughed. "Someone put him in for a commendation yet?"

The third shoved Yardin against the wall. "It took a freak to save the day."

"Pathetic," the last spat.

All four pushed their way past Yardin. Their laughter continued down the corridor until they reached the bend and disappeared from view.

Yardin seethed along the wall. He kicked at the tile at his side, screaming into his balled-up fists.

Thel reached for him once more. "David... I didn't mean..."

"Stop," he snapped. "I don't want to hear it."

"They're assholes," Thel said. She refused to give up on their date. To her, there was no reason for it. A thousand years had done little in the way of social graces, yet somehow the world drowned in complexities she failed to comprehend. "You can't listen to them."

"No?" Yardin said. Cold eyes washed over her. He puffed up his chest to make himself larger than her, yet it wasn't able to hide the tears clinging to the corners of his eyes. "I should listen to a freak like you instead?"

"Freak?" Thel said. "You can't mean that. I—"

"Don't belong here," Yardin seethed. "None of you monsters do."

"David…"

"Stay away from me!" Pivoting on his heels, Yardin stomped down the hall and away from Thel.

Thel stood in the silence left behind by his departure. The cheers and admiration from her fellow officers no longer lifted her spirits. Yardin's anger swallowed all of it up and left her feeling more dejected than ever.

CHAPTER THIRTY-NINE

The Windsor Lake Ballroom was filled to capacity. Over seventeen-hundred attendees had paid their entry fees and brought their checkbooks to the festivities. Appetizers filled banquet tables with enough selections at each station to feed every starving child in the city. If only they had paid for the pleasure.

Chatter had been minimal. The prerequisite greetings passed along in muted tones before tables were selected and groups were ushered in like cattle for the feast.

The true cost came at the required speeches during the meal. Among the clattering of forks against plates, and the refilling of wine glasses with each pass of the many staffers on duty for the evening, the dulcet tones of the City Council, the Mayor, and of course those in charge of the Lumos Development Corporation made their pitch for the Four Points Project.

They were six speakers deep when Ruiz tuned out. He was miserable, surrounded by the preening politicians and money-grubbing opportunists he always hated. Now, in his role as commissioner, somehow he had become one of them. It failed to affect his bank account, though. He was merely part of the crowd, a servant to more than the city, and they all treated him that way as well. With every glance from his neighbors, from the well-wishers across the room, Ruiz saw nothing but more demands.

Gerry Folsom stood on stage, his speech long-winded as usual. He carried on about the Great Restoration of Portents: the masterful marketing campaign behind the Four Points Project and so many other good deeds around town of late. It moved the city away from the darkness of the last few years—of the death and destruction that had glommed onto Portents.

Four Points was the beginning, and the crowd ate up the pitch as easily as they consumed the mountain of refreshments provided with their ticket.

Ruiz couldn't care less. Four Points, to him, didn't matter in the least. Let the city rebuild. He was there to keep people safe from harm, and the project failed to address how that would happen when his resources were taken for protective services at construction sites instead of on patrols. Those patrols had already become strained with the influx of so many refugees in the wake of the Courtyard's collapse. Myths and legends lived among them, worked and played on their streets, and the chaos created by their arrival had yet to be resolved.

A nudge roused him from his daze. He shifted his weight from the hand supporting him on the table and turned. His wife's eyes met his. She leaned in close.

"Clap."

"Huh?"

"Clap," she said as she demonstrated, like he was a child. "It makes it seem like you're listening."

He sat at attention, hands before him. Joining the chorus, Ruiz realized Folsom's speech had ended at some point, concluding the lengthy presentation for the night.

As those around him stood for another round of drinks and food, Ruiz settled against his chair. His wife shifted to his side.

"I'm sorry," he said.

"You should be," Michelle replied. "Your gorgeous wife is sitting next to you on our first night out in months. Where is your head?"

"Not here."

It should have been. His wife certainly deserved that much. Michelle had put up with a lot over his career. The late hours had always been common. Now they were obscene. He put too much on himself, always forgetting what truly mattered. And damn, she looked stunning in her backless blue dress and pearl earrings. Even the way her hair had been pushed up and tied off set his heart racing.

His irritation, though, won out. When he moved for his plate, her hand blocked him. She lifted him from his seat and dragged him away from the mingling crowd.

"These people see you as a pillar of the community," she said in disbelief.

Ruiz almost laughed. "They see me as a wishing well they can pump for favors. I may as well have a quarter slot imprinted on my forehead."

"Alejo…"

"Watch." He pointed at the approaching figure. Renfield looked smug from the successful fundraiser. His coffers were as full as his ego, a dangerous combination.

"A lovely speech, Renfield," Ruiz said with a gracious grin.

"Thank you, Commissioner," Renfield said. He took Michelle's hand. "Wonderful to meet you."

"Michelle."

He bowed his head. "Michelle."

Pleasantries dealt, he returned to Ruiz. "I hoped to talk to you about security arrangements at the construction sites."

A groan escaped Michelle.

Ruiz nodded to their visitor. "Set up a meeting with my office."

Renfield took the news well, even without a firm answer. He walked off, the next required engagement already caught in his hungry eyes. Before he was six feet away, a member of the City Council replaced him.

Morris Finn was one of the old guard—a rarity considering how many had been killed in Cerberus' invasion. A grumbly, overweight man, Morris never gave the close call a thought. He was too focused on his priorities above all others.

"Ah, Ruiz," he said, barely able to say the name, much less look at the man. He weaseled between Ruiz and his wife, chewing vigorously through a plate full of cheese. "There is a dinner next week to discuss the Council's initiative on the extra-normal refugees. You'll be there?"

Ruiz hadn't heard of a meeting, much less the term extra-normal. The announcement staggered him slightly, and he fought to recover. "I—"

Morris failed to notice. "I'm sure you understand our concern about such creatures living next to tax-paying citizens."

"Well, they have—"

Morris smiled and patted the man's shoulder before starting away. "I'm glad we see eye-to-eye on this."

He was gone before Ruiz could respond, not that he would have been heard in the slightest. "We… don't…"

His fists squeezed tight at his sides. He felt a vein threatening to pop out of his temple.

Michelle helped him retreat farther away from the crowd and into the lobby. "Alejo."

"I told you."

"You did, but—"

He shook his head. "I… I need a few minutes."

Pleading eyes begged for the reprieve, and Michelle let out a sigh. "You do."

"Are you sure?"

"Go before I change my mind," Michelle said. She kissed his cheek. "I'll play diplomat."

"I don't deserve you."

"No, you don't."

"Thank you," he said and rushed for the door.

The cool air hit him immediately. The sudden change refreshed and revived him. Taking a deep breath, Ruiz left the walkway behind to avoid any unwanted company. The last thing he needed was another chat.

Unfortunately, that's exactly what he walked into.

"Bad night?"

Loren leaned against the side of the building, hands deep in his pockets, and a dour expression on his face.

Ruiz grumbled under his breath, then joined the man. "Why do I get the feeling it pales in comparison to yours?"

CHAPTER FORTY

He felt like a heel. The last thing Ruiz needed was someone else to pile on their crap, when he already had the entire city breathing down his neck. Loren had found his way to Windsor Lake, nonetheless. He certainly couldn't cover the entry fee, and to hell with the dress code. Instead, he waited impatiently outside, for what he didn't know. Not until Ruiz joined him.

"It's not a competition," Loren said. "But, yeah. My night sucked."

"What happened?"

Ruiz didn't hesitate to ask, which made it worse for Loren. His former superior, and dear friend, appeared battle-worn and bleary-eyed. The wall did much more than support Ruiz. It looked to be the only thing keeping him on his feet.

Loren kicked off the wall, angry at his selfishness. "You've got enough going on. You don't need to hear about my problems."

"If it keeps me out here instead of in there?" Ruiz asked. He waved Loren back. "Tell me already."

Every detail spilled from his lips about every little thing that had plagued him since the death of Patrick Marsh. The knights, the murders, and the keys. His list grew to include how Myers had pulled him into the affair in the first place and the griffin attack. Ruiz was kind enough not to laugh, though he spared a moment to show Loren the photo he'd saved on his phone of Loren's flailing.

"And then there's Soriya…"

Ruiz's eyes went wide. "I'm sorry, what?"

"She's back, Ruiz," Loren said. "Somehow she's back."

Ruiz fell silent, clearly letting the news wash over him. With a slight shake of his head, he rolled his finger for Loren to continue. The former detective buttoned up the case for Ruiz, with the prophecy looming over them now that the killer had four of the five keys.

None of it—not the threat against them or the constant barrage of attacks—brought out more frustration than when Loren mentioned his problems with Gabe. He relayed the classes skipped and the subway rides to the city without permission with such a fury, Ruiz nearly intervened.

Finally, with everything said and done, Loren circled back to the wall and let out a deep, cleansing breath. The weight of the matter lifted for a second.

"Wow," was all Ruiz could say.

"See?"

"Yeah," Ruiz muttered, running a hand through his hair. "You win."

"Told you."

"You're also an idiot."

Loren rolled his eyes. "Of course I am."

Ruiz shuffled closer. "Gabe doesn't need one more person lecturing him, setting boundaries, and trapping him in place. He needs a friend."

"He deserves a normal life."

"That's not your call to make," Ruiz shot back.

"But Gabe needs—"

"Something you refuse to give him. Something you refuse to even give yourself," Ruiz said. "It's why you're still living out of boxes. You've taken some big steps, Greg, but you always prepare to backpedal. You've always got that escape plan in place."

"Now just a—"

"No," Ruiz snapped. "You came here, so you get to put up with me. Your way doesn't work anymore. Not with Gabe in your life. Not with Soriya back, which is too insane to question right now."

Loren pounded his head against the wall lightly. "They're looking to me for answers, Ruiz. For guidance. Me! Even Myers!"

A chuckle escaped Ruiz. "I think Myers is looking for something else."

"Like what?"

"You'll figure it out, eventually." He patted his friend's shoulder. "You're right, though. They are looking to you. So are you going to keep pushing them away out of fear, or are you going to stop running away and be the friend—the family—they see in you?"

Loren sighed. "If I go with the running away option?"

"I will hunt you down and beat the hell out of you."

"I figured," Loren said. He nodded slightly. Ruiz settled at his side once more, and the pair stared into the night sky in silence for a brief time. Loren pondered the advice given, and couldn't help but question the validity of his friend's theory. Had he been ready to run the moment he moved into his new apartment? Is that why he and Gabe had fought so often lately?

Loren pushed his aggravation aside with his unending questioning. He turned to his friend with a gracious smile on his face.

"So what's your deal?"

Ruiz continued to stare into the night. "I'm thinking about stepping down." He shook his head. "No. What I'm really thinking about is walking back into that banquet hall and flipping a buffet table over."

"Sounds like running away to me."

"Yeah," Ruiz said, his jaw clenched. "I realized that the second I opened my mouth. Quite the pair, aren't we?"

"Our lives have never been better."

"And we refuse to see the good parts."

Their laughter hovered between them. Loren motioned to the front doors of the hall. "Get back in there, Commissioner. Help this city like only you can."

"Sound advice," Ruiz said. "Should I repeat it?"

"I think I've got it."

Ruiz patted Loren's back. "Good." When he brought his hand down, his eyes widened. "Oh, hell. Michelle is going to kill me for leaving her in there."

"Nay," Loren said with a wave as they made their way to the front walkway. "She's probably having the time of her life."

The lobby was in full view from their position on the walkway. Michelle shot for the door with fire in her bold eyes.

"Or not," Loren said.

Ruiz straightened his tie and started for the door. "I'm blaming you for this."

"Don't you dare," Loren called out, moving to join him.

"No choice."

"She's still coming this way," Loren said.

"Run."

Loren dashed away from the building, a wave to his so-called dear friend. "You're all heart, Ruiz."

He failed to catch the apologies passed by Ruiz when Michelle met him at the door, or the cursing she threw his way for his long absence.

All Loren heard was Ruiz's advice repeating on him. He truly was a good friend, and exactly what he needed after the long night. Now all Loren had to do was find some way to fix everything.

CHAPTER FORTY-ONE

The lecture filled the car ride home. Every word added to an unending speech about responsibility and life priorities, though Curtis knew nothing about Gabe's sense of either. What he repeated were several notes set up for the other kids they had taken in over the years. He continued to claim his understanding, how all teens went through hard times and wanted to move away from the norm to make their own way, but certain expectations could not be ignored.

The only thing being ignored, though, was Gabe. His needs, his desires, never played into matters. He suffered through the guilt trip in silence. He had heard it all before: the pain he was putting Nicole and Curtis through. Curtis even threw in the concerns from his so-called brothers and sisters, which was a gross exaggeration. They barely acknowledged Gabe's existence, let alone accepted him into their brood.

Gabe stood alone among them; Curtis and Nicole had shuffled him to a spare room opposite the rest of the children. They called it a reflecting space, but to Gabe, the tightly cramped room was an evolved way to put someone in time-out. Like a child, he stamped off the moment they arrived at the home and made his way to the solitary space.

The lecture fell away. None of it mattered to him. School, family, and friends were societal norms that had no place in his life. Curtis' disappointment and Nicole's frustration never entered into the anger coursing through Gabe's entire body. Only Loren's reaction stuck with him and caused him to slam the door shut.

"Why?" he bellowed, tossing his backpack across the room. It bounced off the bed and crashed to the floor, where it settled along the base of the window overlooking the garage roof. "Why didn't he listen? Why doesn't anyone listen to me?"

He lashed out in his aggravation. Shelves of old trophies and photos fell under his sweeping arm. A scream echoed in the space as he kicked out against the bed, the desk, and everything else that seemed to close in around him.

Collapsing on the bed, Gabe grabbed a pillow and jammed it over his face to muffle the scream. Finished, a long breath caught in his lungs, Gabe tossed the pillow aside.

Curtis stood in the doorway, arms across his chest. "You finished?"

"Great," Gabe grumbled. "Another lecture. Just what I need."

Curtis entered and closed the door lightly behind him. He moved for the fallen goods, some dating back to his own childhood. The house had been his parents', one he'd inherited after their passing and revitalized for his own family. Curtis lifted one of the photos, the frame cracked in the corner from the fall.

"No," he said in a low voice. "What you need is a beating." Curtis carefully reset the photo. He rounded the bed, head heavy and shoulders slumped from the long day. "Nicole and I have taken a lot of lumps having you here. All we've tried to do is give you a home, a family, and you have done everything in your power to throw it in our face."

"I had a family," Gabe snapped, unwilling to look at his foster father.

Curtis sighed as he sat on the bed opposite Gabe. "We're not looking to replace them. What happened to them was a tragedy, but keep going down this road, and it will happen to you too. That's the last thing any of us want. Not me or Nicole. Not Greg."

"Like he cares."

Curtis nodded. "You can be as mad as you like with him. He made the right decision tonight. He did what any parent would do to protect someone they love. You get that, don't you?"

"Sure," Gabe replied with a huff.

Curtis threw up his hands and stood. "*Sure*," he said, mimicking the boy. "Gabe—"

"I have homework to finish," Gabe said in a sharp tone. "You mind?"

"Okay," Curtis said. He opened the door, but held the frame. "We'll talk more when you're ready."

The door closed and left Gabe with his solitude. "Great," he muttered, relishing a continuation of the conversation. *What was the point?* he wondered. If they refused to consider his side of events, what he truly desired with his life, then why did they continue to bother? He had certainly tired of the constant arguments.

Shuffling toward the floor, Gabe snatched up his backpack. He tossed it onto the desk and retrieved a pile of folders. His laptop slid along the surface. He pushed it aside to dig into the mountain of assignments he'd ignored for weeks.

Every page carried notes for parent signatures or condemned his lackluster performance, reminding him of his deficiencies. Gabe simply didn't care to live in that world. There were better things to do with his time, and after a few scattered moments in which he failed to answer the same math problem four times, Gabe shoved the folders off the desk and back to the floor.

"Screw this."

Pulling his laptop over, Gabe opened it and the screen came to life. He entered his password, waited for the device to load the home screen, and set to work.

"What was it Malcolm said?" His fingers hovered over the keyboard. "Griffins. Will-o'-the-wisps."

With each entry, more pages loaded. They offered hand-drawn images, fictional representations of the creatures, and their historical origins. Almost every page originated from the same source.

"Arthurian legends."

The stories of old filled his head. Noah always hated them. None ever held his attention; his mind was always geared more toward the practical than the fantastical. However, when Gabe heard them late at night, with his father seated beside the bed in an old wooden rocking chair, Gabe ate them up with a spoon.

The Knights of the Round Table fascinated him. Stories of Arthur and Excalibur, Merlin and Mordred, and so many others sent his dreams to new and amazing places. Looking through them all again on the screen did the same to Gabe's imagination.

"Wait." He stood from the desk. "He mentioned five knights. The Five Knights. There was… there was a book Dad always read."

Gabe rushed from the room. He passed Curtis on his way to the other side of the home.

"What are you—"

"Homework stuff," Gabe said without stopping. "Calculator

and a ruler. Another pencil. Stuff like that."

He was around the corner before Curtis replied. His words were so quick, it was a wonder if Curtis understood a single one, but Gabe pressed on. He reached his room and stepped inside.

The lights were out, his two "brothers" sleeping fitfully along the right-hand wall. Gabe quietly crept to what few belongings he had salvaged from the fire that had consumed his former life. Among them was a book with five raised hands holding swords on the cover.

Gabe grabbed it and moved for the door.

"Gabe?" He turned to see Nicholas rubbing his eyes. He was only ten, orphaned when his parents overdosed while he slept in the other room. "What are you doing?"

"Homework. Don't worry about it."

"When are you coming back to our room?" the boy asked.

"I don't know. I…"

"I wish you liked it here," Nicholas said. "I wish you liked us."

"I…" Words failed Gabe. He moved for the bed and helped Nicholas back under the covers. "I like you, Nicky, I do."

"You're always angry. Always fighting."

Reasons existed, but they all felt false when Gabe looked at the boy. "I'm trying, Nicky. I am."

"They do love you, you know." The boy closed his eyes, halfway to dreamland already. "They love all of us."

"Sure they do, kid." His doubts sat at the tip of his tongue, waiting to spout out in a tirade of curses and frustration Nicholas didn't deserve. Instead, Gabe merely stood and started for the door again. He grabbed a calculator and ruler on his way, then rushed back to his well-deserved prison.

Curtis said nothing. He watched with keen interest, though, as Gabe showcased the procured supplies and disappeared into the room.

With the door closed, Gabe dropped the supplies and opened the book on the desk. The Five Knights were messengers of Merlin, who foresaw a dangerous end for the world. The knights were charged with protecting humanity from the danger however they could, even at the sacrifice of themselves. They built a giant device to achieve this end. They hid it in the center of an immense maze, a tribute to where Merlin first witnessed the vision that had set them on their quest.

Gabe closed the book. The story ran through his thoughts, swirling faster and faster. Back at the laptop, Gabe revisited the case Loren had kept from him, unwilling to let it drop. Local news archives showcased the first victim, Patrick Marsh. They listed his worth and displayed images of the massive estate he'd built in the Riverside District.

The photos included a single image of a hedge maze at the rear of his property.

Gabe jumped to his feet. "I have to tell Loren." He collected the book and the laptop, then shoved them into his bag. From the side pocket, he removed his cell phone—still turned off from his misadventure earlier. The screen lit up, and he paused at the password prompt.

"Wait," he said. "Why should I tell him? He doesn't trust me. He only sees a kid. But I'm not a kid."

He tossed the phone to the bed and reached into his pocket. A single object fell against his palm, and he clutched it tight.

"I'm the Greystone," Gabe said. "Like my parents were. Like Noah was."

He took a deep breath, then moved for the window. Opening it slowly, Gabe held his head out into the night air. Wind rushed through his hair and cooled his cheeks. He lifted his right leg over the sash, only to pause at the threshold.

"I can't do this." Gabe glanced back at the bedroom and the shadow passing beneath the door outside. "This is the wrong move. If I go now, they'll find me. They'll call Loren."

Rushing into action was a mistake. Curtis and Nicole would realize his escape before he reached the end of the street. The limited public transportation at such a late hour caused another problem for Gabe.

He needed to wait. "Tomorrow. I can get there tomorrow."

Gabe closed the window. His body struggled with the decision, hands lingering for a long moment on the sill. To hold back—to plot and plan, in general—went against his every instinct. He knew it was the smarter play, and that carried him back to the bed where he sat impatiently as the clock ticked away the seconds.

"Tomorrow," Gabe repeated, convincing himself of the plan's validity. He rubbed at tired eyes. The late hour finally hit him. As he bent down to remove his socks, Gabe noticed the fallen textbooks on the ground.

"I have to go to school tomorrow," he said with a groan. He lifted the texts from the carpet and dropped them back on the desk. He shook his head as another minute ticked away on the clock. It was going to be a long night and an even longer day. "Which means I have to do my homework. Crap."

CHAPTER FORTY-TWO

"There," Loren said, hammer in hand. He finished nailing the corner of the plywood set over the shattered window. Another piece covered the hole in the door, though nails failed to secure it in place. Duct tape ran around the edges, a makeshift solution that eroded with every passing second. It was enough, though, and a tired Loren stepped back from his do-it-yourself project. "That should do until maintenance can get here."

He couldn't wait to have that conversation. How the hell could he explain that the damage inflicted on his apartment, as well as to the hallway stairs and the roof, had been caused by a mythological ball of light capable of burning at extreme temperatures? He wondered if that would be a tougher sell than disclosing the theft of the plywood from the basement to cover the damages in the interim.

Sleep had eluded him. The constant whipping wind and the creaking noises from the exposed corridor outside his apartment had put him on edge until he'd surrendered. Malcolm had retired to the bedroom, but Loren had heard the shuffling of feet more than once from behind the door. No doubt, the man's burns continued to plague him and kept him from a peaceful rest as well.

Loren lowered the hammer to the coffee table. He lifted the water glass beside it and enjoyed a long sip.

Malcolm shuffled into the room. His phone buzzed in his hand. Raising it close, he swiped across the screen. His eyes widened, and he nearly lost his footing.

Loren lowered the glass. "Malcolm? Are you all right?"

The knight steadied himself on the side of the couch. He placed the phone face down along the armrest, then offered a somber smile.

"Yes," he said. "Yes, I'm fine."

"Can I get you anything?" Loren asked. He ran a mental check of his pantry. "There might be some Pop-Tarts hiding somewhere. Or a stray piece of bread?"

Malcolm sat along the end of the couch. "All I need is your word."

"My word?" Loren said. He took a seat on the chair opposite his company.

Malcolm's hands clasped before him. "You're a lucky man, Greg. So many turn to you. You affect so many lives through your deeds. I want your word you won't take that for granted, that you'll see how truly blessed your life is."

The request surprised Loren and mirrored his discussion with Ruiz from the night before. A distant stare caught the photos on the wall. "It's… difficult for me, Malcolm."

"Because of your wife," Malcolm said, tracking his wayward gaze.

Loren stood. He moved toward the photo of Beth. His fingers grazed the frame. "I wonder if I'm cursed sometimes. That I'll always lose those I care about."

Malcolm joined him. "Perhaps this will help." A hand returned from his pocket with a small object. He held it out to Loren. "It's one of the few relics I keep close to me. It's always brought me a measure of comfort, even on the darkest of days."

"What is it?" He took the object and let it sit on his palm. It was a small red crystal. Jagged edges formed the shape of a heart, a beastly face etched into the surface with teeth biting its own tail. When he ran his fingers along the surface, the object glowed.

"A keepsake passed down to me," Malcolm answered. "A dragon's heart."

Loren shook his head. "I can't accept this."

Malcolm closed his hand around Loren's and the crystal. "Please. It will do you more good now."

"Yeah, right," Loren grumbled. "Like I've been doing such a bang-up job of things so far. I try, I really do. If only I could make things right. That's been my goal from the beginning."

"You'll get there," Malcolm said with a fatherly smirk. "Things have a way of coming back around on you. Everything in life is cyclical. The end is the beginning is the end. Remember, we always return to the start to make sense of the future."

Loren nodded, though the words failed to penetrate. He was

too busy watching the small light emanating from the crystal. Taking a seat, Loren let out a long breath. "Well, whatever happens, I'm glad you're here to help make sense of things. I certainly haven't earned your faith, but thank you for sticking with me."

Malcolm glanced at the phone on the armrest. His gaze dropped to the floor, his words barely a whisper. "If only I could stay."

Loren's brow furrowed. "What do you mean?"

Malcolm straightened his shoulders, throwing off his exhaustion. The smile returned to his face, and he started for the door.

Loren jumped to his feet. "Where are you going?"

"For a walk," the man replied.

"Malcolm," Loren said. "It's not safe. You can't—" He stopped himself. Ruiz's words circled back on him. So did Malcolm's. After everything he had done to push people away, he still hadn't learned a damn thing, had he? "I'm doing it again, aren't I?"

Malcolm reached for Loren's shoulder and squeezed lightly. "You're a good man, Greg."

"But you need a walk."

His hand fell away, and he opened the door. "I won't be long."

Loren hesitated. He wanted to reach out and grab the handle, to shut the door and trap the man inside the apartment. It was for his safety, after all. Yet, the withdrawn and sullen look in Malcolm's eyes told him the walk was necessary—more than necessary after all the anguish he had suffered over the last few days. Who was Loren to stand in his way?

A slight nod escaped Loren. With that, the door closed behind Malcolm. Loren stood in the apartment, alone for the first time in days. They all needed time to figure things out.

CHAPTER FORTY-THREE

The Ravonna overlooked the harbor. It had once been a world-class destination for travelers to Portents. The tourist industry had taken a slight hit with the coming of the Heads of Cerberus. Innocent blood falling like rain had that effect on such industries. The hotel closed, hoping to attract new owners to take on the risk of operating in such a chaotic metropolis.

Soriya sought the quiet afforded by the vacant property. Traveling took her all night, the city as wide awake as her own thoughts. She fled, afraid to face the mistakes made with Gabe and Malcolm and the danger she had put them in through her stupidity.

By the time morning arrived, Soriya had settled on the rooftop of the Ravonna, where she kneeled in the center. The sun rose along the horizon and brought with it a semblance of peace. Dawn broke to offer a sign of hope, one Soriya desperately clung to.

Her memories continued to plague her. The entire last year was nothing but a blank, lost as much as the Bypass was to her. Soriya felt disconnected from everything. When she reached out for a slim strand of recognition, it all seemed to vanish.

The loss terrified her. Using the peace of the morning light as a guide, Soriya tucked her legs beneath her. The Greystone sat in front of her. No longer a warm comfort, the stone was cold to the touch. It had become another shattered shard of her past.

Mentor had taught her many meditation techniques over the years. While not the easiest of students when it came to their lessons, Soriya had listened. Peeling back the layers of her mind, fragments existed. Pieces of her story remained, the very strands of her life waiting to be tied in place. Loren was one and Mentor another. Their shared experiences might not have been easily accessed, but the remnants gave her a starting point.

Soriya pushed away the world. Closing her eyes, she imagined a lock on a door. If she could only find the key within herself, everything would return in an instant. She knew the Greystone lay at the core. It always had with her life, ever since finding the stone under the burning wreckage of her former life.

Within her mind's eye, Soriya pushed against the door. It shoved back, a tug of war for control. With each jolt, sweat ran down her brow. Tension built up in her limbs. Peace faltered and the morning's hope clouded over, cutting the light off completely.

Frustration erupted. Soriya shot to her feet and kicked at the ground. The Greystone, caught in her path, skidded to the corner.

"No," Soriya breathed. She bounded after it. Her hand snatched the precious item before it fell off the edge. She stood at the precipice, cradling the Greystone close. Staring down to the ground below, Soriya wondered if it would be better to let it all go.

She didn't belong in the world—not like this. The stone had always defined her existence. What was she without purpose and without a past?

Soriya crept to the edge. She spread her arms and wondered if the Bypass would accept her this time.

Doubts kept her still. Eventually, they led her back to the roof's center. Soriya tucked the stone away, defeated once more. Quick steps carried her down the stairs of the Ravonna and back to the city.

The past remained out of reach. Everything fell away from her whenever she tried to reconnect, to find her way back into the world. Only one thing felt right to her. Only one thing felt pure and brought with it a sense of self and purpose currently withheld from the stone and everything else.

She needed a fight. She wanted nothing more than to feel blood on her knuckles and a foe cowering at her feet. Just the thought sent a wave of ecstasy through her body. It completed her in a way nothing else had since her return. Cracking her knuckles, the recently revived protector of the city left behind the light of the day for the shadows of the night to come.

Soriya stalked off, looking for a fight and, with it, some semblance of the life so thoroughly taken from her.

CHAPTER FORTY-FOUR

Loren paced the length of the living room for what felt like the thousandth time. It had been hours since Malcolm's departure. Loren had taken advantage of his solitude at the start; he had shaved and showered. As refreshed as could be, he'd eaten breakfast and quickly realized Malcolm had been smart to disregard the Pop-Tart offer. The pastry had been stale, the frosting little more than rotten sugar coating his teeth.

That had been as far as the distractions took him. Now, all that remained was the nervous energy that came from waiting. With each successive lap around the room, Loren cursed himself for letting the man out of his sight for even a second.

The dragon's heart rested in his hand. Clutched tight before him, Loren stared at the curious crystal. He revisited every word spoken by Malcolm and every mannerism committed to memory. Something had happened; something had changed in the man from the previous night, but Loren couldn't connect the dots. His own exhaustion kept the mystery running in an endless loop through his mind, like his continuing circuit through the apartment.

"Come on, Malcolm," Loren muttered under his breath. "Where are you?"

Steps approached in the corridor. Loren paused his pacing, an ear to the door. He tucked the crystal heart deep into his pocket. The steps slowed. Loren ripped the door open when a shadow passed under the frame.

"Malcolm!" he exclaimed. "Where have you—"

Myers stood in front of the door, hair tucked back behind her ear and a hand raised to knock.

"Myers?"

She raised an eyebrow. "Not the best welcome I've received."

Loren shook his head, then stepped out of the way to let her in. "What are you doing here?"

"We released Buchwald's son," Myers said.

"What? When?"

"Last night."

Loren's hand fell upon his brow. He peered at the boarded-up window. "Then he could have…"

"I'm afraid so," Myers said.

"I interrogated him. He knew my name. He… I led him right here." Buchwald had been in custody and the second he was released, the attack occurred? The thought left Loren cold. "Now we have nothing."

"I've put eyes on him. If he's behind this, we'll get him, Loren." Myers leaned against the wall at his side. "If it isn't him, though…"

Loren nodded. She was right. While the possibility existed, there was every chance of Buchwald's innocence as well. The lack of answers frustrated him, causing him to push from the wall for another circuit through the room.

Myers raised a hand to stop him. "Maybe Malcolm knows something we can use."

"Malcolm?"

"Yeah," Myers said. "Where is he?"

Loren couldn't look at her. "He went for a walk."

"You let him go?" The words boomed throughout the apartment.

Loren held up his hands before him. "I've been yelling at myself all morning, so don't bother."

"We need to find him," Myers said. Fear sat in her eyes. "Did he give any indication where he might go?"

"No," Loren said. His hands fell to his hips, and he circled around the couch. "He was fine. Tired from everything that had happened with the Wisp, but otherwise okay. He was coming out to check on me—on my repair job, of all things—and…" Loren stopped at the far side of the couch. A small object rested along the arm, left by Malcolm in his haste to depart. Loren's eyes went wide. "He saw something on his phone."

Loren snatched the device from the couch. He flipped it over, fingers swiping at the screen. "It's locked."

Myers was at his side in seconds. "Try 1, 2, 3, 4."

Loren lowered the phone. "Really?"

Myers shrugged. "Who thinks they're going to lose their phone?"

"I lose mine constantly."

"What's your password?" Loren's silence brought a smug grin to her face. "See?"

Loren punched in the code. The home screen came to life. "I'm in."

"Check his messages."

"I am," Loren said, working as fast as his fingers allowed. They fought against him in his haste for answers.

"See if someone—"

"Myers," Loren snapped. He shifted away for some space. "I am."

Myers backed off a step. "Got it."

Few text chains were listed among his messages. Most of them were from businesses with PIN codes or offering special discounts. The top one, however, was clearly meant for Malcolm, though the number led to no known contact. The message simply read: IMAGE.

Loren clicked on it. "Oh, no."

"What is it?"

Loren passed along the phone. "Malcolm isn't clearing his head."

A young woman sat tied to a chair, her mouth gagged and eyes screaming for help. A knife held tight to her throat completed the photo and the extremely clear message for Malcolm Appleton.

"He's heading right into the killer's hands."

CHAPTER FORTY-FIVE

When Malcolm turned twelve, his uncle on his mother's side took him for a drive around Portents. His uncle drove a convertible. The make and model escaped Malcolm's memory—not that the typical twelve-year-old cared for such details. All Malcolm focused on was the air rushing through his hair as they flew through the city into the deep woods that stretched along her northern border.

At the edge of Rose Riley Forest, they stopped and exited the vehicle. Malcolm's uncle led him to the overpass, and the city spread before them. There, his uncle told him a tale he would carry for the rest of his life. He spoke of the knights and their destiny.

Malcolm, of course, being a curious kid with aspirations of future greatness, had questioned everything. He'd wanted to know about the knights' journey, about what they brought with them, and who they'd trusted with the task ahead.

His uncle had taken each in turn, especially the last. When it came to trust, the knights had only each other. When the time arrived to pass on their task, they had to be sure to choose wisely—for the prophecy was no joking matter and had to be handled with tremendous care.

He still remembered the solemn look in his uncle's eyes, washing over him as he told Malcolm the truth, and later understood the reason behind the drive when, on Malcolm's eighteenth birthday, the key was passed down to him.

His life became more than a story. His entire existence served a purpose greater than any he could ever share with the people around him. They would never understand, never be able to fathom his role as a knight, and Malcolm treasured that responsibility.

The task came at a significant cost, however. A normal life was no longer in the offering. With the resources at his uncle's disposal, Malcolm was able to live a comfortable life within the city. He wanted for nothing—a modest home and all the books he could ever hope to devour.

Companionship, though, fell away from him. There were his fellow knights, of course, but beyond that Malcolm swore loyalty only to his mission as guardian of the key. To compromise that, to give his trust to someone, remained out of reach. His story would remain his alone.

Or so he thought.

There was always more to the story, more to life than the comforts of home and the treasures of a vivid imagination. Life happened, whether desired or not, and when Malcolm met Lynette Neary, he realized how empty his own had been.

That connection pulled at him now, and Malcolm realized the true cost of his desire. By the time he reached the warehouse district and the precise location for his meeting, Malcolm was all out of curses. Only concern remained.

They had a daughter together—Jessica. For a handful of years, their lives were pure bliss. But his responsibility always weighed on him. His task remained, and he saw the danger in the city growing wilder with each passing year. Birdmen soared overhead and gremlins haunted auto shops. Something always spooked him, waiting to leap out when he least expected it.

Fights increased between him and Lynette. He begged her to leave Portents behind, and with it, their love. She refused and left him with only one option. He walked away from them, pushing them away to keep them safe from his responsibility, to keep them protected from the threats in the dark should they become too much to handle.

What a fool he had been. Malcolm should have stayed with them, been a guardian to them more than any other. Instead, he'd selfishly turned his back and closed himself off from all hope of life and love and any semblance of true happiness.

His hidden life—his great secret—demanded compensation now.

"I'm here," Malcolm called into the darkness of the warehouse. He held the door open with one hand to let the light of the midday sun wash over the space. Crates were covered on all sides, the contents of the space long since abandoned like so much of the district. "I came alone."

The door slammed shut and plunged him into shadow. Small windows along the ceiling allowed brief flickers of light, but hid more than they showed. Malcolm wound his way through the warehouse, deeper and deeper through the forgotten contents of the past, until the crates faded and the floor opened up.

A masked figure stood behind Jessica. The knife glinted in his hand, held tight to her neck, just like the picture from that morning. Malcolm recognized the blade as Geoffrey's—a trophy from another dead knight.

"That was smart," the masked figure said. Wide eyes peered through the mask, never blinking and never wavering from Malcolm. "For her sake."

"Let her go," Malcolm said.

Jessica tried to raise her hands, tried to kick at the chair, but the bindings were too tight and kept her locked in place. Her gag swallowed her cries, but the tears made her fear crystal clear for Malcolm to see.

"Please. You have me," Malcolm continued, edging closer. "She has nothing to do with us. Let her go."

"The key first."

Jessica knew nothing of the key or the knights. Malcolm had considered telling her for years. He envisioned driving her out to the overlook just as his uncle had done and sharing the tale of Merlin's prophecy. He wondered if it would spark her imagination as it had for him.

Those were the dreams of his youth, however. Thanks to the masked man, only terror remained.

"I..."

His grip on Jessica's throat tightened. "The key or she dies."

The second the photo had been sent to his phone, Malcolm lost any other option. He removed the chain from around his neck and held the key before him.

"Take it."

The masked man left Jessica behind. He circled the chair and stood before Malcolm. The key fell into his open palm. His eyes gleamed as he accepted the gift. Malcolm took a step forward, his hands reaching for Jessica to free her.

"Thank you," her abductor said in a calm voice. The knife shot out and pierced Malcolm's midsection. Malcolm felt a hand on his back. The cold of the key mixed with the heat of the blade in his gut as the masked man plunged the knife deeper. "Thank you for your service."

The blade twisted hard, then retracted. Malcolm's hands shot to the gaping wound soaking his shirt. He staggered two steps for Jessica. A cry rose from her, muted by the gag wrapped tight across her lips. Tears flowed to match his own. He still had to rescue her. He was her father and had to save her from the horrible choices he'd made in his life.

The last piece of the fail-safe now rested in the killer's hands. Malcolm had failed in his grand quest. And with that failure complete, Malcolm Appleton fell.

CHAPTER FORTY-SIX

"He has a daughter?"

Horns blared. The car swerved across two lanes, then back to the right, before passing through a red light. Tires screeched to a halt all around them. Angry screams trailed after the blitzing Impala. Loren had insisted on driving, his mistakes compounding on top of each other with every block passed.

"Eyes on the road, Loren!" Myers shouted. She clung for her life, hand locked on the handle hanging above the passenger-side door. Her other pushed up against the crushed roof. "They gave you a license?"

"Not helping, Myers," he replied.

She took a sharp breath, barely able to look ahead. Her saving grace was the report sent ahead on her phone. "Yes," she said. "He has a daughter. Jessica Neary."

"He never said a damn word," Loren said through clenched teeth. Malcolm had stayed with him for days. He never bothered to share the little detail that he had a family. It wasn't the sharing that troubled Loren. His ignorance haunted him. He had never thought to ask more about Malcolm, only hoping to keep him safe from the danger hunting him. Then there were the constant distractions—the griffin, Gabe, not to mention Soriya's return.

Myers laid a hand on his shoulder. "He probably didn't think anyone knew about her."

Loren slammed his hands against the steering wheel. "I can't believe I let him go."

"He made a choice."

No, Loren thought. Malcolm had no choice, not if Loren understood anything about the man, and he truly thought he did. Someone was in danger because of Malcolm's role as a knight. Even if it had been a complete stranger, Malcolm would have made the same decision. There was no helping some heroes—they had to play the part no matter the odds against them—and Malcolm was a hero through and through.

He had stood by Loren over the last few days, offering both a friendly ear and moral support. Loren could do no less now. He sped around the corner of Highgate, down Westmark and the row of broken-down warehouses that dominated the southern district.

"Is that it?" Loren pointed ahead.

"Yes." Myers double-checked the message left on Malcolm's phone with the detailed instructions for the meet. "That's the one."

Loren slammed on the brakes in front of the warehouse. The car continued to rock back and forth after they departed for the looming structure.

Myers guided them away from the road to a loading area near the rear. "There's an entrance over here."

Both drew their weapons, Myers with her police-issued Glock and Loren with his taser. Myers took the lead, her authority requiring the role. Loren, however, pulsed with anxiety and nearly shoved her aside when the door opened.

"Malcolm!" Loren called into the dark.

Myers slapped at his arm, and a stiff glare shot his way. Their presence had been a secret until Loren had given it away.

"Sorry," he whispered. He wasn't thinking; the thought of Malcolm's peril drew him forward without caution or prudence.

Myers said nothing. She crept forward around the rows of crates throughout the warehouse. Loren stuck close to cover their rear flank. What felt like hours, but was less than a minute in reality, carried them from the entrance to the main floor of the building.

When Myers halted, Loren crashed into her. He spun at her hesitation, and his eyes caught sight of the body on the floor.

"Malcolm!"

Loren was at his side in an instant. Dropping his weapon to the ground, Loren ran a hand over the knife wound to Malcolm's midsection. His other checked for a pulse, though he knew the outcome long before he made the effort. The pale skin and blue lips from the lack of blood flow made it clear Malcolm's injuries had long since won out.

His friend was dead.

While Loren cradled the deceased, Myers rushed for the bound Jessica. She screamed at their presence, begging for release, and Myers did her best to comply as quickly as possible. Once the straps on her legs and hands fell away, Jessica leaped from the chair and collapsed at her father's side.

She removed the gag, soaked with tears. "Dad! No, no, no…"

Loren wanted to reach for her, his hands covered in Malcolm's blood. Instead, he fell away from the dead.

"Is he—"

Loren shook his head. "He's gone."

Myers nodded. Taking out her phone, she called in the murder. This was still her case, after all, and more was at stake than a single man's demise.

Loren could do nothing, just as he had since Malcolm left him that morning. He'd never felt so powerless and lost. Every time he thought he'd figured out the road ahead, something dragged him back down to the depths. Murder and mayhem, he always called it. The notion sickened him. This, however, was his world, and he had to face it.

More than that, he had to stop the son of a bitch who killed his friend.

"Backup is on the way," Myers said, rejoining him. Jessica continued to grieve for her fallen father. Myers helped Loren to his feet, and the pair stepped away from the scene. "He was the last knight, Loren. What happens now?"

"The end."

"So we stop it."

"Not without help," Loren said. He peered at the dead. He couldn't lose anyone else, yet he also couldn't handle things alone. That wasn't who he was any longer, if it ever was. Alone, there was every chance of failure. Malcolm had trusted him and he refused to let the man down again. Not after this. Not after everything.

"We need Soriya."

CHAPTER FORTY-SEVEN

They waited for officers from the Ninth Precinct to take custody of the scene. An ambulance joined them, and a pair of EMTs helped escort Jessica Neary from the warehouse for a thorough examination.

Her sorrow lingered over the scene. Her father was dead.

Loren, though, knew it was a miracle she remained alive. The killer could have easily taken Jessica's life as well. Nothing and no one would have been able to stop him. The fact he'd left her alive spoke to the focus behind the murderer's intentions.

The keys were all that mattered. With all five in hand, the killer's next move became a mystery.

Myers nudged Loren on the arm. She cocked her head toward their car, and the pair headed over. Loren started for the driver's seat, but Myers cut him off.

She held out her hand. "Please."

"Please, what?"

She waited. "For my sanity. Let me drive."

Loren sighed. He dropped the keys into her hand.

"Good," she said. "We should head to Central and—"

"Myers," Loren interrupted with an icy stare.

She groaned. "After we find Soriya."

"Thank you."

The time for going it alone, for dividing their forces, was at an end. They needed to regroup. For a second, Loren took out his phone and almost dialed Gabe. The kid had stood by his side through every challenge over the last year. They had been in the trenches, fighting the monsters in the dark. He deserved to know what was happening, to be a part of it, or at the very least find out what happened to Malcolm.

Loren noted the late hour on the phone and returned the device to his pocket. Tomorrow was another school day, and Loren had already done enough damage to the kid's academic standing with their recent misadventures. He'd made a promise to Nicole and Curtis to be better.

Slipping into the car, Myers started the engine, and they were off. "Any ideas where she might be?"

Loren lifted Myers' radio from the central console. He turned the volume up before propping it against the dash. "She has a way of letting you know."

Myers disagreed with the plan. Even silent, her thoughts were clear in the way her jaw clenched and how her hand clutched the steering wheel. She'd always been reticent about including Soriya in their affairs. It was a lesson that had taken years for Loren to learn, and he wasn't about to falter now, not with the threat against them.

It didn't take long for news to come down. The radio crackled as the report rang out about a violent altercation at a dockside tavern. As more details filtered through the static, Loren lifted the radio up and nodded to Myers, who spun the wheel. The Impala screeched across three lanes of traffic to complete the U-turn for the RDJ ramp.

"You sure it's her?"

Loren grinned. "You heard the call."

"A fight at a bar?" Myers asked with a scoff. "I hear lots of calls like that."

"Sure," Loren replied. "Who doesn't love a good barroom brawl? But everyone against one person? Let alone one woman?"

Myers raised an eyebrow. "Should I feel offended?"

Loren shook his head. "It's her, Myers."

No other words were needed. The car launched up the on-ramp, and they raced out of downtown for the Riverside District. They skirted around light traffic, ignoring the speed limit, though the Impala wasn't a fan.

It felt like ages, but took little more than fifteen minutes to reach the docks. Myers led them around the harbor until they settled along the business district to the north.

With each tick of the clock, tension rose throughout Loren's body. He couldn't help but feel nervous about his decision to pursue Soriya, when everything said the priority was in tracking down the keys to save the city. Calling it an act of faith bordered on sacrilege to the former detective, but there was some truth to it.

"How close are we?" Loren asked, his nerves winning out.

Myers turned the corner, then tapped the brake to slow down. "I'd say we're here."

Shards of glass spread across the street. Both picture windows on the property had been broken, with stools and tables scattered along the sidewalk out front.

Myers parked down the block. "Loren—"

He grabbed the handle and opened the door. "Let me—"

"Maybe we should wait until backup arrives," Myers interjected.

Loren stepped out into the cold. "Let me talk to her, Myers. She's confused and overwhelmed."

"You forgot dangerous," Myers said coldly.

"I never forget that with her." Loren held tight to the crumpled roof of the car. Pleading eyes begged for the chance.

Myers groaned, hand still squeezing the wheel. "Be careful."

Loren pushed from the car. He ran up the block, the wind whipping into him. Leaning against the gale, Loren stomped over the broken glass for the front of the tavern.

Bodies lay in every direction, bloodied and bruised from the brawl. Strong men and weak men, old and young, there was no rhyme or reason behind who fell where and with whom by their side. Soriya had pounded her way through them all without regard or restraint.

Loren made his way over to the closest victim. He wore a bandanna over greasy black hair. Three teeth were missing from his gaping mouth and dried blood clung to his cheeks. The newcomer reached down, a finger to the man's wrist in search of a pulse. Through contact, Loren heard the soft thump of a heart.

"Thank heaven for small favors."

Soriya stood in the middle of the chaos. Blood dripped from her knuckles, fists tight to her sides. She loomed over her victims, and her chest heaved with every breath as if she couldn't calm down—or didn't want to.

"Soriya?" Loren called. He held his hands before him. Soft steps carried him across the bar to her position. "Soriya, it's me, Loren. I'm here to talk. I only want to help."

She spun toward him, right fist raised to strike. Soriya screamed and launched at him.

Loren sidestepped the blow, but caught a kick to his side. He staggered away, immediately put on the defensive by her assault.

Soriya struck with reckless abandon. She wasn't looking at him at all. No kindness or compassion rested in her deep brown eyes. Only anger remained, which escaped her in a flash of furious fists and devastating kicks.

Loren took each in stride. He blocked blows and backpedaled away from the sweeping swing of her legs, which threatened to send him to the floor like so many others.

"Soriya, it's me!" he yelled. "It's Loren!"

Her fist shot out. An inch from his face, it stopped. Soriya blinked hard, then her eyes snapped wide. "Loren? Loren, I—" Her hand fell away. She peered around the room as if for the first time all night. "Oh. What… What have I done?"

Tears stung her cheeks. Her knees buckled under her. Loren scooped her to his side, supporting her weary frame.

"I've got you, Soriya. We'll figure this out."

"Something is wrong with me, Loren," she said through her tears. "I never should have come back. Why did I ever come back?"

CHAPTER FORTY-EIGHT

Flashing lights filled the street. The police, already stretched thin, flooded the area around the tavern. Emergency workers rushed in and out of the place, working as quickly as possible on the extensive number of injuries to the patrons of the establishment.

Loren led Soriya away toward the shadows of the docks. Myers followed closely, a hand to her holster. Her lack of trust increased with every glare shot in Soriya's direction.

Soriya earned every ounce of the detective's wrath. She had lost control, and felt the same urges fighting their way back to the surface with each breath taken. The calm of the water helped to an extent, but she still pushed away from Loren for some space as a precaution.

Staggered steps distanced her from the pair of guardians watching over her. Myers closed in on Loren. Her low voice carried on the wind so Soriya could hear, which the stone bearer knew to be intentional.

"Loren, this isn't a good idea," Myers said.

"She wasn't in her right mind."

Myers pulled at him. "But she is now?"

"Please," Loren said. "Just give us a few minutes."

Soriya's shame grew by leaps and bounds. Loren's reticence, his worry, brought with it a level of guilt she had never known. There had always been purpose in her actions, yet closing her eyes and seeing the tavern again, Soriya found nothing but cold rage in her heart.

With each remembrance of her struggle, though, more came to light. The shadows in her mind took shape, the pain of her missing year came into focus—unlocked by her fury where peaceful meditation had come up short.

"Soriya?"

She looked away from him. Water rippled toward the docks below their position on the outer harbor. Soriya leaned lightly against the railing on the side of the walkway. "I know what happened, Loren."

"At the bar?" Loren asked. He indicated the tavern up the road. "Did they—"

"No. Not the bar," Soriya replied. "They didn't do... they didn't deserve what I did to them. All I saw was rage, lost to my own confusion, but... but it unlocked something inside me."

"What?"

She let out a deep breath. Her eyes closed, picturing the tale as she told it. "When the Bypass expelled me—when I lost my link with forever—I didn't come back whole. A piece of me is still inside."

"What are you saying?" Loren said as he moved to her side. "How is that possible?"

"Look at me, Loren." She spread her hands out to her sides. The wind whipped through her hair and covered her weeping eyes from view.

"You seem fine," he said, the words weak and distant.

"I'm not," she snapped. "Not even close. I've lost something vital. Knowledge of who I am and what we've been through. And more."

Loren nodded slowly. "Your connection with the Greystone."

Soriya clutched the railing. "I wasn't supposed to come back like this. Not this soon. Something happened."

"Like what?"

"Someone else came through the Bypass."

"You... You mentioned something like that before," Loren said. "A shadow, you said."

"It was there," Soriya answered. "The night I returned. Somehow, their release forced me back."

"Who?" Loren pressed. "Soriya, do you know who it was?"

She clasped her eyes shut. Squeezing the railing with every ounce of frustration in her weary frame, Soriya did everything she could to remember. She felt the cold of the concrete floor in the Bypass Chamber and the hum of the floating green orb over her. The smell of old candles in the domicile filled her nostrils—balsam and sandalwood.

The shadow was there. It stood at the edge of the platform, looming in the thick dark of the world. Without even a glance back, the shadow stalked off toward the stairs and the city beyond.

"No," Soriya muttered. She fought through her memory for something—some trace of recognition. "No, I—"

"It doesn't matter."

Soriya's eyes snapped open. Both she and Loren turned to see Myers standing beside them.

"Myers?" Loren asked with a furrowed brow.

The detective sighed, hands in her pockets. "Look, I get you've been through the wringer. We've all been there. Or as close as us regular people are likely to get, anyway."

"Good save," Loren grumbled.

"The point is," Myers said. "We have more pressing concerns."

"Myers, we—"

"She's right, Loren," Soriya interrupted. "What's happened?"

Loren kicked at the ground. Myers waited, then stepped forward in his silence. "Malcolm Appleton is dead."

Soriya's eyes shot wide. "How?"

"I screwed up," Loren said.

She reached for him. "Loren—"

Myers cleared her throat. "The killer has the five keys is what it boils down to, and we don't have a clue where he's headed."

They had come to her for help. Soriya stood in disbelief, ashamed at her selfishness. Her every thought centered on her own failings, her own situation, when a greater threat waited for them all. Malcolm was dead—something that might have been avoided had she stayed at Loren's instead of taking off the way she had.

"What can we do?"

Loren paced across the walkway. "Malcolm spoke about how everything is cyclical before he took off this morning."

"I don't—"

Loren stopped Myers with a look. "He mentioned how the end becomes the beginning and how we return to the start to figure out our own futures." He groaned, frustrated. "Malcolm was trying to tell me something, but I was so wrapped up in the case—in Gabe and everything else—I missed it."

"This isn't on you, Loren," Myers said. "None of us would have—"

"Return to the start?" Soriya breathed. "Return to the start…"

She moved for the railing and closed her eyes. This time, she pushed outward, away from recent events. Her troubles melted away. Only the past remained, the distant and peaceful times she once shared with Mentor in the confines of the Bypass Chamber.

She hadn't lied to Malcolm about hearing stories of the five knights or the comfort it brought her. Part of the tale mentioned a last stand against the forces of darkness at the place where they had first settled in the area. The fail-safe had been hidden there, tucked away from sight within the confines of a maze, but where would such a maze exist in Portents?

"The first victim," Soriya said. "Who was it again?"

"Patrick Marsh," Loren replied, clear confusion on his face.

"We've been over his estate," Myers said. "It's a dead end."

"No." Soriya shook her head. "There was a reason he had to be first."

"Soriya." Loren let out a sigh. "The place is empty. Nothing left but fifty acres of hedges that I can't imagine anyone is going to want to trim."

"Hedges?" Soriya asked. "As in a hedge maze?"

Myers and Loren shared a glance, then nodded in unison.

A wild laugh escaped Soriya. She rushed toward their waiting car. "That's what Malcolm was trying to tell you."

Myers called after her. "What?"

"The Marsh Estate," Soriya said. "The fail-safe is there."

CHAPTER FORTY-NINE

The sun faded from the sky when Gabe arrived at the Marsh Estate. The manor towered before him. Shutters rattled against the second-floor windows on the front of the edifice, and tree branches scraped along the glass. The maze stretched from the back of the property, a wrought-iron gate clanging loudly in the wind to block it off from the rest of the estate.

This is a terrible idea.

The thought trailed him the entire day. School had been the usual nightmare, made all the worse when he remembered the history exam he'd put off all week. Even with the test finally out of his way, there had been the jeers of his contemporaries, the snickering of girls at his idiocy, and the battering of jocks for his quiet nature.

Kam had come through for him, though. The one blessing of his day-long visit to the educational prison had been her willingness to drive him into the city. Questions sprang up at the request, but Gabe managed to quell them during their travels. He had offered a story about a sick uncle. The tale had bordered on enough grossness—stomach flu—to dissuade Kam from pressing further.

He'd wanted to tell her the truth, and to have her take him the full-length of his journey. Kam never would have left him though and, for that, Gabe was lucky to have her as a friend.

After she'd dropped him off, the sounds of late-afternoon traffic echoing through the downtown spires, Gabe had been on his own with only the mission at hand. Without his phone—left on the desk at the Dunlop home intentionally—Gabe was on his own. He took a deep breath. With his schoolbag tight to his back, Gabe took his first step toward his destination.

His journey through twisting avenues and blocks of greenery ate away what little remained of the sunshine. Eventually, Gabe found his way to Augusta and Twelfth and the home of Patrick Marsh.

Loren should have been with him. He would have known what to say, most likely a flip remark about the excesses of the idle rich rather than instructions on how to proceed. For all his *teachings*, Loren had been a safety net more than anything else. Gabe missed that feeling more than he cared to admit.

Their partnership lay shattered with the return of Soriya. He needed to prove—to himself, more than anyone else—that his path as the Greystone was the true one.

The maze offered him that answer, and Gabe moved toward it with a confident stride. Halfway up the way, however, a light beamed down the street. Gabe spun around to see a car heading for the estate. He rushed toward a row of thick brush covering much of the first level of the manor. Ducking behind a tall bush, Gabe peered around as the car pulled into the driveway. It journeyed past the garages on the left and the house on the right for the gate in the center.

Gabe edged farther down the row of bushes. Each shift brought another rustle of branches and the crunching of leaves beneath his sneakers, but the bristling wind of the night muted his actions.

Stepping from the vehicle was a young man. His tightly cropped hair remained perfectly in place despite the spinning gale. He wore a jacket that hugged a muscular frame. In one hand, he carried a single chain from which hung several keys.

"It's him," Gabe whispered.

His research had been correct. The estate held the secret of the five knights. But if the killer was here, it meant his collecting days were at an end. All the keys were in his possession.

"Malcolm…"

Gabe's eyes filled with tears at the realization. Somehow, Loren's protection had failed. Thinking of that made Gabe realize Loren might have fallen as well. Gabe had no way of finding out—no phone to call him or message to leave him for a solid answer.

There was no time for the fear that sat in his heart over the possible loss of Loren. The killer stood before the wrought-iron gate. With one key, he snapped open the bolt barring entry to the maze beyond.

Then he was gone, lost to the hedges and the darkness within.

Gabe hesitated for a long moment. Malcolm's words filled his memory. *Your time will come.* Gabe felt his presence with every fiber of his being. Taking a step out from the bushes, Gabe crept across the driveway. The killer was here, and with him, a danger to the entire city.

Gabe entered the maze, the Greystone in his hand. He might have been alone, but he carried every lesson learned from Loren, from Malcolm, and from so many others. They all stood with him as the darkness of the maze swallowed him whole.

It fell on him now. Only Gabe could stop the killer.

CHAPTER FIFTY

Myers' frantic words filled the line. Thel missed most of them. Her own rush to grab her coat and keys covered up the ranting and raving of her partner. The gist of the situation rang through, including the location. That was enough for Thel.

"I'm on my way."

She hung up. The phone fell from her hand into her pocket. Keys jangled between her fingers as she ripped the apartment door open and stepped into the hall. Slamming the door, the lock clicking into place, Thel ran for the stairs and the street beyond.

She should have been with Myers the entire time. After handling the masked thieves from the convenience store—and Yardin's tantrum—Thel had decided some rest was in order. There had been no word from Myers, and no sign of a break in the Patrick Marsh case.

Still, Thel felt guilty about her absence. Her thoughts continued to hang on Yardin's behavior and the hate in his eyes at her actions. It wasn't her fault he couldn't handle Thel's abilities. It was who she'd always been. Her sisters had never hidden from the world. Why should Thel? All Thel wanted to do was protect others. Everything she had done since her return had been to make up for the awfulness of her siblings and their past misdeeds.

Hitting the sidewalk, Thel made a beeline for the subway station. She tucked her hands deep into her pockets and leaned into the wind blowing up the lane. Cars passed infrequently, the night sending everyone indoors.

There were exceptions, of course. A couple passed by Thel as she crossed the road. They smiled and laughed with each other, separate from everyone else somehow. They held no doubts about their place in the world, or who they belonged with. It drove daggers through Thel, who tried hard not to look back at them with envy.

When she failed, Thel realized others occupied the street. A pack of shadows lingered around the corner. They were tall, husky individuals packed close together, and when she noted their presence, they immediately turned away from her.

Thel's pace quickened. Hurried steps carried her away from the road and down another block. A dozen others joined them as the pack of shadows closed in on her. Sweat dotted her brow, panic in her eyes, as Thel searched for an open shop or a sign of help from a passerby.

The block was empty, however, leaving her to the crowd at her backside. Thel's frantic walk turned to a run, and she raced for a nearby alley to cut her way to the next block.

The second she turned into the alleyway, Thel slammed into the chest of a massive figure. She fell back from the collision to see five men looming over her. All wore masks to hide their identities, yet their deep gazes made their intentions clear.

Thel turned back to the street, but the way was blocked. The initial shadows closed in around her, wearing the same style of store-bought masks as the rest of the group.

"Hey!" Thel tried to push through them, only to be pushed back to the center.

Hands snatched at her arms. They pulled violently in multiple directions, all vying for a piece of her. Thel kicked out at those closest, unable to connect with any of them thanks to their long reach.

"Back off!" Swinging out, Thel forced the hands from her body. She retreated a step, looking for room in the crowd. "You want to play rough? Let's play rough."

Her song filled the air. She willed the melody into existence, envisioning the strings falling on the masked puppets for her to control. She wanted them to feel the same panic, the same terror, that coursed through her body.

They failed to move. The song affected none of them.

"Nice try," the clear leader of the pack said. He pointed at his ear. Plugs sat deep within to block her ability.

"Oh, shit," Thel muttered.

She turned and met the first blow. The fist slammed into her cheek, which sent her toward the wall of the alley. Another hand grabbed her and kept her locked in the gathering's center. A fist from the right caught her on the nose. Cartilage crunched and blood gushed from the impact.

Unable to see, Thel failed to defend the next strike—a kick that sent her crashing to the ground. More blows struck from all around her. They drove into her gut and across her face without a care. The figures cursed her name. They spat through their masks at her bleeding form.

"Stop," Thel pleaded. "Don't… Why… Why are you doing this?"

They backed away for a second. Thel took the reprieve to work her way to her knees. From out of the crowd, one figure stepped forward. He delivered a driving blow to her left cheek. His scream was guttural and filled with so much hate, Thel couldn't help but wonder at the owner.

A second strike arrived, and Thel caught the man by the wrist. She pulled forward and swiped upward with her free hand. The mask fell off to expose her attacker.

"David?"

Yardin stared at her with disgust. Bloodshot eyes and sneering teeth filled her view. "You're a freak," he spat at her. "You don't belong here."

He yanked his wrist free from her. A slap crashed against her cheek.

Blood dripped from her lips and she wiped it clear. "Because I embarrassed you? That's what this is about?"

"Shut her up, Yardin," the leader said in a cold voice.

"Gladly," Yardin said. He removed the baton from his hip and whipped it across her face. Thel crashed to the ground. The rest of the pack closed in once more.

"This is a message to all freaks!" the leader exclaimed with pride.

Her body surrendered to their assault. There was no more pain from their blows, only disappointment and sadness. She had tried to embrace her second chance at life, only to find others willing to rip it from her because of the differences they held. Hate won out over acceptance. Thel knew it always would.

As the world fell to darkness, sirens rang out. The beating paused, panicked steps squeaking against the concrete. Someone must have seen the fight and called for help.

"We need to go!" a voice yelled.

"But—" Yardin's concern was evident even from a single word. Time stood against them, though.

"Now!"

The shadows retreated into the darkness. Thel, however, didn't move. She curled up tighter along the cold ground, broken far beyond her wounds.

CHAPTER FIFTY-ONE

The hedge maze fell behind Gabe. He had wound through the twists and turns, careful to keep his distance from the killer ahead of him, yet close enough not to become lost in the loops and dead ends riddled throughout the maze.

A final corridor opened to a clearing. Birch trees, with golden leaves hanging off the branches, shimmered in the breeze. An outcropping of rocks stood at the heart of the open space. They formed an archway that led to a cave.

Gabe waited for the killer to enter. Cautious steps took him from the safety of the hedges toward the looming darkness of the underground structure. Part of him wanted nothing more than to walk away. His nerves, the doubts spouted by so many others, infected his every thought.

The stone in his hand kept him from turning away. It pushed him forward, the path ahead the only way to prove his worth to Loren. This was his life, as it had been his brother's and his parents' before him. He refused to relinquish the stone, or the life he'd desired for so long.

Pebbles slipped under his sneakers, clattering against the rocky entryway. Gabe slid into the cave. Darkness enveloped him, and the world disappeared from view. He hugged the wall at his right, using it for support as he continued to descend along the stony path until he arrived at the base.

An immense cavern opened before him. Natural reflective surfaces caught what little light remained from the outer world and glowed dimly to illuminate the space.

Stone pathways ran in wide curves, angling deeper and deeper into the earth. Pillars supported the cave to keep it from collapsing. Stalactites loomed overhead. They dripped moisture in soft rhythm with Gabe's steps.

"Incredible," Gabe whispered. The cave was an impossibility, too huge to exist within the confines of a city like Portents. The ceiling stretched more than a hundred feet into the air, yet Gabe's descent had been nowhere near that deep.

He journeyed along the path, lost to the marvels around him. The glow intensified, as if welcoming Gabe to the grand cavern. So caught up in the world around him, Gabe slid along the edge of the curving path. He caught the pillar to his right. His hand dug into the rock for support.

Gazing down, Gabe realized how high up he stood. He leaned slightly over, listening to the falling pebbles that slipped loose from beneath his feet and fell over the side. They failed to make a sound for several seconds, then hit the bottom with a trickle of noise.

"Whoa," Gabe said. "Watch that first step."

His own presence muffled the existence of another until Gabe stopped. The footfalls of the killer boomed through the cavern, unafraid to be heard as he thought himself alone.

Gabe shifted away from the edge, an increased wariness with every step forward. "Just take it slow," he told himself. Hands in front of him, the Greystone ready at a moment's notice, Gabe worked around the spiraling loops of the stone path, which straightened out to lead into a neighboring cavern as expansive as the first. Rounding the turn into this secondary cave, Gabe halted.

"What is this now?"

An iron gate barred entry to a tertiary structure within the cavern system. Thick beams of metal blocked the view, but Gabe recognized the shallow shifting of water on the other side. The sound was lost behind the moving and muttering of the killer.

He stood at the iron gate beside a mechanism with four open slots. The killer pondered over the machine while he removed the keys from his chain. Placing the first into position, the killer turned the key and heard a ratcheting sound echo from above.

The gate inched apart with the key's use. The killer could hardly contain his joy and jumped for the next open slot. He peered over the mechanism, then back to the keys. Several seconds passed as he matched the markings between them and settled on the correct one.

With each key, the gate widened. Pulleys and winches groaned to life with the turning. The old machine released the gate from the lock until it stood open.

All around them, the ground rumbled. The cavern shook with the arrival of the keys after so long. The tremors caused Gabe to lose his footing on the path. He stumbled forward, away from the cover of the stone pillar and into plain view.

The killer was likewise affected. He staggered away from the machine. The lone key still on his chain almost fell from his hand, but he fought to keep it close. Tucking the key away, the killer struggled to right himself. When he turned back toward the stone path, his eyes widened at the company exposed before him.

"Who the hell are you?" he exclaimed.

Gabe took a deep breath. He stood tall and pushed aside all fear as he approached the killer. "Me? I'm the guy who's putting an end to this. And to you."

"You?" The killer laughed. He slapped his knee, the arrogance behind the cry enough to cause Gabe's teeth to grind loudly. Standing once more, the killer carried a large hunting knife. He spat at the ground, then wiped the remnants from his lips. "A mere child?"

"No," Gabe replied. "A Greystone."

Gabe raised the stone. He didn't know what to do, his instincts nowhere near as sharp as his target's. Before Gabe could act, the killer was already racing toward him, the knife held high and a blood-curdling scream on his lips.

"I was meant for this, boy!"

The blade came down in a sharp arc. Gabe leaped back, tucking the stone and his arms close to his body to avoid losing them in the strike. His body slammed against the wall at his back. The Greystone nearly dislodged from his grip, and he shoved it into his pocket for fear of losing it.

The killer slashed at the air. He closed in for the kill. "No one else could have done this."

Gabe dove clear of the blade. He worked his bag off his back. Snatching the straps, Gabe shot it forward. The knife sank deep into the fabric and stuck there.

"Insolent child!"

Gabe smiled, pulling the blade away from the killer. He tried to grab the knife for himself, but his attacker slapped the pack away. His bag skittered along the narrow turn in the path to the edge.

Gabe jumped after the bag to grab the weapon before it fell off the stony path. He fumbled with the strap, unable to get a grip in his haste, and the bag dropped into the darkness.

The move cost Gabe dearly. The killer snatched Gabe's ankle and twisted hard. Crying out in pain, he clutched the wound to dull the sudden sharp agony rushing up his leg. Gabe kicked out with his other leg, hoping to drive the killer away, but it was too late.

A hand snatched at Gabe's jacket and lifted him. Gabe felt his feet leave the ground, weightless in the strength carried by his attacker. The path's edge loomed closer and closer. Panic filled Gabe's terrified eyes.

"Wait," he pleaded. "Stop."

"I can't," the killer said, unmoved. "Not when I'm so close."

"Don't you—"

Without another word, without a moment's hesitation, the killer let go of Gabe's jacket. For a second, Gabe waited to hit the stone path and feel the cold ground again.

But there was nothing beneath him but air. The deep chasm welcomed him into its dark embrace.

CHAPTER FIFTY-TWO

There had been so much death. The Squire hated it all. Each one was necessary. They had all brought him to the end of his holy mission.

With the fall of the boy into the chasm below, the Squire pulled away from the edge and back to the mechanism with the four keys. He didn't wait to hear the boy's death cry. His own hurried steps blocked it out. Death pained him, needless death all the more. The innocent had suffered long enough with the threat over them every day. It was time to make things right.

The Squire moved for the open gate, then stopped to return to the keys in the mechanism. His hand settled upon his knight's—the bow looped twice-over—and closed his eyes. A silent call rang out. When he opened his eyes again, the light, once dim and distant along the phosphorescent ceiling, crackled with energy. It took shape and streaked toward him. The Squire faced the ball of light, unafraid.

The Wisp sped to greet him, hovering before his face. Its crackling bore a pattern, like words being spoken. It was a language he had failed to learn during their time together, not that he'd cared to. His word was law in their relationship, but he held his tongue until the rumbling settled and a group of stone griffins joined them.

"And where were you to stop that interfering wretch?" the Squire asked.

The griffins said nothing, as was their way. The Wisp, however, spun wildly with way too much to say, and the Squire promptly ignored him. No answer was necessary.

The fault lay with him. He had sought to complete his holy mission on his own, only to be hampered immediately by an outsider. A kid, no less. How could no one see what he was trying to do for them? The Squire sought to save the world. Portents would always be a danger, would always seek to destroy itself from within and spill out to the rest of the planet if left unchecked. Only the Squire recognized the inevitability of the threat. Only the Squire had the will to change their destiny—to save everyone.

He stepped forward, tall and proud before his guardians. "Protect the estate," he said, his voice booming throughout the cavern. "This is my time now. I won't tolerate further delays."

They took off into the air. The flapping of wings sent the Squire back a step, a hand over his brow to watch his army depart. The Wisp lingered. It spun around with crackling light energy. He waited impatiently. The Wisp failed to notice, and he flicked at the creature.

"Secure the maze for me," he said. "Burn anything that dares enter its borders."

The Wisp shot down the path like a bullet from a gun. The light faded, which left the Squire blinded for a brief second until his eyes readjusted. His guardians were set; their tasks put before them. He had no doubts about their abilities or about his own.

His mission stood beyond the open gate. Passing the mechanism, the Squire looked over the four keys used in the proceedings. All but Appleton's were necessary; the glyphs on their handles matched the etchings in the machine. Appleton's was required elsewhere, for some greater purpose.

He stepped through the open gate and made his way down the stony path. The incline made his progress slow, but he never tarried nor stumbled in his travels. The Squire pressed on without hesitation to the next task and the eventual end to come.

A body of water spread before him. The pond ran as far as his eyes could see in all directions from the shallow beach at the base of the incline. The Squire peered around for some sign of his next task, for some clue as to the test to come, but found none.

He stepped forward, and the tip of his shoe touched the water. Bending low, the Squire ran his fingers against the cool liquid and let it soak his skin.

The second he touched the water, the world shook. The Squire stumbled back quickly, up the incline and away from the pool. Stone walls rumbled, the very earth threatened to vibrate uncontrollably, and from the center of the pond, a statue rose.

Climbing higher and higher upon its platform, the statue towered over the Squire. Intricate carvings showed the image to be that of a woman shrouded in fine adornments. A cloak settled upon her brow, but large glowing eyes stared out at the deep pool.

Her hands were clasped before her and gripped tightly to the hilt of a sword. The weapon shone against the reflective surface of the water, pure steel compared to the stone of the woman holding it. It pointed to the pool, which rippled in all directions from the rising of the statue.

The Squire required no introduction to the newcomer. He knew her from every tale told of Camelot.

"The Lady of the Lake."

She made no motion, poised and still in the pool. The Squire waited, his impatience nearly spilling out of him. This was the next test, but no answer came.

The Squire edged to the water once more. He peered into the basin and trailed the guiding light of the Lady's glowing eyes. His own sparked, and he stared up at the sword.

"Of course."

A smile grew on his face. Despite the rumbling around him, and the world shifting dangerously beneath his feet, the Squire felt nothing in his confident stride. He took a step into the water and then another.

He was ready to claim his place among the knights. At last, he was ready to complete his sacred task.

CHAPTER FIFTY-THREE

They parked away from the estate. The presence of a car in the driveway caused them to tense up. Myers drew her sidearm. Loren followed suit the second he was outside the car, the taser clunky compared to her Glock. Myers threw him his keys, still wary about letting him behind the wheel again.

Loren didn't need the argument. There was enough going on, including corralling the third member of their party. Soriya hesitated at the car, fists clenched tight at her sides. Fear rested in her eyes, the memory of her barroom brawl clear even to Loren. Neither wanted a repeat, but Loren knew they couldn't proceed without her.

"Let's go."

They inched up the driveway. Each scanned the manor to the right and the garages to the left. No signs of life presented, no threats leaped out of the darkness. The statues that had been present along the cornices of the domicile were no longer visible. Loren held back the question when they approached the car.

"Buchwald's son?"

Myers shook her head. "He drove a red Subaru. Station wagon is a bold choice these days." She smirked at him. "It's certainly no Impala."

"I'm just glad it still runs," Loren grumbled.

Soriya sighed from the wrought-iron fence, a hand to the swinging gate. "Could we?"

"You upset her about the Impala crack," Loren said, elbowing Myers lightly.

"She should watch you drive." Myers pushed ahead for the maze. "We really doing this?"

"Nothing screams secrets like a giant hedge maze," Loren

commented.

"It's this way," Soriya said definitively.

They made it three steps into the first turn when a whipping sound filled the air. Shadows streaked across the sky. Loren ducked against the side of the hedge. He grabbed Myers and dragged her to his side. Soriya dropped to the ground. She rolled for cover under the overgrown branches.

Griffins soared overhead. Their wings beat rapidly to keep them afloat until they reached the manor. Each one took up position along the rooftop, then settled in. Once their wings stopped beating, they appeared lifeless, yet Loren feared their prying eyes. He poked Myers ahead, and the trio turned the first corner until the hedges obscured them.

"Keep low," Loren said. Both nodded in agreement, and they journeyed away from the entrance. It wasn't until four turns later that their bodies relaxed.

The moment passed quickly. The ground beneath them shuddered. A tremor ripped through the hedge maze and shook the branches in all directions. Terror struck them when the sensation intensified rather than fade.

"What is this?" Myers asked.

Loren shot a look at Soriya. "The fail-safe?"

"We're too late?"

"No," Soriya replied sharply. "I refuse to be too late."

"Soriya," Loren said. She was already out of reach, her wide gait unafraid of discovery. There was only the threat ahead, with no regard to the danger behind them.

Loren moved to follow, but Myers stopped him. "Let her go, Loren. She's always been big on rushing into danger. It's always served her well. Not so much for anyone around her…"

"Myers."

The detective failed to hear him. "Right, Greystone?" Soriya halted at the bend in the maze. Myers rushed up to her. "Isn't that your go-to move, and everyone else is left to pick up the pieces?"

Soriya's jaw clenched, her fist poised for another fight. Loren jumped between them. "This is the last thing we need." They shared a glare and Loren wondered if getting in their way was his worst mistake of the night. He remained firm in his presence until both took a sharp breath. They backed away slowly, turning in opposite directions. Soriya didn't hesitate, didn't question her choice.

"You know what you're doing, Soriya?"

"The tremors grow stronger this way," she said without looking. She stepped forward. Loren shot his hand out.

"Hold up."

"Loren."

He shifted close. "Myers wasn't wrong. We do this together. I'm not losing anyone else if I can help it." Myers passed as he spoke. Their eyes met. "Anyone."

Myers huffed. "I didn't know you cared."

"You didn't ask," Loren shot back.

Another wave of tremors hit. Soriya tore away from Loren and started deeper through the maze.

"We have to hurry." Her brisk pace forced Loren and Myers into a jog after her.

Myers grumbled with every step. "Of course we have to hurry. Can't be doomsday without a ticking clock."

They reached the end of the corridor. Soriya gazed around the bend, then countered in the other direction. Scanning the possibilities, she closed her eyes for a brief second before committing to their course.

The shadows grew around them. The manor was out of view and the darkness claimed them. Soriya led them around turns without hesitation. Her thin gaze pushed through the shadows for the path ahead, helped along by the persistent tremors, which intensified the closer they raced toward the maze's center.

When Loren turned, Myers was at his side. He could practically feel her heart pounding, the sweat dotting her brow.

"A little scared?"

"Try a lot." Myers stopped to catch her breath. Looking up, she paused and her gaze widened. "And with good reason."

It soared across the sky like a glittering firework. The ball of light pierced the darkness, crackling with energy and streaking toward the manor. Suddenly, it stopped and hovered above them for a long breath.

"Is that—"

Loren nodded. "The Will-o'-the-wisp."

Myers inched closer to him. "Do you think it saw us? Can it see us?"

Light flashed overhead. The Wisp snapped forward, then streaked toward them like a dart.

"That answer your question?" Soriya pulled at Loren and Myers. The Wisp closed in, burning the very air in its murderous rage. "Run. Now!"

CHAPTER FIFTY-FOUR

Ruiz pored over the latest report. He could barely see the words on the page, let alone comprehend the nuances of the subject matter. For all he knew, it may as well have been someone's grocery list rather than a critical piece to close the Newburn investigation.

Setting the work aside, Ruiz rubbed at his eyes. He peered toward the windows along the right-hand side of the office. Lights beamed from the street and the park. The statue of William Rath stood against the battering winds up and down Evans Avenue as the branches from the brush surrounding the monument shook.

They weren't the only things shaking, however. Ruiz reached for his coffee cup, the beverage long since cooled from neglect. The liquid inside rippled like a small wave and the cup teetered along the desk's edge. He snatched it up at the expense of two pens and a small pile of file folders left to be reviewed.

"What the hell?" The room quaked. Tremors sent several frames from their hooks on the wall. Ruiz tried to salvage what he could as he staggered across the office for the open door. "Janet? Janet, do you have any idea—"

The floor was empty. Few lights remained on throughout the open corridor, mostly near the elevators and stairwell.

Of course, Janet wasn't around. The late hour struck Ruiz. He should have been home long ago. His wife certainly made that clear in her earlier call. Dinner was waiting—hell, life was waiting—and still he stood in place, wondering about a random tremor.

The weary commissioner cursed under his breath. Slow steps carried him back to the open office door. A second tremor hit, and Ruiz grabbed the frame to keep himself steady. Curiosity turned to blistering concern. He raced for the elevators and signs of life, his need for answers overwriting any desire for home.

"Someone has to know what the hell is going on around here," he muttered. His finger slammed against the elevator call button.

"I know," a voice called out from the shadows. The stairwell door shut behind her, and the figure of a woman took shape as she approached.

"Leslie?" Ruiz said, surprised. She wore a heavy coat, her soft shoes silent on the carpet. He stepped away from the elevators as the doors opened, drawn back into the darkness with his unexpected company. "What do you mean you—"

"It's the Marsh Estate, Ruiz," Leslie said without prompting.

"The Marsh Estate? What is—"

"There's a secret hidden on the property," Leslie pressed. "That's why he was killed. Why the others were as well."

Ruiz knew it to be true. Loren had shared that much with him; the story of the knights and their fail-safe to destroy the city repeated through his head. There was no question about the validity of the claim, only how a City Council member might have learned about it.

"You're talking about an open investigation." Ruiz circled her slowly. "How did you come by any of this information?"

"It's why I came back to Portents. It's why I took the City Council position and why I'm here now. Protecting this city is all that matters."

"From what?" Ruiz shook his head, afraid of the answer. "Who the hell are you, Leslie?"

"Someone trying to help," she said in a soft voice. "Take my advice or don't, Ruiz. The choice is yours."

Leslie turned for the stairs. Ruiz's hand shot out and latched onto her arm. "Hold it," he snapped. "You show up here tonight like this, spouting about secrets at the Marsh Estate, about knowing why the man was murdered."

"It's the truth."

"Then why wait until now?" he asked. "What kind of game are you playing with Portents? So concerned about it, yet you stayed quiet from the start."

"I…" Her head fell to her chest. "You're right. I should have said something. I held my tongue, and it cost men their lives. It's the way things have always been for me, for who I represent. That has to change. You can help us change that."

"Us?" Ruiz's hand slipped away. "What the hell are you talking about?"

"Something that will have to wait." Leslie stood tall and proud. "Time is running out, Ruiz. Get to the Marsh Estate. Fix my mistake before there's nothing left to fix."

She was gone before Ruiz could find the words to stop her. He stood alone in the darkened corridor, unsure what to believe.

When the earth shook again, Ruiz started back to the elevators. The control dinged at his command, and the doors opened. A gangly officer, Corben Daniels, nearly jumped at the sight of Ruiz.

"Sir?" he said. "I was just making the rounds. Didn't realize anyone was still up here."

"No rational people, that's for sure," Ruiz whispered under his breath. He stepped away from the open doors, placed his mug down on the nearest desk, and returned. "We need to move."

"We?" Daniels asked with a furrowed brow. "Sir?"

Ruiz entered the elevator, and the doors closed behind him. He slammed his finger on the button for the first floor. "I need every available unit. Something's happening at the Marsh Estate."

CHAPTER FIFTY-FIVE

What the hell am I doing here?

The question plagued Myers as she hauled ass around another corner of the maze. Her life had been so much simpler only a few days earlier. She might have had doubts about her role as Head Detective, but ever since Patrick Marsh's death nothing had felt right.

Her early mistake about Marsh's secret trips to Lowtown started the ball rolling on a cavalcade of crap piled against her. Now, instead of leading the investigation into a man's murder, she ran for her life from a ball of light behind the pair who were actually in charge.

That's how it always was with Loren and Soriya. Myers might have forgotten that in the year since her last invitation to the chaos that was their everyday existence, but it came roaring back in the Marsh family hedge maze.

They were the heroes of the story. That was their role. Myers, though, had never been more than a damsel in distress. Her life had nearly been extinguished during Henry Erikson's mad plan to murder his brothers on a quest for immortality. Then, there had been the hail of bullets sent her way by Robert Standish. Loren had saved her both times.

Myers tired of being rescued, of feeling less than capable. Of course, facing off against a crackling ball of energy with murderous intentions wasn't exactly in her wheelhouse.

A hand snatched Myers by the wrist and pulled. She fell forward to the hard earth. Less than a second later, the Wisp rushed by and crashed against the far wall. Branches burned. Flames spread out from the ball of light until an entire section of the maze was nothing more than ash.

Myers peered up to see Loren still holding her wrist. "Thanks," she said with muted contempt. *Another rescue. Par for the course.*

"Come on," Loren said, helping her to her feet. He turned to Soriya, who was already at the end of the row. "Now where?"

Soriya pointed behind them. The Wisp was already back. Its slight detour continued to burn. "Move. Move!"

The pair ran; their feet pounded against the thick grass beneath them. Heat rose with the approach of the Wisp, and sweat soaked their brows despite the cool wind slamming into them. They turned just as the Wisp reached them.

Myers' coat singed at the merest touch. Flames sparked along the tails and she shook it off before the rest joined in the burn.

"Damn," she said. "That was my favorite jacket."

"Mourn it later." Loren pulled at her. "Please tell me we're almost there, Soriya."

The Greystone held her tongue. Silence supplied her answer.

Myers swiped at the sweat along her forehead. She tucked her hair back while maintaining her stride. "We can't outrun it."

"What other choice do we have?"

Soriya stopped before the next turn. Her eyes flared, and she leaped for them. "Down!"

Tackling the pair, Soriya covered as much of them as possible. The Wisp soared over her, a scream in the air. Crackling energy sparked. A pained wince spread across Soriya's face. The smell of cooked flesh became prominent.

"Soriya?" Loren left Myers behind to give Soriya a hand. Her back had been scorched, a clear hole through her clothing. Deep red welts dotted the skin where the Wisp brushed by her.

"Hurry," Soriya said, her voice strained. She pushed away from Loren, staggered steps toward the next turn. "We have to hurry."

They fell silent, listening to the scream on the wind. The Wisp circled around them, then streaked down from a new angle. They dove for cover. Quickly, they rounded the nearest turn with no regard for how close they were to the center of the maze or whether their next choice would damn them.

After their fourth turn, a straightaway opened up. A clearing appeared at the end of the wide corridor.

"This is it," Soriya said. "The heart of the maze."

Rushing steps carried them to their goal. The hedges fell away until only a smattering of birch trees, with shimmering golden leaves, rose from the sides of a rock formation in the clearing. The stone created a gaping door into the earth, the cave less inviting than the hedge maze at their backs.

"What's down there?" Myers asked.

"Let's find out," Loren said.

Soriya and Loren took the lead. Even after everything they had been through, even with their injuries and the threat of worse ahead, they didn't hesitate. Myers, though, stared into the night sky at their current predicament. The Wisp had found them. The growing light snapped like a firecracker as it streaked toward them.

"It won't stop," Myers said, her voice little more than a whisper. She peered at the cave before them, confined and unknown, then back to the Wisp and the danger it presented. She called to the others, "I'll stay behind."

Loren halted. "What? Forget it, Myers. That thing—"

"Will chase us down wherever we go," Myers snapped. "You don't know what's down there, Loren. There might be nothing but a dead end."

"It's not—"

Myers silenced him with a glare. "I can keep the Wisp occupied. Buy you some time to end this."

Loren reached for her hand. "Myers… I…"

"Loren," Soriya called from the mouth of the cave. "We need to go."

"Shut it, Soriya!" Loren yelled. He squeezed Myers' hand and leaned close. "Are you insane? I'm not just going to leave you."

The heat from the Wisp grew with every passing second. There was no more time for arguing.

"You heard Soriya. You need to go." Myers patted his chest lightly. "You're the hero. Let me play my part."

Myers took a step away from him. Loren moved to follow, only to find Soriya's hand on his shoulder. "Come on, Loren."

"Dammit," Loren grumbled. "Sam…"

"Go," she replied with a wink. "I've got this."

They stepped into the cave and the darkness swallowed them whole. Myers waited for some sign from them. Nothing came, only the marked increase of crackling in the air. Light filled the clearing as the Wisp arrived.

Myers bolted down the long straightaway into the maze. The Wisp trailed her every step. It burned everything around them as it rushed toward her.

"Oh, Sam," Myers said. "What the hell were you thinking?"

CHAPTER FIFTY-SIX

Loren wanted to turn back. Every step felt like a betrayal—not only of Myers, but of every fiber of his character. The choice was necessary, however, and he continued to repeat that through his mind as he journeyed into the cave's darkness.

Soriya easily handled the steeper-than-expected slope. Loren, though, required a more cautious step, and his hand jutted out to the nearest wall for support more than once. Luckily, the gradient receded after a time, leveling off for them to step confidently forward.

Before them, the cavern opened up. Lights emanated from the ceiling, reflections caught upon the rock, causing enough illumination to guide their way. Where it came from, how it seemed to glow and then ebb like a living, breathing organism escaped Loren, just as all other thought did the second he reached the stone path suspended over the deep chasm of the cavern.

"How?" The question echoed from his lips into the open space of the expansive underground network. They must have traveled only fifteen feet down from the entrance. Yet, standing inside the cavern, it appeared they were more than a hundred feet beneath the surface.

Loren peered back toward the cave's mouth. Even from his position, he could still see the light of the Wisp in the distance. Seeing it made him remember Myers. She was buying them precious time. He couldn't let it go to waste.

Along the twisting stone path, Soriya was well ahead of him already. The burn marks along her back did little to slow her down. Loren caught up at a jog, careful to remain on the narrow path. His gaze continued to flit from wonder to wonder all around them.

"How can something like this be hidden down here?" Loren

asked. "This place is massive."

No reply came; the silence was more than a little unnerving. Her steps attempted to fill the quiet. Pebbles scattered under her feet to the steep edges of the path.

"Hey," Loren called. "Give me something, Soriya. This is your wheelhouse, not mine."

"It used to be," she replied in a distant voice.

Loren wasn't the only one dealing with more than the case, and her vacant stare confirmed her pain.

She brushed his hand off her shoulder. "I told you, Loren. I'm not the same."

"I know. I'm sorry," he said, wanting nothing more than to slap himself for saying anything. The cavern, though, continued to impress. "It's this place. It's like the Courtyard—hidden in plain sight. A, what did you always call it? A microcosm. Our world, only separate somehow. Right?"

"Right," Soriya said quietly. Pressing ahead, Soriya led them down the winding path of the first cave into the connecting structures. She obviously wanted nothing to do with the conversation, unable to look past the memories lost thanks to her rebirth. Her body tensed in a way Loren had never seen before, ready to crack at the slightest obstacle, which only added more pressure to their task.

Rounding another corner, Soriya paused. "Look."

Loren almost slammed into her backside. Shifting away from her, his foot slipped off the side of the path. Loren clutched the pillar at his side as he tumbled. Slowly, his foot found solid ground again, and he returned to the path's center.

"A little warning next time," he muttered.

Soriya was already at the open iron gate and the mechanism at the side. Loren joined her, trying not to think about the possibility of a fall or how far down the chasm went.

His brow furrowed when he approached the lock for the gate. "Four keys. Why are there only four?"

"I thought all five were needed for the fail-safe?"

Loren hated the lack of answers. He had come to rely on Soriya's knowledge over the years. Her struggles piled atop his own. Speculation was all he could manage. "There must be another lock."

Heading through the open gate, Loren and Soriya stuck close

together. She didn't bother with the Greystone, her fists clenched and ready for a fight. Loren led with his weapon, not even close to prepared for conflict.

The slow crashing of waves greeted them in the next chamber. A large pool spread before their eyes, with a monument positioned in the middle staring down at them. The statue carried a sword pointing toward the water.

"The Lady of the Lake?" Loren exclaimed. There were few references he knew from the lore, but that one screamed out to him as he looked upon the serene visage of the statue. "Why not? All we're missing now is the—"

Falling pebbles and shifting rock ended his rant. Soriya jutted out her hand, blocking him from the path back the way they had traveled.

"Did you hear that?"

"It's the rock, Soriya," Loren said. "The tremors are causing shifts and—" Pebbles ran down from the entrance to the inner chamber. There were too many to be natural, and shuffling steps followed them. Loren raised his weapon. "Hands where we can see them!"

The figure held an unsteady hand on the wall to his right. His steps were awkward, unable to put any pressure on his right foot. Scrapes marked his skin. They covered his raised left hand and trailed along his arm and across his face.

"Always giving orders," Gabe said.

Loren's taser fell away. He pushed through Soriya. "Gabe?"

He was at Gabe's side when the boy fell. His knees slammed to the stone, his ankle completely swollen and unable to support his weight.

"Gabe!"

"Hey, Loren," he said with a smug smirk. "I could use a hand."

"What are you doing here?" Loren helped the boy up while propping him along his shoulder to keep his ankle from touching the ground.

"Is there going to be more yelling at me?" Gabe responded. "Because if there is, I might reconsider the whole falling-to-my-death thing."

Loren sighed. He swallowed the argument and pulled Gabe close for a hug. "How did you figure it out?"

"Research," Gabe said. "My dad used to read me stories about the five knights. In it, the knights protected a great secret kept in the heart of a massive maze. When I started looking into the victims, I learned about the hedge maze Marsh had built in his own backyard."

Loren chuckled, pride beaming in his eyes. "Who taught you to investigate?"

"I do listen." He shrugged. "Sometimes."

Soriya joined them. Her hand fell on Gabe's shoulder and squeezed lightly. "Where is he, Gabe?"

Loren glared at her. She was right, of course. Their reunion would have to wait, and so would Loren's concern over Gabe's injuries.

"I'm not sure," Gabe said. "I was lucky to catch the ledge when he dropped me. Took me some time to climb my way up, but I thought I heard him in the water."

Loren spun around. The lake filled the rest of the cavern. "Where would he go?"

Soriya held her tongue. She started for the water.

Loren moved to follow, and a groan escaped Gabe. He shifted for the closest wall for Gabe to grab onto.

"You'll stay here?"

"Yeah," Gabe said with a nod. "It's starting to feel better, but I'd only hold you up."

Loren ran his hand along the kid's arm. "Rest. We'll handle this."

Soriya continued to peer around the cave. Loren joined her at the water's edge. The Lady of the Lake offered nothing, only a cold stare into the dark.

"Any ideas?" Loren asked.

Soriya pulled off what was left of her jacket, then rolled up her sleeves. "Just the one."

"Great," Loren grumbled. He tossed his coat aside. He looked at his taser and the dark water ahead of them. The last thing he wanted was to electrocute himself. With a groan, Loren dropped the weapon onto his coat. "Figures."

"Ready?"

"For a swim to nowhere?" Loren shot back. "Why not?"

CHAPTER FIFTY-SEVEN

There was no outflanking the Wisp. With every turn, it pursued Myers, scorching the very ground. The only saving grace was in Myers' complete awareness of the path back to the middle of the maze.

She simply had to survive long enough to use it.

Slamming into a dead end remained a constant concern. Panic helped her overloaded senses retrace their frantic journey through the maze. The burning branches predicted her movements, the crunched grass another sign of where she had been before.

The Wisp cared little about their destination. It had one goal in mind, and with each turn, closed the gap. Myers ducked to the side, knowing the dead end ahead, just to throw off the Wisp for a second. It spun through the air past her. The heat seared her arm; her reaction time was too slow to avoid the blow.

Myers cried out, then tucked the singed extremity to her torso. Her hand fell over the wound. The warmth coursed through her body, but she pushed it aside like she had so much since the case began.

She wished Thel was with her. A lullaby for the Wisp was definitely in order. She could have used one herself, for that matter.

Why she thought this was the right move escaped her. Myers wanted nothing more than to prove she belonged in the role of Head Detective, that there was more to her than her criminal past. Her lies condemned her to the endless cycle—her hidden past nothing more than a cry for vindication every time it stood revealed to those around her.

Ruiz didn't care. Somehow, the man was able to look past all that and saw something deeper in Myers. She only wished she could do the same, yet with each stumbling step and each pulse of agony from her singed arm, Myers knew she would never pass her own muster. Doubts would always remain in the back of her mind, that last mistake waiting to overtake her.

She only hoped it wasn't tonight and wasn't in front of Soriya and Loren. *Not now. Not with so much at stake.*

The Wisp burned through the hedges row by row. Entire sections caught flame, the smoke filling the sky to give away the monster's position. It didn't do a lick of good for Myers. She continued deeper through the maze, away from the cave and the safety of the group. She cursed her selfless act almost as much as she hoped for its success.

So lost in her own head, Myers missed a crucial turn. She steamed ahead, huffing and puffing for more time, only to rush right into the brambles of a wall.

"No," she muttered. Myers spun around to backtrack. Her foot slid on the grass. She caught herself, found her balance, but the split-second error cost her.

The Wisp blocked her way.

Its crackling intensified. Joy radiated from the Wisp with each rotation. The light bounded back and forth with every step Myers took, taunting her.

"Dammit," Myers said. There was no move to make, no place to run. She held out a hand and beckoned the creature toward her. "Well? Let's get this over with already."

The Wisp cried out, no longer screaming in anger but filled with elated ecstasy. It streaked for the dead end, directly for Myers' chest.

Myers waited, counting the seconds in her mind. The heat was unbearable, like standing on the surface of the sun. At the last moment, Myers leaped aside.

Her leg took the brunt of the assault; her pants immediately flash-fried from the impact. Layers of nerves deadened from the collision and Myers collapsed against the ground. Tears of pain stung her eyes.

The Wisp slammed into the brambles. Ratty branches twisted around the ball of light as the tremendous energy radiating from its core consumed them. The scream returned, and the orb fought to free itself from the burning hedge without success.

Myers staggered to her feet. Her leg slid out from under her, but she held firm. A slight smile escaped her lips, and then she took off again.

She had no choice now. The Wisp would be free in moments, and the chase would resume. Her leg made any chance of extending their dance impossible.

Myers needed to change the game. There was only one way to do that. She retraced her steps until she found the central corridor once more.

The cave stood in the distance. The darkness waited for her. Behind her, the light returned to the sky, the crackling nothing more than the rage of a child.

Myers ran for the cave, hoping it held the key to stopping the creature once and for all.

CHAPTER FIFTY-EIGHT

They dove deeper, kicking hard through the water for some sign of where they needed to go. Instead of getting darker as they traveled, the pool seemed to lighten. Twin white beams showered down on them from the surface. They illuminated a small inlet near the base of the pool.

Pushing through the tightness in his chest, his lungs begging for more oxygen to complete the journey, Loren cut through the water for the small pinhole. It widened as they closed in, Soriya in the lead with Loren a few strokes behind.

Water lay on the other side, but not the same as where they had been. This pool was bright as day, shining and blue compared to the murk that lay inside the cave. When they passed through, Loren's equilibrium shifted. It was as if the entire axis of the world had spun around them, and they were no longer diving but rising with each stroke.

Piercing the surface, Loren and Soriya fought for breath. Waves crashed against the rocky shoreline before them. A small beach offered them an escape from the water, and they made a beeline for it before their bodies completely gave way from the strain.

No tremors trailed their movements. The world around them stabilized, and for a fleeting second, Loren believed the threat had passed. All optimism vanished when they arrived at the water's edge.

Reaching the shore, they looked on in stunned silence as a castle took shape. Ramparts spread into the distance, and a drawbridge lowered to welcome them to the newest cavern. Flags shook from an unseen wind. The cave offered a brighter light than those previously traversed, as globes ran in thick rows across the ceiling, like mini-suns connected by charged cables.

"You've got to be kidding me," Loren said, getting to his feet. His sneakers squished from the water, but he made no move to drain them. He simply continued up the tiny beach until he reached the end of the drawbridge. "A castle?"

Soriya pushed through him. Her lips trembled from their swim. "Keep moving, Loren. Gawk later."

"I can do both."

Soriya glared at him. "Not well."

It was not a true castle. The ramparts and the flags certainly gave the illusion of a massive structure within the cavern. There was nothing beyond the drawbridge and the single wall barring their approach. No other chambers appeared to be present. No other towers or battlements caught their attention.

A display on the far side of the drawbridge near the ironclad gate appeared to block all visitors. Five alcoves were positioned against the outer wall of the castle. Suits of armor filled four of them. The fifth was empty, except for the armor's helmet lying at the base.

On the other side of the door stood a large boulder. From its peak, a sword hilt jutted out. The hilt was hollowed out in a singular shape—that of the last of the five keys.

The killer, adorned in the missing armor, stood before the stone. He held the last key before him, his head lowered as if in prayer for the task ahead. Prayer completed, he slipped the key—Malcolm's, Loren realized from the heart-shaped handle—into the sword's hilt.

The gate unlocked with a great heave. The metal remained in place until the armored killer took hold of the sword in the stone and released it from the cage. Iron bars raised as the pulley worked quickly to open the way behind the castle wall.

A laugh rose from the killer. He raised the sword before him, then spun around in triumph.

Loren's eyes widened. "Of course."

The truth about Buchwald's missing possessions suddenly became clear. There was only one person with the means and the opportunity to take the belongings of the dead man. Only one person had been with him in death, one who had listened to his tales with a keen ear and a desperate heart to wash away the tragedies of his past. This had never been the work of Buchwald's son—a manchild who hated the tales as much as he adored them—but the singular mind of a soldier offered the mission of a lifetime.

"Adam!" Loren cried out.

Adam North, Buchwald's neighbor, scanned the newcomers with wide eyes. "Not any longer," he shouted from across the drawbridge. "I'm not Adam North, or even the Squire, as Joseph named me."

He backed away for the open gate. The second he crossed the threshold, a deep thrumming erupted around them. Earth rumbled beneath their feet and stone crashed down from above.

All around them, the world shook. The tremors increased with every step toward the castle and every breath taken. None affected Adam, who continued to hold the sword over his head as he grinned.

"Now and forever, I am the final knight," he shouted. "And this is the end."

CHAPTER FIFTY-NINE

They were too late.

The quakes continued. From all around them, the earth rumbled and roared. It trembled and heaved; the ground cracked beneath their steps.

Soriya fought back a scream. No matter the lessons learned, the defeats faced, and the sacrifices made, Soriya had always been too late when it came to protecting those she loved. Now, her entire city would pay the price for her failure.

"No," she whispered. Her fists slammed down on her legs. "Not this time."

They ran across the drawbridge. Their pace slowed at the midpoint; the chains holding the bridge in place shook and threatened to snap with each step. Ancient wooden beams split from the shifting tension and the bridge tottered. Soriya's body careened toward the edge and the waiting abyss below.

Before she could tumble off the side, Loren snatched Soriya's hand. Gripping it tight, he led her the rest of the way. At the open gate, he paused for a breath, but she continued.

"Soriya…"

"No," she snapped, dismissing his concern. "There's still time. Hurry, Loren. We have to…"

The words left her as she passed through the open gate. A small armory, with swords, shields, and more, lay tucked in the corner against the wall of the castle. Of course, there was no actual castle; the front wall was merely a placeholder to denote the knights' origins more than anything real. Instead of a royal courtyard, or the entrance to the main chambers of the grand leaders of some ancient empire, there was nothing but open space.

The chained lighting above rattled in their cages as they illuminated ten thousand square feet of terrain. Before them, uneven rocks made up the ground, with small peaks in different places. None were as prominent as the one at the far end of the chamber. It rose like the top of a mountain, yet stood only ten feet higher than the rest of the room.

What caught Soriya's eye and silenced her reassuring words lay beyond the peak. Two massive tumblers, hundreds of feet in length, connected to the earth. They pounded against the ceiling—the foundation of her city—signaling a finale to Portents that always plagued her nightmares.

"We can stop this," she muttered. Her body shook worse than the tremors offered. "We have to—"

"There is no stopping this," Adam bellowed from across the room. He waved the sword for them to see. "The tumblers will cause downtown to crumble. Portents will fall and all her secrets, all the threats she has harbored for so long, will be buried."

"How?" Loren asked. Both turned to him, perplexed by the question. Loren shrugged at Soriya. "Well, how can this possibly do what he says? The way we got down here, wherever the hell here is, it can't be anywhere close to Portents anymore, can it?"

"You've lived here how long?" Adam shouted. "You've seen what this place is like. There are doors around every corner, connecting the city with myriad dimensions within a single space. Temples and pyramids. Great chasms of darkness and insane churches promising light in the heart of forever."

"What?" Loren exclaimed. "The heart..."

Adam continued, unable to hear the strained recollection of the former detective. "All of it is Portents. No matter where you travel. The same holds true here. The city lies above us, though the way was long and the path twisted. Portents will fall. Tonight marks its end."

The tumblers were monstrous, their power everything Adam believed. It wasn't the prospect of Portents' spires collapsing that caused Soriya anguish, though. It wasn't the cries of the innocent as they watched their world burn from the snapping of power lines and electrical systems throughout the downtown area. Those would have shattered anyone else.

Soriya's pain came from the loss of one thing and one thing alone.

"The Bypass," she said in sharp realization.

The glowing gateway to eternity held her only chance to fix herself, to pull herself back together, and find out what had happened to her. If the city fell, so would the Bypass, and every chance at answers would be gone.

"Loren—"

"That's not going to happen, Adam." Loren stepped past Soriya. She followed, and their pace carried them across the uneven plain of rock and stone. "That doesn't need to happen. You see nothing but danger. That's not reality."

Adam scoffed. "You're deluding yourself. Monsters surround you every day, and you turn a blind eye to them. You have done nothing more than provide a band-aid to a city that threatens all life on this planet."

Where Soriya saw wonder in the lives of the many myths and legends in her city, where she once experienced exceptional displays of courage and magic and pure bliss as the protector of Portents, the self-anointed knight saw only threats. He stood, afraid of the world, rather than part of it.

Adam climbed the peak at the far end of the room. Beyond him, a large crevasse separated them from the twin tumblers pummeling the earth. He loomed over Loren and Soriya, refusing to listen to a word said, or entertain the possibility of another view than the one taught him by a dead man.

"I am saving the world," Adam said. "I will bring about a peace the likes of which no one has ever seen. No more war. No more fear."

"I can't let you do this, Adam," Loren replied.

"There is no stopping me," the knight shot back.

"Watch me." Soriya rushed at him without hesitation. He held the key to stopping the tumbler. He must, and if he did, then there was still a way to save her city… including the Bypass.

"Fool," Adam laughed. "I rule here. I control the fail-safe, and all who guard it."

As if the tremors weren't enough to cause their unsteady steps, the room now quaked with a rage unseen. Soriya tumbled to the left, unable to find her footing on the shifting rock.

Loren moved for her, her partner always there for her, even when she didn't deserve it. He stayed close to keep her upright.

"Another guardian?"

Soriya held no answer, her silence even more damning thanks

to Adam's rising laughter.

"A final one," the knight said.

From the depths of the chasm, a loud roar echoed through the chamber. Earth crumbled from the walls, torn apart by something climbing out of the deep dark.

The tumblers shook from the arrival, but continued their task. Every second brought them closer to completion, with millions of lives at stake.

Soriya and Loren, however, had greater concerns at the moment. They felt it in the quaking ground and heard it in the deep screeches that rose with the beating of wings and the scraping of talons.

"Aw, don't tell me," Loren said, his eyes wide with fear.

The creature leaped from the depths of the crevasse. It landed at the precipice of the chasm. Thick claws dug swaths of rock from the ground. A snarl screamed from its lips, and ruby red eyes threatened to swallow them whole.

The final guardian stood before them.

The dragon had arrived.

CHAPTER SIXTY

Flashing red and blue lights reflected off the houses in the Riverside District. Every lost second felt like an hour in Ruiz's mind. His phone vibrated fiercely against his hip, from both the continued rumbling of the ground and the constant flow of calls coming in.

He didn't need to see who they were from. The mayor's office was a given because of the current situation. His refusal to look centered on his wife's calls, however. He held no answers, the meeting with Leslie Gates still at the forefront of his mind. Without answers, only panic remained, and he wasn't ready for that kind of talk with anyone.

The men at his side said nothing. They each received their orders at the station and followed them to the letter. Four squad cars joined the procession. They blitzed away from Central for the district before eventually reaching Augusta and the lone estate on the block.

Smoke rose in the distance. The rear of the property featured large rows of hedges, converted into some sort of maze. Flames were visible as the cars approached, flickering like candles against the pounding wind.

The first squad car reached the driveway. Sirens blared, then cut out as another wave of tremors erupted upon their arrival. The earth cracked beneath the initial patrol. The driveway split, which caused the lead car to tip over the edge into a small pit.

"Brake!" Ruiz yelled. "Stop the car!"

They nearly rear-ended the others. All skidded to a halt to avoid crashing into the first. The occupants of the vehicle scrambled from their squad car, but found themselves trapped within the roiling ground.

Ruiz exited the car, slamming the door shut behind him. Officers followed suit to join him at the curb.

"It's getting worse," Ruiz muttered. The tremors thrummed through his body. The entire city rattled from the rippling waves of quakes erupting from somewhere deeper on the estate.

His officers were clearly nervous. They tossed each other wary looks, their silence more a sign of respect than anything else. All waited for their orders from Ruiz. He suddenly understood what Loren had been trying to tell him the previous night.

Finally, one stepped forward, gun in hand. "What should we do, sir?"

Ruiz took a sharp breath. The manor loomed on their right, the maze behind it. Rising smoke signaled the trouble and there was only one way to get there.

"Set up a perimeter around the property," Ruiz said. He kept his voice loud and assured, refusing to let them notice the sweat on his brow or his own fear peeking through. He hardly knew the men surrounding him. Most had been with the department less than a year, after the great purge that had come at the hands of Cerberus. In that crisis, he had sent those men into war for the city. This, though, was something else, something far more dangerous and unknown.

He motioned to the closest officers. "You four, come with me."

They didn't hesitate to follow. As they passed, the perimeter team helped those caught in the pit. The four at Ruiz's sides were all armed. Their eyes scanned the area with every step along the shattered driveway.

Ruiz led them toward the iron gate, which clattered awkwardly against the bars. The tremors had upended portions of the fence.

A quiet voice spoke up next to him. "How is this happening?"

The kid was barely in his twenties. Frayed nerves caused his hands to shake. Ruiz shot him a grin. "New to Portents?"

"David Yardin, sir," the officer said. "And yes. Four months in."

Ruiz nodded. "You'll be asking 'how is this happening' quite a bit, Yardin."

Roger Atley stopped shy of the gate. He was one of the old guard who'd managed to survive and still had the decency (or madness, some might say) to continue with the department. Atley brushed back hair that refused to flatten. The wind pushed the strands into twin horns atop his head.

"Into the maze, sir?" he asked.

The flames made it clear the twisted paths of the maze held the key to whatever the hell had taken his city by storm. The tremors helped confirm Ruiz's hypothesis; their intensity strengthened with each step forward.

Why Leslie had failed to explain further pissed Ruiz off to no end. Going in blind was a mistake, one that forced him to hesitate for a second. Before he could reassert himself, before he reached the gate to take his first step into the unknown, the hair on the back of his neck prickled.

"I…" Ruiz spun around, eyes thin as they cut through the shadows of the night. Something shifted in the distance and he turned for the manor.

The others joined him, guns at the ready. Atley let the gate go, a curious expression on his face. He pointed toward the rooftop of the grand manor. "Aren't those statues like the thing that grabbed Loren off the street earlier this week?"

Ruiz's entire body tensed up. He coiled like a snake on guard. Atley was right. On the cornices of the roof were several statues. They weren't gargoyles, Ruiz realized. Their misshapen figures looked more like a cross between a lion and an eagle—exactly as Loren had described the creature that had attacked him.

"Those are more than statues," Ruiz whispered.

Each one leaped from the rooftop. Their stone frames slammed to the ground, cracking the earth with their landing. They raised their talons, sharp and thick, and growled as they approached. Several did the same to the perimeter squad.

Ruiz and the others backed up, the gate confining them to the driveway. Yardin cringed at Ruiz's side. "What do we do now?"

"Survive, Yardin," Ruiz replied as he took aim at the closest statue. "That's all we ever do in Portents."

CHAPTER SIXTY-ONE

Myers slid down the slope at the cave's mouth. She crashed along the stone path, and the breath was lost from her lungs for a moment. Her eyes struggled to adjust, as did her body, as she fought to stand. Pain shot up her leg, her gait a staggered mess.

The cavern spread before her. The wonder of it, though, faded behind the burning light rising from outside. The Wisp closed in on her, leaving her no time to admire the massive structure or marvel at the absolute batshit insanity that was Portents.

She could only run for her life.

"This was a bad idea." Her words trailed behind her. Despite the pain, Myers pushed ahead, using every ounce of strength left in her weary and beaten frame to rush along the stone pathways.

The crackle of rock being sheared from the ceiling of the cave's mouth caused her heart to leap in her chest, but Myers refused to look behind her. Heat rose along her back, even with the distance between them.

Panicked eyes scanned the depths of the cave and into the chasm below. "Come on," Myers muttered. "There has to be something I can use. Somewhere I can hide from this son of a bitch."

She found none. The stone path was wide enough for her to travel, but offered little in the way of cover. The farther she journeyed, the less there was in terms of support. Only the big drop into the darkness below remained constant.

The first cavern fell away, the light of the Wisp screaming along the ceiling to track her position. Myers rounded another turn in the byzantine structure. A gate stood open at the end, leading to a tertiary cavern. Along the wall, Myers noticed a shadow.

"Gabe?" she called, scrambling closer.

The kid rubbed at his ankle. It swelled to twice the size of the other beneath his ripped-up pant leg. "Detective Myers?"

Myers reached for his hand. "On your feet, Gabe. We need to move."

"Move?" Gabe said, confused. When he realized her own injuries, Gabe shifted away from her waiting hand. Instead, he used the wall at his back to shimmy his way onto unsteady feet. "Why? What's going—"

Light filled the opening of the cave. The iron above melted from the Wisp's presence and dripped in long streams.

"Oh, shit," Gabe said.

"My sentiments exactly."

They turned away from the gate. Myers hastened to the water's edge, frantically searching for a way out, an escape hatch from the creature intent on her death.

"Where are you going?" Gabe asked.

"How should I know?" she snapped, lost before the pool of dark water.

Gabe's jaw fell open. "You… You didn't have a plan?"

"Does it look like I had a plan?" Myers threw her hands in the air. Her leg screamed, begging for a reprieve. She had little choice in the matter. They were trapped.

The Wisp floated over them. It took its time, savoring their fear.

Myers wanted to scream. Trapping herself was one thing, but she'd dragged Gabe into her mistake as well. The boy, however, continued to gaze ahead at the pond.

His eyes widened. "The water."

"No thanks," Myers said. "I'm not a good swimmer."

His hand hooked under her arm. "Learn fast."

"Gabe…"

The Wisp sensed their movement. No longer content to savor its victory, it shot forward.

"Don't think," Gabe said. He pushed Myers toward the water. "Just do it!"

They dove in. Sharp kicks propelled them as deep as possible. Several feet below the surface, Myers spun around.

The Wisp rushed at them without fear and without a second thought. It streaked toward the water like a blistering sun. The surface bubbled with the sudden influx of heat. With too much momentum built up, the ball of light slammed against the water. Immediately, the Wisp screamed. Its cohesion split—the crackling streams of light dispersed in a hundred directions until nothing remained but darkness.

Gabe pulled at Myers' arm. He pointed further along the pool and led her away from the shore. They surfaced, each coughing for breath.

The kid scanned the cavern as he splashed his way around in a tight circle for signs of the Wisp. "It worked?" Surprise quickly faded when he caught Myers' glare. He cleared his throat. "I mean, it worked."

"Good recovery," Myers said with a laugh. "And even better thinking."

"Thanks."

Quakes rippled around them, ending their reprieve. Debris snapped loose from the ceiling of the cavern and crashed into the surrounding water.

"So much for celebrating," Myers grumbled. The tremors were far worse than they had been.

"We have to help them," Gabe said. "Loren and Soriya. They need—"

Myers groaned. "Let me guess. More swimming is involved?"

Gabe nodded. "Ready?"

"Never," Myers replied. "Not that I ever let it stop me."

She took in a lungful of air and dove once more. This wasn't over yet.

CHAPTER SIXTY-TWO

The mammoth creature roared upon its arrival to the cavern. At least thirty feet tall, the dragon's thick armored hide of red scales shined beneath the ancient lights above. The beast swung its tail against the ground, then clawed the rocky earth with wide talons. Smoke rose from massive nostrils and crimson eyes flared with fury.

The final guardian blocked Soriya and Loren from both Adam and the twin tumblers. There was no time to waste, not with the doomsday device continuing to ramp up to full power. Each crash into the foundations of Portents sent another wave of tremors through Soriya's city. Somewhere above, buildings crumbled and people suffered.

Soriya acted the only way she knew how. She charged at the dragon, fists before her. The beast screamed, unleashing a blistering streak of flame toward Soriya. She ducked beneath the blast, the searing heat enough to cause the very ground to melt. Once clear of the dragon's opening strike, Soriya kicked off the ground and launched toward her target.

A claw swung at her from the left. Soriya tucked her legs tight to her chest in mid-air, avoiding the collision, then shot them out once more. Feet connected solidly with the dragon's chest, yet failed to move the beast even an inch.

Instead, the creature screamed in anger. Soriya followed suit, her own bellow one of defiance in the face of the threat. Behind her, Loren moved for the platform and the knight atop. His was the path of reason. For Soriya, though, only rage remained, and she fought not only to control it but to use what it offered in her fight against the mythic beast.

Circling around, Soriya jumped atop the resting talon of the dragon. It lifted at the sensation to shake her loose. Soriya clung to the dragon's arm and swung free before the beast knocked her off. Hands caught the beating wing of the creature and propelled her way onto it. Soriya raced along the back of the dragon, while the beast cried out at the loss of its target.

The Greystone fell into her hand. She held the weapon along her palm as she took her position atop the flailing dragon. Closing her eyes, Soriya pictured the Uruz rune—used a hundred times over the years—to deliver her the strength she needed to save her city from danger. Soriya imagined the strength flowing through her arms and fed that same will back into the stone with a prayer on her lips.

Fists flew freely. She pummeled the back of the beast. The stone, however, gave her nothing in return. No rune and no glowing power came at her call. There was only her wrath. Her lack of connection damned her once and for all.

The blows did little to affect the dragon, which soared from the ground. The incline shook Soriya loose, and she lost her grip on the dragon's back. She fell, reaching out for anything to slow her descent. The Greystone slipped away, and all her attention went with it. The stone clattered to the ground; it skittered to the edge of the deep chasm.

"No!" Soriya cried out. The dragon's tail shot out at her scream and connected soundly with her falling form. Soriya spun through the air from the blast until she slammed into the peak.

The stone was at her side. Soriya grabbed it, the Greystone cold to the touch. It offered her nothing. No, this fight was for her and her alone.

Soriya slowly stood to face the dragon once more. She needed a new plan… and fast.

"Adam!" Loren shouted. He clambered to the base of the peak and began to climb.

"This is the only way," the knight bellowed back. The power of the tumblers and the might of the dragon enthralled him. His entire quest had reached its pinnacle. There was no backing out now— not for him.

"You're wrong," Loren said. "Every danger Portents has seen, we've stopped."

"So far," Adam snapped. "Until something faster and stronger comes along. What happens then?"

"We get faster. We get stronger." Loren continued to climb, his words rising along with him. "We stop the danger, like we always have."

Adam shook his head. "I thought the same once. I was a soldier, hoping to make a difference in the world. There was nothing but horror on all sides of the conflict. I came home, believing there was something here to hold on to—family and friendship and love. It was all ripped away from me by disease and death."

Loren should have realized the truth sooner. There was the flag from his father's passing in Adam's apartment and the loss of his mother to a terrible illness. Adam had seen nothing but tragedy follow tragedy in his life, including his tour of duty.

"What you've been through—"

"Will never happen to another."

Loren pointed at the tumblers. "This isn't some magic switch. Destroying Portents doesn't suddenly take away every bad thing that happens to the rest of the world. It won't change bad people to good, and good people to great. There will still be pain and suffering."

Adam pondered the words. For a brief second, Loren thought they'd reached him. That the boy finally understood what he was truly doing. Then Adam raised the sword higher and his eyes flared.

"No," he said with utmost confidence. "This fixes everything."

"Is that what Buchwald told you?" Loren asked, grasping for the peak. "He sold you a fairy tale!"

"He gave me a mission!" Adam yelled. "This… this is all I have left."

Loren had felt the same for so long. Whether it had been his wife's cold case demanding to be solved, or a mystery with Soriya hunting monsters of myth and legend, Loren had never focused on anything that really mattered in his life. He had never had the strength to connect with people and build something greater for himself.

Sure, he'd solved his wife's murder. He'd even struck out on his own. But what did he have to show for it? What did he have to live for?

The answer had been obvious all along:

So much.

"No, Adam," Loren said, joining the knight at the peak. "There's more to life. You've let fear win out. I was the same way once."

He watched Soriya launch at the dragon and the tumblers continue their rampage on the city.

"I wish you could see that," Loren said. "I wish you could hear me. You're not giving me a choice, Adam. This ends now."

Soriya rushed the beast. When the dragon turned in her direction, she cut at an angle to avoid the plume of smoke that erupted from its open maw. The assault finished, Soriya was back on her way, fist primed to strike.

It was a ludicrous endeavor. The dragon dismissed her every blow with the tiniest of motions. Claws swiped in near misses. The massive tail of the dragon whipped every stray pebble from the ground at her. They pelted Soriya's skin and knocked her asunder.

The Greystone remained at her side, yet did nothing to assist. Her silent pleas went unanswered, the summons of strength ignored like her attacks on the beast.

There had to be something she could do other than annoy the dragon. Soriya whirled away from the swinging tail. She ducked under it and struck out against the scales lining the beast's underbelly. No weakness presented. No missing scale or open wound stood out to be exploited and conquered with a lucky blow.

The dragon had stood the test of time in the cavern's pit.

Soriya could barely stand at all.

Her undoing came from exhaustion at the battle. The strike against the dragon's underbelly went too long without deviation; she had remained in place for an extra moment, lost in thought at the hopes of a plan where none existed.

The dragon took advantage of her lull. A claw snapped across and caught Soriya in the chest. It drove her away from the beast. Her body slammed against the cold stone earth.

All breath left Soriya. She gasped and her body went numb. When the dragon lifted its claw, Soriya remained on the ground.

Her eyes closed.

*****

"Soriya!" Loren screamed from the peak. He could do nothing but watch her fall, the struggle against the dragon an impossible task from start to finish. She had been nothing but an annoyance, now beaten.

"It's over," Adam whispered in Loren's ear. During Loren's distraction, the knight had snuck up from behind. With a slight push, Loren toppled from the peak. He hit the rock side, then tumbled to the ground with a crashing thud.

"You'll thank me for this," Adam called. Loren held back a laugh as he worked his way to his knees. Manic eyes stared at him. "Not in this life, but the next, you'll see I was right."

Adam raised the sword high, directing it across the cavern. Loren followed the tip to see the dragon rushing toward him. The beast roared as smoke rose in a thick cloud from its nostrils.

"Kill him."

CHAPTER SIXTY-THREE

Loren raised his hands slowly. Heat continued to blast him in the face with each exhaled breath from the dragon.

He had faced many threats over the years. Mad creatures and crazed killers. People and monsters alike had tried to end his life for simply doing his job in protecting the city. None, however, had ever come close to the stature of the great dragon. The creature filled his entire view, practically swallowing the world without trying.

Loren took a step from the platform, his hands still in the air before him. "Maybe we can talk about this?"

The dragon snorted, and another dark plume of smoke wafted into the air. It obscured the monster's ruby red eyes, which flickered for only a moment. Then the dragon raised its left claw, talons poised to strike.

Loren dove for cover. The claw ripped at the base of the platform, tearing away layers of stone. The ground quaked with the beast's movements. Loren fell to his hands and knees, then shot up to his feet. The heat was still on him as Loren ran for his life.

"Reasoning with a dragon," he muttered between heaving breaths. "Can't imagine why that didn't work."

He turned away from the fallen Soriya. Still unconscious, Loren couldn't let anything happen to her, no matter the circumstances. Instead, Loren shot left across the chamber and toward the small armory tucked by the castle wall.

Halfway across the room, the dragon's tail whipped out at him. It smashed to his right. The ground separated, plates of stone shifted as if floating on lava rather than part of the earth. Loren stumbled toward the tail, struggling to keep his balance, while staring warily at the spikes along the beast's tail.

He leaped from stone to stone before the tail slammed down. Breath left Loren as he sailed clear of the devastation. He fell to the ground, struggling to resume his course. There was no pause from the dragon, however. The tail was back in the air, and Loren fought for every inch across the chamber.

"Move it, Greg," he said. "Move it!"

With a screech, the dragon soared above. Wings flapped furiously to carry the massive weight of the creature. The force of the wind propelled Loren forward. He toppled toward the castle wall and crashed headfirst against the stone at its base.

Wheeling around, the dragon still hovering over the cavern, Loren saw the armory to his left. A rack of weapons appeared on display. Swords with chipped blades, shields cracked and split open from wars long since passed, and even spears with rusted edges occupied the space.

He made it only a single step when the dragon smashed to the ground. Dust and debris kicked up from the impact. Loren covered his face. Tucking tight to the wall, he tried to inch toward the nearest sword—something that might make a difference against such an enemy.

The dragon's claw struck. It pounded the ground, cutting Loren off from the weaponry and any hope.

Loren reeled for the safety of the open gate and the drawbridge beyond. Perhaps with the tremors, he might lure the beast across the gap and somehow cause it to fall into the chasm below.

The way was cut off immediately by the fall of the dragon's other claw. He was left with no escape. The beast loomed closer and closer, sharpened teeth ready to make an end of Loren.

He couldn't believe it. After everything he had been through, everything Loren had seen and done over the years, he couldn't let it end in abject failure. The city deserved better.

As the dragon opened its maw and shot forward, Loren's eyes snapped shut. He raised his hands at the creature. "Stop! Just stop!"

Silence took hold of the chamber. Pebbles continued to trickle down, and the tremors rang out thanks to the work of the tumblers, but for Loren there was nothing but absolute quiet for a long breath.

When Loren opened his eyes, the dragon was before him. Mouth now closed, the beast sat, legs tucked under it and a curious look in its fiery eyes. Their shared bewilderment caused Loren to nearly fall over.

"What?" he asked in amazement at the pause in the dragon's attack. "How?"

Nothing made sense. Loren should have been dead. He held no weapon, carried no protection, yet the dragon had stopped.

A light beamed from his pocket. Reaching inside, Loren removed the item he had been carrying since his apartment that morning. Malcolm had called it a good luck charm—one he'd hoped Loren could use when he needed it most. But it was more than that.

Loren smiled and lifted the crystal in his palm for the mythic beast to see.

"The dragon's heart."

CHAPTER SIXTY-FOUR

Chaos overwhelmed the estate. The perimeter team, containing more than a dozen officers, found themselves swarmed by griffins in a matter of seconds. Gunshots rang out, drowning out the cries from Ruiz's men. Yet even through the cacophony of screeches and weapons fire, Ruiz felt each blow his men took, each terrified yelp of pain and agony as the statues rushed for them.

Things weren't any better at the iron gate. Ruiz and the four officers at his side fired at every approaching threat in unison. Bullets chipped away at the stony hide of each creature. Eyes were pierced and wings perforated, but nothing stopped their approach or silenced their growling.

"Keep driving them back!"

Ruiz's rally cry spurred Atley and Yardin forward. The other two—Cliffords and Daniels—watched their flanks as they advanced. The griffins staggered back with each blow; their stonework shattered around the edges. In the gap between clips, though, the hard work of the officers was easily undone.

Atley pointed wildly. "Watch yourselves! There's—"

A griffin shot down from the heavens. A latecomer to the party, it flew from the back of the manor, using the shadows for cover. Crashing to the driveway, it rolled toward Atley. As it passed, talons spread and sliced the officer across the leg.

"Dammit!" Atley cried. He fell to his knee and his hand covered the deep gash, to no avail. Blood poured down his leg, thick and dark like the night itself.

Yardin turned at his colleague's fall. Panicked eyes failed to assess the threat fast enough, and the griffin was upon him before Yardin could raise his weapon to attack. The statue leaped up; its wings caught the young officer in the chest. He launched into the air, passing Ruiz, before crashing along the iron gate.

"Yardin!" Ruiz yelled. He took aim and opened fire. His entire clip emptied in seconds. Each bullet found its mark in the griffin's face until only the remnants of a nose and the curl of its smirk remained.

The blinded beast swung out at anything nearby, only to catch a fellow griffin along the shoulder. Both toppled to the ground. Cliffords and Daniels were on them immediately, firing to keep the creatures on the ground.

Ruiz rushed for Yardin. "You all right?"

Yardin shook the blow away, blinking rapidly. His left arm hung limp. "I'm fine, sir."

"Tell me another one," Ruiz replied. Cliffords and Daniels each lifted Atley, and they retreated for the gate. Ruiz waved them forward as the griffins closed in once more. "How bad is it, Yardin?"

"Might be broken, sir," he said, wincing with each step.

"Where to, Commish?" Cliffords asked.

Atley was barely holding it together. His wound was far too deep to treat while dealing with the threat.

Ruiz looked around frantically for an answer. A group of officers from the perimeter rushed for the garage doors, and Ruiz moved to follow.

"Come on," he called. "We'll take cover and regroup."

They ran for the doors. Griffins snatched at officers who fell too far behind. One was lifted from behind his cruiser and carried into the night. His cry silenced with a bloody thud in the distance.

Two officers snatched the handles on the garage door and opened it with a whine. Everyone rushed inside before the door closed once more. Darkness filled the space. Ruiz found a light switch nearby and flipped it. Bulbs illuminated throughout the three-car garage.

Only one contained a car. Marsh had been a recluse, so his transportation needs had clearly been limited. The other two ports appeared to be mostly for storage. There were garbage cans and overstuffed shelving units. Tucked in the corner were tools—trimmers and shovels.

Ruiz helped Yardin into the back. He found a pile of rags. Tying two together, Ruiz wrapped it around the man's shoulder and placed his broken arm inside. Yardin held back a scream with each movement, but the pain rippled across teary eyes.

Atley was similarly treated by the others. They wrapped a rag tight against his gaping wound to staunch the bleeding. Atley's pale skin was nearly translucent. He needed medical attention, and soon.

Claws swiped at the door from the outside. Fists pounded as growls grew more ferocious. The door cracked and split from the pressure.

"Grab whatever you can use," Ruiz said. He patted Yardin and Atley lightly. "Reload and back us up. We have to put these bastards down."

"There are too many, sir," Cliffords said.

Ruiz took a sharp breath, hands on his hips. The man wasn't wrong, but what could be done? Spinning around, Ruiz settled on the car in the far port. His eyes gleamed.

"Anyone know how to hot-wire a car?"

The task went quickly. Daniels, it turned out, had had a wilder youth than he'd ever mentioned, including a turn with a street racing crew in Venture Cove. He set to work on the car, sparking wires tucked beneath the dash on the semi-classic sedan until the engine roared to life.

"You sure about this, sir?" he asked when Ruiz hopped behind the wheel.

"You feel like doing this?"

Daniels ran his hand along the back of his neck. "Well, no, but—"

"Get ready!" a voice bellowed from the other side of the garage. "Here they come!"

"Now or never, Daniels."

The officer took a step back. "Good luck, sir."

"Luck? What has luck ever done for us?" Ruiz closed the door, then slammed on the accelerator. The car jolted forward. It crashed through the wooden garage door and out onto the driveway.

Griffins penetrated the garage at the other end, but a number at the rear of the group turned at the sudden deafening sound. They screamed as Ruiz spun the wheel. The car screeched in a wide arc, his foot down to the floor.

The car slammed into the wall of enemies. Griffins fell on all sides, while three clung onto the hood. Ruiz reached the end of the group and hit the brake. The three launched backward and skidded across the street. One slammed into the side of a patrol car. Another hit a thick tree trunk where it shattered in half.

The numbers were thinned, but the battle continued. Ruiz hopped free from the car. Not two steps from the vehicle, a loud crash sent Ruiz tumbling to the driveway. He wheeled around, weapon at the ready. A griffin shredded the roof of the car. Satisfied with the destruction, the beast turned to Ruiz and screeched at him.

Ruiz opened fire. The statue staggered back from the initial impacts. The left eye disappeared, as did half of the beast's head, yet it remained atop the car. Ruiz reared back, kicking from the blacktop beneath him to gain some distance.

Clicking sounds rang out from Ruiz's gun. The clip was spent.

The griffin leaped from the car. Talons slashed at the air as the beast landed before Ruiz. It raised a claw, ready to end his life.

"Back off!" Shots erupted from the right. Rapid fire pounded against the side of the statue, chipping away at the stone. The griffin turned with a shriek and was met with one last bullet, which crashed against its beak. The stone swayed for a moment, then shattered along the driveway.

Daniels was at Ruiz's side in an instant. He discharged his empty clip and reloaded. Pausing his assault, the officer held out his hand for the commissioner, who happily took it.

"Looking any better?" Ruiz asked as Daniels helped him to his feet. Gunfire filled the air. The griffins, those left standing from Ruiz's assault, had infiltrated the garage where they met a barrage of gunfire from the officers inside. Those without weapons swung shovels to keep the griffins at bay.

Daniels kept his eyes forward, scanning for another attacker. "Slightly?"

Ruiz raised his sidearm. "Then keep shooting."

"Yes, sir."

Sirens blared and bright lights filled the sky. It was the sweetest sound Ruiz had ever heard. More officers rushed from their patrol cars to join the fight. They battered the griffins on two fronts.

"We seem to be wearing them down!" Daniels exclaimed.

Ruiz laughed. "Way to bring the sunshine on this shitstorm of a day, Daniels."

The griffins fell. That much was true. The tremors, though, continued. They grew stronger with every passing moment, and Ruiz could do nothing about them.

That fight lay with someone else.

"Come on, Greg," Ruiz muttered as he led his officers forward for a final push against the enemy. "I know you're in the middle of this. Save the goddamn day already."

CHAPTER SIXTY-FIVE

The dragon's gaze trailed the crystal. Loren held the crimson item up, slowly moving it from side to side. Awestruck at the incredible shift in fortune, Loren scanned the glowing crystal with renewed appreciation.

Malcolm had spoken about the guardians of the fail-safe and of the knights. Buchwald had clearly been a believer in the guardians. His stories had inspired Adam to reach out to the creatures at his beck and call, not only for protection, but to stamp out his enemies before they could stop him.

Each of the knights had their preference when it came to their role. Jeremy Newton had focused on history—accumulating relics from the past to study and inform their future. Geoffrey had viewed the world like a soldier, always the defender—never afraid to stand and fight. Marsh had held the most power in the group, or so it had seemed, with the maze hidden on his property.

Malcolm had not needed guardians by his side. After everything Loren had learned of the man, only one thing had mattered to Malcolm Appleton: people. He'd trusted in those around him, in their strength of character, to make a difference in the world. The dragon's heart stood as a testament to that statement, and Loren wielded it proudly to honor the sacrifice of a man gone too soon.

The dragon's reticence to strike, however, wore on the knight from his perch. Adam struck the ground with his sword, fury in his wide eyes.

"I said, kill him!"

The dragon looked back, a huff of smoke escaping. Then he returned to the heart and Loren, torn between the two.

Loren approached with the heart before him. "He's—" Loren paused, brow furrowed at the mythic creature. "He?"

The dragon nodded at this assumption.

"Cool." Loren grinned. He held it high for Adam to see. "He's not your puppet any longer and I'm done playing around."

Loren moved for the weapons rack. He dismissed the cracked shields and the dull tips of the spears. Snatching a glistening blade from the armory, Loren gripped the hilt in his right hand. The crystal remained in his left, pulsing brighter in tune with the belly of the mythic beast.

Loren winked at the dragon as he passed for the platform. His steps were confident, despite the twisted landscape and the constant tremors. The tumblers pounded away, any chance of success ticking away with each pulse. Loren picked up his pace, drawn in by the ranting of the knight atop the peak.

"I've trained for this fight my whole life!" Adam bellowed. He tightened his grip on his sword, both hands along the large hilt where the central key remained locked.

Loren climbed along the side of the platform. Each step was precarious, his hands of little use this time around. Still, he dug his heels in along the narrow ledge and rose until he met Adam at the top.

"In a way," he said. "So have I."

"The dragon serves the knights," Adam snapped, inflamed at his guardian's hesitance. "I am the last of them. Only I could have made it this far. You are nothing compared to what I have done here. To what I have achieved. And that trinket is nothing compared to this sword. It was forged in the great beast's fire."

Loren brought his own weapon to bear. "Get the sword away from you. Got it."

"You'll fail."

Loren leaped at the knight. "We'll see."

CHAPTER SIXTY-SIX

The sword's weight pulled at Loren. He struggled to keep the blade upright, while also maintaining a solid grip on the ruby crystal in his other hand.

The weight carried over to the fight itself. This wasn't a battle between two foes. It went far beyond that. The tumblers pounded away at the foundation of the city. Even the dragon played into the affair, a nervous glare whipping from opponent to opponent for some sign of whom to side with.

Each carried a key to victory.

Adam held the advantage. His own strength was built from a manic desire to destroy—to complete the mission laid out before him by Joseph Buchwald. He gripped the hilt of the sword with both hands, his armor glinting beneath the bending and breaking lights above.

He charged at Loren, a scream on his lips. The former detective fell back on his heels immediately. Blades clanged loudly as steel sparked against steel. Loren nearly lost the sword from the initial blow. It took all his strength to raise the weapon once more, and just in time as Adam struck with increased fury.

"You will not stop me!"

Loren dropped to one knee, the sword more of a shield than anything else. He took blow after blow, but offered none of his own. Nothing matched the frenzy of the knight. His determination kept Loren limited. When Loren did move, it was to spin away from the striking sword for some distance.

It was another error in judgment. Loren found the edge. The deep chasm stretched out before him, and he struggled to right himself. As he groped for solid ground, Adam kicked at his left hand.

Blistering pain caused his hand to open. The dragon's heart fell from his grasp to the ground. Adam kicked at the crystal and sent it tumbling off the peak toward the dragon.

Loren's eyes flared. He leaped for the dragon's heart. Fingers grazed the crystal, but then it was gone—falling away and out of reach. The heart bounded off the side of the peak, clattering along the shifting rock of the cavern.

The dragon pounced for it without hesitation. His movement, though, was awkward, and the beast's tail whipped wildly about him in his search for the prize. The tail slammed along the ground and connected with the edge of the cracked, uneven stone floor. The heart went soaring away from the peak, from the dragon, and into the open expanse of the room—lost from sight.

"No," Loren cried, hand still reaching for the lost heart. He scanned the room frantically for signs of the crystal, his one hold on the dragon and his only leverage in the fight.

"The dragon is mine again," Adam's voice boomed.

A shadow loomed over him. Loren caught the shape of a rising sword, ready to impale him against the rock.

"Only if you hold the sword," Loren said. The blade crashed down, and Loren rolled hard to his left, away from his attacker. The sword pierced rock, missing its target by inches.

Loren swept his leg in a wide arc and caught Adam behind the knees. The knight fell, his sword still caught in the rock. Leaping to his feet, Loren ripped the sword from the earth.

"Which you don't hold anymore."

Adam screamed. He jumped to his feet, then charged at Loren. He slammed into the man; the weight of the armor knocked Loren to the ground. The impact forced Adam's sword loose. It clattered against the stone peak and tumbled over the edge.

"No!" Adam leaped for the weapon, to no avail.

The sword fell into the chasm and vanished into the darkness.

Loren quickly shifted away from the edge.

The knight, filled with renewed anger, focused on the sword still in Loren's grip. He grabbed at it, and the two struggled along the weapon's hilt for control.

"Dammit, Adam, don't do this," Loren said.

"I have to!" Adam shouted. His head shot forward and caught Loren on the chin. The sword sailed free. Adam caught it by the hilt and leveled the blade against Loren. "I don't need the dragon any longer. You've still failed. The tumblers are at their peak. The city will fall. Just. Like. You."

Loren peered down. Adam had maneuvered him toward the edge, far closer to the end of the peak than he realized. Adam didn't bother with the sword. He lowered the blade and jutted out his hand. It caught Loren in the chest and sent him tumbling over the side.

Loren fell.

Hands flailed for purchase on the rocky wall. The widening chasm seemed to reach up to greet him. Deep blackness consumed all the light in the room. He reached out for a ledge to catch before the darkness took him completely.

Instead, someone caught him.

"I've got you, Loren," Soriya said, her hand squeezing his tightly. "Just hold on."

CHAPTER SIXTY-SEVEN

Light shined from above. The water had been so dark except for the twin beams from the statue above, which offered a clear path to the pinhole at the bottom. Gabe pushed for every inch gained and rushed for an end to their journey as his lungs burned from a lack of oxygen.

Myers, however, paused. Eyes went wide, clear disorientation from passing through the pinhole between lakes. She spun around, a hand over her mouth to cover a gasp. Forward momentum ceased in her panic and she sank back into the dark.

Gabe dove after her. His ankle screamed at the sudden reversal, the pain nothing compared to his growing fear. Myers reached for him as her eyes glazed over. She needed air desperately.

His arms wrapped around her, and Gabe swam for the surface. Every stroke sent a wave of pain through him, but when her head lolled to the side, he pushed harder for the bright lights above.

Breaking through the surface, Gabe shifted Myers' arm over his shoulder, then rushed toward the nearby beach. "Detective," he said between gasps of air. "Stay with me."

Gabe helped her to the beach, dragging along sand and rock. The world shook around them, but nothing compared to his own shaking—out of fear for his unmoving companion.

"Myers?" He moved in close, a finger to her pulse. Her heart beat slowly. "Thank God. Come on, Myers, we need to—"

She shot upright. Water sprayed from her mouth and covered Gabe's entire face. Myers turned on her side, wracked by a series of deep coughs to clear her airway.

"That was the worst thank you I've ever experienced," Gabe sputtered. He swiped at the water and spittle running down his cheeks. "Better?"

"Getting… there," Myers said. She gulped air like it was a pint of beer. Her hands were before her, as if directing the oxygen toward her lungs. Myers stopped when she realized their surroundings. "What the hell?"

"I think it gets stranger," Gabe said. He stood and held out a hand for her, which she promptly took. Myers stumbled at first, unsteady from the swim. "What happened back there?"

"Are you kidding?" she asked with shocked eyes. "The entire world twisted, like we were caught in a damn hourglass. Didn't you feel that?"

He had. But the notion of worlds twisting and warping with the slightest movement had become more common in his experience. Rather than diminish her shock, Gabe merely smirked. "Pretty hard not to feel everything that's going on, am I right?"

Myers groaned and followed him. They carefully crossed the drawbridge at the open gate of the castle wall. The wooden beams threatened to teeter into the chasm below, but held together for their trek.

Gabe pushed through the majesty of the cavern—the incredible nature of the castle ramparts and the massive flags adorning its lone tower. The lights alone were a marvel. They appeared to have been installed in the early days of electricity, yet continued to run as if no time had passed at all.

Both halted when they passed the castle gate. The main chamber lay before them, including the twin tumblers along the far wall. The mechanism beat ceaselessly against the rock above, somehow connected to everything everywhere. For all the wonder the chamber provided, for all the terror that came with the sight of the tumbler device, it was the dragon staring at them that finally coaxed a reaction from Myers.

"Just when you think you've seen everything…"

Gabe chuckled under his breath. The moment stuck in his throat as he noticed Loren fighting for his life along a peak of rock and stone in front of the tumblers. The killer—now adorned in full armor—knocked Loren from the hill.

"Loren!" Myers exclaimed. She raced off and was a dozen staggered steps ahead before she turned back to her companion. "Gabe?"

It was happening again, just like at the subway. He could hear Loren's words echoing in his mind. The threat against Loren was real, his death imminent without assistance. Yet the danger was to the entire city, not one man.

"Gabe?" Myers called again.

Gabe shook his head. "Go."

"What are you going to do?"

"Good question." In the distance, the knight loomed atop the peak. He beamed triumphantly at the tumblers. Gabe pointed ahead. "Go. Help Loren."

Myers ran without another look back.

Gabe, however, knew there was more to do. He scanned the room. His gaze washed over the weapons to his left and fell upon the dragon. The great beast with its crimson scales and ruby eyes failed to notice his presence. It looked around feverishly for something.

Slow steps brought Gabe deeper into the room. He stretched out his ankle with each one. His resolve muted the pain. His fists opened and closed at his sides, priming for the fight with the killer ahead. The floor shifted with each tremor; the world threatened to split apart and drop into the darkness below with each pump of the tumblers, yet Gabe continued on for the man behind it all.

He stopped when his left shoe kicked something. It clattered a short distance ahead, then came to rest among a patch of pebbles. Gabe crouched to retrieve the item. The small crystal glowed, pulsing as if breathing.

"What do we have here?" Lifting it up, Gabe felt a shadow shift at his side. The dragon recognized the delicate crystal in Gabe's hand. It bent low, its mouth salivating over the glowing item. Gabe clutched it tighter. "Something you want, huh?"

He waved the object back and forth. The dragon tracked the movement, practically swaying to the rhythm. Gabe's eyes thinned, locked on the peak and the tumblers beyond.

"Yeah," he said. "I can work with this."

CHAPTER SIXTY-EIGHT

Adam had won. He stood before the tumblers, enthralled by their power. They pulsed faster and faster, the ancient fail-safe ready for one final push through the foundations of the city.

Everything had built to this moment. It started when Joseph Buchwald had shared with him the truth about the knights, about the key, and about their purpose. Adam's solemn vow to the dying man had launched the greatest mission of his life, and now it had reached its crescendo.

"I did it," Adam said. He closed his eyes, picturing the pride of his knight. Buchwald had dreamed of this day for so long. The danger would no longer threaten the rest of the world. There would be no more darkness to hold back, no more fear of monsters and myths and death. "I saved the world. The mission… it's over."

Portents would fall. With it, the sickness that oozed from every alleyway, from the very shadows themselves, would not be allowed to thrive. The world would be safe, and no one would suffer needlessly again. He had taken that burden on—suffered through war, through the death of his father and the disease that had claimed his mother. Constant tragedy dogged his existence. It ended today with the completion of his task.

"What do I do now?"

Adam paused, opening his eyes to the world as if for the first time. The question never entered matters before. Only the mission mattered. First, it had been his promise to Buchwald, then fulfilling that promise. Murder had been an unnecessary evil in his quest. So many had died at his hands, and all for their keys to enact the fail-safe.

Adam had worried endlessly over the safety of the world—over the lives of the innocent outside Portents' borders and their futures. He had never thought about his own life after his victory.

Adam staggered away from the tumblers, which roared to finality. "I… I can't die here," he whispered. "Not now."

Fear struck him and he stumbled along the peak. His heart pounded in his chest. His body felt the weight of the armor constricting his movements and covering his entire frame like a body-wide noose.

"Off… Have to get this… off." Gloves fell from his hands. He ripped off straps and peeled off layers with reckless abandon. Chunks of armor clanged to the cold stone at his feet. The chest plate, his boots, every inch of his body desired nothing more than freedom from the armor and its tiresome burden.

He had completed the mission, but there was more to do, wasn't there? Why had he not thought of that before?

Relieved of his knighthood, forsaking the role bequeathed to him by Buchwald and those who came before him, Adam retreated from the peak. When he turned to climb down, however, someone blocked his way.

Startled eyes widened. The boy he'd killed, who had fallen off the cavern's path into the chasm below, stood before him.

"Where do you think you're going?"

"We have to get out of here!" Adam screamed. Hands flailed before him to showcase the chaos as it finally snapped into focus for him. The roof collapsed above. The walls threatened to surrender once and for all from the constant pounding of the tumblers. "We have to run!"

He rushed at the boy, who pushed Adam back with a stiff hand.

"Not yet," the kid said. He clenched his fists tight, his legs bent and ready for a fight. "Time for round two."

CHAPTER SIXTY-NINE

"Move, boy!" The killer swiped at the air between them.

Gabe barely cleared the strike. Frantic eyes shot to the ground, his footing precarious along the peak. He maintained a tight grip on the pulsing crystal, the dragon unable to tear its gaze away.

"Does it look like I'm standing still?"

Gabe's tone clearly struck the killer as glib, as his reaction was decidedly unfriendly. He threw a right cross, which forced Gabe farther back along the narrow peak.

Panic filled the killer's every move. He leaped with reckless abandon, terrified for some reason. This was in stark contrast to how Gabe had found him previously. That man had been committed to a cause, willing to kill his way to the tumblers in order to activate the fail-safe. The figure before him no longer carried a shred of confidence or a sense of purpose.

The killer pointed to the glowing crystal. "The heart doesn't matter. With the sword lost, all hope of control is at an end."

Gabe suddenly understood what the killer was going through. The way his eyes wavered on the tumblers—the key to control the device had somehow fallen out of reach to them all. "The end… it scares you, doesn't it?"

"I fear nothing!"

The killer leaped at Gabe, clumsily extending too far against his foe. It took little effort for Gabe to sidestep the strike. With the killer's arms exposed, Gabe snatched his wrists and tossed him back along the peak.

The fight was pointless. No matter what had happened between them the first time around, Gabe now saw the truth in the once-proud killer. He was just a frightened kid, overwhelmed by the consequences of his actions—a soldier following the orders of a dead man instead of choosing his own path.

"I think you fear everything," Gabe said. He stepped forward, forgetting about the pain in his ankle and about Loren's struggle to survive beneath his very feet. There was no time for such concerns. The city needed saving and as Gabe's eyes flitted from the killer, to the tumblers, then to the dragon and back again, he knew only one way to see it through. "But most of all? I think you fear failure."

"What?"

Gabe held the heart over his head. The dragon stared intently, lifting from the ground with the strong beat of its wings.

The killer's eyes went wide. "What are you doing?"

"This is for Malcolm, you son of a bitch."

"Don't!"

Gabe launched the pulsing crystal at the tumblers on the other side of the chasm.

The dragon raced after the heart. It soared over Gabe, talons clawing ahead for its prize. Shooting forward like a comet, the dragon opened its gaping maw and swallowed the heart.

Successful in its goal, the dragon tried to rear up. Its momentum, though, caused the beast to crash against the ancient tumblers. Delicate machinery smashed on impact; centuries-old pulleys and winches snapped under the weight of the massive creature.

The dragon clawed at the wall, trying to climb over the falling debris. With each frantic kick, more and more of the doomsday device shattered. The mechanism fell into the deep abyss. Pulleys wrapped tight against the dragon's legs. Falling lights crashed upon its wings, and the mythic creature joined the tumblers in the dark underbelly of the chasm.

The killer fell to his knees. Horror struck his youthful face as he watched his mission end before its rightful conclusion.

"I failed," he muttered beneath his hands.

The entire chamber continued to shake uncontrollably. The tumblers, the mechanism behind the destruction above, had also held the room together. With it gone, the ceiling broke apart and the ground itself tipped and upended with each successive tremor.

Gabe shifted for the edge, careful to work his way down the side with his wounded ankle. When he looked back, the killer remained on his knees, lost to his failure.

"Don't just sit there," Gabe cried. "Get up!"

The killer appeared disheartened and broken. "Why?" he asked.

"There's nothing left for me out there."

"That's not true," Gabe said. He started up once more, a hand out for his enemy. "Please, you have to—"

The lights above snapped loose from their moorings. Boulders dislodged and crashed down like comets from space. The killer gazed up, arms spread to welcome the end.

"No!" Gabe yelled.

The killer was gone in an instant. The chamber claimed him, but it was the mission that had truly taken his life.

Gabe stood before the fallen rock, aghast at the loss. He never stood a chance at changing the killer's fate.

All Gabe could do was escape the destruction raining down from above. He slid along the peak to the base, his ankle screaming with every shift. He stared up at the oblivion heading his way.

All he could do now was run.

CHAPTER SEVENTY

Soriya wasn't strong enough. She struggled to maintain her grip on Loren's hand. Her fingers were slick with sweat. Loren's weight certainly didn't help matters, but she thought better than to mention it at the moment.

The Greystone held the answer but remained silent at her side. With it, she could have easily drawn the strength to save her dear friend. If she could have been the ever-loyal protector, the person she had always been to both Loren and her city, this would have been over long ago.

She couldn't. And the Greystone wouldn't. She was failing, and even Loren realized it as he fought for the side of the pit.

"Loren," Soriya said through clenched teeth. "You're slipping."

His free hand picked at the rock, to no avail. "Can't… find a good grip."

There was no ledge to stand on, no outcropping of rock or vine to snatch. The rock face offered nothing—a hazardously vertical incline that only led into the deep dark below.

Overhead, debris fell. Machinery clanged loudly as it crashed along the far wall and into the abyss. A strong bounce would send something their way and end all hope of a rescue. Almost as instantly as the collapsing chamber would. Both realized the ticking clock in their struggle.

"I'm not strong enough," Soriya said. She tried to pull, afraid of losing what little grip remained.

"Soriya…"

"If I could access the Greystone," she continued. She struggled to see him through teary eyes. Her failure, the price of her rejection from the Bypass, haunted her more now than ever before. It was too high a price for her return, and she cursed herself. "If I could just use the stone, I could… I… I can't save you, Loren."

"It's okay, Soriya."

"It's—"

"Listen to me," Loren interrupted, a piercing gaze locked on her. "You have to go. This place is going to collapse."

"I'm not leaving you."

"I need you to," he replied. His words boomed over the devastation surrounding them. Despite the rending destruction throughout the chamber, in that moment, the world melted away until only the two of them remained. "For Gabe. I should have handled things better with him, been a better friend to him, and more."

She shook her head, refusing to listen. They were not the words of a survivor. They were the words of a man giving up—surrendering to the inevitable. Soriya couldn't let it happen, couldn't let this be goodbye… not like this and not when it was all her fault.

Soriya pulled harder. "Help me, Loren."

"It's your turn to help me, Soriya," he said. Tears spilled from his eyes. He looked down into the dark, then smiled up at her. "Tell Myers—"

"Tell me what?"

Myers' hand shot down into the pit and snatched Loren by the wrist.

"Sam?" Loren exclaimed.

Soriya nearly fell away from the chasm, shocked to see the snarky detective at her side. Myers gritted her teeth. "Well? Are we doing this or not?"

Strengthening her grasp on the man's hand, Soriya pulled with renewed vigor. The pair lifted him out of the dark.

Both cried out from the strain. Loren crossed the ledge and snatched the shaking floor with his toes. He collapsed into their arms, laughing and crying at the same time.

"It was my turn to save you, Loren," Myers said.

"I appreciate it."

Soriya did as well. She said nothing of the sort, still distraught over almost losing a man who meant more to her than she remembered. Grateful barely covered her feelings toward Myers, though the detective would hardly care to hear it.

Myers was too busy looking around the chamber. She blew the hair from her face, then grabbed Loren by the hand once more.

"You can both appreciate me later," she said. The entire chamber fell around them. From the ramparts of the castle to the peak
on the other side of the cavern, everything shook as the fail-safe
gasped its last breath. Myers pulled them ahead for the shattered
drawbridge and the rippling lake beyond. "We need to get the hell
out of here before we're all crushed to death."

CHAPTER SEVENTY-ONE

They ran for the drawbridge. Soriya remained behind the others, covering their rear while continually scanning the cavern for falling debris. Loren stuck close to Myers, but when she quickened her pace, he struggled to join her. He slowly fell back a step and his legs wavered on the uneven rock.

"Loren?"

He waved her off. "I'm fine, Myers."

"Then let's go already," the detective replied. She cocked a thumb toward the exit. "I've had my fill of this place."

"No Wi-Fi?" Loren joked.

"That's a serious offense to me." Myers reached for him once more. He tried to fight her off, wanting to stand on his own, but he stumbled a step and she caught him. "Come on, tough guy. Lean on me for this one."

He nodded, and they started up again. Their injuries hampered their progress, but they continued to make their way forward. With each crash, all eyes shifted wildly through the cavern. Eventually, Myers peered back and noticed Soriya had stopped moving.

"Greystone?"

"Keep going," Soriya answered. "I'm right behind you."

Myers shrugged, the response enough for her. There would never be genuine concern from the woman. Their history made that impossible, and until they came to grips with that, there was only so far they were each willing to go. Still, Soriya was grateful for Myers' presence in the cavern. Her decisiveness in racing to Loren's side had saved the man's life. For that, Soriya would always be glad to call the detective an ally.

Soriya had slowed for a reason. Something had caught her attention while watching the world break apart all around her. Or rather, some*one* had caught her attention.

Gabe stood in the center of the chamber. His twisted ankle caused him to shift uneasily along the ground, but he never moved very far. He kept staring at the damaged foundation and the now-destroyed doomsday device.

"Gabe!" She was at his side in a second. Her hand pulled him away from his clearly troubled thoughts.

"Did we lose?" Gabe asked. "This place…"

"Is no longer needed," Soriya said with confidence. "What lies above—the city—will survive. But here and now? It's becoming disconnected."

"How do you know? I thought—"

"Call it faith."

Gabe hesitated on the crumbling ramparts and the torn flags. "It's all going away. All this wonder. Lost to the world now."

Her hand settled on his arm. Warm eyes greeted him. "There will be other wonders, Gabe. I promise."

He turned and winced with deep pain. Soriya lifted his arm over her shoulder and behind her neck.

"Here," she said. "One step at a time."

"Thanks."

"I'm proud of you, Gabe," Soriya said as she led them ahead. "If anyone should be the Greystone, I'm glad it's you."

"You mean that?" he asked, nearly stumbling at her admission.

She smirked. "With all my heart."

They crossed the drawbridge. Careful steps along the shattered wooden beams gave them access to the narrow beach and the water beyond. Ripples rushed toward them, caused by Myers and Loren, who were well on their way to the other side.

No questions were asked, merely a glance once they had reached deep enough into the water. Gabe filled his lungs and dove into the pool. Soriya followed closely, a constant eye on his progress.

The pinhole passed without issue, and the light diminished almost immediately. They were back in the world—the microcosm, as Loren had described it. Both broke through the surface to grab a long breath.

Quakes continued. Sharp stalactites plummeted from above. Soriya and Gabe swam for the shore. Once out of the pond, they turned back.

The Lady of the Lake statue crumbled. Rock from above crashed against her visage, shattering the serene look of the aged figure. The sword tipped, and her head split in the opposite direction until the entire statue fell into the water.

"Hey!" Myers called from the secondary chamber. "Move it, you two! I can't carry everyone!"

"You I can handle," Soriya said. "Her? Her I could do without."

Gabe laughed. "She's growing on me."

Soriya lifted him against her side once more, and they rushed to the iron gate. The stone path stood chipped in several areas, but the way was mostly clear. Their travels took them around wide turns and back to the slope at the mouth of the great cave.

Myers and Loren were ahead, climbing the last bit to the surface. As Soriya and Gabe moved to follow, the quakes increased. A crack formed above and the entire ceiling dropped.

"Move," Soriya cried. "Move!"

An entire wave of debris crashed to the ground. The stone path shattered behind them, crumbling into the void below. Soriya pushed Gabe higher, forcing him up toward the surface.

Loren's voice bellowed from the other side of the falling rock. "Gabe! Soriya!"

With one last heave, Soriya and Gabe leaped from the cave. They landed on the soft grass, pulled clear by Myers and Loren.

The cave collapsed. The outcropping of rock fell inward, then sank to the ground, leaving nothing but a slight mound of stone and a rising cloud of dust.

Soriya worked her way to her feet. Gabe joined her, and they offered a silent farewell to the wonder of the world beneath their feet—never to be seen again.

"It's gone," Gabe whispered. "And the city?"

No quakes followed them. No wisps tracked them with their crackling light, and no griffins screeched for their blood. There was only the clear sky above, the half-moon a beacon in the star-filled night.

"You did it, Gabe," Soriya said.

Gabe sighed with relief. Portents was safe.

CHAPTER SEVENTY-TWO

Calm settled in the clearing. Loren caught his breath. He looked around at the trio who had accompanied him. They were with him every step of the way, without question. Each bore the weight of their own burdens, troubled by their pasts, their histories, or simply their age, yet none of it had mattered in the end. They had stood together and come out on the other side.

He couldn't help but beam at them. For so long, Loren had believed himself alone in the world—his own doing, through his selfish need to solve his wife's murder. Yet, these three, along with so many others, reminded him day-in and day-out that his life was intertwined with theirs. They were never alone and could never be alone. They were better as a whole, and Loren had never felt that as clearly as he did in the silence of the clearing.

"Is everyone all right?" he asked. Soriya and Gabe turned away from the starry sky. Myers pushed from the trunk of the birch trees—its leaves no longer glistening gold, but faded from the destruction of the cave—to join him. "Myers?"

"I'm fine, Loren." Her body was still singed from her time with the Wisp, yet she played it off by hiding the pain in her eyes when she rubbed at her wounds. "I—"

Loren moved for her and pulled her in for a hug. "You saved my life."

"I owed you one." Myers retreated a step, her cheeks flush and her gaze unable to meet his own. She forced a laugh. "Just don't make a habit out of it."

He joined her in laughter. There was more to say. More hung between them and had for the past year, but there would be time for that later. His feelings toward Myers were still a jumbled mess. He hoped to sort them out, eventually. He needed to.

Myers clearly understood, shuffling along the grass. She hitched her thumb toward the corridor of the maze. "I should—"

Loren nodded. "Yeah. Me too. I need to—"

He peered at Gabe, who watched the scene awkwardly. The boy waved Loren toward Myers, the former detective's eyes flaring in disagreement.

"He did good, Loren." Myers offered a thumbs up for the boy, then stepped away from the gathering.

"That was…" Gabe hesitated, searching for the words as Loren approached. "Have you ever spoken to a woman before?"

"Gabe." Loren ignored the jab, mostly because he didn't have a single rebuttal to share. He pulled the boy close. "Come here."

"This is a trick, right?"

Loren let him go. "What do you mean?"

"This is the part where you start yelling at me again, isn't it?"

Loren chuckled. "I think Nicole can handle that."

"Oh," Gabe whispered. A fear worse than any Loren had noticed during their time underground or facing the nightmares of Portents over the past year filled the boy's face. "She's going to kill me. Crap. They both are, aren't they?"

Loren wrapped an arm around Gabe's shoulders. "I might be able to talk them down. It's not every day your foster kid saves the city."

Sadness rested in Gabe's tired eyes. "I couldn't save him, though. The knight."

"Adam didn't have a reason to live," Loren replied. "The mission was all he had. That's not life."

Gabe slowly nodded. Loren hoped he heard every word, and that they sunk in through his thick teenage skull. The mission—be it as a knight or a Greystone—could not be the only thing in their lives. There had to be more, and Loren knew if Gabe was to learn such a lesson, it would have to come from him.

A shadow shifted to his right. Loren spun on his heels to catch the subtle movement. "And where are you skulking off to?" he called to Soriya.

She closed her eyes. "I was a liability, Loren. I almost wrecked everything. Worse, I almost lost you."

Loren scoffed in disbelief. He staggered from Gabe and reached for Soriya. "You stood face-to-face against a dragon. You didn't hesitate, didn't pause to think about what would happen to you. All that mattered was the city. All that mattered was everyone else. You did all that, knowing you couldn't use the Greystone." He shook his head and held her close. "You're the bravest damn soul I know, and I missed you."

Tears dotted her eyes. "I missed you too, Loren."

Shuffling grass woke them to the world. The peace of the night shattered as armed officers rushed through the final corridor of the maze toward them. Ruiz took the lead, bruised and battered from a fight, but ready for the next.

"What the hell is going on?" he said when he arrived at the clearing.

All four occupants shot a look at each other, each holding back a grin. Loren stepped forward, hands before him. "Welcome to the party, Commissioner."

Ruiz grumbled. He jammed his sidearm into his holster, then waved down the rest of the officers at his back. "I take it we're celebrating now?"

"Sounds good to me," Myers said with a clap of her hands. She passed Ruiz, patting his back before moving toward the maze and the flashing lights in the distance. "You're buying the first round, Chief."

CHAPTER SEVENTY-THREE

The walk back took time. A pair of officers helped Gabe along the twisting path of the maze. Myers pushed ahead of the pack rather than listen to Ruiz's constant questions during their journey. Something had struck her when she'd seen the others and not her partner, Thel.

Soriya held back, as was her way. Despite everything they had been through, Loren hoped she would be all right. They would always be able to lean on each other. She simply needed to reach out. Looking back, however, Loren worried for her. A somber gaze, distant and lonely, rested in her weary eyes. The doubts returned in the silent aftermath of their struggle. Some fights never truly ended.

Loren stuck close to Ruiz, who helped him along. His former superior questioned everything. He started with the maze itself to the cave structure hidden from the world, but his ceaseless queries carried through to the shattered remains of the griffins, which greeted them at the driveway of the towering manor.

Answers were difficult to give, but they came. Loren shared their experiences, the massive structures hidden beneath the estate, and the entire world they had found on the other side of the lake. Each answer brought a clear chill to Ruiz. He tried to hide his fears, but they spilled out when they arrived at the flashing lights and the many patrols stationed along the perimeter.

"I want this place searched top to bottom," he commanded to everyone in range. Ruiz eyed his subordinates, showcasing every structure in sight along the expansive estate. "If there's any access to a cavern or castle or whatever the hell else, I want it sealed!"

The crowd scattered, their marching orders disseminated from captains and lieutenants as groups formed. Gabe and Myers headed for the ambulances, the latter already on her phone. Loren stuck close to Adam North's car in the driveway, using the vehicle to hold himself upright. His entire body wanted to give way, exhausted from everything.

He grinned at Ruiz. "You know, you're pretty good at giving orders."

"And you're lousy at following them." Ruiz sighed. He looked over his friend with growing concern. "You should get yourself checked over, Greg."

Loren shrugged. "Maybe after they finish with Gabe and Myers."

"What about Soriya?"

Loren laughed as Ruiz whipped around in search of the young warrior. "Oh, she vanished as soon as she could."

"She's really back." Ruiz shook his head. He leaned along the hood of the car. Loren sat alongside him, a cold stare at the hedge maze. For a second, he imagined Soriya's shadow among the branches. Then it was gone, as if it had never been there.

"I…" He still worried about her. That look of longing, the sadness in her step over what had been lost in her revival, continued to haunt him. "Yeah, I hope so." Loren let out a long breath. The cold air wafted slowly before him. He turned curiously to his friend. "How did you know to come here?"

Ruiz huffed. He stared ahead, refusing to meet Loren's question head-on. "I'm still trying to figure that out."

"Anything I should be concerned about?"

Ruiz's brow furrowed. "Don't you have enough already?"

A chuckle escaped from Loren. Ruiz knew him too well.

The Commissioner's hand settled along Loren's shoulder. "These knights with their prophecy? This was bigger than anything we've faced before."

Adam's words echoed in Loren's mind. His concern over the growing danger of Portents and the day the city would be unable to contain it. Ruiz's fear felt cut from the same cloth.

"We stopped it."

"Then why does it feel like this is only the start?"

"You've seen what this place is like. There are doors around every corner, connecting the city with myriad dimensions within a single space. Temples and pyramids. Great

chasms of darkness and insane churches promising light in the heart of forever."

It wasn't the first time he had heard about the heart. Whatever it was, whatever threat loomed before them, Loren knew it was coming and far sooner than he would have liked. All he could do was hope their shared strength would be enough in the end.

Ruiz stood, hands shuffling deep into his pockets. He paced the front of the car, then stopped and turned to Loren. "Come back to work."

Loren nearly fell over. "What?"

"We need you."

"I'm right here," Loren replied.

After everything that had happened, how could he possibly go back to the force? So much of Loren's former life had revolved around solving crimes, tracking down killers and battling back demons both within and without. He had lost so much time on his own personal mission.

"I can't," he said. "Work—wearing the badge again—would be moving backward. I'm done doing that."

Ruiz bit his lower lip. He nodded with each word spoken, completely understanding, yet unable to accept the answer. "Then not as a cop. As a consultant. You can help us, and Portents, just like you have been."

Loren cocked an eyebrow. He pushed from the car and met the man's locked gaze. "Are you sure about this, Commissioner?"

"Not one bit," Ruiz admitted. He extended his hand.

Loren took a breath and accepted the hand. "Then, I guess, I'm in. And thanks."

A groan echoed across the driveway. Myers, her wounds bandaged, stopped short of their handshake and rolled her eyes. "Does this mean I have to work with him again?"

Loren pulled away from Ruiz. "Is it too late to change my mind?"

"If I have to suffer, you have to suffer."

"Hey," Myers called. "I'm standing right here."

All three broke into a laugh. It carried on the wind, swirling deep into the night, and helped push away thoughts of the nightmares to come.

CHAPTER SEVENTY-FOUR

Rose Riley Forest overlooked the city from the west. It climbed along the ridgeline separating Portents from the suburbs and helped create a natural border to contain the spires of downtown and the burgeoning masses living therein.

Flashing lights danced along the buildings. They rushed away from the towers on Evans Avenue and the old stonework of Grant Park. Each headed for Riverside and the dangers unleashed. From within the confines of downtown, smoke rose. The tremors may have silenced, but the damage done remained for all to see. The terror of the act and the consequences of the misdeed would take a long time to part from the minds of every soul in the city.

No sound reached the forest. Not the cries of the innocent, injured at the height of the quakes, or the tears of those afraid to shut their eyes in case they returned. Amid the billowing branches and the rising trees, there was nothing but peace in the night.

It was a peace that was rapidly coming to an end.

From every direction along the ridge, figures stepped from the shadows. They wore heavy black cloaks to shelter them from the elements. White masks hid their faces from the world, protecting their identities and their intentions.

Dozens stepped out among the trees to survey Portents. It had always been their way and when the call had arrived with the first tremor, they had come running—abandoning all others for the sake of their cause.

They would always stand in solidarity for the protection and safety of Portents. That had always been their mission, and after too long away from the city, they had finally returned.

Each stared out over Portents at the smoke, the wisps of flame, and the flashing lights. Their city was in pain. It suffered at the whims of a lone attacker with far grander dreams than any of them could have imagined. They should have been involved, should have heeded the signs long ago. That hesitation could no longer stand, and the figure at the center of the gathering made it clear with her deep words.

"It's started."

The gentleman to her left stepped forward with a nod. "The ringing of the bell," he said, in memory of the revitalized Saint Sebastian's Church and the prophecy noted along its tower walls.

Another woman approached from the other side of the central figure. "The fall of the knights."

The story of the five knights had been known to more than the line of Greystones and their charges. The knights were a last resort, and with that safety net removed, things would now move much more quickly.

"We have seen the signs," the masked man replied. "The end is coming."

Murmurs rose from the crowd. Each felt the shift in the air. This was not an isolated incident, though those below would see things otherwise. The citizens of Portents, and their protectors, never looked past the moment at the entire picture. The future stood at the precipice. One push would send it faltering into the dark forever.

"Then the Luminaries have returned just in time." She caught their glaring eyes even through their masks. Doubts hid there, along with questions about their role and how it must change to meet the coming future before it was too late.

"Or so you hope," the gentleman to her right said.

"Renfield." The name slipped out, and she bit her tongue. Anger met her, though she tried to wave it down. "The masks—"

"Protect us," Renfield answered. "They allow us to work in secret, to preserve the city and make ready, though we are far from prepared."

"The project proceeds—"

"Yes, yes," Renfield said dismissively. "Not quickly enough. You know this, Leslie."

The central figure let the name ring out to those around her. Slowly, she removed her mask. The cool breeze grazed her cheeks. Leslie Gates filled her lungs, shucking away the traditions of their order with a solemn look at her brethren.

"You're right, Renfield," she said in a calm voice. "However, we can't hide as we have in the past. It's time to become the light we've always claimed to be."

"How?" the woman to the left said. She took her mask off, and the wide eyes of Julia Tuttle met Leslie's. "After all our fallen sister did? They will never accept us."

"They will have no choice." The damage Karen Winters had inflicted with her rise to power would always taint the cause of the Luminaries. But it could not stop them from trying. "I know someone who will be of great help, not only to our efforts, but to all of Portents."

They joined together, accepting her at her word. They never questioned, only sought a way to protect Portents. Leslie let them have their quiet moment of peace in the midst of the forest. She knew their work was only truly beginning.

And time was not on their side.

CHAPTER SEVENTY-FIVE

Myers raced to the hospital as soon as she received the news. She had wondered why there had been no sign of Thel at the Marsh Estate. With every call to her partner's cell phone, that wonder turned quickly to worry until there was nothing left but dread at the thought of what could have happened amid the dangerous tremors from the knight's fail-safe.

The news was worse than she'd imagined. In Myers' heart, she'd believed Thel to be all right, merely delayed because of the chaos unfolding. Images of upended cars in massive potholes or jammed doors from fallen support beams had flashed before her eyes, but none had been life-threatening.

None had put Thel in the ICU at Mercy Hospital.

All relief at helping Loren close out the case departed when Myers passed through the doors. As she rushed across entire wards for some sign of her partner, her steps frantic and confused by the hospital's byzantine layout, Myers put aside her former doubts.

Through it all, she had fought against her role as Head Detective, but tonight her duty had trumped any fear of inadequacy. She had to remain, had to carry on, not out of obligation but because of who she had grown to be as a person—outside the shadow of her father's tragic past and her own base lies in achieving her position.

She had to carry on for her partner as well.

"Thel!" Myers yelled through the ICU. She found her in a private room. The door opened with the passing of a pair of nurses taking vitals during their rounds. Myers caught the door, her badge all the permission needed to enter. "I came as soon as I heard."

The sight of her partner stopped Myers in her tracks. Thel's left eye was covered by bandages, her cheek swollen and pulsing in red. A cast covered her right forearm, held tight against her abdomen with a sling. Both feet were elevated, the right by a pillow with gauze wrapped tight against her ankle. The left was suspended and covered in a cast that ran from the middle of her foot to just below her knee.

"Thel…" Myers slowed her approach, stunned by the damage sustained. Thel's nose was clearly broken, her lips as swollen as her left cheek, though a darker shade of red as dried blood clung to the deeper scrapes. "What happened? Who—"

"Please," a nurse said, cutting her off. The woman held a finger to her lips. "She's been through a trauma. She needs time."

Myers nodded. It was Thel who waved her forward, her voice small and broken like the rest of her. "It's… it's okay."

The nurse failed to agree. She rolled up her sleeves, ever prepared to protect her patients, even against themselves.

"Please," Thel said.

A deep sigh escaped the nurse. "A few minutes." Gentle eyes met her patient. "Then rest."

Unable to nod in agreement, Thel winked with her only open eye. The nurse passed Myers for the door, hesitated at the threshold over her decision, then continued into the hallway.

Myers crept close to her partner with a hand to the railing. "Thel. What the hell—"

"What happened to you?" Thel asked.

The question stopped Myers. "What?"

"You look like crap."

Myers glanced at the bandages decorating her body. Her burns ached, the pain dulled by a cocktail of drugs still working through her system. "Who cares about me? What happened to you?"

Thel looked away. "They jumped me, Sam."

"Who?" Myers asked. "Did you see?"

"I…" Thel paused, something right at the tip of her tongue. "No."

Myers noted the hesitation. "Are you sure?"

Thel refused to meet Myers' question. She stared up at the panels on the ceiling. "They came for me, Sam," she said in a terrified voice. "Because of what I am."

"What's that?" Myers said with a smirk. "A badass detective and an adequate singer?"

Thel struggled to smile. "Adequate?"

"Compared to me."

"Ha," Thel exclaimed, then winced. She settled deeper into her pillows for support. "Oh, that hurt."

Myers was glad to bring a smile to the surface. It failed to remove the intense outrage bubbling underneath her own. Thel had done nothing but help the city since her return to the world. She had only hoped to fit in, to make a difference after all the pain her sisters inflicted in their previous lives.

The assault against her was a hate crime and not the first to show up in Portents over the last year. More and more had cropped up of late. The threats grew with the number of Courtyard refugees found living among the so-called regular people in the city.

That hate shattered her friend. Myers could tell the pain was more than physical for Thel. Her every fear had become justified by a single act. Someone had taken away her hopes and dreams. Myers refused to let that stand.

"I'm going to find these bastards," she said. "They're going to pay for what they did."

"Sam…"

"Rest." Myers ran her hand lightly along Thel's left arm. "I'll visit tomorrow."

Myers left Thel in the dim light of the room. She wanted to say more, wanted to hear more details, but Myers could tell with each pressured look her partner needed the rest. She retreated to the hall to swipe at tired, tear-stained eyes. The door closed behind her, and she settled along the frame for a long breath.

"She say anything?" a voice asked across the hall.

Myers opened her eyes, straightening her back and clearing her throat. "Not much," she said. "You sure you're up for keeping watch?"

The uniformed officer raised the sling on his left arm slightly. "I'll be fine. It's her I'm worried about."

"She'll be all right. Especially when we catch these monsters." Myers stepped away from the door. A smile slipped from her lips. "She'll be glad you're here."

David Yardin nodded. "Happy to do it."

His partner, Cliffords, approached from down the hall. His gaze tracked every movement in the ICU. He passed by them for the right side of the door to Thel's room, where a folding chair had been set up.

Myers looked them over carefully. "No one gets past you two, got it?"

Both nodded. It was enough to allow Myers to walk away. She needed sleep, but more than that, she needed to get started at making things right for Thel.

Yardin called after her as she headed out for the night. "Don't worry, Detective," he said with a smirk. "We'll keep a close eye on her."

CHAPTER SEVENTY-SIX
One Week Later

Loren scrambled through the living room. He picked up every stray magazine and flipped over couch cushions to hide even the merest strand of dust or crumb residue. He couldn't remember the last time he felt so nervous.

Rolling his eyes at yet another broken-down cardboard box beneath the coffee table, Loren bent to retrieve it. A quick dash through the kitchen and the box fell atop the others in a massive heap in the corner. He studied the pile and wondered what had taken him so long to get rid of them. A grin spread across his face.

"Guess I just needed the proper motivation." A knock at the door roused him from his musings. "Speaking of which…"

Loren was back in the living room when the second round of soft rapping hit the door. The entire slab had been replaced by the maintenance staff earlier in the week, as had the window overlooking the street below. None of the staff had been keen on the damage, or the lack of explanation to the scorch marks littering the building that had forced them to repaint much of the property. Loren knew they would make it up to him with a rent increase when his renewal came up.

His shaking hand hesitated at the knob. Loren took a calming breath, then opened the door.

Curtis and Nicole stood in the hall. Before them was Gabe, who anxiously peered through Loren to the rest of the apartment.

"Hey," Loren said, clearing the threshold. "Come on in."

Gabe rushed in at the invitation. He spun around, a curious eye at every detail in the room and at the owner of the apartment. Nicole joined him in his search of the place. She offered Loren little more than a glare. Her frustration might have ebbed, but was still very much alive.

Curtis stopped before Loren to shake his hand. "Thanks for having us."

Loren offered the couch on the far side of the room. "Please."

Gabe shook his head. He leaned along the wall, arms across his chest. "What the heck is going on, Loren?"

"Gabe…"

"I've been calling you all week."

Loren had answered when he could, but mostly he'd remained silent in the aftermath of their adventure. He hadn't told Gabe about working with Myers on Thel's assault, or about his new position with the police department. Each message sent had offered little in the way of information, and it had done nothing but antagonize the boy, if his agitation was any indication.

"How's school been?" Loren asked.

"Huh? Boring." Gabe shot back. His shoulders slumped at the question. "Wait. Are you back on the normal-life kick? Are you getting rid of me?"

Nicole sighed. "He's been on edge all week."

"But he's towed the line," Curtis added. "Even caught up on his homework."

Gabe huffed. "With supervision."

Curtis smirked. "To and from school. Homework with the other kids in common spaces. It's been a nice, quiet week."

Nicole nodded. "Absolutely."

That was not the impression Gabe gave. His eyes begged for an escape from his wardens. Loren couldn't help laughing.

Gabe shifted closer to Loren. "Come on. What is going on?"

Loren looked over the young man, no longer quite the kid he had been. Sweat dotted Loren's brow, and he dabbed at it before sweeping his arm around Gabe to lead him through the apartment.

"Give us a few minutes?"

Nicole and Curtis shared a knowing stare, then settled against the sofa cushions.

Once in the hallway, Loren let Gabe go. "Sorry about this last week."

"I don't need apologies, Loren," Gabe replied. "I need answers."

"Now you sound like me."

Gabe groaned his disapproval at the comparison.

Loren paused at the door to the spare bedroom. "I screwed up before, Gabe. After everything you had gone through, I didn't understand what you needed. I thought it was normalcy—a home, a family, and a separation from the world that took so much from you. The world I'm always caught up in."

"It's my world too, Loren. It always will be." Gabe's eyes fell to the floor. His look was distant, clearly lost to visions of his parents and his brother. They were always with him, just like Beth always would be for Loren.

"I see that now," Loren said. "I wasn't an anchor to your past, holding you back. I was a link to memories you will always cherish, no matter the pain that comes with them."

Loren opened the door to the spare bedroom and stepped inside. He took a slow step, a deep breath caught in his lungs. His heart pounded in his chest.

"Connections have never been easy for me," he said to Gabe. "But I've spent too long running from them—running from life."

Gabe held to the door frame, leaning hard. "Going somewhere with this?"

"You might say that." Loren reached up to the ceiling fan and pulled the chain. The entire room illuminated. The stacks of boxes were gone. In their place was a bed with a desk to the right. A basketball hoop hung from the closet door in the corner. There was a mirror on the wall above a wide dresser. "What do you think?"

"No more boxes?" Gabe asked, surprised. "Finally decided to finish moving in?"

"I was hoping you'd join me."

Gabe fell back a step. "What?"

"The room is yours if you want it," Loren said. "Nicole and Curtis are helping me work it out with the foster system. There's still a ton of work to do but, thanks to them and about a million favors called in by Ruiz, I've been granted probationary status."

Gabe lingered in the room. He paced around the bed, over to the window, and then to the closet. He repeated the circuit twice, passing Loren with each revolution.

Loren finally stopped him. "Well? Say something."

Gabe wrapped his arms around Loren's chest and squeezed hard.

Loren smiled. The world blurred through watery eyes. "Can I

take that as a yes?"

"No more pushing me away?" Gabe asked.

Loren stepped back, hands on the young man's shoulders. "We're in this together, Gabe. It's time to move forward, don't you think?"

CHAPTER SEVENTY-SEVEN

He should have done this long ago.

Loren lingered outside Gabe's bedroom. Peering through the thin crack left by the open door, he watched the newest addition to the apartment sleep soundly. There was a peace in having Gabe in the room, so accepting and so willing to look past the flaws in Loren's character, though they were glaringly obvious to the rest of the world.

The kid stuck with him through everything. Even when pushed away—forced into a situation that didn't account for all his needs—Gabe still rose above it all to help. The risk, while terrifying to Loren, didn't matter to Gabe as long as he was able to save someone else.

Gabe brought hope back into Loren's world, something he never imagined possible. He could do no less for the young man. It was time for them to move forward, to face the dangers of the city together.

Loren closed the door and started down the hallway. So much had changed in the last week. Gabe's arrival to the apartment was a huge component of that feeling, but barely scratched the surface in actuality. There had also been Soriya's return. The impact of that revelation continued to stagger Loren. Myers' call was just as surprising. It had opened another door in his life Loren thought closed long ago.

Fingers grazed the frame hanging on the wall. "You knew, didn't you?" Beth's smiling face beamed at him. Her voice may have quieted over the last year, but her advice continued to ring through his thoughts and always would.

So many surprises had entered his life of late, but none compared to Ruiz's offer. The job remained an unknown, though the first shreds of work had already slipped into his hands thanks to Myers.

She was hard at work on Thel's case, the siren still recovering from her injuries at the hands of an angry mob. Their identities continued to elude the department, which had brought Myers to Loren's door once more for help. She'd hated to ask, almost as much as Loren disliked disappointing her with a lack of progress.

Loren let the case linger in his mind as he paced the hall. At the entrance to the living room, he paused. A shadow shifted in the darkness.

"Hey!" Loren rushed for the lamp beside the couch and pulled the cord. "Who the hell are you and what—"

Soriya stood near the open window. Her shoulders slumped forward, and her head leaned limply against the glass. The torn and frayed state of her clothes matched the turmoil she must have been feeling inside.

"Hello, Loren," she said in a quiet voice.

Loren settled, a hand over his heart. "You scared the hell out of me, Soriya. What are you doing here?"

"I had to come," she said. Slowly turning from the glass, Soriya offered a sad smirk. "To say goodbye."

Loren moved for her. "Hey. Don't give me that. After everything we've been through… I lost you once. I won't let it happen again."

At his touch, Soriya reeled. Her arms closed across her chest, and she slipped away from the light for the shadows in the room. "There is a piece of me missing."

"You went through hell itself, Soriya," Loren replied. "That takes a toll. But you're here now and we can figure this out. We can figure anything out, like we always have."

"Things are too different," Soriya said with a shake of her head. "I'm too different."

"You're—"

"Please," she interrupted. Her eyes begged for him to listen. Loren sighed, then nodded. "This is hard enough. Loren, I have to find out why I came back. Here and now."

"And we will. Give it time. We could—" He stopped himself this time. She had clearly made her decision long before her arrival to the apartment. Discussing it further was pointless, and Loren realized that in her stance, in her wayward glances for the window and the world outside. Her arrival had been a courtesy. "How? If you're going to go through with this—if you're going to leave again to find what's missing—at least tell me how."

"The Bypass, Loren," she answered. "I have to go back."

CHAPTER SEVENTY-EIGHT

The glowing green sphere floated pristinely in the center of the chamber. Cold stone stretched along the floor, cracked from the tremors but intact throughout. The domicile remained in the corner, though neglect had left it home to cobwebs more than anything or anyone. Treasures hid in the shadows, untouched even with the return of their owner to the space.

Soriya took in her home with nothing but emptiness in her heart. This should have been a cherished moment for her, a great resurgence of spirit to be in the place of her power and the key to her very life. She had lived in harmony among the books and relics for over two decades.

Yet, when it came time to recall a single occurrence, Soriya's memory blurred. Moments remained, small recollections like the tale of the knights. Most, however, were as lost as she was after her expulsion from the Bypass.

Soriya stepped onto the platform. The pillars at her side towered to the ceiling forty-feet above, their surfaces fractured from past battles, but still standing. They struggled on with their task. Soriya couldn't follow their example. She had lost too much, especially her connection to the Greystone.

Soriya couldn't just wait and hope for the best—she needed to act.

She needed the truth about what had happened to her.

"You'll lock the chamber like I showed you?" she asked. Her eyes remained ever forward on the spinning green Bypass. Thin flickers of shadow flitted along the surface, then dove deeper and out of sight again.

Loren stood outside the domicile. He held back, his reservation clear in every glance and every sharply spoken word. "I will, but…"

A heavy sigh caused the stone bearer to turn toward him. "This is a mistake, Soriya."

She respected the opinion. It was why she had gone to him rather than vanish from the face of the earth again. Loren had never been one to handle loss of any kind. She couldn't leave without giving him the chance to talk her out of her decision. Lost memory or not, missing spirit or not, there was no one in the world she trusted more than Greg Loren.

"It's mine to make," she replied.

Loren stepped closer, a hand to the nearest pillar. "The answers aren't in there," he said, pointing to the Bypass. "We can find them together. Here."

She had believed that once. When she'd returned, in the aftermath of her mistake with the Will-o'-the-wisp, Soriya had tried to find her answers. Nothing had come but a rising fury that threatened to overtake her. It took all her control to rein it in, and she feared what that meant for those around her.

"I'm not whole, Loren," Soriya said. "I can't remember pieces of my past. What I've done? What I've failed to do? I don't feel connected to this place. I don't feel anything except…" She swiped at her eyes. "This isn't life, Loren."

She looked at the floating orb of green light once more. Another step brought her within reach, and her hand shot to the surface. She grazed eternity with her fingertips.

"The Bypass took that from me," she continued. "I have to find out why. I have to see what is still hidden from me. Please tell me you understand."

Loren bit his lip. His reflection shone on the rapidly spinning globe. "I do," he said. "I don't like it, but I do."

"Thank you." She peered back, the sad gaze of her partner washing over her. Soriya took in the world around her. The pillars, the domicile, and the stairs leading back to her city, were a reminder of all that she'd lost. She lingered for a moment on the floor at the base of the platform.

Loren tracked her, almost reading her thoughts. "Leave it to me, Soriya."

Her brow furrowed.

"The shadow?"

He was right, of course. The shadow from her memories continued to haunt her. There was something in its shape, in its presence, that sent an icy chill up her spine. She felt the importance of its identity, as if the shadow held the key to everything of late.

"I'll figure out who else came through, Soriya," Loren said. "I promise."

She nodded. "And I promise to come back."

"You damn well better," Loren said.

A smirk formed on her lips. Soriya took in a deep breath, the Bypass before her.

"See you soon."

With that, Soriya stepped through the veil to the infinite and the answers waiting within.

ACKNOWLEDGEMENTS

This book would not have been possible without the support of my incredible patrons. They are the true heroes, having to put up with all my quirks and panic attacks. A hefty thank you to:

Matt Patrick
Sally Hall
Sara Frandina
Paul Sardella
Vicki Wilkinson

I wanted to give a special thanks to my old friend, B, who deserves much of the credit for my career path whether he realizes it or not. The years spent imagining great adventures and going on grand quests in the backyard or down the street provided endless creative fuel for the stories we always wanted to share with the world.

ABOUT THE AUTHOR

Lou Paduano is the author of the Greystone series of urban fantasy adventures, which follow Detective Greg Loren and Soriya Greystone as they hunt myths, monsters, and legends in the city of Portents.

He is also the author of the conspiracy thriller series, The DSA, a serialized tale about a clandestine government agency trying to discover the true power behind humanity's future.

 He lives in Grand Island, New York with his wife and three daughters. Sign up for his e-mail list for free content as well as updates on future releases at loupaduano.com.

THE GREYSTONE SAGA
AVAILABLE NOW

Follow the adventures of Soriya Greystone and Detective Greg Loren as they hunt dangerous myths and legends in the city of Portents.

BOOK ONE - SIGNS OF PORTENTS
BOOK TWO - TALES FROM PORTENTS
BOOK THREE - THE MEDUSA COIN
BOOK FOUR - PATHWAYS IN THE DARK
BOOK FIVE - A CIRCLE OF SHADOWS
BOOK SIX - ALPHA AND OMEGA

GREYSTONE-IN-TRAINING

For years, Soriya trained to become the Greystone.
Follow the trials that made her the protector
Portents needed to fend off the darkest of threats.

BOOK ONE - HAMMER AND ANVIL
BOOK TWO - THE GIFTS OF KALI
BOOK THREE - THE FINAL GAUNTLET

GREYSTONE LOST TALES

ARMY IN THE OBELISK
THE LAST KING

GREYSTONE CONTINUES IN…

Soriya's past is revealed at last!

On a quest to reclaim the missing piece of her soul, Soriya Greystone journeys through the Bypass itself. Deep at the heart of eternity, she is offered a choice: a heaven of her own making or a chance to return to Portents for a lifetime of pain and conflict.

The true choice waits for her, though. One she must navigate with Mentor by her side. But what sin haunts him? How does it tie to the day Soriya lost her parents and all memory of her previous life?

While the past is revealed to Soriya, Greg Loren confronts a deadly present in Portents. A mad bomber has struck, killing indiscriminately with the push of a detonator.

As the dead pile up, Loren and Detective Sam Myers are in a race against time to figure out the reason behind the bombings before the killer strikes again.

www.ingramcontent.com/pod-product-compliance
Lightning Source LLC
Chambersburg PA
CBHW021245190726
48289CB00005B/1489